THE EARLY SPENSER
THREE COMPLETE NOVELS

BOOKS BY ROBERT B. PARKER

The Godwulf Manuscript

God Save the Child

Mortal Stakes

Promised Land

Three Weeks in Spring
(with Joan Parker)

The Judas Goat

Wilderness

Looking for Rachel Wallace

Early Autumn

A Savage Place

Ceremony

The Widening Gyre

Love and Glory

Valediction

A Catskill Eagle

Taming a Sea-horse

Pale Kings and Princes

Crimson Joy

THE EARLY SPENSER

Three Complete Novels

THE GODWULF MANUSCRIPT
GOD SAVE THE CHILD
MORTAL STAKES

Robert B. Parker

DELACORTE PRESS/SEYMOUR LAWRENCE

A Seymour Lawrence Book
Published by
Delacorte Press/Seymour Lawrence
Bantam Doubleday Dell Publishing Group, Inc.
666 Fifth Avenue
New York, New York 10103

A portion of *The Godwulf Manuscript* appeared in the October 1973 issue of *Argosy*.

Design by Richard Oriolo

Library of Congress Cataloging in Publication Data

Parker, Robert B., 1932–
The early Spenser: three complete novels / Robert B. Parker.
p. cm.
Contents: The Godwulf manuscript—God save the child—Mortal stakes.
ISBN 0-385-29728-9
1. Spenser (Fictitious character)—Fiction. 2. Detective and mystery stories. American. I. Parker, Robert B., 1932– Godwulf manuscript, 1989. II. Parker, Robert B., 1932– God save the child, 1989. III. Parker, Robert B., 1932– Mortal stakes, 1989. IV. Title.
PS3566.A686A6 1989 89-1613
813′.54—dc19 CIP

Manufactured in the United States of America
Published simultaneously in Canada
First Delacorte edition
June 1989

10 9 8 7 6 5 4 3 2 1

BG

THE GODWULF MANUSCRIPT

This, like everything else,
is for Joan, David, and Daniel

1

The office of the university president looked like the front parlor of a successful Victorian whorehouse. It was paneled in big squares of dark walnut, with ornately figured maroon drapes at the long windows. There was maroon carpeting and the furniture was black leather with brass studs. The office was much nicer than the classrooms; maybe I should have worn a tie.

Bradford W. Forbes, the president, was prosperously heavy—reddish face; thick, longish, white hair; heavy white eyebrows. He was wearing a brown pin-striped custom-tailored three-piece suit with a gold Phi Beta Kappa key on a gold watch chain stretched across his successful middle. His shirt was yellow broadcloth and his blue and yellow striped red tie spilled out over the top of his vest.

As he talked, Forbes swiveled his chair around and stared at his reflection in the window. Flakes of the season's first snow flattened out against it, dissolved, and trickled down onto the white brick sill.

It was very gray out, a November grayness that is peculiar to Boston in late fall, and Forbes's office seemed cheerier than it should have because of that.

He was telling me about the sensitive nature of a college president's job, and there was apparently a lot to say about it. I'd been there twenty minutes and my eyes were beginning to cross. I wondered if I should tell him his office looked like a whorehouse. I decided not to.

"Do you see my position, Mr. Spenser," he said, and swiveled back toward me, leaning forward and putting both his hands palms down on the top of his desk. His nails were manicured.

"Yes, sir," I said. "We detectives know how to read people."

Forbes frowned and went on.

"It is a matter of the utmost delicacy, Mr. Spenser"—he was looking at himself in the glass again—"requiring restraint, sensitivity, circumspection, and a high degree of professionalism. I don't know the kind of people who usually employ you, but . . ."

I interrupted him.

"Look, Dr. Forbes, I went to college once, I don't wear my hat indoors. And if a clue comes along and bites me on the ankle, I grab it. I am not, however, an Oxford don. I am a private detective. Is there something you'd like me to detect, or are you just polishing up your elocution for next year's commencement?"

Forbes inhaled deeply and let the air out slowly through his nose. "District Attorney Frale told us you were somewhat overfond of your own wit. Tell him, Mr. Tower."

Tower stepped away from the wall where he had been leaning and opened a manila file folder. He was tall and thin, with a Prince Valiant haircut, long sideburns, buckle boots, and a tan gabardine suit. He put one foot on a straight chair and flipped open the folder, no nonsense.

"Carl Tower," he said, "head of campus security. Four days ago a valuable fourteenth-century illuminated manuscript was stolen from our library."

"What is an illuminated manuscript?"

Forbes answered, "A handwritten book, done by monks usually, with illustrations in color, often red and gold in the margins. This particular one is in Latin and contains an allusion to Richard Rolle, the fourteenth-century English mystic. It was discovered forty years ago behind an ornamental façade at Godwulf Abbey, where it is thought to have been secreted during the pillage of the monasteries that followed Henry the Eighth's break with Rome."

"Oh," I said, "that illuminated manuscript."

"Right," Tower said briskly. "I can fill you in with description and pictures later. Right now we want to sketch out the general picture. This morning President Forbes received a phone call from someone purporting to represent a campus organization, unnamed. The caller said they had a manuscript and would return it if we would give a hundred thousand dollars to a free school run by an off-campus group."

"So why not do so?"

Again Forbes answered. "We don't have one hundred thousand dollars, Mr. Spenser."

I looked around. "Perhaps you could rent out the south end of your office for off-street parking," I said.

Forbes closed his eyes for perhaps ten seconds, inhaled audibly, and then went on.

"All universities lose money. This one, large, urban, in some ways undistinguished, loses more than most. We have little alumni support, and that which we do have is often from the less affluent segments of our culture. We do not have one hundred thousand dollars."

I looked at Tower. "Can the thing be fenced?"

"No, its value is historical and literary. The only market would be another university, and they would recognize it at once."

"There is another problem, Mr. Spenser. The manuscript must be kept in a controlled environment. Air-conditioned, proper humidity, that sort of thing. Should it be kept out of its case too long, it will fall apart. The loss to scholarship would be tragic." Forbes's voice sank at the last sentence. He examined a fleck of cigar ash on his lapel, then brought his eyes up level with mine and stared at me steadily.

"Can we count on you, Mr. Spenser? Can you get it back?"

"Win this one for the Gipper," I said.

Behind me Tower gave a kind of snort, and Forbes looked as if he'd found half a worm in his apple.

"I beg your pardon?" he said.

"I'm thirty-seven years old and short on rah-rah, Dr. Forbes. If you'll pay me, and do your Pat O'Brien impressions somewhere else, I'll see if I can find the manuscript."

"This gets us nowhere," Tower said. "Let me take him down to my office, Dr. Forbes, and lay it all out for him. I know the situation and I'm used to dealing with people like him."

Forbes nodded without speaking. As we left the office he was standing at his window, hands clasped behind his back, looking at the snow.

The administration building was cinder block, with vinyl tile, frosted glass partitions, two tones of green on the corridor walls. Tower's office was six doors down from Forbes's and not much bigger than Forbes's desk. It was done in beige metal. Tower got seated behind his desk and tapped his teeth with a pencil.

"It's really slick how you can charm a client, Spenser."

I sat across from him in the other chair. I didn't say anything.

"Sure," he said, "the old man's kind of a ham, but he's a damn good administrator, and a damn fine person."

"Okay," I said, "he's terrific. When I grow up I want to be just like him. What about the Godwulf Manuscript?"

"Right." He took an eight-by-ten color print from his manila folder and handed it to me. It showed an elegantly handwritten book lying open on a table. The words were in Latin and around the margins in bright red and gold were drawn knights and ladies and lions on their hind legs, and vines and stags and a serpentine dragon being lanced by an armor-clad hero on a plump and feminine horse. The first letter at the top left on each page was elaborately drawn and incorporated into the design of the margins.

"It was taken three nights ago from its case in the library's rare book room. The watchman punched in there at two and again at four. At four he found the case open and the manuscript gone. He can't say positively that it wasn't there at two, but he assumes he would have noticed. It's hard to prove you didn't see something. You want to talk to him?"

"No," I answered. "That's routine stuff. You or the cops can do that as well as I could. Have you got a suspect?"

"SCACE."

"SCACE?"

"Student Committee Against Capitalist Exploitation. Revolution at the far-left fringe of the spectrum. I don't know it the way courts want it known; I know it the way you know things like that if you're in my line of work."

"Informer?"

"Not really, though I've got some contacts. Mostly, though, it's a gut guess. It's the kind of thing they'd do. I've been here for five years. Before that I was with the Bureau for ten. I've spent a lot of time on radicals, and I've developed a feel for them."

"Like the late director developed a feel for them?"

"Hoover? No, he's one reason I quit the Bureau. He was a hell of a cop once, but his time came and went before he died. I got enough feel about the radical kids not to classify them. The worst of them have the same things wrong that zealots always have, but you can't blame them for getting rigid about some of the things that go on. That ain't Walt Disney World out there." He nodded out his window at the blacktop quadrangle where the slush was beginning to collect in semi-fluid patterns as the kids sloshed through it. A thin and leafless sapling leaned against its support stake. It was a long way from home.

"Where do I find SCACE? Do they have a clubhouse with college pennants on the wall and old Pat Boone records playing day and night?"

"Not hardly," Tower said. "Your best bet would be to talk to the secretary, Terry Orchard. She's the least unpleasant of them, and the least unreasonable."

"Where do I find her?"

Tower pressed down an intercom button and asked someone to bring him in the SCACE file.

"We keep a file on all college organizations. Just routine. We're not singling SCACE out."

"I bet you've got a thick one on the Newman club," I said.

"Okay, we don't pay as much attention to some as others, granted. But we're not persecuting anybody."

Tower's door opened and a post-coed blonde in high white boots came in. She was wearing something in purple suede that was too short for a skirt and too long for a belt. Above that was a scarlet satin long-collared shirt with puffed sleeves and a deep neck. Her thighs were a little heavy—but perhaps she thought the same of me. She laid a thick brown file folder on Tower's desk, looked me over like the weight guesser at a fair, and left.

"Who was that," I asked, "the dean of women?"

Tower was thumbing through the file. He extracted a typewritten sheet.

"Here," he said, and handed it across. It was a file on Terry

Orchard: home address: Newton, Mass. college address: none. Transient.

"Transient?" I said.

"Yeah, she drifts. Mostly she lives with a guy named Dennis Powell, who's some kind of SCACE official. She also used to live sometimes with a girl over on Hemenway Street. Connelly, Catherine Connelly. It's all there in the file."

"Yeah, and the file is a year old."

"I don't have the staff. The kids come and go. They're only here four years, if that. The real romantic radicals like to think of themselves as free floaters, street people. They sleep around on floors and sofas and Christ knows where else. Your best bet would be to get her after class."

Again the intercom, again the purple skirt.

"See if you can get Terry Orchard's schedule from the registrar's office for me, Brenda." All business. Competent. Professional. No hanky-panky. No wonder he lasted ten years with the Feds.

She was back in about five minutes with a Xerox copy of an IBM printout of Terry Orchard's schedule. She had a class in the psychology of repression that ended at three in Hardin Hall, fourth floor. It was 2:35.

"Picture?" I asked Tower.

"Right here," he said. He looked at the massive watch on the broad, snakeskin band that he wore. It was the kind they call a chronometer, which will tell you not only the time but the atmospheric pressure and the lunar cycle.

"Three o'clock," he said. "Plenty of time; Hardin Hall is two buildings away across the quad. Take the elevator to the fourth floor. Room four-o-nine is to your left, about two doors down the corridor."

I looked at the picture. It wasn't good. Obviously an ID shot. Square face, rather thick lips, and hair pulled tight back away from her face. She looked older than the twenty her file had said she was. But most people do in ID shots. I reserved judgment.

"Okay," I said. "I'll go see her. How about a retainer? Forbes telling me how indigent you all were has me nervous."

"One will come to you in the mail from the comptroller. A week's worth in advance."

"Sold," I said. I gave him back the file and the picture.

"Don't you want it?"

"I'll remember," I said. We shook hands. I left.

The corridors were beginning to fill with students changing classes. I pushed through into the quadrangle. The thin elm sapling I'd seen from Forbes's window wasn't as lonely as I thought. Five cousins, no less spindly, were geometrically spaced about the hot top quadrangle. Three sides of the quadrangle were bordered with gray-white brick buildings. Each had wide stairs leading up to multiple glass-door banks. The buildings were perfectly square, four stories high, with gray painted casement windows. It looked like corporate headquarters for White Tower Hamburgers. The fourth side opened onto the street, where MBTA trains rumbled.

Under one of the saplings a boy and girl sat close together. He was wearing black sneakers and brown socks, flared dungarees, a blue denim shirt and a fatigue jacket with staff sergeant's stripes, a Seventh Division patch, and the name tag GAGLIANO. His thick black hair blossomed out from his head in a Caucasian afro and the snow streaked the rose-colored lenses of his gold-rimmed glasses. The girl had on bib overalls and a quilted ski parka. On her feet were blue suede hiking boots with thick corrugated soles and silver lacing studs. Her blond hair was perfectly straight and halfway to her waist. She wore a woven leather headband to keep it out of her eyes. I wondered if it was a mark of advancing years when you no longer wanted to neck in the snow.

A black kid in a Borsalino hat came out of the library across the quadrangle. He had on a red sleeveless jumpsuit, black shirt with bell sleeves, high-heeled black patent leather boots with black laces. A full-length black leather trench coat hung open. A Fu Manchu mustache swept to the chin on each side of his mouth. Two kids in football jackets exchanged looks as he went by. They had necks like pilot whales. A slim black girl in an Angela Davis haircut and huge pendant earrings trailed a gentle scent of imported bath soap past me as I went into Hardin Hall, the third building on the quadrangle.

The elevator that took me to the fourth floor was covered with obscene graffiti that some proprietous soul had tried to doctor into acceptability, so that phrases like "buck you" mingled with the more traditional expletives. It was a losing cause, but that didn't make it a bad one.

Room 409 had a blond oak door with a window in it, just like the other six classrooms that lined the corridor on each side. Inside I could see about forty kids facing a woman seated up front at a table. She wore a dark maroon silk granny dress with a low scooped neckline. The dress was covered with an off-white floral design that looked like hydrangea. Her long black hair was caught back with a gold barrette. She wore large round horn-rimmed glasses, and was smoking a corncob pipe with a curved amber stem. She was speaking with great animation and her hands flashed with large rings as she spoke and gestured. A number of students were taking notes, some watched her closely, some had their heads down on the desk and were apparently asleep. Terry Orchard was there, back row, looking out the window at the snow. She looked like kids I'd seen before, the real goods, faded Levi's jacket and pants, faded and unironed denim shirt, hair pulled back tight in a pigtail like an eighteenth-century British sailor. No makeup, no jewelry. On her feet were yellow leather work shoes that laced up over the ankle. She wasn't built so you could tell from where I was, but I would have bet my retainer that she wouldn't be wearing a bra. There are kids that get their anti-establishment milkman's overalls in the Marsha Jordan Shop with their own charge card. But Terry wasn't one of them. Her clothes exclaimed their origin in Jerry's Army-Navy Store. She was better-looking than her picture, but still looked older than twenty.

2

The bell rang and the teacher stopped—apparently in mid-sentence—put her corncob pipe in her mouth, folded up her notes, and started out. The kids followed. Terry Orchard was one of the first out the door. I fell in beside her.

"Excuse me," I said, "Miss Orchard?"

"Yes?" No hostility, but very little warmth either.

"My name is Spenser and I'd like to buy you lunch."

"Why?"

"How about, I'm a Hollywood producer casting for a new movie?"

"Get lost," she said without looking at me.

"How about, if you don't come to lunch with me I'll break both your thumbs and you'll never play pool again?"

She stopped and looked at me. "Look," she said, "what the hell do you want anyway? Why don't you go hang around down at the convent school with a bag of candy bars?"

We were down one flight of stairs now and turning toward the next flight. I took a card out of the breast pocket of my jacket and handed it to her. She read it.

"Oh, for crissake," she said. "A private eye? Jesus. Is that corny! Are you going to pull a gat on me? Did my old man send you?"

"Miss Orchard, look at it this way, you get a free lunch and half a million laughs afterward talking to the gang back at the malt shop. I get a chance to ask some questions, and if you answer them I'll let you play with my handcuffs. If you don't answer them, you still get the lunch. Who else has been out with a private eye lately?"

"A pig is a pig," she said. "Whether he's public or private, he works for the same people."

"Next time you're in trouble," I said, "call a hippie."

"Oh, crap, you know damn well . . ."

I stopped her. "I know damn well that it would be easier to argue over lunch. My fingernails are clean and I promise to use silverware. I'm paying with establishment expense money. It's a chance to exploit them."

She almost smiled. "Okay," she said. "We'll go to the Pub. They'll let me in dressed this way. And this is the only way I dress."

We had reached the ground level and headed out into the quadrangle. We then turned left out onto the avenue. The buildings around the university were old red brick. Many of the windows were boarded, and few of the rest had curtains. Along the avenue was some of the detritus that gathers at the exterior edge of a big university: used-book shops, cut-rate clothing stores featuring this year's freaky fashions, a porno shop, a school of astrology-reading in a storefront, a term-paper mill, three sub joints, hamburger, pizza, fried chicken joints, and a place selling soft ice cream. The porno shop was bigger than the bookstore.

The Pub was probably once a gas station. It had been painted entirely antique green, glass windows and all. The word PUB was gold-leafed on the door. Inside were a juke box, a color TV, dark wooden tables and high-backed booths, a bar along one side. The ceiling was low and most of the light came from a big Budweiser sign in the rear. The bar was mostly empty in midafternoon; a group in one booth was playing cards. In the back a boy and girl were talking very softly to one another. Terry Orchard and I took the second booth from the door. The table top was covered with initials scratched with penknife and pencil point over a long period of time. The upholstery of the booth was torn in places and cracked in others.

"Do you recommend anything?" I asked.

"The corned beef is okay," she said.

A fat, tough, tired-looking waitress wearing sneakers came for our order. I ordered us both a corned beef sandwich and a beer. Terry Orchard lit a cigarette and blew smoke through her nostrils.

"If I drink that beer you're an accomplice. I'm under twenty-one," she said.

"That's okay, it gives me a chance to show contempt for the establishment."

The waitress set down two large schooners of draft beer. "Your sandwiches will be out in a minute," she said, and shuffled off. Terry took a sip.

I said, "You're under arrest." Her eyes flared open, and then she smiled, grudgingly, over the glass.

"You're nowhere near as funny as you think you are, Mr. Spenser, but you're a hell of a lot better than I figured. What do you want?"

"I'm looking for the Godwulf Manuscript. The university president himself called me in, showed me his profile, dazzled me with his elocution, and assigned me to get it back. Tower, the campus cop, suggested you might help me."

"What is a Godwulf Manuscript?"

"It's an illuminated manuscript from the fourteenth century. It was in the rare book room at your library; now it isn't. It's being held for ransom by an unidentified campus group."

"Why did Super Swine think I could help?"

"Super Swine—you must be an English major—he thought you could help because he thinks SCACE took it, and you are the secretary of that organization."

"Why does he think SCACE took it?"

"Because he has an instinct for it, and maybe because he knows something. He's not just a storefront clotheshorse. When he's not getting his nails manicured and his hair styled with a razor, he is probably a pretty shrewd cop. He didn't tell me everything he knows."

"Why not?"

"Sweetie, no one ever tells me everything he knows; it is the nature of the beast."

"You must get a swell view of life looking at it through a keyhole half the time."

"I see what's there."

The waitress brought our sandwiches, large, on dark bread, with pickles and chips. They were sweet pickles, though. I ordered two more beers.

"What about the manuscript?" I asked.

"I don't know anything about it."

"Okay," I said, "tell me about SCACE then."

Her face was less friendly now. "Why do you want to know about SCACE?"

"I won't know till I've learned. That's my line of work. I ask about things. And people don't tell me anything, so I ask about more things, and so on. Now and then things fall into place."

"Well, there's nothing to fall into place here. We're a revolutionary organization. We are trying to develop a new consciousness; we're committed to social change, to redistribution of wealth, to real liberty for everyone, not just for the bosses and the rip-off artists."

Her voice had become almost mechanical, like the people who do telephone canvassing for dance studios. I wondered how long it had been since she'd actually thought about all those words and what they really meant.

"How you go about getting these things instituted?"

"By continuous social pressure. By pamphleteering, by marching, by demonstrating our support for all causes that crack the establishment's united front. By refusing to accede to anything that benefits the establishment. By opposing injustice whenever we find it."

"Making much progress?" I asked.

"You bet your life. We're growing every day. There were only three or four of us at first. Now there are five times that many."

"No, I meant injustice."

She was silent, looking at me.

"I haven't made much progress that way either," I said.

A tall, big-boned blond kid wearing a plaid shirt and Levis came into the Pub and looked around. He was clean-shaven and wild-haired, and when his eyes got used to the dimness he headed over to us and slid in beside Terry Orchard. He picked up her half-filled glass, drained it, set it down, and said to her, "Who's this creep?"

"Dennis," she said, "be nice."

He squeezed her arm hard with one hand and repeated the question. I answered for her.

"My name's Spenser."

He turned his head toward me and looked very hard at me. "I'm talking to her, not you, Jack. Shut up."

"Dennis!" She said it with more emphasis this time. "Who the hell do you think you are? Let go of my arm."

I reached over and took hold of his wrist. "Listen, Goldilocks," I said, "I bought her a beer and you drank it. On my block that entitles you to get your upper lip fattened."

He yanked his hand away from me. "You think maybe the long hair makes me soft?"

"Dennis," Terry said, "he's a private detective."

"Freaking pig," he said, and swung at me. I pulled my head out of the way and slipped out of the booth. The punch rammed against the back of the booth; the kid swore and turned toward me. He was not planning to quit, so I figured it best end swiftly. I feinted toward his stomach with my left hand, then hooked it over his lowered guard and turned my whole shoulder into it as it connected on the side of his face. He sat down hard on the floor.

Terry Orchard went down on her knees beside him, her arms around his shoulders.

"Don't get up, Dennis. Stay there. He'll hurt you."

"She's right, kid," I said. "You're an amateur. I do this kind of thing for a living."

The big old tough waitress came around and said, "What the hell is going on? You want the cops in here? You want to fight, go outside."

"No more trouble," I said. "I'm a movie stunt man and I was just showing my friend how to slip a punch."

"And I'm Wonder Woman and if you do it again, I'm calling the blues." She stomped off.

"The beer offer still holds," I said. The kid got up, his jaw already beginning to puff. He wouldn't want to chew much tomorrow. He sat down in the booth beside Terry, who still held his arm protectively.

"I'm sorry, Mr. Spenser," she said. "He isn't really like that."

"What's he really like?" I asked.

His eyes, which had been a little out of focus, were sharpening. "I'm like I am," he said. "And I don't like to see Terry sitting around boozing with some nosy goddamn gumshoe. What are you doing around here anyway?"

The left hook had taken some of the starch out of him. His voice was less assertive, more petulant. But it hadn't made him any sweeter.

"I'm a private detective looking for a stolen rare book, the Godwulf Manuscript. Ever hear of it?"

"No."

"How'd you know I was a private cop?"

"I didn't till Terry said so, but you got the look. If your hair were much shorter it would be a crew cut. In the movement you learn to be suspicious. Besides, Terry's my woman."

"I'm not anybody's woman, Dennis. That's a sexist statement. I'm not a possession."

"Oh, Christ," I said. "Could we cut the polemics a minute. If you know of the manuscript, know this also. It has to be kept in a climate-controlled atmosphere. Otherwise it will disintegrate. And then it will be worthless both to scholars and to you, or whoever the book-nappers may be. The university hasn't got the money to ransom it."

"They got the money to buy football players and build a hockey rink and pay goddamn professors to teach three hours a week and write books the rest of the time."

"I'm not into educational reform this week. Do you have any thoughts on where the missing manuscript might be?"

"If I did I wouldn't tell you. If I didn't I could find out, and when I found out I wouldn't tell you then either. You aren't peeking over the transom in some flophouse now, snoopy. You're on a college campus and you stick out like a sore thumb. You will find out nothing at all because no one will tell you. You and the other dinosaurs can rut around all you want—we're not buying it."

"Buying what?"

"Whatever you're selling. You are the other side, man."

"We aren't getting anywhere," I said. "I'll see you."

I left a five on the table to cover the lunch and left. It was getting dark now and the commuter traffic was starting. I felt the beer a little, and I felt the sadness of kids like that who weren't buying it and weren't quite sure what it was. I got my car from where I'd parked it by a hydrant. It had a parking ticket tied to the windshield wiper. Eternal vigilance, I thought, is the price of liberty. I tore the ticket up and drove home.

3

I was living that year on Marlborough Street, two blocks up from the Public Garden. I made myself hash and eggs for supper and read the morning's *New York Times* while I ate. I took my coffee with me into the living room and tried looking at television. It was awful, so I shut it off and got out my carving. I'd been working on a block of hard pine for about six months now, trying to reproduce in wood the bronze statue of an Indian on horseback that stands in front of the Museum of Fine Arts. The wood was so hard that I had to sharpen the knives every time I worked. And I spent about half an hour this night with whetstone and file before I began on the pine. At eleven I turned on the news, watched it as I undressed, shut it off, and went to bed.

At some much later time, in the dark, the phone rang. I spiraled slowly upward from sleep and answered it after it had rung for what seemed a long time. The girl's voice at the other end was thick and very slow, almost like a 45 record played at 33.

"Spenser?"

"Yeah."

"It's Terry . . . help me."

"Where are you?"

"Eighty Hemenway Street, apartment three."

"Ten minutes," I said, and rolled out of bed.

It was 3:05 in the morning when I got into my car and headed for Hemenway Street. It wasn't till 3:15 when I got there. Three A.M. traffic in Boston is rarely a serious problem.

Hemenway Street, on the other hand, often is. It is a short street of shabby apartment buildings, near the university, and for no better reason than Haight-Ashbury had, or the East Village, it had become the place for street people. On the walls of the building Maoist slogans were scrawled in red paint. On a pillar at the entrance to the street was a proclamation of Gay Liberation. There were various recommendations about pigs being offed scrawled on the sidewalk. I left my car double-parked outside 80 Hemenway and tried the front door. It was locked. There were no doorbells to push. I took my gun out, reversed it, and broke the glass with the handle. Then I reached around and turned the dead lock and opened the door from the inside.

Number three was down the hall, right rear. There were bicycles with tire locks lining both walls, and some indeterminate litter behind them. Terry's door was locked. I knocked; no answer. I knocked again and heard something faint, like the noise of a kitten. The corridor was narrow. I braced my back against the wall opposite the door and drove my heel, with 195 pounds behind it, against the door next to the knob. The inside jamb splintered, and the door tore open and banged violently against the wall as it opened.

Inside all the lights were on. The first thing I saw was Dennis Goldilocks lying on his back with his mouth open, his arms outspread, and a thick patch of tacky and blackening blood covering much of his chest. Near him on her hands and knees was Terry Orchard. Her hair was loose and falling forward as though she were trying to dry it in the sun. But it wasn't sunny in there. She wore only a pajama top with designs of Snoopy and the Red Baron on it, and it was from her that the faint kitten sounds were coming. She swayed almost rhythmically back and forth making no progress, moving in no direction, just swaying and mewing. Between her and

Dennis on the floor was a small white-handled gun. It or something had been fired in the room; I could smell it.

I knelt beside the blond boy and felt for the big pulse in his neck. The minute I touched his skin I knew I'd never feel the pulse. He was cool already and getting colder. I turned to Terry. She still swayed, head down and sick. I could smell something vaguely medicinal on her breath. Her breath was heaving and her eyes were slits. I pulled her to her feet, and held her, one arm around her back. She was almost all the way under. I couldn't tell from what, but whatever it was, it was an o.d.

I walked her into the bathroom, got her pajama shirt off, and got her under the shower. I turned the water on warm and then slowly to full cold and held her under. She quivered and struggled faintly. The sleeves of my jacket were wet up past the elbows and my shirt-front was soaked through. She pushed one hand weakly at my face and began to cry instead of mew. I held her there some more. As I held her I kept listening for footsteps behind me. The door had made a hell of a lot of noise when I kicked it open, and the gunshot must have been a loud one long before that. But the neighborhood was not, apparently, that kind of neighborhood. Not the kind to look into gunshots and doors splintering and such. The kind to pull the covers up over the head and burrow the face in the pillow and say screw it. Better him than me.

I got a hand up to her neck and felt her pulse. It was quicker—I guessed about sixty. I got her out of the shower and across to the bedroom. I didn't see a robe, so I pulled the blanket off the bed and wrapped it around her. Then we waltzed to the kitchen. I got water boiling and found some instant coffee and a cup. She was babbling now, nothing coherent, but the words were intelligible. I made coffee with her balanced half over one hip, my arm around her and the blanket caught in my fist to keep her warm. Then back to the living room to the day bed—there were no chairs in the kitchen—and sat her down.

She pushed aside the coffee and spilled some on herself and cried out at the pain, but I got her to drink some. And again some. And one more time. Her eyes were open now and her breath was much less shallow. I could see her rib cage swell and settle regularly beneath the blanket. She finished the coffee.

I stood her up and we began to walk back and forth across the apartment, which wasn't much of a walk. There was the living room, a small bedroom, a bath, and a kitchenette, barely big enough to stand in. The living room, in which the quick and dead were joined, held only a card table, a steamer trunk with a lamp on it, and the studio couch on whose bare mattress Terry Orchard had drunk her coffee. The blanket I had pulled off the bed had been its only adornment, and as I looked into the bedroom I could see a cheap deal bureau beside the bed. On it was a candle stuck in a Chianti bottle beneath a bare light bulb hanging from a ceiling.

I looked down at Terry Orchard. There were tears running down her cheeks, and less of her weight leaned on me.

"Sonova bitch," she said. "Sonova bitch, sonova bitch, sonova bitch."

"When you can talk to me, talk to me. Till then keep walking," I said.

She just kept saying sonova bitch, in a dead singsong voice, and I found that as we walked we were keeping time to the curse, left, right, sonova bitch. I realized that the broken door was still wide open and as we sonovabitched by on the next swing I kicked it shut with my heel. A few more turns and she fell silent, then she said, half question—

"Spenser?"

"Yeah."

"Oh my God, Spenser."

"Yeah."

We stopped walking and she turned against me with her face hard against my chest. She clenched onto my shirt with both fists and seemed to be trying to blend into me. We stood motionless like that for a long time. Me with my arms around her. Both wet and dripping and the dead boy with his wide sightless eyes not looking at us.

"Sit down," I said after a while. "Drink some more coffee. We have to talk."

She didn't want to let go of me, but I pried her off and sat her on the day bed. She huddled inside the blanket, her wet hair plastered down around her small head, while I made some more coffee.

We sat together on the day bed, sipping coffee. I had the impulse to say, "What's new?" but squelched it. Instead I said, "Tell me about it now."

"Oh, God, I can't."

"You have to."

"I want to get out of here. I want to run."

"Nope. You have to sit here and tell me what happened. From the very first thing that happened to the very last thing that happened. And you have to do it now, because you are in very big trouble and I have to know exactly how big."

"Trouble? Jesus, you think I shot him, don't you?"

"The thought occurred to me."

"I didn't shoot him. They shot him. The ones that made me take the dope. The ones that made me shoot the gun."

"Okay, but start with the first thing. Whose apartment is this?"

"Ours, Dennis's and mine." She nodded at the floor and then started and looked away quickly.

"Dennis is Dennis Powell, right?"

"Yes."

"And you live together and are not married, right?"

"Yes."

"When did the people come who did this?"

"I don't know exactly—it was late, about two thirty maybe."

"Who were they?"

"I don't know. Two men. Dennis seemed to know them."

"What did they do?"

"They knocked on the door. Dennis got up—we weren't asleep, we never go to sleep till very late—and asked, 'Who is it?' I couldn't hear what they said. But he let them in. That's why I think he knew them. When he opened the door they came in very fast. One of them pushed him against the wall and the other one came into the bedroom and dragged me out of bed. Neither one said anything. Dennis said something like, 'Hey, what's the idea?' Or 'Hey, what's going on?' One of them had a gun and he held it on both of us. He never said anything. Neither one. It was spooky. The other guy reached in his coat pocket and came out with my gun."

"Is that your gun on the floor?" I asked.

She wouldn't look but nodded.

"Okay, then what?" I asked.

"He handed my gun to the first man, the man with the gun, and then he grabbed me and turned me around and put his hand over my mouth and bent my arm up behind me and the other man shot Dennis twice."

"With your gun?"

"Yes."

"Then what?"

"Then—" She paused and closed her eyes and shook her head.

"Go on," I said.

"Then the man that shot Dennis made me hold the gun in my hand and shoot it into Dennis. He held my wrist and squeezed my finger on the trigger." She said it in a rush and the words nearly ran together.

"Did he have on gloves?"

She thought a minute. "Yes, yellow ones. I think they might have been rubber or plastic."

"Then what?"

"Then the one who was holding me made me lie down on the bed. I didn't have anything on but my top. And the other one poured some kind of dope in my mouth and forced it shut and held my nose till I swallowed it. Then they just held me there with a hand over my mouth for a little while. Then they left."

I didn't say anything. If she'd invented that story coming out of a narcotic coma, she was some kind of special species and nothing I could handle. She might have hallucinated the whole thing, depending on what she had taken. Or the story might be true.

"Why did they make me shoot him after he was dead?" she asked.

I discovered as I answered that I believed her. "To hook you on a paraffin test. When you fire a handgun cordite particles impregnate your skin. A lab man puts paraffin over it, lets it dry, peels it off, and tests it. The particles show up in the wax."

It took a minute to register. "A lab man, you mean the police?"

"Yes, honey, the police."

"No, can't we get out of here? I'll go home. You won't say anything. My father will pay you. He has money. I know he can give you some . . ."

"Your boyfriend, dead in your apartment, killed with your gun, you gone? They'd come and get you and bring you back. Do you know a lawyer?"

"A lawyer, how the hell would I know a freaking lawyer?" She looked desperately toward the door. "I'm splitting, screw this scene." Her voice had gotten harsh and tough with fright, and I noticed her lapse into the jargon of her peer group as her fright increased. When she'd been clinging to me she talked like a young girl in college. When she wanted to get away from me her voice and language changed. I held her against me with my arm around her shoulder.

"Listen," I said. "You are in trouble enough to pull up over your head and tie a knot in. But you're not in it alone. I'll help you. It's my line of work. I'll get you a lawyer in a bit. Then I'll call the cops. Before I do, though—" She started to speak and I squeezed her. "Listen," I said, "When the cops come don't say anything, don't talk to them, don't argue with them, don't be hostile, don't be smart. Do not say anything to anybody till you talk to the lawyer. His name is Vincent Haller. He'll see you soon after you go downtown. Talk only with him present and say only what he says you should. Have you ever been busted?"

"No."

"Okay. It's not anywhere near as bad as you think it is. No one will hurt you. No one will grab you under a bright light and hit you with a hose. You'll be okay, and you won't be in long. Haller will take care of you."

She nodded. I went on.

"Before I make my call—do you have any idea why the men did this?"

"No."

"Do you use drugs?"

"Yes."

"Do you know what they gave you?"

"No. It tasted like paregoric and smelled like ether. It wasn't anything I'd tried. Whatever it was, was a downer though."

"Okay. Get dressed. I'm going to call."

4

The first of Boston's finest to arrive were two bulls from a radio car. They came in, told us not to touch anything, got our names, frisked me, took my gun, and looked closely at us till the homicide people came. They came, as they always do, in large numbers: technicians, photographers, someone from the medical examiner's. Two guys in white coats to carry out the corpse and some dicks to investigate the crime and question the suspects. In this case the crew was led by the commander of the homicide bureau, Lieutenant Martin Quirk. I'm six foot one and he was taller than I am, taller and thicker. His hands and fingers were thick and his lips were thick and his nose was broad. His thick black hair was cut close. He was clean-shaven at four A.M. and his shoes gleamed with dark polish. His shirt was freshly ironed and his tie neatly knotted. His suit was immaculate and sharply creased. He wore a Tyrolean hat with a feather in it and a white raincoat, which he never took off. His face was pockmarked and there was a short scar at one corner of his mouth.

He stood now looking at me with his raincoat open and his hands in his hip pockets. "This is sure a lucky break for us, Spenser, having you on this to help us out. We need slick professionals like yourself to straighten us out and all. Keep us from forgetting to look for fingerprints, missing clues, and stuff."

"I didn't plan to get into this, Lieutenant. The kid called me for help, and I came over and found her. And him. She was badly drugged. I got her sobered up a little and called you."

"How did she know you?" Quirk asked.

"I'm on a case that she's involved in."

"What case?"

"Looking for a missing rare manuscript stolen from a university."

"What university?"

"If it seems pertinent, I'll tell you."

"If I want to know, you'll tell me." Quirk's voice squeezed out sharp and flat like sheet metal.

"I'll tell you if you need to know it. I don't make a living telling cops everything they want to know about clients."

"I don't make a living taking crap from hole-in-the-wall shysters like you, Spenser."

A thin, blue-jowled sergeant named Belson drifted in between Quirk and me.

"Come on, Lieutenant, this don't get us far. Both the girl and the victim are university students, and there's a fair bet that it's the same university that hired Spenser."

Quirk looked at me, then Belson. "Do you know him?" he asked, nodding at me.

"Yeah, he used to work out of the Suffolk County D.A.'s office about five years ago. I hear he got canned."

"Okay, get his story." He turned to me. "You're not working for the D.A. now, boy, you're working my side of the street, and if you get in my way I'll kick your ass right into the gutter. Got that?"

"Can I feel your muscle?" I said.

Quirk looked at me without saying anything, then turned away and walked over to the girl.

Belson shook his head and pulled out a notebook.

"Start up with the lieutenant, Spenser, and you'll end up looking like you went through a pepper mill."

"I won't be able to sleep without a night light," I said.

Belson shrugged. "Okay. Start from the beginning. You're in the business. I don't have to lead you."

I told him, omitting, mostly from stubbornness, the name of my client, but including, because it was sure to come out anyway, the incident in the Pub that afternoon, when I had knocked the kid down.

Belson shook his head again. "How could anyone get mad at a sweetheart like you? I would have thought he'd have been hypnotized with the way you're so agreeable."

I let that go.

"You're sure you might not have been hustling his chick just a little, Spenser? And maybe you were over here hustling her again and he came home and caught you, and an argument developed?"

"Yeah, and I pulled out my fourteen-dollar Saturday night special and let fly at him. Come off it, Belson. You're just talking for the hell of it. You know I didn't do it. You know I wouldn't use a piece of cheap tin like that gun. If I had, you know I would have covered it better than this."

"Okay, maybe I don't like you for it. I've known you a long time, and it's not your style. But it could happen. You got nothing against girls, I can recall. It could be his gun and you had to take it away from him and it went off. Lotta people get killed by people in a way that ain't their style."

"And I shot him four times in the chest getting it away from him?"

"Could be to cover it up, make it look different."

"You're fishing, Frank," I said.

"Maybe."

"Have you heard the girl's story yet?"

"Nope, lieutenant's getting that now."

"He's going to love it," I said.

"Of course you got it before you called us," Belson said.

"She was way under from something. I had to bring her out."

"And then you had to ask her what happened and then she had to tell you. And then you had to fix up a story maybe."

"Wait till you hear the story. You don't think I'm smart enough to work up something like that. You guys are cops, not priests.

Calling you isn't a ritual act. I called you as soon as my judgment told me it was both feasible and prudent."

Belson set fire to a half-smoked cigar before he said anything. Then he said, "You talk good for a dumb slug; feasible and prudent, my, my."

From the other side of the room Quirk spoke over his shoulder without turning his head. "Belson, bring the private license over here."

Belson nodded me toward Quirk and I walked over. Quirk was straddling the only straight chair in the room, with his forearms crossed on the back. Before him Terry Orchard was on the couch. She had on a denim shirt and Levi's again, but her hair was still wet and tight on her skull. She looked awfully small.

"Spenser," he said without looking up. "She says she won't say anything unless you say it's all right. She says you told her not to talk to us without a lawyer."

"Right enough, Lieutenant. I knew you wouldn't want to take advantage of her when she was confused, or perhaps in a state of shock."

"We're going to take her in."

"I thought you might."

"We'd like you to come along, too," Quirk said.

"I wouldn't miss it," I said.

Terry looked at me with her eyes very wide and dark. I said to her, "Haller will be there. Just do as I said."

The assistant M.E., a small man with thick glasses and gray curly hair, came over to Quirk.

"I'm through," he said. "If you are too, we'll haul him off."

"Any opinions, Manny?" Quirk asked.

"Yeah, I'd guess he was shot in the chest."

"That med school training really gives you insight," Quirk said. "Anything that I need to know that you can tell me now?"

"Shot sometime within the last five or six hours, cause of death presumable gunshot. I don't see any other signs. Got any corroborative testimony?"

Quirk looked at Belson.

"Spenser says the kid was dead when he arrived at three fifteen and that the blood had gotten tacky and the skin was cool," Belson said.

The assistant M.E. said, "That seems about right, but it could be a couple hours earlier for all I can prove here."

Quirk nodded. "Okay, thanks, Manny." And then to the two white-coated interns, "Take him away."

They bundled Dennis Powell onto the stretcher. He'd already started to stiffen and he was getting awkward to handle. They straightened his arms out down by his side, put his ankles together, wrapped the tarp around him, and strapped him into the stretcher. Then they dollied him out. They had to stand him up to get him out the apartment door, and when they did the top of him lolled against the straps. Terry made a noise and looked away. The stretcher bumped down the stairs and out to the ambulance. A few curious early risers stood around staring. The two harness bulls who'd showed up first kept them away from the door. A little fat dick in a long blue overcoat with a button missing came in after letting the stretcher out.

"Nothing, Lieutenant. Nobody heard nothing, nobody saw nothing, nobody knows nothing. Half of them are goddamn faggots, anyway."

"Jesus Christ," Quirk said. "Just give me information; don't review the witnesses' sex life for me."

"Okay, Lieutenant. I mean I figured that being as they was faggots you might not want to take their word. You know how these goddamn perverts are."

"No, I don't know, and I don't want you to tell me. Stay around, ask questions. See what you can find out about these two. Try to remember you're on the homicide squad, not the vice squad. When I want a fag count, I'll let you know."

The dick hustled out. Quirk shook his head. Belson was looking up at the ceiling, puffing the cigar butt that was barely clearing his lips by now.

"Take 'em downtown, Frank," Quirk said to Belson. "I'll clean up here and be along."

As we started out I said to Belson, "I'm still double-parked out there. Let me get it off the street before some zealous meter maid gets it hauled off."

Belson said, "Why don't you follow me downtown. Then we won't have to drive you back later."

I nodded and grinned. "See? I told you you didn't think I did it."

"I don't think anything," Belson said. "But you'll be down to look out for the little girl."

Belson took Terry into the squad car and they drove off. I got my car out from behind another white and blue police car with the seal of the city on the side, and followed Belson's car up Hemenway to Boylston, down Boylston to Clarendon, right on Clarendon, then up the Stanhope Street Alley and in behind headquarters.

5

We went in the back door, off Stanhope Street by the parking area that says RESERVED FOR PRESS. There were no cars there. You only go in the front door if you're newsfilm material. If they put the arm on you in a disadvantaged neighborhood you go in past the empty press lot.

The Homicide Division was third floor rear, with a view of the Fryalator vent from the coffee shop in the alley and the soft perfume of griddle and grease mixing with the indigenous smell of cigar smoke and sweat and something else, maybe generations of scared people. Vince Haller was leaning against one of the desks outside Quirk's frosted glass cubicle. He was wearing a white double-knit suit, and over one shoulder he carried a camel's-hair coat with big leather buttons. His gray hair was long and modish and he had a big Teddy Roosevelt mustache. He was a couple of inches taller than I was, but not as heavy.

"Gentlemen?" he said in his big actorish voice.

I gave him a wave and Belson said, "Hello, Vince."

"I'd like a chance to talk to my client."

Belson looked at Terry Orchard. "Is this man your attorney?"

She looked at me and I nodded. She said, "Yes."

"You can talk with her at my desk there." Belson nodded at a scarred and cluttered desk outside Quirk's enclosed cubicle. "We'll stay out of earshot."

"Has she been charged, Frank?" Haller asked.

"Not yet."

"Will she be?"

"I don't know. The lieutenant will be along in a minute. He takes care of that stuff. We'll want to talk with her a lot, though, either way."

"Has she been advised of her rights?"

Belson snorted. "Are you kidding. If she were shooting at me with a flame thrower I'd have to advise her of her rights before I shot back. Yes, she's been advised."

"Have you, Miss Orchard?"

"Yes, sir." She was numb and scared, and entirely submissive.

"Okay, come over here and we'll talk." She did and Belson and I stood silently watching them. I suddenly realized how tired I was. I'd slept about three hours. As we stood there, Quirk came in with two other dicks. He looked over at Haller and Terry Orchard, said nothing, and walked into his cubicle. Belson went in after him.

"Stick around," he said. And closed the door. The two dicks sat down at desks, and looked at nothing.

At the other end of the office a black cop with thick hands and a broken nose was talking into a telephone receiver cradled on one shoulder. An old guy in green coveralls came through dragging a cardboard carton with a rope handle and emptying the ashtrays and wastebaskets into it. Haller was still talking to Terry. And I thought about all the times I'd spent in shabby squad rooms like this. Sometimes it felt like all the rooms I was ever in looked out onto alleys. And I thought about how it must feel to be twenty and alone and be in one at 5:30 A.M. and not sure you'd get out. The steam pipes hissed. I wanted to hiss back.

More than that I wanted to run. The room was hot and stuffy. The air was bad. I wanted to get out, to get in my car and drive north. In my mind I could see the route, over the Mystic Bridge up Route 1, north, maybe to Ipswich or Newburyport where the houses were stately and old and the air was clean and cold and full of the sea. Where there's a kind of mellowness and a memory of another time and another America. Probably never was another America though. And if I headed out that way I'd probably be sitting around the police station in Ipswich, smelling the steam pipes and the disinfectant and wondering if some poor slob deserved what he was getting.

Quirk came out of his office. And looked at Haller. Then turned to me.

"Come in and talk."

I did. I told the same story to Quirk that I had to Belson. Exactly the same way. Quirk listened without a word. Looking straight at me all the time I talked. When I was through he said, "Okay, wait outside."

I did. He called Terry Orchard in. Haller went with her. The door closed. I sat some more. The dick at the end of the room still talked into the phone. The two that had come in with Quirk continued to sit and look elaborately at nothing. The sun had come up and shone into one corner of the room. Dust motes drifted in languidly.

"I can't stand it anymore," I said. "I'll confess, just don't give me the silent treatment anymore."

The two detectives looked at me blankly. "Confess what?" one of them said. He had long curly sideburns.

"Anything you want, just no more of the cold shoulder."

Sideburns said to his partner, "Hey, Al, ain't he a funny guy? Right before you go off duty after working all night it's really great to have a funny guy like him around so you can go home happy. Don't you feel that way, Al?"

Al said, "Aw, screw him."

More silence. I got up and walked to the window. There was a heavy wire mesh across it so suspects wouldn't jump out, drop three stories to the ground, and run off. The windows were grimy, with a kind of ancient grime that seemed to have sunk into the glass. Three floors below a thin Puerto Rican kid with pointed shoes came out of the back of the coffee shop with a bucket and poured hot dirty water into the street. It steamed in the cold briefly. I looked at my watch. 6:40. The kid had got up awful early to come in and mop the floor. I wondered how late tonight he'd be there.

Belson came out of Quirk's office with Terry, through the squad room, and out. Haller came out too, and walked over to me.

"They've gone down to the lab. I think they'll book her," he said. I didn't say anything.

He said, "Quickly, I wanted to check her story with you. She was asleep with her boyfriend in their apartment. Two men apparently known to Powell entered. Shot Powell, forced her to shoot Powell's body, drugged her, and left. She called you. You came. Sobered her up, got her story. Called the cops."

"That's it," I said.

"She knows you because the university employed you to find a missing rare book."

"Manuscript," I said.

"Okay, manuscript. . . . You got in touch with her because the campus security man suggested that an organization she was part of might have taken it. She had your card. In trouble, she called you."

"Right again," I said.

"As stories go it's not a winner," Haller said.

"I know," I said.

"She's convincing when she tells it, though," said Haller.

"What's its effect on Quirk?" I asked.

"Hard to say. He doesn't show much, but I don't think he's easy about it. I think he'll book her, but I don't think he's sure she's guilty."

"What do you think?" I asked.

"All my clients are innocent."

"Yeah," I said, "of something, anyway."

While we waited, the shift changed. Al and Sideburns left. The black cop with the phone departed. The day people came in. Faces shaved, wind-reddened. Smelling of cologne. Some of them had coffee in paper cups they'd bought on the way in. It smelled good. No one offered me any. Belson came back into the office with Terry. They went back into Quirk's office. Haller with them. Quirk yelled from inside.

"Spenser, come in. You might as well hear the rest."

I went in. It was crowded in there. Quirk was behind his desk. Terry in a straight chair beside it. Belson, Haller, and I standing against the wall. Quirk's desk was absolutely bare except for a tape recorder and a transparent plastic cube that on all sides contained pictures of a woman, children, and an English setter.

Quirk turned the recorder on. "All right, Miss Orchard, your story and Spenser's match. But that proves nothing much. You had plenty of time to arrange it before we were called. Can you think of any reason why two men would wish to come and kill Dennis Powell?"

"No, I don't know—maybe." Terry spoke barely above a whisper, and she seemed to sway slightly in the chair as she spoke.

"Which is it, Miss Orchard?" Quirk's voice was almost entirely without inflection and his thick, pockmarked face was entirely impassive. Terry shook her head.

Haller said, "Really, Lieutenant, Miss Orchard is about to fall from the chair." When Haller talked, the orange level light on the recorder flared brightly.

"Which is it, Miss Orchard?" Quirk said again, as if Haller hadn't spoken.

"Well, I think he was involved in the manuscript."

"Which manuscript?"

"The one that Mr. Spenser is looking for, the whatchamacallit manuscript."

I said, "Godwulf," and Quirk said, "Is it the Godwulf Manuscript, Miss Orchard?"

She nodded.

Quirk said, "Say yes or no, Miss Orchard; the recorder can't pick up signs."

"Yes," she said.

"How was he involved?"

"I don't know, just that he was, and some faculty member was. I heard him talking on the phone one day."

"What did they say?"

"I can't remember."

"Then why do you think it involved the theft of a manuscript?"

"I just know. You know how you remember having an idea from a conversation but don't remember the conversation itself, you know?"

"Why do you think a faculty member is involved, Miss Orchard?"

She shook her head again. "Same reason," she said.

"Do you think one of the men who you say killed Powell was a professor?"

"No."

"Why not?"

"I don't know. They didn't look like professors."

"What did they look like?"

"It's hard to remember. It was so fast. They were both big and had on dark topcoats and hats, regular felt hats, like businessmen wear. The one who shot Dennis had big sideburns, like Prince Albert, you know, along his jaw. He was sort of fat."

"Black or white?"

She looked startled. "White," she said.

"Why would the theft of a manuscript cause two big white men in hats and topcoats to come to your apartment at two thirty A.M. and kill Powell and frame you?"

"I don't know."

"Why—" Quirk stopped. Tears were running down Terry Orchard's face. She made no sound. She sat still with her eyes closed and the tears coming down her face.

I said, "Quirk, for crissake . . ."

He nodded, turned to Belson.

"Frank, get a matron and book her."

Belson took her arm. She stood up.

There was no sign that she heard him, or that she heard anything.

Belson took her out. Haller went with her.

Quirk said, "So far you're out of it, Spenser. I got nothing to hold you for. But if something does come up I want you to be where I don't have to look for you."

I got up. "There are whole days at a time, Lieutenant, that go by without me ever giving a real goddamn about what you want."

Quirk took my gun out of his desk and handed it to me, butt first. "Beat it," he said.

I put the gun away, went down the stairs three flights and out the front door. There were no cameramen, no TV trucks. It was cold and the wet snow-rain had frozen into gray lumpy ice. I went around the corner, got in my car, drove home, drank two glasses of milk, and went to bed.

6

The phone woke me again. I squinted against the brutal bright sunlight and answered.

"Spenser?"

"Yeah."

"Spenser, this is Roland Orchard." He paused as if waiting for applause.

I said, "How nice for you."

He said, "What?"

I said, "What do you want, Mr. Orchard?"

"I want to see you. How soon can you get here?"

"As soon as I feel like it. Which may be a while."

"Spenser, do you know who I am?"

"I guess you're Terry Orchard's father."

He hadn't meant that. "Yes," he said. "I am. I am also senior partner of Orchard, Bonner and Blanch."

"Swell," I said. "I buy all your records."

"Spenser, I don't care for your manner."

"I'm not selling it, Mr. Orchard. You called me. I didn't call you. If you want to tell me what you want without showing me your scrapbook, I'll listen. Otherwise, write me a letter."

There was a long silence. Then Orchard said, "Do you have my address, Mr. Spenser?"

"Yeah."

"My daughter is home, and I have not gone into the office, and we would very much like you to come to the house. I expect to pay you."

"I will come out in about an hour, Mr. Orchard," I said, and hung up.

It was a little after noon. I got up and stood a long time under the shower. I'd had about four and a half hours' sleep and I needed more. Ten years ago I wouldn't have. I put on my suit—I wasn't sure you could get onto West Newton Hill without one—made and ate a fried egg sandwich, drank a cup of coffee, and went out. I should have made the bed. I knew I would hate finding it unmade when I came back.

It was cold and bright out. It took five minutes for the heater in the car to get warm enough to melt the ice on my windows, and another five minutes for it to melt. I had no ice scraper.

By the Mass Turnpike it is less than ten minutes from downtown Boston to West Newton. From West Newton Square to the top of West Newton Hill is a matter of fifty thousand dollars. Status ascends as the hill rises, and at the top live the rich. It is old rich on West Newton Hill. Doctor rich, professor rich, stockbroker rich, lawyer rich. The new rich, the engineer rich, and the technocratic rich live in developments named after English kings in towns like Lynnfield and Sudbury.

Roland Orchard looked to be a rich man's rich man. His home was large and white and towering as one came up the hill toward it. It occupied most of the lot it was built on. New rich seem to want a lot of land for a gardener to manicure. Old rich don't seem to give a damn. Across the front and around one side of the house was a wide porch, empty in the winter but bearing the wear marks of summer furniture. Above the door was a fan-shaped stained glass window. I rang the bell. A maid opened the door. Her black skin, devoid of make-up, shone as though freshly burnished. Her almond-colored eyes held a knowledge of things that West Newton Hill didn't want to hear about.

She said, "Yes, sir."

I gave her one of my cards. The one with only my name on it.

"Yes, Mr. Spenser. Mrs. Orchard is expecting you in the study."

She led me down a polished oak-floored hall, past a curving stairway. The hall—it was more like a corridor—ran front to back, the depth of the house. At the far end a floor to ceiling window opened out onto the backyard. The coils of a grapevine framed the window. The rest was dirty snow. The maid knocked on a door to the left of the window; a woman's voice said, "Come in." The maid opened the door, said "Mr. Spenser," and left.

It was a big room, blond wood bookcases built in on three walls. A fieldstone fireplace covered the fourth wall. There was a fire going, and the room was warm and smelled of woodsmoke. Mrs. Orchard was standing when I came in. She was darkly tanned (not Miami, I thought, West Palm Beach, probably) and wearing a white pants suit and white boots. Her hair was shag cut and tipped with silver, and the skin on her face was very tight over her bones. She had silver nail polish and wore heavy Mexican-looking silver earrings. A silver service and a covered platter on a mahogany tea wagon stood near the fire. A chiffon stole was draped over the back of the couch, and a novel by Joyce Carol Oates lay open on the coffee table.

As I walked toward her she stood motionless, one hand extended, limp at the wrist, toward me. I felt as if I were walking into a window display.

"Mr. Spenser," she said. "It's very nice of you to come."

"That's okay," I said.

I didn't know what to do with her hand, shake it or kiss it. I shook it, and the way she looked made me suspect I'd chosen wrong.

"My husband had to go into the office for a bit; he should be back soon."

I said, "Uh huh."

"He might have stopped off at the club for handball and a rubdown. Rolly works very hard to stay in shape."

"Uh huh."

"What do you do, Mr. Spenser? You look to be in excellent condition. Do you work out?"

"Not at the club," I said.

"No," she said. "Of course not."

I took off my coat. "May I sit down?" I said.

"Oh, I'm sorry, of course, sit down. Will you have some coffee, or tea? I had some sandwiches made up. Would you like one?"

"No, thank you, I ate before I came. I'll take coffee though, black."

"You must pardon me, Mr. Spenser, my manners are really much better. It's just that I've never been involved with policemen and all. And I have never really spoken to a private detective before. Are you carrying a gun?"

"I thought I'd risk West Newton without one," I said.

"Yes, of course. You're sure you won't have a sandwich?"

"Look, Mrs. Orchard, I spent most of last night with your daughter and a corpse. I spent the rest of last night with your daughter and the cops. The last I knew she was in jail for murder. Your husband says she's home. Now he and you didn't get me out here to make sure I was eating properly. What do you want?"

"My husband will be along soon, Mr. Spenser; he'll explain. Rolly handles these things. I do not." She looked straight at me as she talked and leaned forward a little. She had large blue eyes, and she wore eye shadow, I noticed. I bet the eyes got her a lot that she wanted. Especially when she looked right at you and leaned forward a little as she talked. She turned slightly on the couch and tucked one leg under the other, and I got the long line of her thigh and the jut of her sharp breasts. Her body looked lean and tight. A little sinewy for my taste. She kept the pose. I wondered if I was supposed to bark.

She picked up the book. "Do you read much, Mr. Spenser?"

"Yeah," I said.

"Do you enjoy Miss Oates?"

"No."

"Oh, really? Why on earth not?"

"I'm probably insensitive," I said.

"Oh, I don't think so, Mr. Spenser. What little I've heard Terry say of you suggests quite the contrary."

"Where is Terry?"

"In her room. Her father has asked that she talk with no one except in his presence."

"How's she feel about that?"

"After what she's gotten herself into and what she's putting us through, she's learning to do what she's told."

There was a triumphant undertone in Mrs. Orchard's voice. I said nothing.

"Would you put another log on the fire, Mr. Spenser? It seems to be going low, and Rolly always likes a blazing fire when he comes in."

It was a way of establishing relationships, I thought, as I got a log from the basket and set it on top of the fire—get me to do her bidding. I'd known other women like that. If they couldn't get you to do them little services, they felt insecure. Or maybe she just wanted another log in the fireplace. Sometimes I'm deep as hell.

The door to the study opened and a man came in. He wore a dark double-breasted blazer with a crest on the pocket, a thick white turtleneck sweater, gray flared slacks, and black ankle boots with a lot of strap and buckle showing. His hair was blond and no doubt naturally curly; it contrasted nicely with his tan. He was a slender man, shorter than I by maybe an inch and maybe ten years older. Under the tan his face had a reddish flush that might be health or booze.

"Spenser," he said, and put out his hand, "kind of you to come." I shook hands with him. He wasn't being the top-exec-used-to-instant-obedience. He was being the gracious-man-of-affluence-putting-an-employee-at-ease.

He said to his wife, "I'll have coffee, Marion."

She rose and poured him coffee. She put several small triangular sandwiches on a plate, put the coffee cup in the little depression on the plate that was made to hold it, and placed it next to a red leather wing chair.

Orchard sat down, carefully hiking his trouser legs up at the knee so they wouldn't bag. I noticed he had a thick silver ring on his little finger.

"I'm sorry to have kept you waiting, Spenser, but I don't like to stay out of work if I can help it. Married to the job, I guess. Just wanted to make sure everything was running smoothly."

He took a delicate sip of coffee and a small bite of one of the sandwiches.

"I wish to hire you, Mr. Spenser, to see that my daughter is exonerated of the charges leveled against her. I was able to have her released on bail in my custody, but it took a good deal of doing and

I had to collect a number of favors to do it. Now I want this mess cleared up and the suspicion eliminated from my name and my home. The police are working to convict. I want someone working to acquit."

"Why not have Terry join us?" I said.

"Perhaps later," Orchard said, "but first I want to speak with you for a time."

I nodded. He went on. "I would like you to give me a complete rundown of the circumstances by which you became involved with Terry up to and including last night."

"Hasn't Terry told you?"

"I want your version."

I didn't want to tell him. I didn't like him. I did like his daughter. I didn't like his assumption that our versions would differ. I said, "Nope."

"Mr. Spenser. I am employing you to investigate a murder. I want a report of what you've discovered so far."

"First, you may or may not be hiring me. You've offered. I haven't accepted. So at the moment I owe you nothing. That includes how I met your daughter, and what we did."

"Goddammit, Spenser, I don't have to take that kind of insolence from you."

"Right," I said, "you can hire another Hawkshaw. The ones with phones are in the yellow pages under SLEUTH."

I thought for a moment that Orchard was going to get up and take a swing at me. I felt no cold surge of terror. Then he thought better of it, and leaned back in his chair.

"Marion," he said, "I'll have some brandy. Would you join me, Mr. Spenser?" I looked at my watch; it was two thirty. He really handled stress well. I decided what the flush under the tan was.

"Yeah. I'll have some. Thank you."

Marion Orchard's face looked a little more tightly stretched over her good bones as she went to the sideboard and poured two shots of brandy from a decanter into crystal snifters. She brought them back to us, handed one to me and one to her husband.

Orchard swirled it in his glass and took a large swallow. I tried mine. It was the real stuff okay, barely liquid at all as it drifted down my throat. A guy who served brandy like that couldn't be all bad.

"Now look, Spenser. Terry is our only child. We've lavished every affection and concern on her. We have brought her up in wealth and comfort. Clothes, the best schooling, Europe. She had her own horse and rode beautifully. She made us proud. She was an achiever. That's important. We do things in this family. Marion rides and hunts as well as any man."

I looked at Marion Orchard and said, "Hi ho, Silver."

Orchard went on. I was not sure he'd heard me.

"Then when it came time for college, she insisted on going to that factory. Can you imagine the reaction of some of my associates when they ask me where my daughter goes to school and I tell them?" It was a rhetorical question. I could imagine, but I knew he wasn't looking for an answer. "Against my best judgment I permitted her to go. And I permitted her to live there rather than at home." He shook his head. "I should have known better. She got in with the worst element in a bad school and . . ." He stopped, drank another large slug from his snifter, and went on. "She never gave us any trouble till then. She was just what we wanted. And then in college, living on the very edge of the ghetto, sleeping around, drugs. You've seen her, you've seen how she dresses, who she keeps company with. I don't even know where she lives anymore. She rarely comes home, and when she does it's as if she were coming only to flaunt herself before us and our friends. Do you know she appeared here at a party we were giving wearing a miniskirt she'd made out of an old pair of Levi's? Now she's gotten herself involved in a murder. I've got a right to know about her. I've got a right to know what she'll do to us next."

"I don't do family counseling, Mr. Orchard. There are people who do, and maybe you ought to look up one of them. If you'll get Terry down here we'll talk, all of us, and see if we can arrange to live in peace while I look into the murder."

Orchard had finished his brandy. He nodded at the empty glass. His wife got up, refilled it, and brought it to him. He drank, then put the glass down. He said, "While you're up, Marion, would you ask Terry to come down."

Marion left the room. Orchard took another belt of brandy. He wasn't bothering to savor the bouquet. I nibbled at the edge of mine. Marion Orchard came back into the room with Terry.

I stood and said, "Hello, Terry."

She said, "Hi."

Her hair was loose and long. She wore a short-sleeved blouse, a skirt, no socks, and a pair of loafers. I looked at her arms—no tracks. One point for our side; she wasn't shooting. At least not regularly. She was fresh-scrubbed and pale, and remarkably without affect. She went to a round leather hassock by the fire and sat down, her knees tight together, her hands folded in her lap. Dolly Demure, with a completely blank face. The loose hair softened her, and the traditional dress made her look like somebody's cheerleader, right down to loafers without socks. Had there been any animation she'd have been pretty as hell.

Orchard spoke. "Terry, I'm employing Mr. Spenser to clear you of the murder charge."

She said, "Okay."

"I hope you'll cooperate with him in every way."

"Okay."

"And, Terry, if Mr. Spenser succeeds in getting you out of this mess, if he does, perhaps you will begin to rethink your whole approach to life."

"Why don't you get laid," she said flatly, without inflection, and without looking at him.

Marion Orchard said, "Terry!" in a horrified voice.

Orchard's glass was empty. He flicked an eye at it, and away.

"Now, you listen to me, young lady," he said. "I have put up with your nonsense for as long as I'm going to. If you . . ."

I interrupted. "If I want to listen to this kind of crap I can go home and watch daytime television. I want to talk with Terry, and maybe later I'll want to talk with each of you. Separately. Obviously I was wrong; we can't do it in a group. You people want to encounter one another, do it on your own time."

"By God, Spenser," Orchard said.

I cut him off again. "I want to talk with Terry. Do I or don't I?"

I did. He and his wife left, and Terry and I were alone in the library.

"If I told my father to get laid he would have knocked out six of my teeth," I said.

"Mine won't," she said. "He'll drink some more brandy, and tomorrow he'll stay late at the office."

"You don't like him much," I said.

"I bet if I said that to you, you'd knock out six of my teeth," she said.

"Only if you didn't smile," I answered.

"He's a jerk."

"Maybe," I said. "But he's your jerk, and from his point of view you're no prize package either."

"I know," she said.

"However," I said, "let's think about what I'm supposed to do here. Tell me more about the manuscript and the professor and anything else you can remember beyond what you told Quirk last night."

"That's all there is," she said. "I told the police everything I know."

"Let's run through it again anyway," I said. "Have you talked with Quirk again since last night?"

"Yes, I saw him this morning before Daddy's people got me out."

"Okay, tell me what he asked you and what you said."

"He started by asking me why I thought two big white men in hats would come to our apartment and kill Dennis and frame me."

That was Quirk, starting right where he left off, no rephrasing, no new approach, less sleep than I had and there in the morning when the big cheeses passed the word along to let her out, getting all his questions answered before he released her.

"And what did you answer?" I said.

"I said the only thing I could think of was the manuscript. That Dennis was involved somehow in that theft, and he was upset about it."

"Can you give me more than that? How was he involved? Why was he involved? What makes you think he was involved? Why do you think he was upset? What did he do to show you he was upset? Answer any or all, one at a time."

"It was a phone call he made from the apartment. The way he was talking I could tell he was upset, and I could tell he wasn't talking to another kid. I mean, you can tell that from the way people talk. The way his voice sounded."

"What did he say?" I said.

"I couldn't hear most of it. He talked low, and I knew he didn't want me to hear, you know, cupping his hand and everything. So I tried not to hear. But he did say something about hiding it . . . like 'Don't worry, no one will find it. I was careful.' "

"When was this?" I asked.

"About a week ago. Lemme see, I was up early for my Chaucer

course, so it would have been Monday, that's five days ago. Last Monday."

The manuscript had been stolen Sunday night.

"Okay, so he was upset. About what?"

"I don't know, but I can tell when he's mad. At one point I think he threatened someone."

"Why do you think so? What did he say that makes you think so?"

"He said, 'If you don't . . .' No . . . No . . . he said, 'I will, I really will. . . .' Yeah. That's what it was . . . 'I really will.' But very threateny, you know."

"Good. Now why do you think it was a professor? I know the voice tone told you it was someone older, but why a professor? What did he say? What were the words?"

"Well, oh, I don't know, it was just a feeling. I wasn't all that interested; I was running the water for a bath, anyway."

"No, Terry, I want to know. The words, what were his words?"

She was silent, her eyes squeezed almost shut, as if the sun were shining in them, her upper teeth exposed, her lower lip sucked in.

"Dennis said, 'I don't care' . . . 'I don't care, if you do.' . . . He said, 'I don't care if you do. Cut the goddamn thing.' That's it. He was talking to an older person and he said cut the class if the other person had to. That's why I figured it must be a professor."

"How do you know he wasn't talking about cutting a piece of rope, or a salami?"

"Because he mentioned class or school a little before. And what could they be talking about angrily that had to do with salami?"

"Okay. Good. What else?"

There wasn't anything else. I worked on her for maybe half an hour more and nothing else surfaced. All I got was the name of a SCACE official close to Powell, someone named Mark Tabor, whose title was political counselor.

"If you think of anything else, anything at all, call me. You still have my card?"

"Yes. I . . . my father will pay you for what you did last night."

"No, he won't. He'll pay me for what I may do. But last night was a free introductory offer."

"It was a very nice thing to do," she said.

"Aw, hell," I said. "What you should try to do is this. You should try to keep from starting up with your old man for a while. And you should try to stay around the house, go to class if you think you should, but for the moment let SCACE stave off the apocalypse without you. Okay?"

"Okay. But don't laugh at us. We're perfectly serious and perfectly right."

"Yeah, so is everyone I know."

I left her then. Said good-bye to her parents, took a retainer from Roland Orchard, and drove back to town.

7

Driving back to Boston, I thought about my two retainers in the same week. Maybe I'd buy a yacht. On the other hand maybe it would be better to get the tear in my convertible roof fixed. The tape leaked. I got off the Mass Pike at Storrow Drive and headed for the university. On my left the Charles River was thick and gray between Boston and Cambridge. A single oarsman was sculling upstream. He had on a hooded orange sweat shirt and dark blue sweat pants and his breath steamed as he rocked back and forth at the oars. Rowing downstream would have been easier.

I turned off Storrow at Charlesgate, went up over Commonwealth, onto Park Drive, past a batch of ducks swimming in the muddy river, through the Fenway to Westland Ave. Number 177 was on the left, halfway to Mass Ave. I parked at a hydrant and went up the stone steps to the glass door at the entry. I tried it. It was open. Inside an ancient panel of doorbells and call boxes covered the left wall. I didn't have to try one to know they didn't work.

They didn't need to. The inner door didn't close all the way because the floor was warped in front of the sill and the door jammed against it. Mark Tabor was on the fourth floor. No elevator. I walked up. The apartment house smelled bad and the stair landing had beer bottles and candy wrappers accumulating in the corners. Somewhere in the building electronic music was playing at top volume. The fourth flight began to tell on me a little, but I forced myself to breathe normally as I knocked on Tabor's door. No answer. I knocked again. And a third time. Loud. I didn't want to waste the four-flight climb. A voice inside called out, "Wait a minute." There was a pause, and then the door opened.

I said, "Mark Tabor?"

And he said, "Yeah."

He looked like a zinnia. Tall and thin with an enormous corona of rust red hair flaring out around his pale, clean-shaven face. He wore a lavender undershirt and a pair of faded, flare-bottomed denim dungarees that were too long and dragged on the floor over his bare feet.

I said, "I'm a friend of Terry Orchard's; she asked me to come and talk with you."

"About what?"

"About inviting people in to sit down."

"Why do you think I know what's her name?"

"Aw, come off it, Tabor," I said. "How the hell do you think I got your name and address? How do you know Terry Orchard is not a what's his name? What do you lose by talking with me for fifteen minutes? If I was going to mug you I would have already. Besides, a mugger would starve to death in this neighborhood."

"Well, what do you want to talk about?" he asked, still standing in the door. I walked past him into the room. He said, "Hey," but didn't try to stop me. I moved a pile of mimeographed pamphlets off a steamer trunk and sat down on it. Tabor took a limp pack of Kools out of his pants pocket, extracted a ragged cigarette, and lit it. The menthol smell did nothing for the atmosphere. He took a big drag and exhaled through his nose. He leaned against the door jamb. "Okay," he said. "What do you want?"

"I want to keep Terry Orchard out of the slam, for one thing. And I want to find the Godwulf Manuscript, for another."

"Why are the cops hassling Terry?"

"Because they think she killed Dennis Powell."

"Dennis is dead?"

I nodded.

"Ain't that a bitch, now," he said, much as if I'd said the rain would spoil the picnic. He went over and sat on the edge of a kitchen table covered with books, lined yellow paper, manila folders, and the crusts of a pizza still in the take box. Behind him, taped to the gray painted wall with raggedly torn masking tape, was a huge picture of Che Guevara. Opposite was a day bed covered by an unzipped sleeping bag. There were clothes littered on the floor. On top of a bureau was a hot plate. There were no curtains or window shades.

I clucked approvingly. "You've really got some style, Tabor," I said.

"You from *House Beautiful* or something?" he said.

"Nope, I'm a private detective." I showed him the photostat of my license. "I'm trying to clear Terry Orchard of the murder charge. I'm also looking for the Godwulf Manuscript, and I think they're connected. Can you help me?"

"I don't know nothing about no murder, man, and nothing about no jive ass manuscript." Why did all the radical white kids from places like Scarsdale and Bel-Air try to talk as if they'd been brought up in Brownsville and Watts? He stubbed out his Kool and lit another.

"Look," I said. "You and Dennis Powell roomed together for two years. You and Terry Orchard are members of the same organization. You share the same goals. I'm not the cops. I'm free-lance, for crissake, I'm labor. I work for Terry. I don't want you. I want Terry out of trouble and the manuscript back in its case. Do you know where the manuscript is?"

"Naw, man. I don't know anything about it."

He didn't look up from the contemplation of his Kool. His voice never varied. Like Terry, he showed no affect. No response to stimulus. It was as though he'd shut down.

"Tell me this," I said. "Does SCACE have a faculty adviser?"

"Oh, man, be cool. SCACE ain't no frat house, baby. Faculty adviser . . . Man, that's heavy."

"Do any faculty members belong to SCACE?"

"Maybe. Lot of people belong to SCACE. That's for me to know and you to guess."

"What's the big secret?"

"Lots of dudes can get in trouble for joining organizations like SCACE. The imperialists don't like opposition. The fat cats don't like organizations that are for the worker. The superoppressors are scared of the revolution."

"You forgot to mention the capitalist running-dog lackeys," I said.

"Like you, you mean? See what happened to Terry Orchard? The pigs have framed her already. They'll do anything they can to stamp us out."

"Look, kid, I don't want to sit up here and argue Herbert Marcuse with you. The cops are professionals. You can sit here in your hippie suit and drink wine and smoke grass and read Marx and play revolution like Tom Sawyer ambushing the A-rabs all you want. That bothers the cops like a tick fly on an elephant. If they wanted to stamp you out, they'd come in here and stamp and you'd know what a stamping was. They don't have to get frilly and frame some twenty-year-old broad to get at you. They've got guys in the station house in Charlestown that they keep in a cage when they're not on duty."

He gave me a tough look. Which isn't easy when you weigh 150 pounds.

"How about a faculty member that might be associated with SCACE?"

He let the smoke from his cigarette out of his nose and mouth slowly. It drifted up around his head. Long years of practice, I thought. He looked straight at me with his eyes almost closed for a long time. Then he said, "Where would the movement be now if someone had saved Sacco and Vanzetti?"

"Sonova bitch," I said. "You're almost perfect, you are, a flawless moron. I don't think I've ever seen anyone stay so implacably on the level of absolute abstraction."

"Screw you, man," he said.

"That's better," I said. "Now we're getting down where I live. I've got no hope for you, punk. But I promise you that if that kid gets burned because you don't tell me what you could tell me, I will come for you. You martyr that kid and I'll give the movement another martyr."

"Screw you, man," he said.

I walked out.

I went back down the four flights of stairs, as empty as when I went up. Some sleuth, Spenser, a real Hawkshaw. All you've found out is you get winded after four flights of stairs. I wondered if I should go back up and have a go at shaking some information out of him. Maybe later. Maybe he'd stew a little and I could call on him again. I didn't even know he knew anything. But talking to him, I could feel him holding back. I could even feel that he liked knowing something and not telling. It added color to the romance of his conspiracy. Out in the street the air was cold and it tasted clean after the mentholated smoke and the stale air of Tabor's room. A truck backfired and up on Mass Avenue a bus ground under way in low gear.

My next try was the campus. The student newspaper was located in the basement of the library. On the blond oak door cut into the cinder block of the basement corridor an inventive person had lettered NEWS in black ink.

Inside, the room was long and narrow. L-shaped black metal desks with white Formica tops were sloppily lined up along the long wall on the left. A hand-lettered sign made from half a manila folder instructed the staff to label all photographs with name, date, and location. The room was empty except for a black woman in a red paisley dashiki and matching turban. She was fat but not flabby, hard fat we used to call it when I was a kid, and the dashiki billowed around her body like a drop cloth on the sofa when the living room's going to be painted. A plastic name plate on her desk said FEATURE EDITOR.

She said, "Can I help you?" Her voice was not cordial. No one seemed to be mistaking me for a member of the academic community.

I said, "I hope so." I gave her a card. "I'm working on a case, and I'm looking for information. Can I ask you for some?"

"You surely can," she said. "All the news that's fit to print, that's us."

"Okay, you know there's a manuscript been stolen."

"Yep."

"I have some reason to believe that a radical student organization, SCACE, is involved in the theft."

"Uh huh."

"What I'm looking for are faculty connections with SCACE. What can you tell me?"

"Why you want to know about faculty connections?"

"I have reason to believe that a faculty member was involved in the theft."

"I have reason to believe that information is a two-way go, sweetie," she said. "Ah is a member ob de press, baby. Information is mah business."

I liked her. She was old for a student, maybe twenty-eight. And she was tough.

"Fair enough," I said. "If you'll drop the Stepin Fetchit act, I'll tell you what I can. In trade?"

"Right on, brother," she said.

"Two things. One, what's your name?"

"Iris Milford."

"Two, do you know Terry Orchard?"

She nodded.

"Then you know she's a SCACE member. You also may know she's been arrested for murder."

She nodded again.

"I think the manuscript theft and the murder are connected." I told her about Terry, and the murder, and Terry's memory of the phone call.

"Someone set her up," I said. "If someone wanted her out of the way they'd just have killed her. They wanted to kill Powell. They wouldn't go to the trouble and take the risk just to frame her. And they wanted to kill Powell in such a way as to keep people from digging into it. And it looked good—a couple of freaky kids living in what my aunt used to call sin. On drugs, long-haired, barefooted, radical, and on a bad trip, one shoots the other and tells some weird hallucinogenic story about guys in trench coats. The Hearst papers would have them part of an international sex club by the second day's story."

"How come you're messing it up, then? If it's so good. How come you don't believe it?"

"I talked to her right after it happened. She's not that good a liar."

"Why ain't it a trip? Maybe she really thinks she's telling you true. You ever been on a trip?"

"No. You?"

"Baby, I'm fat, black, widowed, pushing thirty, and got four kids. I don't need no additional problems. But she could think it happened. Got any better reason for thinking she's not guilty?"

"I like her."

"All right," she said. "That's cool."

"So, what do you know?"

"Not a hell of a lot. The kid Powell was a jerk, sulky, foolish. On an ego trip. Terry, I don't know. I've been in classes with her. She's bright, but she's screwed up. Jesus, they're so miserable, those kids, always so goddamn unhappy about racism and sexism and imperialism and militarism and capitalism. Man, I grew up in a tarpaper house in Fayette, Mississippi, with ten other kids. We were trying to stay alive; we didn't have time to be that goddamn unhappy."

"How about a professor?"

"In SCACE, you got me. I do know that there's a lot of talk about drug dealing connected with SCACE."

"For instance?"

"For instance, that Powell was dealing, and had big connections. He could get you smack, anything you wanted. But especially smack. A kid that can get unlimited smack is heavy in some circles."

"Mob connection?"

"I don't know. I don't even know whether he really could get a big supply of smack. I just tell you what I hear. Kids like to talk big —especially to me, because I live in Roxbury, and they figure all us darkies are into drugs and crime, 'cause we been oppressed by you honky slumlords."

"I want a professor," I said. "Try this. Name me the most radical faculty members in the university."

"Oh, man, how the hell do I know? There's about thirty-five thousand people in this place."

"Name me anyone, any that you know. I'm not the Feds. I'm not going to harass them. They can advocate cannibalism for all I care. I only want to get one kid out of trouble. Make me a list of any you can think of. They don't have to be active. Who is there that might be involved in stealing a manuscript and holding it for ransom?"

"I'll think on it," she said.

"Think on it a lot. Get any of your friends who will think on it too. Students know things that deans and chairmen don't know."

"Ain't that the truth."

"How about an English professor? Wouldn't that be the best bet? It was a medieval manuscript. It was important because it referred to some medieval writer. Wouldn't an English professor be most likely to think of holding it for ransom?"

"Who's the writer it mentions?" she asked.

"Richard Rolle."

"How much they want for him?"

"A hundred thousand dollars."

"I'd give them some dough if they'd promise not to return it. You ever read his stuff?"

I shook my head.

"Don't," she said.

"Can you think of any English professors who might fit my bill?"

"There's a lot of flakes in that department. There's a lot of flakes in most departments, if you really want to know. But English . . ." She whistled, raised her eyebrows, and looked at the ceiling.

"Okay, but who is the flakiest? Who would you bet on if you had to bet?"

"Hayden," she said. "Lowell Hayden. He's one of those little pale guys with long, limp blond hair that looks like he hasn't started to shave yet, but he's like thirty-nine. You know? Serious as a bastard. Taught a freshman English course two years ago called The Rhetoric of Revolution. You dig? Yeah, he'd be the one, old Dr. Hayden."

"What's he teach besides freshman English?"

"I don't know for sure. I know he teaches Chaucer, 'cause I took Chaucer with him." I felt a little click in the back of my head. Something nudged at me. A Chaucer class had been mentioned before. I tucked the inkling away. I knew I could dredge it up later when I had time. I always could.

"Mrs. Milford, thank you. If you come up with anything, my number's on the card. I have an answering service. If I'm not there, leave a message."

"Okay."

I got up and looked around the basement room. "Freedom of the press is a flaming sword," I said. "Use it wisely, hold it high, guard it well."

Iris Milford looked at me strangely. I left.

The corridor in the basement of the library was almost empty. I looked at my watch. 5:05. Too late to find anyone in the English Department. I went home.

In my kitchen I sat at the counter and opened a can of beer. It was very quiet. I turned on the radio. Maybe I should buy a dog, I thought. He'd be glad to see me when I came home. The beer was good. I finished the can. And opened another. Where was I? I ran over the last couple of days in my mind. One: Terry Orchard didn't kill Dennis Powell. That was a working hypothesis. Two: the missing manuscript and the murder were two parts of the same thing, and if I found out anything about one, I'd know something about the other. That was another working hypothesis. What did I have in support of these hypotheses? About half a can of beer. There was that click I had when I talked with Iris Milford. Chaucer. She's had a Chaucer course with Lowell Hayden. I drank the rest of the beer and opened another can. It came back. Terry was up early for her Chaucer course the day Dennis had been telling some professor on the phone to cut his class. I looked at my face, reflected in the window over the sink. "You've still got all the moves, kid," I said. But what did it give me? Nothing much, just a little coincidence. But it was something. It suggested some kind of connection. Coincidences are suspect. Old Lowell Hayden looked better to me all the time. I got another beer. After three or four beers everything began looking better to me.

I got a pound of fresh scallops out of the refrigerator and began to make something called Scallops Jacques for supper. It was a recipe in a French cookbook that I'd gotten for a birthday present from a woman I know. I like to cook and drink while I'm doing it. Scallops Jacques is a complicated affair with cream and wine and lemon juice and shallots, and by the time it was done I was feeling quite pleasant. I made some hot biscuits for myself, too, and ate the scallops and biscuits with a bottle of Pouilly Fuissé, sitting at the counter. Afterward I went to bed. I slept heavily and for a long time.

8

I slept late and woke up feeling very good, though my mouth tasted funny. I went over to the Boston YMCA and worked out in the weight room. I hit the light bag and the heavy bag, ran three miles around their indoor track, took a shower, and went down to my office. I was glistening with health and vigor till I got there. You never felt really glistening in my office. It was on Stuart Street, second floor front, half a block down from Tremont. One room with a desk, a file cabinet, and two chairs in case Mrs. Onassis came with her husband. The old iron radiator had no real control and the room, closed for three days, reeked with heat. I stepped over the three-day pile of mail on the floor under the mail slot and went to open the window. It took some effort. I took off my coat, picked up the mail, and sat at my desk to read it. I'd come down mainly to check my mail, and the trip had been hardly worth it. There was a phone bill, a light bill, an overdue notice from the Boston Public Library, a correspondence course offering to teach me karate at home in my spare time, a letter from a former client insisting that while I had found his wife she had left again and hence he would not pay my bill, an invitation to join a vacation club, an invitation to buy a set of socket wrenches, an invitation to join an automobile club, an invitation to subscribe to five magazines of my choice at once-in-a-lifetime savings, an invitation to shop the specials on pork at my local supermarket, and a number of less important letters. Nothing from Germaine Greer or Lenny Bernstein, no dinner invitations, no post cards from the Costa del Sol, no mash notes from Helen Gurley Brown. Last week had been much the same.

I stood up and looked out my window. It was a bright day, but cold, and the whores had emerged, working the Combat Zone, looking cold and bizarre in their miniskirts, boots, and blond wigs. Being seductive at twenty degrees was heavy going, I thought. Being horny at twenty degrees wasn't all that easy either. Things were slow for the whores. It was lunchtime, and the businessmen were beginning to drift down from Boylston and Tremont and Back Bay offices to have lunch at Jake Wirth's or upstairs in the Athens Olympia. The whores eyed them speculatively, occasionally approached one, and were brushed off. The businessmen didn't like to look at them and hurried off in embarrassment when approached, visions of the day's first Bloody Mary dancing in their heads.

I closed the window, threw most of the mail away, locked the office, and headed for my car. The drive to the university was easy from my office, and I was there in ten minutes. I parked in a slot that said RESERVED FOR UNIVERSITY PRESIDENT and found my way to Tower's office. The secretary was wearing a pink jumpsuit this day. I revised my opinion about her thighs. They weren't too heavy; they were exactly the right size for the jumpsuit. I said, "My name's Spenser. To see Mr. Tower." She said, "Yes, Mr. Spenser, he'll be through in a minute," and went back to her typing. Twice I caught her looking at me while she pretended to check the clock. You haven't lost a thing, kid, I thought. Two campus cops, in uniform, looking unhappy, came out of Tower's office. Tower came to the door with them.

"This is not Dodge City," he said, "you are not goddamn towntamers—" and shut the outer office door behind them as they left. "Dumb bastards," he said. "Come on in, Spenser."

"I'll see you again on the way out," I said to the secretary. She didn't smile.

"What have you got, Spenser?" Tower asked when we were in and sitting.

"A bad murder, some funny feelings, damn little information, some questions, and no manuscript. I think your secretary is hot for me."

Tower's face squeezed down. "Murder?"

"Yeah, the Powell killing. You know about it as well as I do."

"Yeah, bad. I know, sorry you had to get dragged into it. But we're after a manuscript. We're not worried about the murder. That's Lieutenant Quirk's department. He's good at it."

"Wrong. It's my department too. I think the manuscript and the murder are connected."

"Why?"

"Terry Orchard told me."

"What?" Tower wasn't liking the way the talk was going.

"Terry remembers a conversation on the phone between Dennis Powell and a professor in which Dennis reassured the professor that he'd hidden 'it' well."

"Oh, for crissake, Spenser. The kid's a goddamn junkie. She remembers anything she feels like remembering. You don't buy that barrel of crap she fed you about mysterious strangers and being forced to shoot Dennis, and being drugged and being innocent. Of course she thinks the university's involved. She thinks the university causes famine."

"She didn't say the university. She said a professor."

"She'll say anything. They all will. She knows you're investigating the manuscript, and she wants you to get her out of what she's gotten herself into. So she plays little-girl-lost with you, and you go panting after her like a Saint Bernard dog. Spenser to the rescue. Balls."

"Tell me about Lowell Hayden," I said.

Tower liked the conversation even less. "Why? Who the hell is employing who? I want to know your results, and you start asking me questions about professors."

"Whom," I said.

"What?"

"It's whom, who is employing whom? Or is it? Maybe it's a predicate nominative, in which case . . ."

"Will you come off it, Spenser. I got things to do."

"Me, too," I said. "One of them is to find out about Lowell

Hayden. His name has come up a couple of times. He's a known radical. I have it on some authority that he's the most radical on campus. I have it on authority that Powell was pushing heavy drugs and had heavy drug connections. I know Hayden had an early Chaucer class on the morning that Powell was talking to a professor about cutting his early morning class."

"That adds up to zero. Do you know how many professors in this university have eight o'clock classes every day? Who the hell is your authority? I know what's going on on my campus and no one's pushing heroin. I don't say no one's using it, but it's isolated. There's no big supplier. If there were, I'd know."

"Sure you would," I said. "Sure, what I've got about professors and Lowell Hayden adds up to zero, or little more. But he is all I've got for either the murder or the theft. Why not let me think about him? Why not have a look at him? If he's clean, I won't bother him. He probably is clean. But if he isn't . . ."

"No. Do you have any idea what happens if it gets out that a P.I. in the employ of the university is investigating a member of the university faculty? No, you don't. You couldn't." He closed his eyes in holy dread. "You stick to looking for the manuscript. Stay away from the faculty."

"I don't do piecework, Tower. I take hold of one end of the thread and I keep pulling it in till it's all unraveled. You hired me to find out where the manuscript went. You didn't hire me to run errands. The retainer does not include your telling me how to do my job."

"You'll stay the hell away from Hayden, or you'll be off this campus to stay. I got you hired for this job. I can get you canned just as easy."

"Do that," I said, and walked out. When you have two retainers you get smug and feisty. In the quadrangle I asked a boy in a fringed buckskin jacket where the English Department was. He didn't know. I tried a girl in an ankle-length o.d. military overcoat. She didn't know either. On the third try I got it; first floor, Felton Hall, other end of the campus.

Felton Hall was a converted apartment building, warrened with faculty offices. The main office of the English Department was at the end of the first floor foyer. An outer office with a receptionist/ typist and a file cabinet. An inner office with another desk and woman and typewriter, secretary in chief or administrative assistant, or some such, and beyond that, at right angles, the office of the chairman. The receptionist looked like a student. I asked to see the chairman, gave her my card, the one with my name and profession but without the crossed daggers, and sat down in the one straight-backed chair to wait. She gave the card to the woman in the inner office, who did not look like a student and didn't even look one hell of a lot like a woman, and came back studiously uninterested in me.

Somewhere nearby I could hear the rhythm of a mimeograph cranking out somebody's midterm or a reading list for someone's course in Byzantine nature poetry of the third century. I got the same old feeling in my stomach. The one I got as a little kid sitting outside the principal's office.

The office was done in early dorm. There was a travel poster with a picture of the Yugoslav coast stuck with Scotch tape to the wall above the receptionist's desk, the announcement of a new magazine that would pay contributors in free copies of the magazine, the big campy poster of Buster Keaton in *The General,* and a number of Van Gogh and Gauguin prints apparently cut off a calendar and taped up. It didn't hold a candle to my collection of Ann Sheridan pinups.

The mannish-looking inner-office secretary came to her door.

"Mr. Spenser," she said, "Dr. Vogel will see you now."

I walked through her big office, through two glass doors, and into the chairman's office, which was still bigger. It had apparently once been the dining room of an apartment, which had been divided by a partition so that it seemed almost a round room because of the large bow window that looked out over a recently built slum. In the arch of the bow was a large dark desk. On one wall was a fireplace, the bricks painted a dark red, the hearth clean and cold. There were books all around the office and pen and ink drawings of historical-looking people I didn't recognize. There was a rug on the floor and a chair with arms—Tower had neither.

Dr. Vogel sat behind the desk, slim, medium height, thick curly hair trimmed round, black and gray intermixed, clean-shaven, wearing a black pin-striped double-breasted suit with six buttons, all buttoned, pink shirt with a wide roll collar, a white tie with black and pink stripes, and a diamond ring on the left little finger. Whatever happened to shabby gentility?

"Sit down, Mr. Spenser," he said. I sat. He was looking at my card, holding it neatly by the corners before his stomach with both hands, the way a man looks at a poker hand.

"I don't believe I've ever met a private detective before," he said without looking up. "What do you want?"

"I'm investigating the theft of the Godwulf Manuscript," I said, "and I have only the slightest of suggestions that a member of your department might be involved."

"My department? I doubt that."

"Everyone always doubts things like that."

"I'm not sure the generalization is valid, Mr. Spenser. There must be circles where theft surprises no one, and they must be circles with which you're more familiar than I. Why don't you move in those circles, and not these?"

"Because the circles you're thinking of don't steal illuminated manuscripts, nor do they ransom them for charity, nor do they murder undergraduates in the process."

"Murder?" He liked that about half as well as Tower had.

"A young man, student at this university, was murdered. Another student, a young woman, was involved and stands accused. I think the two crimes are connected."

"Why?"

"I have some slight evidence, but even if I didn't, two major crimes committed at the same university among people belonging to the same end of the political spectrum, and probably the same organization, is at least an unusual occurrence, isn't it?"

"Of course, but we're on the edge of the ghetto here. . . ."

"Nobody involved was a ghetto resident. No one was black. The victim and the accused were upper-middle-class affluent."

"Drugs?"

"Maybe, maybe not. To me it doesn't look like a drug killing."

"How does it look to the police?"

"The police don't belabor the obvious, Dr. Vogel. The most obvious answer is the one they like best. Usually they're right. They don't have time to be subtle. They are very good at juggling five balls, but there are always six in the game, and the more they run the farther behind they get."

"Thus you handle the difficult and intricate problems, Mr. Spenser?"

"I handle the problems I choose to; that's why I'm free-lance. It gives me the luxury to worry about justice. The cops can't. All they're trying to do is keep that sixth ball in the air."

"A fine figure of speech, Mr. Spenser, and doubtless excellent philosophy, but it has little relevance here. I do not want you snooping about my department, accusing my faculty of theft and murder."

"What you want is not what I'm here to find out. I'll snoop on your department and accuse your faculty of theft and murder as I find necessary. The question we're discussing is whether it's the easy way or the hard way. I wasn't asking your permission."

"By God, Spenser . . ."

"Listen, there's a twenty-year-old girl who is a student in your university, has taken a course from your faculty, under the auspices no doubt of your department, who is now out on bail, charged with the murder of her boyfriend. I think she did not kill him. If I am right, it is quite important that we find out who did. Now, that may not rate in importance up as high as, say, the implications of homosexuality in Shakespeare's sonnets, or whether he said *solid* or *sullied,* but it is important. I'm not going to shoot up the place. No rubber hose, no iron maiden. I won't even curse loudly. If the student newspaper breaks the news that a private eye is ravaging the English Department, the hell with it. You can argue it's an open campus and sit tight."

"You don't understand the situation in a university at this point in time. I cannot permit spying. I sympathize with your passion for justice, if that is in fact what it is, but my faculty would not accept your prying. Violation of academic freedom integral to such an investigation, sanctioned even implicitly by the chairman, would jeopardize liberal education in the university beyond any justification. If you persist I will have you removed from this department by the campus police."

The campus police I had seen looked like they'd need to outnumber me considerably, but I let that go. Guile, I thought, guile before force. I had been thinking that more frequently as I got up toward forty.

"The freedom I'm worried about is not academic, it's twenty and female. If you reconsider, my number's on the card."

"Good day, Mr. Spenser."

I got even. I left without saying good-bye.

On the bulletin board in the corridor was a mimeographed list of faculty office numbers. I took it off as I went by and put it in my pocket. The mannish-looking secretary watched me all the way out the front door.

9

I walked through the warm-for-early-winter sun of midafternoon across the campus back toward the library. In the quadrangle there was a girl in a fatigue jacket selling brown rice and pinto beans from a pushcart with a bright umbrella. Six dogs raced about barking and bowling one another over in their play. A kid in a cowboy hat and a pea jacket hawked copies of a local underground paper in a rhythmic monotone, a limp and wrinkled cigarette hanging from the corner of his mouth.

I went into the reading room of the library, took off my coat, sat down at a table, and took out my list of English professors. It didn't get me far. There was no one named Sacco or Vanzetti; none had a skull and crossbones by his name. Nine of the names were women; the remaining thirty-three were men. Lowell Hayden's name was right there after Gordon and before Herbert. Why him, I thought. I didn't have a goddamn thing on him. Just his name came up twice, and he teaches medieval literature. Why not him? Why not Vogel, why not Tower, why not Forbes, or Tabor, or Iris Milford, why not Terry Orchard if you really get objective? Like a Saint Bernard, Tower had said. Woof. Why not go home and go to bed and never get up? Some things you just had to decide.

I got up, put the list back in my pocket, put on my coat, and headed back out across campus, toward the English Department. Hayden's office was listed as fourth floor Felton. I hoped I could slip past Mary Masculine, the super-secretary. I made it. There was an old elevator to the left of the foyer, out of sight of the English office. It was a cage affair, open shaft, enclosed with mesh. The stairs wound up around it. I took it to the fourth floor, feeling exposed as it crept up. Hayden's office was room 405. On the door was a brown plastic plaque that said DR. HAYDEN. The door was half open and inside I could hear two people talking. One was apparently a student, sitting in a straight chair, back to the door, beside the desk, facing the teacher. I couldn't see Hayden, but I could hear his voice.

"The problem," he was saying in a deep, public voice, "with Kittredge's theory of the marriage cycle is that the order of composition of *The Canterbury Tales* is unclear. We do not, in short, know that 'The Clerk's Tale' precedes that of 'The Wife of Bath,' for instance."

The girl mumbled something I couldn't catch, and Hayden responded.

"No, you are responsible for what you quote. If you didn't agree with Kittredge, you shouldn't have cited him."

Again the girl's mumble. Again Hayden: "Yes, if you'd like to write another paper, I'll read it and grade it. If it's better than this one, it will bring your grade up. I'd like to see an outline or at least a thesis statement, though, before you write it. Okay?"

Mumble.

"Okay, thanks for coming by."

The girl got up and walked out. She didn't look pleased. As she got into the elevator I reached around and knocked on the open door.

"Come in," Hayden said. "What can I do for you?"

It was a tiny office, just room for a desk, chair, file cabinet, bookcase, and teacher. No windows, Sheetrock partitions painted green.

Hayden himself looked right at home in the office. He was small, with longish blond hair. Not long enough to be stylish; long enough to look as though he needed a haircut. He had on a light green dress shirt with a faint brown stripe in it, open at the neck, and what looked like Navy surplus dungarees. The shirt was too big for him, and the material bagged around his waist. He was wearing gold-rimmed glasses.

I gave him my card and said, "I'm working on a case involving a former student and I was wondering if you could tell me anything."

He looked at my card carefully, then at me.

"Anyone may have a card printed up. Do you have more positive identification?"

I showed him the photostat of my license, complete with my picture. He looked at it very carefully, then handed it back.

"Who is the student?" he said.

"Terry Orchard," I said.

He showed no expression. "I teach a great many students, Mr." —he glanced down at my card lying on his desk—"Spenser. What class? What year? What semester?"

"Chaucer, this year, this semester."

He reached into a desk drawer and pulled a yellow cardboard-covered grade book. He thumbed through it, stopped, ran his eyes down a list, and said, "Yes, I have Miss Orchard in my Chaucer course."

Looking at the grade book upside down, I could see he had the student's last name and first initial. If he didn't know her name or whether she was in his class or not without looking her up in his grade book, how, looking at the listing ORCHARD, T., did he know it was Miss Orchard? Like Tabor, the zinnia head, no one seemed willing to know old Terry.

"Don't you know the names of your students, Dr. Hayden?" I asked, trying to say it neutrally, not as if I were critical. He took it as if it were critical.

"This is a very large university, Mr. Spenser." He had to check the card again to get my name. I hope he remembered Chaucer better. "I have an English survey course of sixty-eight students, for instance. I cannot keep track of the names, much as I try to do so. One of this university's serious problems is the absence of community. I am really able to remember only those students who respond to my efforts to personalize our relationship. Miss Orchard apparently is not one of those." He looked again at the open grade book. "Nor do her grades indicate that she has been unusually interested and attentive."

"How is she doing?" I asked, just to keep it going. I didn't know where I was going. I was fishing and I had to keep the conversation going.

"That is a matter concerning Miss Orchard and myself." Nice conversation primer, Spenser, you really know how to touch the right buttons.

"Sorry," I said. "I didn't mean to pry, but when you think about it, prying is more or less my business."

"Perhaps," Hayden said. "It is not, however, my business; nor is it, quite frankly, a business for which I have much respect."

"I know it's not important like Kittredge's marriage cycle, but it's better than enlisting, I suppose."

"I'm quite busy, Mr. Spenser." He didn't have to check this time. A quick study, I thought.

"I appreciate that, Dr. Hayden. Let me be brief. Terry Orchard is accused of the murder of her boyfriend, Dennis Powell." No reaction. "I am working to clear her of suspicion. Is there anything you can tell me that would help?"

"No, I'm sorry, there isn't."

"Do you know Dennis Powell?"

"No, I do not. I can check through my grade books, but I don't recall him."

"That's not necessary. The grade book won't tell me anything. There's nothing at all you can think of? About either?"

"Nothing. I'm sorry, but I don't know the people involved."

"Are you aware that the Godwulf Manuscript has been stolen?"

"Yes, I am."

"Do you have any idea what might have happened to it?"

"Mr. Spenser, this is absurd. I assume your interest relates to the fact that I am a medievalist. I am not, however, a thief."

"Well," I said, "thanks anyway." I got up.

"You're welcome. I'm sorry I wasn't more useful." His voice was remarkable. Deep and resonant, it seemed incongruous with his slight frame. "Thanks for coming by."

As I left the office, two students were waiting outside, sitting on the floor, coats and books in a pile beside them. They looked at me curiously as I entered the elevator. As it descended I could hear Hayden's voice booming. "Come in, Mr. Vale. What can I do for you?"

On the ground floor were two campus policemen, and they wanted me. I hadn't eluded Mary Masculine after all. She was hovering in the doorway to the English office. One of the cops was big and fat with a thick, pockmarked face and an enormous belly. The other was much smaller, a black man with a neat Sugar Ray mustache and a tailored uniform. They weren't wearing guns, but each had a nightstick stuck in his hip pocket. The fat one took my arm above the elbow in what he must have felt was an iron grip.

"Start walking, trooper," he said, barely moving his lips.

I was frustrated, and angry at Lowell Hayden and at Mary Masculine and the university. I said, "Let go of my arm or I'll put a dent in your face."

"You and who else?" he said. It broke my tension.

"Snappy," I said. "On your days off could you come over and be my dialogue coach?"

The black cop laughed. The fat one looked puzzled and let go of my arm.

"What do you mean?" he said.

"Never mind, Lloyd," the black cop said. "Come on, Jim, we got to walk you off campus."

I nodded. "Okay, but not arm in arm. I don't go for that kind of stuff."

"Me neither, Jim. We'll just stroll along."

And we did. The fat cop had his nightstick out and tapped it against his leg as we went out of the building and toward the street. His eyes never left me. Alert, I thought, vigilant. When we got to my car, the black cop opened the door for me with a small, graceful flourish.

The fat one said, "Don't come back. Next time you show up here you'll be arrested."

"For crissake," I said. "I'm working for the university. Your boss hired me."

"I don't know nothing about that, but we got our orders. Get out and stay out."

The black cop said, "I don't know, Jim, but I think maybe you been canceled." He closed the door and stepped back. I started the car and pulled away. They still stood there as I drove off, the fat one looking balefully after me, still slapping his nightstick against his leg.

10

It was getting dark, and the commuter traffic was starting to thicken the streets. I drove slowly back to my office, parked my car, and went in.

When I unlocked my office door the first thing I noticed was the smell of cigarette smoke. I hadn't smoked in ten years. I pushed it open hard and went in low with my gun out. There was someone sitting at my desk, and another man standing against the wall. In the half-light the tip of his cigarette glowed. Neither of them moved. I backed to the wall and felt for the light switch. I found it, and the room brightened.

The man against the wall laughed, a thin sound, without humor. "Look at that, Phil. Maybe if we give him money he'll do that again."

The man at my desk said nothing. He was sitting with his feet up, my chair tipped back, his hat still on, his overcoat still buttoned up, though it must have been ninety in there, wearing rose-colored gold-rimmed glasses. He looked at me without expression, a very tall man, narrow, with high shoulders, six foot four or five, probably. Behind the glasses one eye was blank and white and turned partly up. Along the right line of his jaw was a purple birthmark maybe two inches wide, running the whole length of the jaw from chin to ear. His hands were folded across his stomach. Big hands, long, square, thick fingers, the backs prominently veined, the knuckles lumpy. I could tell he was impressed with the gun in my hand. The only thing that would have scared him more would have been if I had threatened to flog him with a dandelion.

"Put that away," he said. "If he was going to push you I wouldn't have let Sonny smoke." His voice was a harsh whisper, as if he had an artificial throat.

Sonny gave me a moon-faced smile. He was thick and round, running to fat, with mutton-chop sideburns that came to the corners of his mouth. His coat was off and his collar open, the tie at half-mast. Sweat soaked the big half-moon circles around his armpits, and his face was shiny with it. I put the gun away.

"A man wants to see you," Phil said. I hadn't seen him move since I came in. His voice was entirely without inflection.

"Joe Broz?" I said.

Sonny said, "What makes you think so?"

Phil said, "He knows me."

"Yeah," I said, "you walk around behind Broz."

Phil said, "Let's go," and stood up. Six-five, at least. When he was standing you could see that his right shoulder was higher than his left.

I said, "What if I don't want to?"

Phil just looked at me. Sonny snickered, "What if he don't want to, Phil?"

Phil said, "Let's go."

We went. Outside, double-parked, was a Lincoln Continental. Sonny drove; Phil sat in back with me.

It had started to snow again, softly, big flakes, and the windshield wipers made the only sound in the car. I looked at the back of Sonny's neck as he drove. The hair was long and stylish and curled out over the collar of his white trench coat. Sonny seemed to be singing soundlessly to himself as he drove. His head bobbed, and he beat gentle time on the wheel with one suede-gloved hand. Phil was a silent and motionless shape in the corner of the back seat.

"Either of you guys seen *The Godfather*?" I asked.

Sonny snorted. Phil ignored me.

"Beat up any good candy store owners lately, Sonny?"

"Don't ride me, Peep; you'll find yourself looking up at the snow."

"I'm heavy work, Sonny. College kids are about your upper limit, I think."

"Goddammit," Sonny started, and Phil stopped him.

"Shut up," Phil said in his gear box voice, and we both knew he meant both of us.

"Just having a little snappy conversation, Phil, to pass the time," I said.

Phil just looked at me, and the menace was like a physical force. I could feel anxiety pulse up and down the long muscles of my arms and legs. Going to see Joe Broz was not normally a soothing experience anyway. Not many people looked forward to it.

The ride was short. Sonny pulled to a stop in front of a building on the lower end of State Street. Phil and I got out. I stuck my head back in before I closed the back door.

"If a tough meter maid puts the arm on you, Sonny, just scream and I'll come running."

Sonny swore at me and burned rubber away from the curb.

I followed Phil into the building. We took the self-service elevator to the eleventh floor. The corridor was silent and empty, with marble wainscoting and frosted glass doors. At the far end we went through one marked CONTINENTAL CONSULTING CO. Inside was an empty stainless-steel and coral-vinyl reception room. There is little that is quieter than an office building after hours, and this one was no exception. The lights were all on, the receptionist's desk was geometrically neat. On one wall were staggered prints by Maurice Utrillo.

Phil said, "Gimme your gun."

I hesitated. I didn't like his manner, I didn't like his assumption that I'd do what I was told because he'd told me to, and I didn't like his assumption that if he had to he could make me. On the other hand, I'd come this far because I was curious. Something bothered Broz enough to have him send his top hand to bring me in. And Sonny looked a lot like one of the two hoods that Terry had described. Also, Phil didn't seem much to care whether I liked his assumptions or not.

I noticed that there was a gun in Phil's hand, and it was pointing at an area somewhere between my eyes. I'd never seen him move. I took my gun out of my hip holster and handed it to him, butt first. People were taking it away from me a lot lately. I didn't like that too much either. Phil stowed my gun away in an overcoat pocket, put away his own gun in the other, and stepped to one of the inner doors of the reception room. It was solid, no glass panel. I heard a buzz, and the door clicked open. I looked around and spotted the closed-circuit camera up high in one corner of the reception room. Phil pushed the door open and nodded me through it.

The room was bone white. The first thing I saw was my own reflection in the wide black picture window that stretched the width of the opposite wall. My reflection didn't look too aggressive. In front of the window was a broad black desk, neat, with a bank of phones on it. The room was carpeted with something thick and expensive, in a dark blue. There were several black leather chairs about. Along the side wall was an ebony bar with blue leather padding. Leaning against it was Joe Broz.

There was something theatrical about Broz, as if there were always a press photographer downstage left, kneeling to shoot a picture with his big Speed Graphic camera. He was a middle-size man who stood very straight with his chin up, as if squeezing every inch of height out of what God had given him. He had many teeth—a few too many for his mouth—and they were very prominent and white. His hair was slick black, combed straight back from a high forehead and gray at the temples. The sideburns were long and neatly trimmed. His nose was flat and thick with a slight ski-jump quality to the end that hinted at a break somewhere in the past. He wore a white suit, a white vest, a dark blue shirt, and a white tie. There was a gold chain across the vest, and presumably a gold watch tucked in the vest pocket. I would have bet against a Phi Beta key, but little is sure in life. He had one foot hooked on the brass rail of the bar, and a large diamond ring flashed from his little finger as he turned a thick highball glass in his hands.

"Do you always dress in blue and white?" I asked. "Or do you have the office redone to match your clothes every day?"

Broz sipped a little of his drink, put it down on the bar, and swung fully around toward me, both elbows resting on the bar.

"I have been told," he said in a deep voice that had the phony quality you hear in an announcer's voice when he's not on the air, "that you are a wise-ass punk. Apparently my information was correct. So let's get some ground rules. You are here because I sent for you. You will leave when I tell you to. You are of no consequence. You have no class. If you annoy me, I will have someone sprinkle roach powder on you. Do you understand that?"

"Yeah," I said. "I think so, but you better give me a drink. I feel faint."

Phil, who had drifted to a couch in the far corner and sprawled awkwardly on it, let out a soft sound that sounded almost like a sigh.

Broz moved to his desk, sat, and nodded at one of the leather chairs. "Sit down. I got things to say. Phil, make him a drink."

"Bourbon," I said, "with water, and some bitters."

Phil made the drink. He moved stiffly, and his hands seemed like distorted work gloves. But they performed the task with a bare economy of motion that was incongruous. I'd have to be sure not to make any mistakes about Phil.

I leaned back in the black chair and took a sip of the bourbon. It was a little more expensive than the private label stuff I bought. There was too much bitters, but I decided not to call Phil on it. We'd probably have other issues. There was a knock on the door. Phil glanced at the monitor set in the wall by the door, opened the door, and let Sonny in. He had his trench coat folded over his arm, and his tie was neatly up. His neck spilled over slightly around his collar. He walked quietly over to a chair near the couch and sat down, holding the trench coat in his lap. Broz paid no attention to him. He stared at me with his yellowish eyes.

"You're working on a case." It wasn't really a question. I wasn't sure Broz ever asked questions.

I nodded.

"I want to hear about it," Broz said.

I shook my head.

Broz got a big curved-stem meerschaum pipe out of a rack on his desk and carefully began to pack it from a thick silver humidor.

"Spenser, this can be easy or hard. I'd just as soon it was easy, but the choice is yours."

"Look," I said, "one reason people employ me is because they want their business private. If I spill what I know every time anybody asks me, I am not likely to flourish."

"Your chances of flourishing are not very big right now, Spenser." Broz had the pipe packed to his satisfaction and spoke through a blue cloud of aromatic smoke. "I know you are looking for the Godwulf Manuscript. I know that you are working for Roland Orchard. What I want to know is what you've got. There's no breach of confidence in that."

"Why do you want to know?"

"Let's say I'm an interested party."

"Let's say more than that. Why be one way? You tell me what your interest is; I'll think about telling you what I know."

"Spenser, I'm hanging on to my patience. But it's slipping. I don't have to make swaps with you. I get what I ask for."

I didn't say anything.

From his place Sonny said, "Let me have him, Mr. Broz."

"What are you going to do, Sonny," I said, "sweat all over me till I beg for mercy?"

Phil made his little sighing sounds again. Sonny put his trench coat carefully on the arm of the couch and started toward me. I saw Phil look at Broz and saw Broz nod.

"You been crying for this, you sonova bitch," Sonny said.

I stood up. Sonny was probably thirty pounds heavier than I was, and a lot of it was muscle. But some of it was fat, and quickness didn't look to be Sonny's strong suit. He swung a big right hand at me. I rolled away from it and hit him in the middle of the face twice with left hooks, getting my shoulder nicely behind both of them, feeling the shock all the way up into my back. Sonny was tough. It rocked him, but he didn't go down. He grabbed at my shirtfront with his left hand and clubbed at me with his right. The punch glanced off my shoulder and caught me under the left eye. I broke his grip by bringing my clenched fists up under his forearm, and then drove my right forearm against the side of his jaw. He stumbled back two steps and sat down. But he got up. He was wary now. His hands up, he began to circle me. I turned as he did. He put his head down and lunged at me. I moved aside and tripped him and he sprawled against Broz's desk, knocking over the pipe rack. Broz never blinked. Sonny pushed himself up from the desk like a man doing his last push-up. He turned and came at me again. His nose was bleeding freely and his shirtfront was bloody. I feinted with my left hand at his stomach and then brought it up over his hands and jabbed him three times on that bloody nose, then crossed over with a right hand that caught him in the neck below the ear. He went down face first. This time he stayed. He got as far as his hands and knees and stayed, his head hanging, swaying slightly, with the blood dripping on the azure rug.

Broz spoke to Phil. "Get him out of here, he's messing on the rug." Phil got up, walked over, pulled Sonny to his feet by the back of his collar, and walked him, weaving and swaying, out through a side door.

Broz said, "Sonny seems to have exaggerated his ability."

"Maybe he just underestimated mine," I said.

"Either way," Broz said.

Phil came back in, wiping his hands on a handkerchief. "Ask him again, Joe," he rasped, "now that Sonny's got him softened." His face twisted in what was, I think, a momentary smile.

Broz looked disgusted. "I want you out of this business, Spenser."

"Which business?"

"The Godwulf Manuscript. I don't want you muddying up the water."

"What's in it for me if I pull out?"

"Health."

"You gonna unleash Sonny on me again?"

"I can put ten Sonnys on your back whenever I want to. Or Phil. Phil's not Sonny."

"I never thought he was," I said. "But I hired on to find the manuscript."

"Maybe the manuscript will turn up." Broz leaned back in the big leather executive swivel with the high back, and blew a lungful of pipe smoke at the ceiling. His eyes were squeezed down as he squinted through the smoke.

"If it does, I won't have to look for it anymore."

"Don't look for it anymore." Dramatically, Broz came forward in the swivel chair, his hands flat on the desk. "Stay out of it, or you'll end up looking at the trunk of your car from the inside. You've been warned. Now get the hell out of here." He swiveled the chair around to face the window, putting the high leather back between me and him. What a trouper, I thought.

Phil stood up. I followed him out through the door we'd entered. Broz never moved or said a word. In the anteroom a thin-faced

Italian man with a goatee was cleaning his fingernails with the blade of a large pocket knife, his feet up on the desk, a Borsalino hat tipped forward over the bridge of his nose. He paid us no mind as we went through.

11

I took a cab back from Broz's office to mine. When I got there, I sat in my chair in the dark and looked out the window. The snow was steady now and starting to screw up the traffic. Plows were out, and their noise added to the normal traffic sounds that drifted up through the closed window. "Sleigh bells ring," I thought, "are ya listening." The falling snow fuzzed out all the lights in the Combat Zone, giving them halos of neon red and streetlight yellow. I was tired. My eye hurt. The knuckles of my left hand were sore and puffy from hitting Sonny in the face. I hadn't eaten for a long time and I was hungry, but I didn't seem to want to eat. I pulled a bottle of bourbon out of the desk drawer and opened it and drank some. It felt hot in my stomach.

Where was I? Somewhere along the line I had touched a nerve, and somebody had called Broz. Who? Could be anybody. Broz got around. But it was probably someone today. Broz would have no reason to wait once he knew I was trampling around on his lawn. I couldn't see Broz being tied into the Godwulf Manuscript. It wasn't worth any money. It was impossible to fence. But he'd implied he'd put it back if I dropped out. He knew a lot of people; maybe he could push the right button without being necessarily involved. Maybe he'd been lying. But something had stirred him up. Not only did he want me out of things, but he wanted to know what I knew. Maybe it was simply collateral interest. Maybe it was Powell's murder. Maybe he didn't want me digging into that: I liked that better. Terry's description of the two men included one like Sonny. The other one wasn't Phil. But Phil wouldn't do that kind of trench duty anyway. I was amazed he had done errand duty for me. But why would Broz care one way or the other about a loudmouth kid like Dennis Powell, care enough to send two employees to kill him and frame his girl? Yet somebody's employees did it. It wasn't an amateur job, by Terry's account. Came in, held them up, had her gun, the rubber gloves, the drug they'd brought, the whole thing. It didn't sound like it had been ad-libbed. Did they have inside help? How did they get hold of her gun? And what possible interest would Broz have in the university? He had a lot of interests—numbers, women, dope—but higher education didn't seem to be one of them. Of his line, dope would seem the best connection. It seemed the only place where college and Broz overlapped. Dennis Powell was reputed to be a channel for hard stuff: heroin, specifically. That meant, if it were true, that he had mob connections, direct or indirect. Now he was dead, in what looked like some kind of mob killing. And Joe Broz wanted me to keep my nose out of his business.

But what did that have to do with the manuscript? I didn't know. The best connection I had was the dope and the question of the gun. How did they know she'd have a gun there? She'd lived with another girl before she'd lived with Powell. I took another belt of the bourbon. Uncut by bitters or ice and cheap anyway, it grated down into my stomach. Catherine Connelly, Tower had told me. Let's try her. More bourbon. It wasn't really so bad, didn't taste bad at all, made you feel pretty nice in your stomach. Made you feel tough, too, and on top of it—whatever it was. The phone rang.

I picked it up and said, "Spenser industries, security division. We never sleep."

There was a pause, and then a woman spoke.

"Mr. Spenser?"

"Yeah."

"This is Marion Orchard, Terry's mother."

"Howya doing, sweets," I said, and took another pull on the bourbon.

"Mr. Spenser, she's gone."

"Me, too, sweets."

"No, really, she's gone, and I'm terribly worried."

I put the bottle down and said, "Oh, Christ!"

"Our lawyer called and said the police wished to speak with her again, and I went to her room and she wasn't there and she hasn't been home all day. There's two hundred thousand dollars bail money, and . . . I want her back. Can you find her, Mr. Spenser?"

"You got any ideas where I should look?"

"I . . . Mr. Spenser, we have hired you. You sound positively hostile, and I resent it."

"Yeah, you probably do," I said. "I been up a long time and have eaten little, and had a fight with a tough guinea and drank too much bourbon and was thinking about going and getting a sub sandwich and going to bed. I'll come out in a little while and we'll talk about it."

"Please, I'm very worried."

"Yeah, I'll be along." I hung up, put the cork in the bottle, put the bottle in the drawer. My head was light and my eyes focused badly and my mouth felt thick. I got my coat on, locked the office, and went down to my car. I parked in a taxi zone and got a submarine sandwich and a large black coffee to go. I ate the sandwich and drank the coffee as I headed out to Newton again. Eating a sub sandwich with one hand is sloppy work, and I got some tomato juice and oil on my shirtfront and some coffee stains on my pant leg. I stopped at a Dunkin' Donuts shop in West Newton Square, bought another black coffee, and sat in my car and drank it.

I felt terrible. The bourbon was wearing off, and I felt dull and sleepy and round-shouldered. I looked at my watch. It was a quarter to ten. The snow continued as I sat and forced the coffee down. I had read somewhere that black coffee won't sober you up, but I never believed it. After bourbon it tasted so awful it had to be doing some good.

The plows hadn't gotten to the Orchards' street; my wheels spun and my car skidded getting up their hill. I had my jacket unbuttoned, but the defrosters were going full blast. And, wrestling the car through the snow, I could feel the sweat in the hollow of my back, and my shirt collar was wet and limp. Sometimes I wondered if I was getting too old for this work. And sometimes I thought I had gotten too old last year. I jammed the car through a snowdrift into the Orchards' driveway and climbed out. There was no pathway, so I waded through the snow across the lawn and up to the front door. The same black maid answered the door. She remembered me, took my hat and coat, and led me to the same library we'd talked in before. A fire was still burning, but no one was in the room. I got a look at myself in the dark window: unshaven, sub sandwich stains on my shirt, collar open. There was a puffy mouse under one eye, courtesy of old Sonny. I looked like the leg man for a slumlord.

Marion Orchard came in. She was wearing an ankle-length blue housecoat that zipped up the front, a matching headband, and bare feet. I noticed her toenails were painted silver. She seemed as well groomed and together as before, but her face was flushed and I realized she had been drinking. Me, too. Who hadn't? The ride and the coffee had sobered me up and depressed me. My head ached, and my stomach felt like I'd been swallowing sand. Without a word Marion Orchard went to the sideboard, put ice in a glass from a silver bucket, added Scotch, and squirted soda in from a silver-laced dispenser. She drank half of it and turned toward me.

"You want some?"

"Yes, ma'am."

"Scotch or bourbon?"

"Bourbon, with bitters, if you've got it."

She turned and mixed me bourbon and soda with bitters in a big square-angled glass. I drank some and felt it begin to combat the coffee and the fatigue. I'd need more, though. From the looks of Marion Orchard, she would, too, and planned on getting it.

"Where's Mr. Orchard?" I asked.

"At the office. Sitting behind his big masculine desk, trying to feel like a man."

"Does he know Terry's gone?"

"Yes. That's why he went to the office. It makes him feel better about himself. All he can cope with is stocks and bonds. People, and daughters and wives, scare hell out of him." She finished the drink, took mine, which was still half full, and made two fresh ones.

"Something scares hell out of everybody," I said. "Have you any thoughts on where I should look for Terry?"

"What scares hell out of you?" she asked.

The bourbon was making a lot of headway against the coffee. I felt a lot better than I had when I came in. The line of Marion Orchard's thigh was tight against the blue robe as she sat with her legs tucked up under her on the couch.

"The things people do to one another," I answered. "That scares hell out of me."

She drank some more. "Wrong," she said. "That engages your sympathy. It doesn't scare you. I'm an expert on what scares men. I've lived with a scared man for twenty-two years. I left college in my sophomore year to marry him, and I never finished. I was an English major. I wrote poetry. I don't anymore." I waited. She didn't really seem to be talking to me anymore.

"About Terry?" I prodded softly.

"Screw Terry," she said, and finished her drink. "When I was her age I was marrying her father and nobody with wide shoulders came around and got me out of that mess." She was busy making us two more drinks as she talked. Her voice was showing the liquor. She was talking with extra-careful enunciation—the way I was. She handed me the drink and then put her hand on my upper arm and squeezed it.

"How much do you weigh?" she asked.

"One ninety-five."

"You work out, don't you? How much can you lift?"

"I can bench press two-fifty ten times," I said.

"How'd you get the broken nose?" She bent over very carefully and examined my face from about two inches away. Her hair smelled like herbs.

"I fought a ranked heavyweight once."

She stayed bent over, her face two inches away, her fragrant hair tumbling forward, one hand still squeezing my arm, the other holding the drink. I put my left hand behind her head and kissed her. She folded up into my lap and kissed back. It wasn't eager. It was ferocious. She let the glass drop from her hand onto the floor, where I assume it tipped and spilled. Under the blue robe she was wearing nothing at all, and she was nowhere near as sinewy as she had looked to me the first time I saw her. Making love in a chair is heavy work. The only other time I'd attempted, I'd gotten a charley horse that damn near ruined the event. With one arm around her back I managed to slip the other one under her knees and pick her up, which is not easy from a sitting position in a soft chair. Her mouth never left mine, nor did the fierceness abate as I carried her to the couch. She bit me and scratched me, and at climax she pounded me on the back with her clenched fist as hard as she could. At the time I barely noticed. But when it was over, I felt as if I'd been in a fight, and maybe in some sense I had.

She had shed the robe during our encounter and now she walked naked over to the bar to make another drink for each of us. She had a fine body, tanned all over except for the stark whiteness of her buttocks and the thin line her bra strap had made. She returned with a drink in each hand. Gave one to me and then stroked my cheek once, quite gently. She drank half her drink, still standing naked in front of me, and lit a cigarette, took in a long lungful of smoke, let it out, picked up her robe, and slipped into it. There we were, all together again, neat, orderly, employee and employer. Here's to you, Mrs. Robinson.

"I think Terry is with a group in Cambridge that calls itself the Ceremony of Moloch. In the past, when she would get in trouble or be freaked out on drugs or have a fight with her father, she'd run off there, and they let her stay. One of her friends told me about it."

She'd known that when she'd called me. But she'd gotten me out here to tell me. She really didn't like her husband.

"Where in Cambridge is the Ceremony of Moloch?"

"I don't know. I don't even know if she's there, but it's all I could think of."

"Why did Terry take off?" I didn't use her name. After copulation on the couch, Mrs. Orchard sounded a little silly. On the other hand, we were not on a "Marion" basis.

"A fight with her father." She didn't use my name either.

"About what?"

"What's it ever about? He sees her as an extension of his career. She's supposed to adorn his success by being what he fantasizes a daughter is. She does everything the opposite to punish him for not being what she fantasizes a father is . . . and probably for sleeping with me. Ever read *Mourning Becomes Electra,* Spenser?"

That's how she solved her problem with names; she dropped the Mister. I wondered if I should call her Orchard. I decided not to. "Yeah, a long time ago. But is there anything you could tell me about Terry, or the Ceremony of Moloch, that might turn out useful? It is past midnight, and I've gotten a lot of exercise today."

I think she colored very slightly. "You are like a terrier after a rat. Nothing distracts your attention."

"Well," I said, "there are things, occasionally, Marion."

Her color got a little deeper and she smiled, but shook her head.

"I wonder," she said. "I wonder whether you might not have been thinking of a way to run down my dear daughter Terry, even then."

"Then," I said, "I wasn't thinking of anything."

She said, "Maybe."

I was silent. I was so tired it was an effort to move my mouth.

She shook her head again. "No, there's nothing. I can't think of anything else to tell you that will help. But can you look? Can you find her?"

"I'll look," I said. "Did your lawyer tell you what the cops wanted?"

"No. He just said Lieutenant Quirk wanted her to come down tomorrow and talk with him some more."

I stood up. Partly to see if I could. Marion Orchard stood up with me.

"Thank you for coming. I know you'll do your best in finding Terry. I'm sorry to have kept you up so late." She put out her hand, and I took it. Christ, breeding. Here she was, upper crust, Boston society, yes'm. Thank you very much, ma'am, for the drink and the toss on the couch, ma'am, it's a pleasure to be of service to you and the master, ma'am. I gave her hand a squeeze. I was goddamned if I was going to shake it.

"I'll dig her up, Marion. When I do, I'll bring her home. It'll work out."

She nodded her head silently and her face got congested-looking and red around the eyes, and I realized she was going to cry in a minute. I said, "I'll find my way out. Try not to worry. It'll work out."

She nodded again, and as I left the library she touched my arm but said nothing. As I closed the door behind me I could hear the first stifled sob burst out. There were more before I got out of earshot. They would probably last most of the night. I went out the front door and into the dead, still white night, got in my car, and went back to town. Every fiber of my being felt awful.

12

It was about one thirty when I got back to my apartment. I stripped off my clothes and took a long shower, slowly easing the water temperature down to cool. In the bedroom, putting on clean clothes, I looked at the bed with something approaching lust, but I kept myself away from it. Then I went to the living room in my socks and called a guy I knew who did night duty at the *Globe.* I asked him where I could find the Ceremony of Moloch. He gave me an address in Cambridge. I asked him what he knew about the group.

"Small," he said. "Freaky. Robes and statues and candlelight. That kind of crap. Moloch was some kind of Phoenician god that required human sacrifice. In *Paradise Lost,* Milton lumps him in with Satan and Beelzebub among the fallen angels. That's all I know about them. We did a feature once on the Cambridge-Boston subculture and they got about a paragraph."

I thanked him and hung up and went back into the bedroom for my shoes. I sat down on the bed to put them on, and that was where I lost it. As long as I was up I could move, but from sitting to lying was too short a distance. I lay back, just for a minute, and went to sleep.

I woke up, in the same position, nine hours later in broad daylight, with the morning gone. I went out to the kitchen, measured out the coffee, put the electric percolator on, went back, stripped down, shaved, showered, put on my shorts, and went out to the kitchen again. The coffee was ready and I drank it with cream and sugar while I sliced peppers and tomatoes for a Spanish omelet.

I felt good. The sleep had taken care of the exhaustion. The snow had stopped, and the sunlight, magnified by reflection, was pure white as it splashed about the kitchen. I greased the omelet pan and poured the eggs in. When the inside was right I put in the vegetables and flipped the omelet. I'm very good at flipping omelets. Finding out what was happening with Terry Orchard and the Godwulf Manuscript seemed to be something I wasn't very good at.

I ate the omelet with thick slices of fresh pumpernickel and drank three more cups of coffee while I looked at the morning *Globe.* I felt even better. Okay, Terry Orchard, here I come. You can run, but you can't hide. I considered stopping by to frighten Joe Broz some more but rejected the plan and headed for Cambridge.

The address I had for the Ceremony of Moloch was in North Cambridge in a neighborhood of brown and gray three-decker apartment buildings with open porches across the back of each floor where laundry hung stiff in the cold. I went up the unshoveled path without seeing the print of cloven hoofs. No smell of brimstone greeted me. No darkness visible, no moans of despair. For all I could tell the house was empty, and its inhabitants had gone to work or school. Every third person in Cambridge was a student.

In the front hall there were three mailboxes, each with a name plate. The one for the third floor apartment said simply MOLOCH. I went up the stairs without making more noise than I had to and stood outside the apartment door. No sound. I knocked. No answer. I tried the door. Locked. But it was an old door, with the frame warped. About thirty seconds with some thin plastic was all it took to open it.

The door opened onto a narrow hall that ran right and left from it. To the left I could see a kitchen, to the right the half-open door of a bathroom. Diagonally on the other wall an archway opened into a room I couldn't see. The wallpaper in the hall was faded brown fern leaves against a dirty beige background. There were large stains of a darker brown here and there, as if someone had splashed water against the walls. The floor was made of narrow hardwood painted dark brown, and there was a threadbare red runner the length of the hall. The woodwork was white and had been repainted without being adequately scraped first, so that it looked lumpy and pocked. It had not been repainted recently, and there were many nicks and gouges in it. I could see part of the tub and part of the water closet in the bathroom. The tub had claw and ball feet, and the water closet had a pull chain from the storage tank mounted up by the ceiling. The place was dead still.

I walked through the arch into what must have been the living room. It no longer was. In the bay of the three-window bow along the right-hand wall there was an altar made out of packing crates and two-by-fours that reminded me of the fruit display racks in Faneuil Hall market. It was draped with velveteen hangings in black and crimson and at its highest reach was inverted a dime store crucifix. The crucifix was made of plastic, with the Sacred Heart redly exposed in the center of the flesh-tinted chest. On each side of the crucifix were human skulls. Beside them unmatched candelabra with assorted candles, partially burned. The walls were hung with more of the black velveteen, shabby and thin in the daylight. The floor had been painted black and scattered with cushions. The room smelled strongly of incense and faintly of marijuana and faintly also of unemptied Kitty Litter.

I went back down the corridor, through the kitchen with its oilcloth-covered table and its ancient black sink, and into a bedroom. There were no beds, but five bare mattresses covered the floor. Three of them had sleeping bags rolled neatly at the wall end. In the closet were two pairs of nearly white jeans, a work shirt, something that looked like a shift, and an olive drab undershirt. I couldn't tell if the owners were male or female. The two other bedrooms were much the same. In a pantry closet off the kitchen were maybe a dozen black robes, like graduation costumes. On the shelves were a five-pound bag of brown rice, some peanut butter, a loaf of Bone Bread, and a two-pound bag of granola. In the refrigerator there was a plastic pitcher of grape Kool-Aid, seven cans of Pepsi, and three cucumbers. Maybe they had a bundle in a numbered account in Switzerland, but on the surface it didn't look like the Ceremony of Moloch was a high-return venture.

I went back out, closed the door behind me, and went to my car. The noon sun was making the snow melt and heating the inside of my car. I sat in it, two doors up from the house of Moloch, and waited for someone to come there and do something. It was cold, and the snow had begun to crust over when someone finally showed up. Eight people, in a battered Volkswagen bus that had been hand-painted green. Three of the eight were girls, and one of them was Terry. They all went into what they probably called the temple. It occurred to me that I wasn't exactly sure what to do with Terry now that I'd found her. There wasn't much point in dragging her out by the hair and taking her home locked in the trunk. She'd just take off again and after a while I'd get sick of chasing and fetching.

It was dark now, and cold. A fifteen-year-old Oldsmobile sedan pulled up behind the Volkswagen bus and unloaded five more people. They went into the three-decker. I sat some more. The thing to do was to call Marion Orchard, tell her I'd located her daughter, have her notify the cops, and let them bring her in. I had no legal authority to go in and get her. No question. That was what I had to do. I looked at my watch. 7:15.

I slipped out of my coat, got out of the car, and went to the house of the Ceremony of Moloch. This time I was very quiet going up the stairs. At the door I stood silent and listened. I could hear music that sounded as if it were being played on one string of an Armenian banjo. The smell of incense and pot was very rich. At irregular intervals there were chimes like the ones rung during a Roman Catholic Mass. The thing to do was to call Terry's mother and have the cops come pick her up. I took out my plastic shim and opened the door. Inside the hallway the heat was tangible and stifling. There was no light.

From the living-room altar area came the twanging sound of the music, now quite loud, and the lesser sound of a man chanting. A flickering light fell into the hallway from the living room. Despite the heat I felt cold, and my throat was tight. The chimes sounded again. And I heard a kind of muffled whimper, like someone sobbing into a pillow. I looked carefully around the corner. Suspended by clothesline from the ceiling, in front of the altar I had seen earlier, was a full-sized cross, made of two-by-sixes. To it, in a parody of the Crucifixion, Terry Orchard was tied with more length of clothesline. She was naked, and her body had been marked with astrological and cabalistic signs in what looked to be, in the candlelight, several different colors of Magic Marker. She was gagged with a wide piece of gray tape.

Before her stood a tall, wiry man, naked too, wearing a black hood, his body covered with the same kind of Magic Marker design work. In a semicircle on the floor, in black robes, sat the rest of the people. The music was coming from a tape recorder behind the altar. In his hand the guy with the hood had a carved piece of black wood, about a foot and a half long, that looked like a nightstick. He was chanting in a monotonous singsong in a language I didn't understand and didn't recognize. And as he chanted he swayed in front of Terry in an approximation of the beat from the tape recorder. The seated audience rocked back and forth in the same tempo. Then he made a gesture with the nightstick, and I realized its function was phallic.

I took out my gun and put a bullet into the tape recorder. The explosion of the shot and the cessation of the music were simultaneous, and the silence that followed was paralyzing. I stepped into the room with my gun leveled at all of them, but especially the fruitcake with the hood. With my left hand I took a jackknife out of my pants pocket, and worked the blade open with one hand by holding it in my teeth. No one made a sound. I sidestepped around behind the cross and cut Terry loose without taking my eyes from the audience. When the ropes parted, she fell. I folded the knife shut against my leg and put it away. I reached down without looking and got her up with one hand under her arm. The guy with the hood and the funny nightstick never took his eyes off me, and the steady gaze through the Halloween pumpkin triangles cut in the hood made me very edgy. So did the fact that there was one of me and twelve of them.

My hand still hanging on to Terry's arm, I backed up out of the room, through the narrow hall, and out the still-open door. The cold air of the stairwell rushed up like the wind from an angel's wing in the doorway of Hell. "I'm going to close this door," I said, and my voice sounded like someone else's. "If it opens, I'll shoot at it."

No one said a word. No one moved. I let go of Terry's arm, closed the door, took hold of her arm again, and headed down the stairs. No one came after us. Out the front door and across to my car. We ran. In my mind I could see us from their third floor vantage, outlined sharp against the white snow in the streetlight. No one shot at us. I pushed Terry into the car first, came in behind her, and got it out of there. It was a full block before I looked at Terry. She huddled, still stark naked, still with the tape on her mouth, in the far corner of the seat. She must have been freezing. I reached into the back seat, took my coat from where I'd left it, and gave it to her. She pulled it around her.

"Maybe you ought to take the gag off," I said.

She peeled it carefully, and spit out what looked like a wadded paper towel that had been stuffed in her mouth. She didn't say anything. I didn't say anything. The heater had warmed up and was starting to warm the car. I turned on the radio. We went down along the Charles on Memorial Drive and across the Mass Ave bridge. Boston always looks great from there. Especially at night, with the lights and the skyline against the starry sky and the sweep of the river in a graceful curve down toward the harbor. It probably didn't look too spiffy at the moment to Terry.

I turned off onto Marlborough Street and pulled up in front of my apartment. Terry waited in the car while I went around and opened the door. She was well brought up. She had to walk barefoot across the frozen pavement but showed no sign that she felt it. We went up in the elevator.

Inside my apartment she looked about curiously. As if we'd recently met at a cocktail party and I'd invited her home to see my carvings. I felt the urge to giggle hysterically, but stifled it. I went to the kitchen, got out some ice, and poured two big shots of bourbon over the ice. I gave her one. Then I went to the bathroom and started to run hot water in the tub. She stayed right behind me—like a dog I used to have when it was supper-time, or when he thought I might be about to go somewhere.

"Get in," I said. "Take a long, slow hot bath. Drink another drink. I'll make us some supper, and we'll eat it together. No candlelight, though. A lot of bright overheads."

I took her nearly empty glass, added more ice, and filled it again. I gave it to her, pushed her gently into the bathroom, and closed the door.

"There's some kind of bubble bath or whatever in the medicine cabinet," I said through the door. I waited till I heard her splash into the tub. Then I went to the kitchen. I put on a pot of rice to cook and got four boneless chicken breasts out of the meat keeper. I cooked them with wine and butter and cream and mushrooms. While they cooked I tossed a salad and made a dressing with lime juice and mint, olive oil, honey, and wine vinegar. There were two bottles of Rhine wine in the refrigerator for which I'd originally had other plans, but I could buy some more tomorrow.

By the time I'd gotten the table set in the living room, she was through, and came out of the bathroom wearing a towel with her hair tucked up and some color in her face. I handed her my bathrobe and she slipped into it, modestly closing it before she let the towel slip to the floor. It occurred to me that half the time we'd spent together she'd been without clothes.

I gave her a third drink and freshened up my own. She sat on a stool in the kitchen and sipped it while I put some baking powder biscuits in the oven.

She had not spoken since I'd found her. Now she said, "Do you have any cigarettes?"

I found some thin filter tips in a fancy feminine package that a friend had left in one of the kitchen drawers. I held a match for her as she lit one and inhaled deeply. She let the smoke slip slowly out of her nose as she sipped her drink, holding the glass in both hands. The smoke spread out on the surface of the bourbon and eddied gently back up around her face. I felt my stomach tighten; I had known someone a long time ago who used to do just that, in just that way.

I got out the corkscrew and opened one of the bottles of wine. I poured some into each glass, and then took the biscuits out and served the supper. She sat opposite me at the small table and ate. Her manners were terrific. One hand in the lap, small bites, delicate sips of wine. But she ate everything. So did I. Still no talk. I had the radio on in the kitchen. When I offered her more, she nodded yes. When I got up to get the second bottle of wine, I plugged in the coffee. Its steady perk made a pleasant counterpoint to the radio. When we'd finished eating, I poured the coffee and brought out some applejack and two pony glasses. I put them on the cobbler's bench coffee table in front of the sofa. She sat at one end and I sat at the other, and we drank our coffee and sipped our brandy and she smoked another cigarette, holding her hand primly over the gap in the front of the bathrobe as she leaned over to accept my light. I got out a cigar and we listened some more to the radio. She leaned back against the arm of the couch and closed her eyes.

I stood up and said, "You can sleep in my bed. I'll sleep out here." I walked to the bedroom door and opened it. She went in.

I said, "I'm sorry I don't have any pajamas. You could sleep in one of my dress shirts, I guess."

"No, thank you," she said. "I don't wear anything to bed anyway."

"Okay," I said. "Good night. We'll talk in the morning."

She went in and shut the door, then opened it a crack. I heard her get into the bed. I picked up the dishes and put them in the dishwasher. Then I went in and took a shower and shaved. I felt odd, like my father probably had when we were small and all home and in bed and he was the only one up in the house. I got a blanket out of the closet, shut out the lights, and lay on my back on the couch smoking the rest of my cigar, blowing the smoke across the glowing tip.

I heard the light click on in the bedroom. She called, "Spenser?"

"Yeah?"

"Would you come in here, please?"

I got up, put on a pair of pants, and went in, still smoking the cigar. She was lying on her back in bed with covers pulled up under her chin.

"Sit on the bed," she said.

I did.

"Did you ever work on a farm?" she asked me.

"Nope."

"My grandfather, my mother's father, had a farm in Illinois. He used to milk fifty cows a day, and he had forearms like yours. He wasn't as big as you, but he had muscles in his forearms like you do."

I nodded.

"You're not fat at all, are you?" she said. I shook my head.

"With your clothes on you look as if you might be a little fat, but with your shirt off you're not. It's all muscle, isn't it?"

I nodded.

"You look like . . . like a boxer, or like somebody in a Tarzan movie."

"Cheetah," I said.

"Do you know," she said, "do you know that I've only met you four times in my life, and you are the only person in the entire world I can trust?" As she got to the end of the sentence her eyes filled. I patted her leg and said, "Shhh." But she went on, her voice not quite steady but apparently under control.

"Dennis is dead. My mother and father use me to get even with each other. I thought I could join the Moloch people. They'd dropped out, they weren't hung up on all the crap my father is. I thought they just took you as you were. They don't." Her voice got shakier. "They initiate you."

I patted her thigh again. I had nothing to say. The stub of the cigar was too short. I put it in an ashtray on the night table.

"Do you know what the initiation is?"

"I figured out the first part," I said.

She sat up in bed and let the covers fall away.

"You are the only one in the world, in the whole goddamned sonova bitch world . . ." The tears started to come. I leaned toward her and put my arm around her and she caught hold of me and squeezed.

"Love me," she said in a choked voice. "Make love to me, make me feel, make love to me, make me feel." A fleeting part of my mind thought, "Jesus, first the mother, then the daughter," but the enduring majority of my mind said, Yes, Yes, Yes, as I bore her back onto the bed and turned the covers back from her.

13

In the morning I drove Terry home. Riding out to Newton we mentioned neither the Ceremony of Moloch nor the previous night. We ran through the events of the murder again; nothing new. I described Sonny for her in detail. Yes, that sounded like one of the men. They had brought the drug with them that she'd swallowed. They had brought her gun with them. Yes, she had shared that apartment with Cathy Connelly before Dennis had moved in. They had parted friends and still were, as far as Terry knew. Cathy lived on the Fenway, she said. On the museum side, near the end closest to the river. She didn't know the number. I stopped in front of her house and let her out. I didn't go in. Having slept with mother and daughter within the same twenty-four hours, I felt fussy about sitting around with both of them in the library and making small talk. She leaned back in through the open door of my car.

"Call me," she said.

"I will," I said.

She closed the door and I pulled away, watching her in the rear-view mirror. She went in very slowly, turning once to wave at me. I tooted the horn in reply.

Back to Boston again. I seemed to be making this drive a lot. Turning off Storrow at the Charlesgate exit, I went up the ramp over Commonwealth Ave and looked down at the weeping willows underneath the arch—bare now, with slender branches crusted in snow and bending deep beneath winter weight. There was a Frost poem, but it was about birches, and then I was off the ramp and looking for a parking space. This was not a business for poets anyway.

I parked near the Westland Avenue entrance to the Fenway and walked across the street to a drugstore. There was no listing in the phone book for a Catherine Connelly on the Fenway. So I started at the north end and began looking at the mailboxes in apartment lobbies, working my way south toward the museum. In the third building I found it. Second floor. I rang. Nothing happened. I rang again and leaned on it. No soap. I rang some other buzzers at random. No one opened the door. A cagey lot. I rang all the buttons. No response. Then a mean, paunchy man in green twill shirt and pants came to the front door. He opened it about a foot and said, "Whaddya want?"

"You the super?" I said.

"Who do you think I am?" He was smoking a cigarette that looked as if he'd found it, and it waggled wetly in the corner of his mouth as he spoke.

"I thought you were one of Santa's helpers coming around to see if everything was set for Christmas."

"Huh?" he said.

"I'm looking for a young woman named Catherine Connelly. She doesn't answer her bell," I said.

"Then she ain't home."

"Mind if I check?"

"You better stop ringing them other buzzers too," he said, and shut the door. I resisted the temptation to ring all the buzzers again and run. "Childish," I thought. "Adolescent." I went back to my car, got in, and drove to the university. Maybe I'd be able to locate her there. I parked in a spot that was reserved for Dean Mersfelder and headed for the library basement.

Iris Milford was there in her NEWS office, behind her metal desk.

There were several other members of the staff, obviously younger, doing journalistic things at their metal desks.

She recognized me when I came in.

"Nice eye you got," she said.

I'd forgotten the punch Sonny had landed. It looked worse than it felt, though it was still sore to touch.

"I bruise easily," I said.

"I'll bet," she said.

"Want to have lunch with me?" I asked.

"Absolutely," she said. She closed the folder she was looking at, picked up her purse, and came around the desk.

"Too bad about how you can't make up your mind," I said.

We walked out through the corridor. It was class-change time and the halls were crowded and hot and loud. A miasma of profanity and smoke and sweatiness under heavy winter coats. Ah, where are the white bucks of yesteryear? We wormed our way up to the first floor and finally out past the security apparatus that set off an alarm if someone smuggled out a book, past the scrutiny of a hard-faced librarian alert beside it, into the milling snow-crusted quadrangle. I got a cab and we rode to a restaurant I liked on top of an insurance building, where the city looked clean and patrician below, and the endless rows of red-brick town houses that had crumbled into slums looked geometric and orderly and a little European, stretching off to the south.

We had a drink and ordered lunch. Iris looked out at the orderly little brick houses.

"Get far enough away and it looks kinda pretty, don't it?" she said. "You only get order from a distance. Close up is always messy."

"Yeah," I said, "but your own life is always close up. You only see other people's lives at long range."

"You better believe it," she said. "I'll take another pop."

I ordered us two more drinks.

"Okay, Spenser, what is it? You not the type to feed drinks to a poor colored lady and take advantage of her body. Even one as irresistible as mine. What you want?"

I liked her. She'd been there and seen it done. A tough, wised-up, honest broad.

"Well, if you're not going to come across, I'll take second best. Tell me about Cathy Connelly."

"What you want to know?"

"I don't know, everything, anything. All I know is she was once Terry Orchard's roommate, that she moved out when the Powell kid moved in, that she now lives on the Fenway, and that she wasn't home when I called on her this morning."

"That's about as much as I know. She was in my Chaucer class, and I copied her notes a couple times. I don't know her much better than that."

"She belong to SCACE?"

"Not that I know. She seemed kind of a loner. Didn't belong to anything I know of. You never see her around campus, but that don't mean much because the goddamn campus is so big and crowded that you might not see a woolly rhinoceros around campus."

"Boyfriends?" I asked.

"None that I know. But I'm telling you, I don't hardly know her. What I'm saying could be wrong as hell."

"Where can I get a picture of her?"

"Student Personnel Office, I would guess. That's where we get ones we use in the paper for fast-breaking news stories, like who was elected captain of the girls' field hockey team. Campus security can probably get them for you."

"I don't think so, Iris. Last dealing I had with campus security was when they ejected me from the premises. I think they don't like me."

She widened her eyes. "I thought they hired you."

"They did, but I think they are in the process of making an agonizing reappraisal of that decision."

"You having a good week, Spenser. Someone plunks you in the eye, you get thrown off the campus, you gonna get fired, you can't find Cathy Connelly. I hope you don't depress easy."

"Like you were saying, it's always messy close up."

"What you want Connelly for, anyway?"

"She was Terry Orchard's roommate. She might know how Terry's gun got from her bedside table into a hood's pocket."

"Jesus, she don't look the type."

"There isn't any type, my love."

She nodded, "Ain't that the truth."

"Want dessert?" I said.

She nodded. "Do I look like someone who turns down dessert?"

I asked for a dessert menu.

Iris said, "I can get the picture for you. I'll go over to student personnel and tell them we need it for a feature we're doing. We do it all the time."

"Would you like two desserts?" I said.

After I paid the bill with some of Roland Orchard's retainer and drove her back to the university, she did what she said. I sat in the car with the heater on, and she strolled into the student center and returned twenty minutes later with a two-by-two ID photo of Cathy Connelly. I thanked her.

She said, "Two drinks and a lobster salad will get you almost anything, baby," and went to class.

I drove over to Mass Ave and had a technician I know at a photo lab blow the picture up to eight by ten. Service while I waited cost me twenty-five dollars more of Roland Orchard's retainer, and I still hadn't got the tear fixed in my car top.

I took the picture back to my office and sat behind my desk looking at it. She looked like a pallid little girl. Small features, light hair, prominent teeth, serious eyes. While I was looking at her picture my door opened and in came Lieutenant Quirk. Hatless, wearing a glen plaid overcoat, shoes glossy, pocked face clean-shaven, ruddy from the cold, and glowing with health. He closed the door behind him, and stood looking at me with his hands in his overcoat pockets. He did not radiate cheer.

"Come in, Lieutenant," I said. "No need to knock, my door is always open to a public servant. You've come, no doubt, to ask my assistance in solving a particularly knotty puzzle . . ."

"Knock it off, Spenser. If I want to listen to bullshit, I'll go over to a City Council meeting."

"Okay, have a seat. Want a drink?"

Quirk ignored the chair I'd nodded at and stood in front of my desk.

"Yeah, I'll have a drink."

I poured two shots of bourbon into two paper cups. Quirk drank his off without expression and put the empty cup down. I sipped at mine a little and thought fondly of the stuff that Roland Orchard served.

"Terry Orchard is it, Spenser," he said.

"The hell she is."

"She's it. Captain Yates is taking personal charge of the case, and she's the one."

"Yates. That means you're off it?"

"That's right."

"What else does it mean?"

"It doesn't mean anything else."

I poured two more shots of bourbon. Quirk's hard face looked like he was concealing a toothache.

"Like hell it doesn't mean anything else, Quirk. You didn't make a special trip down here just to keep me informed on personnel shifts in the BPD. You don't like her for it, and you know it. Why is Yates on it?"

"He didn't say."

I sipped some more of my bourbon. Quirk walked over and looked out my window.

"What a really swell view you've got, Spenser."

I didn't say anything. Quirk came back to my desk, picked up the bottle, and poured himself another drink.

"Okay," he said. "I don't like the kid for the murder."

I said, "Me either."

"I got nothing. Everything I've got says she's guilty. Nice simple murder, nice simple solution. Why screw around with it?"

"That's right," I said. "Why screw around with it?"

"I've been on the force twenty-two years. You meet a lot of liars in twenty-two years. I don't think she was lying."

I said, "Me either."

Quirk was walking around the room as he talked, looking at it like he looked at everything, seeing it all, and if he ever had to, he'd remember it all.

"You went to see Joe Broz yesterday."

I nodded.

"Why?"

"So he could tell me to butt out of the Godwulf Manuscript–Terry Orchard affair."

"What did you say?"

"I said we'll see."

"Did you know the manuscript is back?"

I raised one eyebrow, something I'd perfected after years of practice and a score of old Brian Donlevy movies. Quirk appeared not to notice.

"Broz suggested that was possible," I said.

Quirk nodded. "Any idea why Broz wanted you to butt out?"

"No," I said. "Any idea why Yates wanted you to butt out?"

"No, but there's a lot of pressure from somewhere up the line."

"And Yates is responding."

Quirk's face seemed to shut down. "I don't know about what Yates is doing. I know he's in charge of the case and I'm not. He's the captain. He has the right to assign personnel."

"Yeah, sure. I know Yates a little. One of the things he does best is respond to pressure from somewhere up the line."

Quirk didn't say anything.

"Look, Lieutenant," I said, "does it seem odd to you that there are two guys looking into the Terry Orchard thing and both of us are told to butt out within the same day? Does that seem like any kind of coincidence to you?"

"Spenser, I am a cop. I have been a cop for twenty-two years, and I will keep on being one until they lock me out of the station house. One of the things that a cop has to have is discipline. He gets orders, he has to obey them—or the whole thing goes to hell. I don't have to like what's happening, but I do it. And I don't run around crying about it."

"Words to live by," I said. "It was the widely acclaimed Adolf Eichmann who popularized that 'I obey orders' routine, wasn't it?"

"That's a cheap shot, Spenser. You know goddamn well the cops are right more than they're wrong. We're not wiping out six million people. We're trying to keep the germs from taking over the world. To do that you got to have order, and if someone gets burned now and then so someone gets burned. If every cop started deciding which order to obey and which one not, then the germs would win. If the germs win, all the goddamn bleeding hearts will get their ass shot."

"Yeah, sure, the big picture. So some goddamn teenaged kid gets fed to the fishes for something she didn't do. So you know she didn't do it and Joe Broz puts the squeeze on some politician who puts the squeeze on Captain Yates who takes you off the case. But you don't cry. It's good for society. Balls. Why don't you take what you got to the States?"

"Because I haven't got enough. The State cops would laugh and giggle if I came in with what I've got. And because, goddamn it, Spenser, because I can't. I'm a cop. It's what I do. I can't."

"I know," I said. "But I can. And I'm going to. I'm going to have Broz and Yates, and you, too, if I have to, and whoever else has got his thumb in whatever pie this is."

"Maybe you will," Quirk said. "I hear you were a pretty good cop before you got fired. What'd you get fired for?"

"Insubordination. It's one of my best things."

"And maybe Broz will have you shot in the back of the head."

I let that pass. We were silent.

"How much do I have to get for you before you go to the States?"

"I'm not asking you to get a damn thing for me," Quirk said.

"Yeah, I know. If I got you proof. Not suspicion, proof. Then what happens?"

"Then the pressure will go away. Yates is impressed with proof."

"I'll bet," I said.

More silence. Quirk didn't seem to want to leave, but he didn't have anything to say. Or at least he wasn't saying it.

"What do you know about Cathy Connelly, Lieutenant?"

"We checked her out routinely. No record, no evidence of drugs. Roomed with Orchard before her boyfriend moved in. Now lives somewhere over on the Fenway."

"Anybody interview her?"

"Couple of precinct boys in a radio car stopped by. She wasn't home. We saw no reason to press it. Do you?"

"Those two hoods had Terry Orchard's gun with them when they came to the apartment. How'd they get it?"

"If it's true."

"Of course, if it's true. I think it's true. Cathy Connelly seems like the best person to ask about how they got the gun. Terry doesn't know, Powell is dead. Who's left?"

"Why don't you go ask her then?" Quirk said. "Thanks for the drink."

He walked out leaving the door open behind him, and I listened to his footsteps going down the hall.

14

I went over to the university to call on Carl Tower. I hoped the campus cops weren't under orders to shoot on sight. Whether they were, the secretary with the ripe thighs was not. She was friendly. She had on a pants suit today, black, with a large red valentine heart over the left breast. Red platform heels, red enamel pendant earrings. Bright red lipstick. She obviously remembered me. I was probably haunting her dreams.

She said, "May I help you?"

"Don't pull that sweet talk on me," I said.

"I beg your pardon."

"I know what you're thinking, and I'm sorry, but I'm on duty."

"Of all the outer offices in all the towns in all the world," she said, "you had to walk into mine." There was no change in her expression.

I started to say something about, "If you want anything, just whistle," but at that moment Carl Tower appeared at his office door and saw me. I was obviously not haunting his dreams.

"Spenser," he said, "get the hell in my office."

I took off my wristwatch and gave it to the secretary. "If I don't come out alive," I said, "I want you to have this."

She giggled. I went into Tower's office.

Tower picked up a tabloid-size newspaper from his desk and tossed it across at me. It was the university newspaper. Across the top was the headline ADMINISTRATION AGENT SPIES ON STUDENT, and in a smaller drop head, PRIVATE EYE HIRED BY ADMINISTRATION QUESTIONS ENGLISH PROFESSOR. I didn't bother to read the story, though I noticed they spelled my name wrong in the lead paragraph.

"It's with an *s,* not a *c,*" I said. "Like the English poet. S-p-e-n-s-e-r."

Tower was biting down so hard on his back teeth that the muscles of his jaw bulged at the hinge.

"We won't ask for a return on the retainer, Spenser," he said. "But if you are on this campus again, ever, we'll arrest you for trespassing and use every influence we have to have your license lifted."

"I hear you got the manuscript back," I said.

"That's right. No thanks to you. Now beat it."

"Who returned it?"

"It just showed up yesterday in a cardboard box, on the library steps."

"Ever wonder why it came back?"

Tower stood up. "You're through, Spenser. As of this minute. You are no longer in the employ of this university. You have no business here. You're trespassing. Either you leave or I call some people to take you out of here."

"How many you going to call?"

Tower's face got quite red. He said, "You sonova bitch," and put his hand on the phone.

I said, "Never mind. If I whipped your entire force it would embarrass both of us."

On the way out I stopped by the secretary's desk. She handed me back my watch.

"I'm glad you made it," she said.

On the inside of the watch strap in red ink she had written "Brenda Loring, 555-3676."

I looked up at her. "I am, too," I said, and strapped the watch back on.

She went back to typing and I went back to leaving the university in disgrace. Administration agent, I thought as I went furtively down the corridor. Zowie!

15

Back to the Fenway to Cathy Connelly's apartment. I rang the bell; no answer. I didn't feel like swapping compliments with Charlie Charm the super, so I strolled around the building looking for an alternate solution. Behind the apartment was an asphalt courtyard with lines for parking spaces and a line of trash barrels, dented and bent, against the wall, behind low trapezoidal concrete barriers to keep the cars from denting and bending them more. Despite the ill-fitting covers on them, some of the trash had spilled out and littered the ground along the foundation. The cellar entrance door was open, but the screen door was closed and fastened with a hook and eye arrangement. It was plastic screening. I took out my jackknife and cut through the screen at the hook. I put my hand through and unhooked it. Tight security, I thought. Straight ahead and two steps down stretched the cellar. To my left rose the stairs. I went up them. Cathy Connelly was apartment 13. I guessed second floor, given the size of the building. I was wrong. It was third floor. Close observation is my business.

Down the corridor ran a frayed, faded rose runner. The doors were dark-veneer wood with the numbers in shiny silver decals asymmetrically pasted on. The knob on each door was fluted glass. The corridor was weakly lit by a bare bulb in a wall sconce at the end. In front of number 13 a faint apron of light spread out under the door. I looked at my watch; I knocked again. Same result. I put my ear against the door panel. The television was on, or the radio. I heard no other sound. That didn't prove anything. Lots of people left the TV running when they went out. Some to discourage burglars. Some because they forgot to turn them off. Some so it wouldn't seem so empty when they came home. I tried the knob. No soap. The door was locked. That was a problem about as serious as the screen door in the cellar. I kicked it open—which would probably irritate the super, since when I did, the jamb splintered. I stepped in and felt the muscles begin to tighten behind my shoulders. The apartment was hot and stuffy, and there was a smell I'd smelled before.

The real estate broker had probably described it as a studio apartment—which meant one room with kitchenette and bath. The bath was to my left, door slightly ajar. The kitchenette was directly before me, separated from the rest of the room by a plastic curtain. To my right were a day bed, the covers folded back as if someone were about to get in, an armchair with a faded pink and beige shawl draped over it as a slipcover, a bureau, a steamer trunk apparently used as a coffee table, and a wooden kitchen table, painted blue, which seemed to double as a desk. On it the television maundered in black and white. In front of the kitchen table was a straight chair. A woman's white blouse and faded denim skirt were folded over the back of it, underwear and socks tangled on the seat. A saddle shoe lay on its side beneath the chair and another stood flat-footed under the table. There was no one in the room. There was no one behind the plastic curtain. I turned into the bathroom and found her.

She was in the tub, face down, her head under water, her body beginning to bloat. The smell was stronger in here. I forced myself to look. There was a clotted tangle of blood in the hair at the back of one ear. I touched the water; it was room temperature. Her body was the same. I wanted to turn her over, but I couldn't make myself do it. On the floor by the tub, looking as if she'd just stepped out of them, were a pair of flowered baby doll pajamas. She'd been there awhile. Couple of days, anyway. While I'd been ringing her bell and asking the super if he'd seen her, she'd been right here floating motionless in the tepid water. How do you do, Miss Connelly, my name is Spenser, very sorry I didn't get to meet you sooner. Hell of a way to meet now. I looked at her for two, maybe three minutes, feeling the nausea bubble inside me. Nothing happened, so I began to look at the bathroom. It was crummy. Plastic tiles, worn linoleum buckling up from the floor. The sink was dirty and the faucet dripped steadily. There was no shower. Big patches of paint had peeled off the ceiling. I thought of a line from a poem: "Even the dreadful martyrdom must run its course/Anyhow in a corner, some untidy spot." I forget who wrote it.

There were no telltale cigar butts, no torn halves of claim checks, no traces of lint from an imported cashmere cloth sold only by J. Press. No footprints, no thumb prints, no clues. Just a drowned kid swelling with death in a shabby bathroom in a crummy apartment in a lousy building run by a grumpy janitor. And me.

I went back out into the living room. No phone. God is my copilot. I went out to the hall and down the stairs to the cellar. The super had an office partitioned off with chicken wire from the rest of the cellar. In it were a rolltop desk, an antique television set, and a swivel chair, in which sat the super. The smell of bad wine oozed out of the place. He looked at me with no sign of recognition or welcome.

I said, "I want to use your phone."

He said, "There's a pay phone at the drugstore across the street. I ain't running no charity here."

I said, "There is a dead person in room thirteen, and I am going to call the police and tell them. If you say anything to me but yes, sir, I will hit you at least six times in the face."

He said, "Yes, sir." Pushing an old wino around always enlivens your spirits. I picked up the phone and called Quirk. Then I went back upstairs and waited for him to arrive with his troops. It wasn't as long a wait as it seemed. When they arrived Captain Yates was along.

He and Quirk went in to look at the remains. I sat on the day bed and didn't look at anything. Sergeant Belson sat on the edge of the table smoking a short cigar butt that looked like he'd stepped on it.

"Do you buy those things secondhand?" I asked.

Belson took the cigar butt out of his mouth and looked at it. "If I smoked the big fifty cent jobs in the cedar wrappers, you'd figure I was on the take."

"Not the way you dress," I said.

"You ever think of another line of work, Spenser? So far all you've detected is two stiffs. Maybe a crossing guard, say, or . . ."

Quirk and Yates came out of the bathroom with a man from the coroner's. The lines in Quirk's face looked very deep, and the medic was finishing a shrug. Yates came over to me. He was a tall man with narrow shoulders and a hard-looking pot belly. He wore glasses with translucent plastic rims like they used to hand out in the army. His mouth was wide and loose.

He looked at me very hard and said, "Someone's going to have to pay for that door."

Belson gave him a startled look; Quirk was expressionless. I couldn't think of anything to say, so I didn't say anything. It was a technique I ought to work on.

Yates said, "What's your story, Jack? What the hell are you doing here?"

"Spenser," I said, "with an *s* like the English poet. I was selling Girl Scout cookies door to door and they told us to be persistent. . . ."

"Don't get smart with me, Jack; we got you for breaking and entering. If the lieutenant here hadn't said he knew you, I'da run you in already. The janitor says you threatened him, too."

I looked at Belson. He was concentrating mightily on getting his cigar butt relit, turning it carefully over the flame of a kitchen match to make sure it fired evenly. He didn't look at me.

"What's the coroner's man say about the kid?" I asked Quirk.

Yates answered, "Accidental death. She slipped getting in the tub, hit her head, and drowned." Belson made a noise that sounded like a cough. Yates spun toward him. "You got something to say, Sergeant?"

Belson looked up. "Not me, Captain, no, sir, just inhaled some smoke wrong. Fell right on her head, all right, yes, sir."

Yates stared at Belson for about fifteen seconds. Belson puffed on his cigar. His face showed nothing. Quirk was looking carefully at the light fixture on the ceiling.

"Captain," I said, "does it bother you that her bed is turned back, her clothes are on the chair, and her pajamas are on the bathroom floor? Does it seem funny to you that someone would take off her clothes, put on her pajamas, and get in the bathtub?"

"She brought them in to put on when she got through," Yates said very quickly. His mouth moved erratically as he talked. It was like watching a movie with the soundtrack out of sync. Peculiar.

"And dropped them carefully in a pile on the floor where the tub would splash them and she'd drip on them when she got out because she loved putting on wet pajamas," I said.

"Accidental death by drowning. Open and shut." Yates said it hard and loud with a lot of lip motion. Fascinating to watch. "Quirk, let's go. Belson, get this guy's statement. And you, Jack"—he gave me the hard look again—"be where I can reach you. And when I call, you better come running."

"How about I come over and sleep on your back step," I said, but Yates was already on his way out.

Quirk looked at Belson. Belson said, "Right on her head she fell, Marty."

Quirk said, "Yeah," and went out after Yates.

Belson whistled "The Battle Hymn of the Republic" between his teeth as he got out his notebook and looked at me. "Shoot," he said.

"For crissake, Frank, this is really raw."

"Captain don't want an editorial," Belson said, "just what happened."

"Even if you aren't bothered by the pajamas and all, isn't it worth more than routine when the ex-roommate of a murder suspect dies violently?"

Belson said, "I spent six years rattling doorknobs under the MTA tracks in Charlestown. Now ride in a car and wear a tie. Captain just wants what happened."

I told him.

16

I sat in my car on the dark Fenway. The super had, grumbling, installed a padlock on the splintered door to the Connelly apartment while a prowl car cop watched. Belson had departed with my statement, and everything was neat and orderly again. The corpse gone. The mob, the cops, the university had all told me to mind my own business. Not a bad trio; I was waiting for a threat from organized religion. In a few weeks Terry Orchard would be gone, to the women's reformatory in Framingham; twenty years probably, a crime of passion by a young woman. She'd be out when she was forty, ready to start anew. You meet such interesting people in jail.

I got a flashlight and some tape out of the glove compartment and a pinch bar out of my trunk and went back over to the apartment house. The super hadn't fixed the screen on the back door, but he had shut and locked the inside door. I went to a cellar window. It was locked. On my hands and knees I looked through the frost patterns of grime. Inside was darkness. I flashed the light through.

Inside was what looked like a coal bin, no longer used for coal. There were barrels and boxes and a couple of bicycles. I taped a tic-tac-toe pattern on one of the windowpanes and tapped the glass out with the pinch bar. The tape kept the noise down. When the opening was big enough I reached my hand through and unlatched the window. It was not a very big window, but I managed to slide through it and drop to the cellar floor. I scraped both shins in the process.

The cellar was a maze of plastic trash bags, old wooden barrels, steamer trunks, cardboard boxes, clumsily tied piles of newspaper. A rat scuttled out of the beam from my flashlight as I worked my way through the junk. At the far end a door, slightly ajar, opened onto the furnace room, and to the left were the stairway and the super's cage. I could hear canned laughter from the television. I went very quietly along the wall toward the stairs. I was in luck; when I peered around the corner of the super's office he was in his swivel chair, asleep in the rich fumes of port wine and furnace heat, the TV blaring before him. I went up the same stairs to the third floor. No hesitation on the second floor—I learn quickly. The padlock on Cathy Connelly's door was cheap and badly installed. I got the pinch bar under the hasp and pulled it loose with very little noise. Once inside I put a chair against the door to keep it closed and turned on the lights. The place hadn't changed much in the past two hours. The bloated corpse was gone, but otherwise there was nothing different. It wasn't a very big apartment. I could search it in a couple of hours probably. I didn't know what I was looking for, of course, which would slow me down, because I couldn't eliminate things on an "is-it-bigger-than-a-bread-box" basis.

I started in the bathroom, because it was on the left. If you are going to get something searched you have to do it orderly. Start at a point and go section by section through the place, not where things are most likely, or least likely, or anything else, just section by section until you've looked at everything. The bathroom didn't take long. There was in the medicine cabinet some toothpaste, some aspirin, some nose drops prescribed by a doctor in New Rochelle, New York, a bottle of Cope, some lipstick, some liquid make-up, a safety razor, an eyebrow pencil. I emptied out the make-up bottle; there was nothing in it but make-up. The aspirin tasted like aspirin, the Cope appeared to be Cope, the nose drops smelled like nose drops. There was nothing in the lipstick tube but lipstick. There was nothing in the toilet tank, nothing taped underneath the sink, no sign that anything had been slipped under the buckling linoleum. I stood on the toilet seat and unscrewed the ceiling fixture with a jackknife blade—nothing inside but dusty wiring that looked like it wouldn't pass the city's electrical code. I screwed the fixture back in place.

I went over the kitchen next. I emptied the flour, sugar, dry cereal, salt, and pepper into the sink one by one and sifted through them. Other than some little black insects I found nothing. The stove was an old gas stove. I took up the grillwork over the burners, looked carefully at the oven. The stove couldn't be moved without disconnecting the gas pipe. I was willing to bet Cathy Connelly never had. I took all the pans out of the under sink cabinet and wormed under the sink on my back, using my flashlight to examine it all. A cockroach. There was little food in the old gas refrigerator. I emptied it. A couple of TV dinners. I melted them under the hot water in the sink and found nothing. I took the panel off of the bottom and looked carefully in. The motor was thick with dust kitties, and the drip pan was gummy with God knows what.

The living room was of course the one that took time. It was about two in the morning when I found something. In the bottom bureau drawer was a cigar box containing letters, bills, canceled checks. I took it over to the daybed, sat down, and began to read through them. There were two letters from her mother full of aimless amenities that made my throat tighten. The dog got on the school bus and her father had gotten a call from the school and had to leave the store and go get it, younger brother was in a junior high school pageant, momma had lost three pounds, she hoped Cathy was watching what she ate, daddy sent his love.

The third letter was different. It was on the stationery of a Peabody motel. It said:

Darling,
You are beautiful when you are asleep. As I write this I am looking at you and the covers are half off you so I can see your breasts. They are beautiful. I want to climb back into bed with you, but I must leave. You can cut my eight o'clock class, but I can't. I won't mark you absent though and I'll be thinking about last night all the time. The room is paid for and you have to leave by noon, they said. I love you.

There was no date, no signature. It was written in a distinctive cursive script.

For crissake! A clue. A goddamned clue. I folded the note up and put it in my inside coat pocket. So far I was guilty of breaking and entering, possession of burglar's tools, and destruction of property. I figured tampering with evidence would round things out nicely. I wanted to run right out and track down my clue, but I didn't. I searched the rest of the room. There were no other clues.

I turned off the lights, moved the chair, and went out. The door wouldn't stay shut because of the broken padlock. I went out the front way this time, as if I belonged. When I reached my car I put the pinch bar back in the trunk, got in the car, and sat for a bit. Now that I had a clue, what exactly was I supposed to do with it? I looked at my watch. 3 A.M. Searching apartments is slow business. I turned on the interior light in my car, took out my clue, and read it again. It said the same thing it said the first time. I folded it up again and tapped my front teeth with it for about fifteen seconds. Then I put it back in my pocket, turned off the interior light, started up the car, and went home. When I decide something I don't hesitate.

I went to bed and dreamed I was a miner and the tunnel was collapsing and everyone else had left. I woke up with the dream unfinished and my clock said ten minutes of seven. I looked at the bureau. My clue was up there where I'd left it, partly unfolded, along with my loose change and my jackknife and my wallet. Maybe I'd catch somebody today. Maybe I'd detect something. Maybe I'd solve a crime. There are such days. I'd even had some. I climbed out of bed and plodded to the shower. I hadn't worked out in four days and felt it. If I solved something this morning, maybe I could take the afternoon off and go over to the Y.

I took a shower and shaved and dressed and went out. It was only 7:45 and cold. The snow was hard-crusted and the sun glistened off it very brightly. I put on my sunglasses. Even through their dark lenses it was a bright and lovely day. I stopped at a diner and had two cups of coffee and three plain doughnuts. I looked at my watch. 8:15. The trouble with being up and at 'em bright and early was once you were up most of the 'em that you wanted to be at weren't out yet.

I bought a paper and cruised over to the university. There was room to park in a tow zone near the gymnasium. I parked there and read the paper for half an hour. Nowhere was there mention of the fact that I'd found a clue. In fact, nowhere was anyone even predicting that I would. At nine o'clock I got out and went looking for Iris Milford.

She wasn't in the newspaper office. The kid cropping photos at the next desk told me she never came in until the afternoon, and showed me her class schedule pasted on the corner of her desk. With his help I figured out that from nine to ten she had a sociology course in room 218 of the chemistry building. He told me how to get there. I had a half-hour wait in the corridor, where I entertained myself examining the girl students who went by. During class time they were sparse and I had nothing else to do but marvel at the consistency with which the university architects had designed their buildings. Cinder block and vinyl tile seem to suffice for all seasons. At ten minutes to ten the bell rang and the kids poured into the corridor. Iris saw me as she came out of the classroom. She said, "Hell, Spenser. How'd you know where to find me?"

I said, "I'm a trained detective. Want some coffee?"

We went to the cafeteria in the student union. Above the cafeteria entrance someone had scrawled in purple Magic Marker, "Abandon All Hope Ye Who Enter Here."

I said, "Isn't that from Dante?"

She said, "Very good. It's written over the entrance to hell in book three of 'The Inferno.' "

I said, "Aw, I bet you looked that up."

The cafeteria was modernistic as far as cinder block and vinyl tile will permit. The service area along one side was low-ceilinged and close. The dining area was three stories high, with one wall of windows that reached the ceiling and opened on a parking lot. The cluttered tables were a spectrum of bright pastels, and the floor was red quarry tile in squares. It was somewhere between an aviary and Penn Station. It was noisy and hot. The smoke of thousands of cigarettes drifted through the shafts of winter sunlight that fused in throught the windows. Abandon All Hope Ye Who Enter Here.

I said, "Many campus romances start here?"

She laughed and shook her head. "Not hardly," she said. "You want to scuff hand and hand through fallen leaves, you don't go here."

We stood in line for our coffee. The service was cardboard, by Dixie. I paid, and we found a table. It was cluttered with paper plates, plastic forks, and cardboard beverage trays and napkins. I crumpled them together and deposited them in a trash can.

"How long you had this neatness fetish?" Iris asked.

I grinned, took a sip of coffee.

"You find Cathy Connelly?" she asked.

"Yeah," I said, "but she was dead."

Iris's mouth pulled back in a grimace and she said, "Shit."

"She'd been drowned in her bathtub, by someone who tried to make it look accidental."

Iris sipped her coffee and said nothing.

I took the letter from my inside pocket and gave it to her. "I found this in her room," I said.

Iris read it slowly.

"Well, she didn't die a virgin," Iris said.

"There's that," I said.

"She was sleeping with some professor," Iris said.

"Yep."

"If you can find out what eight o'clock classes she had, you'll know who."

"Yep."

"But you can't get that information because you've been banished from the campus."

"Yep."

"Which leaves old Iris to do it, right?"

"Right."

"Why do you want to know?"

"Because I don't know. It's a clue. There's a professor in here someplace. The missing manuscript would suggest a professor. Terry says she heard Powell talking to a professor before he was killed, now Cathy Connelly appears to have been sleeping with a professor, and she's dead. I want to know who he is. He could be the same professor. Can you get her class schedule?"

"This year?"

"All years, there's no date on the note."

"Okay, I got a friend in the registrar's office. She'll check it for me."

"How soon?"

"As soon as she can. Probably know tomorrow."

"I'm betting on Hayden," I said.

"As a secret lover?"

"Yep. The manuscript is medieval. He's a medieval specialist. He teaches Chaucer, which is an early class. Terry Orchard was up early for her Chaucer course the day that Powell threatened some professor on the phone. The conversation implied that the professor on the phone had an early class. Hayden pretended not to know Terry Orchard when in fact he did know her. He's a raging radical according to a very reliable witness. There's enough coincidence for me to wager on. Why don't you get in touch with your friend and find out if I'm right?"

She said, "Soon as I finish my coffee. I'll call you when I know."

I left her and headed back for my car.

17

I was right. Iris called me at eleven thirty the next morning to report that Cathy Connelly had taken Chaucer this year with Lowell Hayden at eight o'clock Monday, Wednesday, and Friday. The only other eight o'clock class she'd had in her three years at the university had been a course in Western civilization taught by a woman.

"Unless she was gay," Iris said, "it looks like Dr. Hayden."

"You took the same course, right?" I asked.

"Yeah."

"Got any term papers or exams, or something with a sample of his writing?"

"I think so. Come on over to the newspaper office. I'll dig some up."

"Don't you ever go to class?"

"Not while I'm tracking down a criminal, I don't."

"I'll be over," I said.

When I got there Iris had a typewritten paper bound in red plastic lying on her desk. It was twenty-two pages long and titled "The Radix Trait: A Study of Chaucer's Technique of Characterization in *The Canterbury Tales.*" Underneath it said "Iris Milford," and in the upper right-hand corner it said "En 308, Dr. Hayden, 10/28." Above the title in red pencil with a circle around it was the grade A minus.

"Inside back page," she said. "That's where he comments."

I opened the manuscript. In the same red pencil Hayden had written, "Good study, perhaps a bit too dependent on secondary sources, but well stated and judicious. I wish you had not eschewed the political and class implications of the *Tales,* however."

I took the note out of my coat pocket and put it down beside the paper. It was the same fancy hand.

"Can I have this paper?" I asked Iris.

"Sure—why, want to read it in bed?"

"No, I'm housebreaking a puppy."

She laughed. "Take it away," she said.

Near my office there was a Xerox copy center. I went in and made a copy of the note and the comment page in Iris's paper. I took the original up to my office and locked it in the top drawer of my desk. I put the copies in my pocket and drove over to see Lowell Hayden.

He wasn't in his office, and the schedule card posted on his door indicated that he had no more classes until Monday. Across the street at a drugstore I looked for his name in the directory. He wasn't listed in the Boston books. I looked up the English Department and called them.

"Hi," I said, "this is Dr. Porter. I'm lecturing over here at Tufts this evening and I'm trying to locate Lowell Hayden. We were grad students together. Do you have his home address?"

They did, and they gave it to me. He lived in Marblehead. I looked at my watch. 11:10. I could get there for lunch.

Marblehead is north, through the Callahan Tunnel and along Route 1A. An ocean town, yachting center, summer home, and old downtown district that reeked of tar and salt and quaint. Hayden had an apartment in a converted warehouse that fronted on the harbor. First floor, front.

A big hatchet-faced woman in her midthirties answered my ring. She was taller than I was and her blond hair was pulled back in a tight bun. She wore no make-up, and the only thing that ornamented her face were huge Gloria Steinem glasses with gold rims and pink lenses. Her lips were thin, her face very pale. She wore a man's green pullover sweater, Levi's, and penny loafers without socks. Big as she was, there was no extra weight. She was as lean and hard as a canoe paddle, and nearly as sexy.

"Mrs. Hayden?" I asked.

"Yes."

"Is Dr. Hayden in?"

"He's in his study. What do you want?"

"I'd like to speak with him, please."

"He always spends two hours a day in his study. I don't permit him to be bothered during that time. Tell me what you want."

"You're beautiful when you're angry," I said.

"What do you want?"

I offered her my card. "If you'll give that to Dr. Hayden, perhaps he'll break his rules just once."

"I will do nothing of the kind," she said without taking the card.

"Okay, but if you'll give him this card when he is through his meditations I'll be waiting out in my car, looking at the ocean, thinking long thoughts." I wrote on the back of the card, "Cathy Connelly?" and put the card down on the edge of the umbrella stand by the door. She didn't slam it, but she closed it firmly. I had the feeling she did everything firmly.

I went back to my car and watched the sun glint on the water. There weren't many boats in the harbor in winter, mostly sea gulls bobbing on the cold water and swooping in the bright sky. A lobster boat came slowly into the harbor mouth past the lighthouse on the point of Marblehead Neck. Behind me, the seafood restaurant on the wharf was filling with lunchtime customers, and ahead of me two tourists were taking pictures of the wharf building. I watched the Hayden apartment. Hatchet face never so much as peeked out a window at me. Her husband as far as I could tell continued to meditate. The waves hit the wharf regularly; the interval between waves was about three seconds. After two hours and twenty minutes Lowell Hayden appeared at the front door and looked hard at me. I waved. He shut the door and I sat some more. Another half hour and Hayden appeared again, this time wearing a tan poplin jacket with a fur-lined hood. Other than that he seemed to be dressed just as he had been the last time I saw him. His wife loomed behind him, much taller. She stood in the open door while he came to the car. Making sure I wouldn't mug him, I guess. He opened the door and got in. I smiled pleasingly.

He said, "Spenser, you'd better leave me alone." His little pale face was clenched and there was a flush on each cheekbone. He looked a bit like Raggedy Andy.

"Why is that?" I said.

"Because you'll get hurt."

"No," I said. "You're not saying it right. Keep the lips almost motionless, and squinch your eyes up."

"I'm warning you now, Spenser. You stay away from me. I have friends who know how to deal with people like you."

"You gonna call in some hard cases from the Modern Language Association?"

"I mean people who will kill you if I say so."

"Oh, Mrs. Hayden, you mean."

"You leave her out of this. You've upset her enough." He looked nervously at the motionless and implacable figure in the doorway.

"She asking you funny questions about Cathy Connelly?"

"I don't know anything about Cathy Connelly."

"Yeah, you do," I said. "You know about spending the night with her in a motel in romantic Peabody. You know that she's dead, and you know how she died."

"I do not." His resonant voice was up about three octaves; for the first time it matched his appearance. He glanced back at the woman in the doorway. "I'll have you killed, you bastard. I don't know anything about this. You leave me alone or you'll be so sorry—you can't imagine."

"You don't really think Joe Broz will kill me on your say-so, do you?"

His pale face went chalk white. The flush left his cheeks and his left eyelid began to flutter. My right hand was resting on the steering wheel and he suddenly dug his fingernails into it. I yanked my hand away and Hayden jumped out of the car and walked very fast to the house.

"You'll see," he shouted back to me. "You'll see, you bastard. You'll see."

He went in past his wife, who closed the door. Firmly.

There were four red scratches on the back of my hand. Lucky it wasn't the wife; they would have been on my throat. I leaned back in the car and took a big lungful of air and let it out slowly. I knew something. I knew that Hayden was it, or at least part of it. He'd overreacted. And he'd made a big mistake threatening me with tough-guy connections. It had to be Broz, and his reaction to the name made it certain. English professors don't know hired muscle unless there's something funny. Here there was something very funny. But exactly what? What was Lowell Hayden's connection with Joe Broz? What did either one have that the other would want? Hayden didn't have money, which was all Broz would want. The connection had to be dope somewhere. Powell was reputed to be a contact for heroin. Powell might be connected with Hayden. Hayden was connected to Cathy Connelly, who was connected to Terry Orchard, who was connected to Powell.

My head began to feel like a mare's nest. I could connect Hayden to Cathy Connelly for sure. The rest was just speculation, and what I knew in my gut wasn't going to get Terry Orchard out of jail. My best hope was Hayden's hysteria. He panicked pretty easily, and if I kept pushing at him, who knows what else might boil to the surface? But first I needed another point of view, a third party, you might say. It was time to go call on old Mark Tabor again. And this time maybe I'd stay longer and lean a little heavier.

18

Mark Tabor was not home when I got to Westland Avenue. I had to walk up four flights of stairs to find that out. I walked back down and sat outside in my car. I spent a lot of time doing that. It was getting dark and colder; I kept the motor running and the heater going. My stomach was making great cavernous noises at six thirty when Tabor showed up. He came down from Mass Ave with his hands deep in the pockets of a pea jacket, the collar up, and his red corona of hair blossoming about the dark coat like an eruption. He turned in at his building and I came up behind him, reaching his door as he was closing it. I hit it hard with my shoulder and it flew open, propelling Tabor across the room. He tripped over the bed as he staggered backward and fell on it. I shut the door hard behind me, for effect. I wanted him scared.

"Hey, man, what the hell," he said.

"The hell is this, stupid," I said. "If you don't answer what I ask I'm going to pound you into an omelet."

"Who the Christ are you, man?"

"My name's Spenser. I was here before, and you proved too tough for me to break. I'm back for another try, boy, only this time I'll try harder."

"I don't know nothing you care about, man."

"Oh, yeah, you do. You know about Lowell Hayden. Tell me. Tell me everything you know about Lowell Hayden."

"Hey, man, all I know is he's a professor, you know. That's all I know."

"No, you know more than that. You know he's in SCACE with you, don't you?" I moved toward him and he scrambled off the bed and backed toward the wall.

"No, man, honest. . . ."

"Yeah, you know that. And you'll tell me. But there's something else."

I was on his side of the bed now and close to him. He tried to jump onto the bed and away from me. I grabbed him by the shirt-front and slammed him back up against the wall.

"Before you tell me about Hayden, I want to speak to you about the manner in which you address me."

I had my face very close to his and was holding him very tight up against the wall. "I want you to address me as Mr. Spenser. I do not want you to address me as 'man.' Do you understand that?"

"Aw, man . . ." he began, and I slapped him in the face.

"Mr. Spenser, boy," I said.

"Lemme go, Mr. Spenser. You got no right to come in here and hassle me."

I jerked him away from the wall and slammed him back up against it.

"We're not here to discuss my rights, stupid, we're here to talk about Lowell Hayden. Is he in SCACE?"

"No, man . . . Mr. Spenser."

I slapped him across the face again, a little harder, twice.

"I'll kill you if I have to, stupid," I said.

"Okay, okay, yeah, he was in SCACE, but he was like a secret member, you know? Dennis Powell brought him in; he said this dude would be like a faculty contact only under cover, you dig? And me and Dennis would be like the only ones to know." He was beginning to sniffle a little as he talked.

"And the manuscript, what about that?" I twisted a little more shirtfront up in my hand and lifted him up on tiptoe for emphasis.

"I didn't have nothing to do with that; that was Dennis and Hayden. Hayden arranged it. I never even saw it."

"Okay, one more: Was Powell dealing hard drugs on campus?"

"Yeah."

"What?"

"Skag, mostly."

"Where did he get it?"

"I don't know."

I slammed him against the wall again.

"Honest to God, Mr. Spenser, I don't know. Ask Hayden, him and Dennis were close as a bastard. He might know. I don't know."

"How did Dennis get killed?"

"I don't know."

"How did Cathy Connelly get killed?"

"I don't know, honest to Christ, I don't know about any of that." He was shaking and his teeth chattered.

I believed him. But I had some hard facts for the first time. I had Hayden connected with Powell. I had Powell connected with heroin, which meant mob connections. If Powell and Hayden were that close, I had Hayden connected to the mob. I had Hayden and Powell both connected to the Godwulf Manuscript, and I had the Godwulf Manuscript connected to Broz. More than that, I had Cathy Connelly connected to both Hayden and Terry Orchard. In fact, I had Hayden connected with two murders.

"Let me go, Mr. Spenser. I don't know anything else."

I realized I was still holding Tabor half off the ground. I let him go. He sank onto the bed and began to cry.

I said, "Everyone gets scared when they are over-matched in the dark; it's not something to be ashamed of, kid."

He didn't stop crying, and I couldn't think of anything else to say. So I left. I had a lot of information, but I had an unpleasant taste in my mouth. Maybe on the way home I could stop and rough up a Girl Scout.

It was raining when I came out, a cold rain about a degree above snow, and in the dark the wetness made the city look better than it was. The light diffused and reflected off things that in the daylight were dull and ugly.

It was nearly eight o'clock. I hadn't eaten since breakfast. I went to a steak house and ate. Halfway through my steak I caught sight of myself in the mirror behind the bar. I looked like someone who ought to eat alone. I didn't look in the mirror again.

It was twenty minutes of ten as I parked in front of my apartment. In front of me was parked an aggressively nondescript car made noticeable by the big whip antenna folded forward over the roof and clipped down. It was Quirk.

When I got out of the car he was waiting for me, and I said, "What the hell do you want, Lieutenant?"

"I want to talk with you. Let's go inside."

Quirk was great for small talk. When we got to my apartment I offered him a drink. He said, "Thanks."

"Okay, Lieutenant, what do you want to talk about? How poor Cathy Connelly fell in the bathtub and hit her little head?"

"What have you got?" Quirk said.

"What do you mean what have I got? You taking a survey for H.E.W.?"

"What have you got on the Connelly thing and on Lowell Hayden and the Powell murder?"

"Say, you must be some kind of investigator; you know all about what I'm up to."

Quirk stood up, walked across the room, and looked out my window. He took a long pull at the bourbon and water in his hand and turned around and looked at me.

"I'm trying, Spenser, I'm trying to ask you polite, and treat you like you weren't a wise-ass sonova bitch, because I owe you. Because maybe I need you to do some stuff for me. Why don't you try to help me through this by trying out your nightclub act on someone else? What have you got for me?"

Quirk was right. I felt lousy about Mark Tabor, and I was taking it out on Quirk. "I got three categories of things," I said. "What I know and can prove; what I know and can't prove; and what I don't know."

Quirk sat in my armchair and looked at me and listened.

"Here's what I know and can prove. Lowell Hayden and Cathy Connelly were lovers. They spent at least one night together in a Holiday Inn in Peabody—Peabody, what a romantic!—and I've got a note he wrote that locks him up on that one. Lowell Hayden and Dennis Powell were in on the theft of the Godwulf Manuscript. Hayden was an anonymous member of a student radical group called SCACE. Powell was dealing heroin. I've got a witness that will confirm that. I told Joe Broz I'd stop messing around with the case if the manuscript were returned. The next day it was returned."

"But you're still messing around," Quirk said.

"Yeah," I said. "I lied."

"Broz probably won't like that."

"Probably won't," I said.

"What else can you prove?"

"Nothing. But here's what I know anyway. Hayden is tied to Broz. It was after I talked to him the first time that Broz warned me off. This afternoon when I talked to him he said he had people who would kill me if he said so. You and I know where to find people like that, but your average teacher of medieval lit doesn't. If Powell was dealing heroin, he was tied to the mob too. That's too big a coincidence—that Powell and Hayden should both be mob connected and connected to each other and not have it mean something. Hayden had to have something to do with drug pushing. That's the only thing that Broz would have in common with a university community. More connection: Hayden's girl friend was a roommate of Powell's girl friend, Cathy Connelly and Terry Orchard, and if Terry's story is true, it would be Cathy Connelly who would have known that Terry had a gun, and where she kept it, and how to get it. If Terry's story is true, the killing of Powell was not amateur work. Now who would have both professional connections and access to knowledge of Terry's gun?"

Quirk said, "Hayden."

"And," I said, "the killing of Cathy Connelly was an amateur production, even though Yates seemed to like it. Powell was dead and Terry was in Charles Street at the time. Of this interlocking quartet who does that leave?"

"Hayden."

"Clues must be your game, Lieutenant," I said. "You're two for two."

"Got some more?"

"Yeah, here's the hard stuff. Why did Powell get killed? Why did Terry get framed? Why did Cathy Connelly get killed? One point—Hayden is not playing with fifty-two cards. I talked to him today, there're pieces missing. Kidnaping that manuscript sounds just about right for him. So if he's it in this game, it may be harder to explain because he is not normal. The reasons he would do things are not predictable reasons."

"You got a nice assortment of possibilities," Quirk said. "So far you're into organized crime, dope pushing, theft, radical politics, adultery, and murder. I'm not saying I agree with you. But if I did, Hayden would look good to me. He would be the handle, and I'd keep turning it until something opened." Quirk stood up. "If you're messing with Joe Broz, you might turn up dead some morning. I'd better know the name of this witness in case you do."

"Tabor," I said. "Mark Tabor, seventy-seven Westland Ave, apartment forty-one."

"Thanks," Quirk said. "Thanks for the drink, too. See you."

I let him out. He was clearly sick with worry about me getting killed.

19

The next morning I went over to the university and put a tail on Hayden. I couldn't think of anything else to do. I knew he was involved in two killings and that Terry was involved in none, but I couldn't prove it. I could nail him for manuscript-naping or whatever, but I was willing to bet that the university wouldn't press charges, and even if they did, with a good lawyer and a first offense what would happen to him? I could threaten to tell his wife about Cathy Connelly, but he wasn't likely to confess to murder to placate his wife. But he knew I knew, and it had to bother him. He might do something stupid, and if I kept after him I might catch him doing it.

So in the fresh of morning when Hayden showed up for his nine o'clock class in pre-Shakespearean drama I was lurking about the north end of the corridor, and when he came out fifty minutes later, I was at the south end of the corridor getting a drink from the bubbler. While he conferred with students in his office about image patterns in *The Play of the Weather* and *Gammer Gurton's Needle,* I studied the announcements and grad school advertisements on the bulletin board down the corridor.

Surveillance on a guy that knows you is hard, and it's much harder when you're trying to do it alone. In the long run it's not possible. Eventually Hayden would catch me and there was nothing to do about it. On the other hand, before he did I might catch him, and anyway, I didn't know what else to do.

Hayden ate lunch in his office from a brown paper bag and a thermos. I didn't. By three o'clock that afternoon I was pretty sure how Hayden would spot me. He'd hear my stomach rolling. At four Hayden went to his *Beowulf* class. As soon as he was safely into his lecture I ducked out and bought half a dozen hamburgers at McDonald's. On the way back I bought a pint of Wild Turkey bourbon at a package store and was back in time to pick Hayden up after class and follow him to the parking lot.

Following him through the rush hour traffic was two-handed work, and I didn't get to my supper until we were through the Callahan Tunnel and into East Boston. By the time we got to Lynn Shore Drive I'd eaten three cold hamburgers and swallowed about two inches of the pint. A cold McDonald's hamburger is halfway between a jelly doughnut and a hockey puck, but the nine-dollar bourbon helped.

I sat at the head of Hayden's street with the motor idling and the heater on until nine o'clock, when I ran low on gas and had to shut off the motor. By ten fifteen I was cold. The hamburgers were long gone, though the memory lingered on the back of my throat, and I was almost through the bourbon. During that time Hayden had not come to me and confessed. He had not had a visit from Joe Broz or Phil, or the Ghost of Christmas Future. The Ceremony of Moloch had not shown up and sung "The Sweetheart of Sigma Chi" under his window. At eleven o'clock the lights in his living room went out and I went home—stiff, sore, tired, crabby, dyspeptic, cold, and about five-eighths drunk.

The next day we did it all again. This time I brought along a satchel of sandwiches and a large thermos of coffee. At the end of the day my stomach felt better, but I didn't know anything more, and I had discovered new dimensions of boredom.

On the third day things picked up. It was raining again. Hard and steady. Everything was frosted with slush. Hayden had a class from four to five, and it was dark when I stood in a doorway across the street and watched him get in his car in the parking lot. He was turning over the engine when two guys got in with him. One in front, one in back. The windshield wipers went on, then the headlights. The car began to back out of its space. My car was parked on a hydrant one hundred feet from the doorway and I was in it with the motor running when Hayden's car turned out of the parking lot. I stayed close behind him. Too close really, but it was dark and wet and I was worried. The two guys that got in his car didn't look like poets to me, and I didn't want to lose Hayden. He was all I had, and if something became of him, nothing much good would become of Terry Orchard.

We turned south on Huntington Avenue, past the new high-rise apartments, a hospital, another college, and out onto the Jamaicaway. Big houses, mostly brick, set well back and sumptuous, lined the road. Elms that had survived the Dutch disease arched over it, and to the right in an extended hollow was Jamaica Pond, wooded and grassy under the gray slush. Hayden's car pulled off the road and parked on the shoulder. I drove on by, turned left into a side street beyond, and parked.

I cut through the backyard of a large brick Dutch colonial house on the corner and came out opposite where Hayden's car was parked on the shoulder across the street. I didn't see any of them. The hard rain and warm weather were causing the wet slush to steam and a fog to rise from the rotting ice on the pond. I ran across the street and came up behind Hayden's car. It was empty. I realized that I had my gun in my hand though I didn't recall taking it from the hip holster. I stopped and listened. No sound but the rain and the cars on the Jamaicaway whooshing past on their way to Dedham and Milton. My stomach buzzed with tension.

There were tracks in the slush leading down toward the pond. I followed them into the mist. Closer to the pond it was so dense I could only see a few feet ahead.

I half expected to see Beowulf jump out of the bog and rip the arm off something. . . . "My God, Holmes, those are the footprints of a gigantic hound. . . ." I was wearing a hip-length wool jacket, and the rain was soaking through along my shoulders. The wet wool smelled like a grammar school coatroom. Ahead of me I heard a kind of low wail. I stopped still in the dark. In front of me there were indistinct figures. I looked at them obliquely as I'd learned to do a long time ago in Korea, and they came into sharper focus. Hayden was the one making the mournful noise. He seemed to be having trouble standing, and one of the other men had him under the arms. He stepped away and Hayden slumped to his knees and began to wail louder. The man who hadn't been holding him brought a long-barreled pistol from his side and placed it against the back of Hayden's head. I turned sideways as you do on the pistol range, and yelled, "Freeze!"

The guy with the gun snapped around and I felt the thump in my side simultaneous to the muzzle flash and before I heard the shot. It felt like I'd been hit in the ribs with a brick. I staggered, steadied myself, let out my breath, and brought my gun down on the middle of his chest . . . slack . . . squeeze . . . and my own shot exploded. He fell over backward. His buddy was shooting now, and a bullet thunked into a tree beside me. Out of the edge of my vision I saw Hayden crawling for some bushes. I ducked behind the tree. There was no pain yet, but my whole left side was numb and I felt a little dizzy. It was quiet again. Up on the Jamaicaway the headlights were fuzzy in the fog and the whoosh of their passage was cottony. The rain droned down. I slid down the tree and stretched out, belly down in the slush, and peered around the edge of the tree. I couldn't see anyone. Still on my belly I began to inch backward.

About ten feet in back of the tree was a big old blue spruce whose bottom boughs skirted out six or eight feet around the bottom. I inched backward under them and lay still. Nothing moved. I was feeling dizzier, and the first twitches of hurt were cutting through the numbness in my side. The slush was cold, and underneath the tree the earth had started to thaw and turn to mud. Inching backward for ten feet had scraped a lot of it up under my coat.

I wondered if I'd die here. Face down under a spruce tree in the mud trying to keep a double murderer from getting shot by two hired thugs. I felt like I wanted to throw up. The noise would locate me. I swallowed it back. More silence while I fought the nausea and the cold.

After what seemed to be the duration of the Christian epoch, I saw him. He had circled the tree where I'd first hidden and stepped out so that had I still been there he'd have been behind me. He was good; it took him maybe a second to realize I wasn't there and where I probably was. He spun and I put three shots into his chest, holding the gun in both hands to keep it steady. His gun bounced out of his hand and plopped softly into the slush. He fell more slowly sideways and joined it. I crawled out from under the tree and over to him. I felt in his neck for the big pulse. There wasn't any. I crawled on over to his buddy. Same thing. I got up and looked around for Hayden. I didn't see him, and getting up was an error. My head spun and I sat down backward. The jar of it set the pain in my side to moving.

"Hayden," I yelled. No sound.

"Hayden, you dumb sonova bitch, it's Spenser. You're all right. They're dead. Come on out."

I got hunched over on one hip and put my gun back in the holster. Then I got both hands onto the trunk of a sapling and pulled myself up.

"Hayden!"

He appeared from behind the bushes. His glasses were gone, and his wet lank hair was plastered down over his small skull.

"They were going to kill me," he said. "They were going to kill me. They . . . they had no right . . ."

Hayden looked at me blankly. His eyes were red and swollen and his face, without glasses, looked naked.

"They were supposed to kill you," he said.

"Yeah, we'll talk about that, but gimme a hand."

The numbness was about gone now, and the blood was a warm and sticky layer over the pain.

"We were allies. We were working together. And they were going to kill me."

He backed away from me, up toward the road. I let go of the tree and took a step toward him. He backed up faster.

"They were supposed to kill you."

I took another step toward him and fell down. He was now backing up so fast he was running. Like a cornerback trying to stay with a wide receiver.

"Hayden!" I yelled.

He turned and ran up toward his car. Sonova bitch. At least he didn't kick me when I fell. I heard his car start but I didn't see him pull away. I was busy with other things. Two more tries convinced me that I'd have trouble walking up the hill, so I crawled. It was getting harder as the dizziness and the nausea progressed.

20

I don't know how long it took me to get up that hill to the street. Every few feet I had to rest, and the last hundred feet or so I had to drag myself along on my stomach. I pulled myself over the curb and rested with my cheek in the gutter of the road and the rain drumming on my back. The pain drummed even harder in my side, and there was a kind of counterpoint throb in my head. Then, suddenly, there was a big red-faced MDC cop standing over me in the glare of headlights and the steady pulse of the blue light. I didn't know how long I'd been out or where I was exactly.

"Just lay there, Jack. Don't move around."

"I'm not drunk," I said.

"I can tell that, Jack. The left side of your coat is soaked with blood."

"I'm not drunk," I said again. It seemed very important to keep saying it. At the same time I knew he knew I wasn't drunk. He'd just said that he knew that. "I'm not," I said. The cop nodded. His face was red and healthy looking. He had a thick lower lip and a fine gray stubble on his chin. His partner brought the folding stretcher and they inched me onto it.

"Jesus Christ," I said.

Then I was looking up at the funny big light that diffuses the glare and the tubes and apparatus and a woman in a white coat, and I realized my coat and shirt were off. "I been shot," I said.

"That was my diagnosis too." She was bending over and looking at my side closely.

"Bullet went right through, banged off a rib, probably cracked it —I don't think it's broken—and went on out. Tore up the latissimus dorsi a bit, caused a lot of blood loss and some shock. You'll live. This will sting." She swabbed something on the wound.

"Jesus Christ," I said.

A nurse wheeled me on the table down to have the rib X-rayed. Then she wheeled me back. The same ruddy-faced MDC cop that had picked me up was sitting on one of the other treatment tables in the cubicle off the emergency room. His partner leaned against the door jamb. He was skinny with pimples.

"I'll need a statement," Ruddy-face said.

"Yeah, I imagine. Look, you know Quirk, homicide commander?"

He nodded.

"Call him, tell him I'm here and need to see him. He'll come down and I'll give the statement to both of you. You been through my wallet yet?"

"Yep."

"Okay, you know my name and my line of work. It's important that Quirk gets what I have to say. A guy might get killed, and he's the key to a couple of murders."

The doctor returned with my X rays and pushed past Pimples into the room. "As I said, rib cracked. I'll tape it and bandage the wound, then we'll put you to bed. In two or three days you'll be back on your feet."

Ruddy-face said to his partner, "Go call the lieutenant, Pooler."

Pooler said, "How come he gets special treatment? I say we get his statement and let Quirk know through channels."

"That's what you say, huh." Ruddy-face took out a big wooden kitchen match and stuck it in his mouth and chewed on it.

"Yeah, how come because the guy's got a private license we have to kiss his ass. Quirk'll get to his statement when he's ready."

Ruddy-face took the match out of his mouth and examined the chewed end.

"You be sure and call the lieutenant by his last name when you see him, Pooler. He'll like that. Makes him feel he's popular with the men."

"Jesus Christ . . ."

Ruddy-face got a very hard sound into his voice. "Goddammit, Pooler, will you call the lieutenant? This guy got shot, two other people got killed. Lieutenant's going to see him anyway. If he knows him maybe he'll want to see him sooner. Why would this guy make up the story? 'Cause he's queer for the lieutenant? If the guy's right and we don't call we'll be directing traffic in South Dorchester Christmas morning."

Pooler went. The doctor was busy wrapping my rib cage and ignored them both.

"Where am I?" I asked her. "Boston City?"

"Yep."

When the doctor got through a nurse wheeled me up to a ward bed. The ruddy-faced cop came with me. His partner stayed down to wait for Quirk. The ward was half-empty and depressing.

"It'll be full by morning," the nurse said. She cranked up the bed and she and the cop slid me onto it.

"Doctor says give you a shot to help you sleep," she said.

"Not yet," I said. "Wait until I've talked with the cops."

Ruddy-face nodded at her that he agreed.

"Okay," she said to Ruddy-face. "Tell the floor nurse when you're through and we'll come in and give him his shot then." She left. Ruddy-face sat down beside the bed.

"How you feel?" he asked.

"Like I been kicked in the side by a giraffe," I said.

He fumbled inside his coat and brought out a pint of Old Overholt.

"Want a shot before the nurse gets back?" he said.

I took the bottle.

"Crank me up," I said. He raised the head end of the bed so I was half-sitting, and I inhaled half his bottle.

I handed him back the bottle. He wiped the top off with his hand in an unconscious gesture of long practice, and took a long pull. He handed it back to me.

"Finish it," he said. "I got another one in the car."

The liquor burned hot in my stomach, and the pain was a little duller. Quirk arrived; Belson was with him. Quirk looked at the bottle and then at Ruddy-face. I put the bottle down empty on the night stand away from Ruddy-face.

"Where'd he get the bottle, Kenneally?"

Ruddy-face shrugged. "Musta had it with him, Lieutenant. How ya doing, Frank?"

Quirk said, "I'll bet." Belson nodded at Ruddy-face.

"Okay"—Quirk turned to me—"lemme have it."

Belson had a notebook out. Ruddy-face got up and moved to the end of the ward, where he broke out a new match and began to chew on it.

"I'm fine, thanks, Lieutenant. Just a little old bullet wound."

"Yeah, good, let's hear it all. There's two carcasses downstairs right now that the MDC people brought in from Jamaica Pond. I want to hear."

I told him. He listened without interruption. When I got through he turned to Belson. "You see the two, Frank?"

"Yeah. One of them is a gofer for Joe Broz, Sully Roselli. I don't know the other one. His driver's license says Albert J. Brooks. Mean anything to you?"

Quirk shook his head and looked at me. I shook mine too.

"CID is looking into him," Belson said.

"Right, now see what you can do about getting a leash on Hayden. Pick up and hold."

"Yates will be disappointed," I said.

"Can't be helped," Quirk said. "Hayden's a witness to attempted murder and two homicides. Got to bring him in."

Quirk looked back at me thoughtfully.

"Two of them in the dark," he said. "Not bad."

He nodded at Belson and they left. As they went out Quirk said to Kenneally, "Tell the nurse we're through. And don't give him any more booze."

By the time the nurse got there I was halfway under again and barely felt the needle jab.

21

I woke up in bright daylight, confused, to the sound of a monotonous deep cough from the other end of the room. I shifted in the bed and felt the pain in my side and remembered where I was. The coughing went on down the ward. I creaked myself around on the bed, dropped my legs over the side, and got myself sitting up. All the beds were full. I had a hospital johnny and an adhesive sash around my torso. Very natty. I stood up. My legs felt spongy, and I braced myself with one hand against the bed. Steady. I walked the length of the bed. Not bad. I walked back to the head. Better. I U-turned, back toward the foot. Then I started down the length of the ward. Slow, shaky, but halfway down I didn't have to hold on. An old man with no teeth mumbled to me from one of the beds.

"You get hell if they catch you out of bed," he said.

"Watch," I said.

I kept going. All the way to the end of the ward, then back, then down the ward again. I was feeling balanced and ambulatory when the floor nurse came in. She had a cheerful Irish face and a broad beam. She looked at me as if I'd messed on the floor.

"Oh, no," she said. "Right back in the bed, there. We're not supposed to be strolling around. Come on."

"Cookie," I said, "we are doing more than strolling. We are getting the hell out of here as soon as we can find our pants."

"Nonsense, I want you to hop right back in that bed. This minute." She clapped her hands sharply for emphasis.

"Don't do that," I said. "I may faint, and you'll have to give me mouth-to-mouth resuscitation." I kept on walking.

She glanced at the name card at the foot of my empty bed. "Mr. Spenser, must I call the resident?"

In the middle of the ward was a large double door. I pushed it open. It was a walk-in closet with baskets on shelves. My clothes were in one of them. I put on my pants, still soggy with the mud half-dried on them.

"Mr. Spenser." She stood in semiparalysis in the doorway. I dropped the johnny and slipped my jacket on over the bandaged body. Shirt and underwear were so blood-soaked and mud-drenched that I didn't bother. I jammed my feet into my loafers. They had been my favorites, tassles over the instep. One tassle was now missing and there were two inches of mud caked all over them. My gun and wallet were missing. I'd worry about that later.

I pushed past the nurse, whose face had turned very red.

"Don't fret, cookie," I said. "You've done what you could, but I've got stuff I have to do and promises to keep. And for a guy with my virility what's a bullet wound or so?"

I kept going. She came behind me and at the desk outside by the elevator a second nurse joined her in protest. I ignored them and went down the elevator.

When I got outside onto Harrison Ave it was a very nice day—sunny, pleasant—and it occurred to me that I didn't have a car or money or a ride home. I didn't have my watch either, but it was early. There was little traffic on the streets. I turned back toward the hospital and my Irish nurse came out.

"Mr. Spenser, you're not in condition to walk out like this. You've lost blood; you've suffered shock."

"Listen to me now, lovey," I said. "You're probably right. But I'm leaving anyway. And we both know you can't prevent it. But what you can do is lend me cab fare home."

She looked at me, startled for a minute, and then laughed. "Okay," she said. "You deserve something for sheer balls. Let me get my purse." I waited, and she was back in a minute with a five-dollar bill.

"I'll return it," I said.

She just shook her head.

I walked over to Mass Avenue and waited till a cab cruised by. When I got in the cabby said, "You got money?"

I showed him the five. He nodded. I gave him the address and we went home.

When he let me out I gave him the five and told him to keep it.

I got a look at my reflection in the glass door of my apartment building and I knew why he'd asked me for money first. My coat was black with mud, blood, and rain. The same for my pants. My ankles showed naked above the mud-crusted shoes. I had a forty-six-hour beard stubble and a big bruise on my forehead I must have gotten when I crawled over the curbstone the night before.

I realized I didn't have a key. I rang for the super. When he came he made no comment.

"I've lost my key," I said. "Can you let me into my apartment?"

"Yep," he said, and headed up the stairs to my place. I followed. He opened my door and I went in. "Thanks," I said.

"Yep," he said. I closed the door.

I wondered if he'd noticed that I looked different. Maybe he thought it an improvement.

Despite the palpable silence of the place I was glad to be home. I looked at my pine Indian still on the sideboard in the living room. I hadn't gotten to the horse yet, and he seemed to flow into a block of wood. I went into the kitchen, took off the coat, pants, and shoes, and stuffed them into the wastebasket. Then I went in and took a shower. I kept the wounded side away from the water as much as I could. I shaved with the shower still running and stepped back in to rinse off the shave cream. I toweled dry and dressed. Gray, hard-finished slacks with a medium flare, blue paisley flowered shirt with short sleeves, blue wool socks, mahogany-colored buckle boots with a side zipper, broad mahogany belt with a brass buckle. I liked getting dressed, feeling the clean cloth on my clean body, I paid special attention to it all. It was good not to be dead in the mud under a blue spruce tree.

In the kitchen I made coffee and put six homemade German

sausages in the fry pan. They were big fat ones I had to go up to the North Shore to buy from a guy who made them in the back of the store. You should always start them on low in a cold fry pan. When they began to sizzle I cored a big green apple and peeled it. I sliced it thick, dipped the slices in flour, and fried them in the sausage fat. The coffee had perked, and I had a cup with heavy cream and two sugars. The smell of the sausage and apple cooking began to make my throat ache. I slipped a spatula under the apples and turned them. I took the sausages out with tongs and let them drain on a paper towel. When the apple rings were done, I drained them with the sausages and ate both with two big slices of coarse rye bread and wild strawberry jam in a crock that you can buy up at the Mass Ave end of Newbury Street.

I listened to the morning news on the radio while I drank the last of my coffee. They mentioned the shooting in the Jamaicaway but gave no names. I was referred to as a Boston private detective. When it was over I switched off the radio, left the dishes where they were, and went to my bedroom. I got a spare gun out of the drawer and put it in an extra hip holster. The hip holster had slots for six extra bullets and I slipped them in and clipped it to my belt with the barrel end in my right back pocket.

I got five ten-dollar bills and a spare set of keys out of my top bureau drawer and slipped them into my pocket. Went to the front closet and got my other jacket. It was my weekend-in-the-country jacket, cream-colored canvas, with a sherpa lining that spilled out over the collar. I was saving it in case I was ever invited down to the Myopia Hunt Club for cocktails and a polo match. But since some-one had shot a hole in my other coat, I'd have to wear it now. It was 8:10 when I left my apartment. Smart, clean, well fed, and alive as a sonova bitch.

22

I took a cab back out to Jamaica Pond. My car was where I'd left it, keys still in the ignition, sunglasses still up on the dashboard. Hubcaps still on the wheels. Ah, law and order. I got in, started it up, and drove on back into town to my office. I opened all the windows to air the place out and checked my mail. Called the answering service to find that Marion Orchard had called three times and Roland Orchard once. I called Quirk to see if they'd found Hayden. They hadn't. I hung up and started to lean back in my chair and put my feet up. My side hurt and I froze in midmotion, remembering the wound, and eased my feet back to the ground. I sat very still for about thirty seconds, breathing in small shallow breaths till things subsided. Then I got up quite carefully and closed the window. No sudden moves.

It was time to start looking for Hayden. I looked down at Stuart Street; he wasn't there. I felt a good deal like going home and lying down on my bed, but Hayden probably wasn't there either. The best

I could think of was go out and talk to Mrs. Hayden. As I was driving out to Marblehead again, the pain in my side began to be tiresome. At first it was almost a pleasant reminder that I was alive and hadn't bled to death in Jamaica Pond. But by now I was used to being alive and was again accepting it as my due, the common course of things; and the pain now served no other purpose than to remind me of my mortality. Also, the drive to Marblehead is among the worst in Massachusetts. It is only barely possible to reach Marblehead from anywhere, and the drive from Boston through the Callahan Tunnel, out Route 1A through East Boston, Revere, and Lynn is narrow, cluttered, ugly, and long. Particularly if you've recently been shot in the side.

There was a sea gull perched on the ridgepole of Hayden's gray weather duplex when I pulled in to the driveway. There was a larger number of people on the wharf than there had been last time, and I realized it was Saturday.

The shades of Hayden's place were drawn, but there was a stir of motion at the edge of one by the front door. I rang the bell and waited. No answer. No sound. I rang again. Same thing. I leaned on the bell and stayed there watching the ocean chop and flutter in the harbor and the bigger waves break against the causeway at the east end of the harbor. Inside I could hear the steady bleat of the bell. It sounded like a Bronx cheer. I felt it was directed at me—or was I getting paranoiac? She was tough; she hung in there for maybe five minutes. Then the door opened about two inches on a chain and she said, "Get out of here."

I said, "We've got to talk, Mrs. Hayden."

She said, "The police have been here already. I don't know where Lowell is. Get out of here."

I said, "Lowell's got one chance to stay alive, and I'm it. You shut the door on me and you'll be slamming the lid on your husband's casket."

The door slammed. Persuasive, that's me. Old silver tongue. I leaned on the bell some more. Another four or five minutes and she cracked. People who can endure bamboo slivers under the fingernails begin to weaken after ten minutes of doorbell ringing. She opened up again. Two inches, on the chain.

I said real quick, "Look. I saved your husband's life last night and got shot in the chest for my troubles and damn near bled to death because your husband ran off and left me. He owes me. You owe me. Let me save his life again. You won't get another chance." The door shut, but this time only for about thirty seconds. As I started to lean on the bell again I heard the chain bolt slide off and the door opened.

"Come in," she said.

She was as sumptuously dressed as she had been on my previous visit. This time it was brown corduroy pants that tapered at the ankles, brown leather sandals with a loop over the big toe, and a gray sweat shirt. Her hair was in the same tight bun, her face as empty of make-up as it had been. Her eyes behind the big pinkish eyeglasses were as warm and as deep as the end of a pool cue.

The apartment smelled of cat food. The front door opened into the living room. Beyond that I could see the kitchen and to the right of it a closed door, which I assumed led to another room. Maybe the master's study. In front of me, opposite the door and along the right-hand wall, rose a staircase.

The living room was big and sunny and looked like the display window at Sid and Mabel's furniture outlet. There were four canvas director's chairs, two blue ones and two orange ones, more or less grouped around a clear plastic cube with an empty vase on it. On the far wall was a blond bookcase with a brilliant coat of shellac on it, which held an assortment of textbook-looking books, mostly paperbacks, and a pile on the bottom shelf of record albums and acoarse-paper magazines without covers, which were probably academic journals. On top of it were a McIntosh amplifier and a Garrard turntable. On each side, standing three feet high on the floor, were two Fisher speakers. The whole rig probably had cost more than my car, and surely more than the furniture. On the floor were two rugs, fake fur in the shape they would have had were they real and skinned out to dry. One was a zebra, one a tiger. House beautiful.

"Sit down," she said, and her thin lips barely moved as she talked. "Coffee?"

"Yes, please." I eased into one of the director's chairs. A fat Angora cat looked at me from the chair opposite, its yellow eyes as blank as doorknobs, its fur snarled and burry. It was the first time I could recall sitting in a director's chair. I had missed little, I decided. Mrs. Hayden appeared with the coffee in a white plastic mug, insulated, the kind you get with ten gallons of gas at an Exxon station. I took it black and sipped. It was instant.

"You say my husband needs your help. Why?"

"He's involved in one larceny and two murders. There is obviously a contract out on him. And if I don't find him before the contractors do, he's going to have all his troubles solved for him with a neat lead injection."

"I don't know what you're talking about."

"I bet you do. But I'm not going to argue with you. I'm telling you that if he doesn't come in under cover, he's dead."

"What makes you think you can help him?"

"That's my line of work. I helped him last night. I can do it again. There's a homicide cop named Quirk who'll help too."

"Why should I trust you?"

"Because I got a hole in the left side of my body to prove it. Because you could trust me last night a hell of a lot more than I could trust your husband."

"Why do you care what happens to him?"

"I don't. But I care what happens to a twenty-year-old kid who'll end up in the women's reformatory unless I can find out the truth from your husband."

"And what happens to him when you find out whatever you think the truth is?"

"He'll live. I can't promise much else, but it's better than what he'll get if Broz gets there first. The Supreme Court has outlawed the death penalty, but Broz hasn't."

"This is ridiculous," she said in her flat thin voice. "I do not know anyone named Broz. I do not know anything about any killings or any girls going to jail. My husband is away for a few days on professional business."

She had her hands in her lap and was twisting the gold wedding ring round and round on her finger. I didn't say anything. Her voice went up half a note.

"It's absurd. You're absurd. It's an absurd fairy tale. My husband is a respected scholar. He is known all over America in his field. You wouldn't know that. You wouldn't know anything about us. You're nothing but a . . . a . . ."

"Cheap gumshoe?" I suggested.

"A snoop! A sneaky snoop! Nothing will happen to my husband. He's fine. He'll be back in a few days. He's just traveling professionally. I told you that. Why do you keep asking me?" Her voice went up another half note. "You bastard. Why are you hounding him?

Why does everyone hound him? He's a scholar, but you won't leave him alone. None of you. You, the police, those men, that girl . . ." Tears began to run down her face; her voice thickened.

"What girl?"

She wailed then. Her face got red and contorted and her mouth pulled back from her lips so that her gums were exposed. Her nose ran a little, and she cried with her whole considerable frame—huge, gasping sobs mixed with a high eerie sound like locusts. She drooled a bit too. I sipped on my coffee and said it again.

"What girl?"

Had she buried her face in her hands, or turned away, or fled the room it would have been tolerable. But she didn't. She sat, looking at me full face, and cried harder and harder till I began to think she would hurt herself. I couldn't keep looking. I got up and walked around the room. I looked out at the harbor. There was dust in random patterns on the windowpane. I put my hands in my pockets and walked back across the room and looked out the other window. She continued to howl. My side hurt and my head throbbed and I felt a little sick.

I looked at her sideways. She was trying to pick up her coffee cup but her hand shook so violently that the coffee sloshed out onto the coffee table and formed a brown puddle on the clear plastic. She kept trying, even though most of the coffee had sloshed out, and finally threw it frantically on the floor. The cat jumped off the chair and went into the kitchen.

She was screaming now steadily, except for the wrenching gasp when she had to breathe. I went over and put one hand on her shoulder. She jerked away and scrambled out of the chair. Both her hands were pushed out in front of her as she backed away from me, across the room. She stopped in the far corner and screamed with her hands straight out before her, palms up, as if pushing against something.

She swore at me now, the curses bubbling out through the screams as if her saliva were viscous, repetitious obscenities, including one I hadn't heard before. Then she stopped. The gasping breaths became more frequent, the screaming interludes shorter. Then she was whimpering. Then she was breathing as if she'd just run three miles, her chest heaving under the sweat shirt, her face wet with tears and sweat and saliva and nasal mucus. The effect of her hysteria had loosened her hair in strands, and it stuck to the wetness on her cheek and forehead. She let her hands drop and straightened up in the corner. Her breathing slowed a little and the air ceased to rasp as it went to and from her lungs.

I said, "What girl?"

She shook her head without speaking. Then she went to the kitchen. I stepped to the kitchen door to make sure she didn't guillotine herself on the electric can opener, but her plan was better than that. She took a bottle of Scotch out of one of the cabinets—they kept it in with the Wheaties—removed the cap, and poured about half a cup into a water glass. She didn't offer me any. She drank it as if it were a nighttime cold medicine. All of it. And poured another. This she carried back out into the living room and placed before her on the glass cube as she sat back down. She wiped her face with the sleeve of her sweat shirt, and pushed her hair back off her face. From one pocket of the corduroy Levi's she took a bent packet of Kents. It took her two matches to get a cigarette going. But she did it and dragged a big lungful through the filter. The cigarette was old and dry and the big drag consumed nearly half of it, leaving a big glowing end which faded into ash and dropped on the floor. She paid it no attention. What looked like a descendant of the shaggy cat I'd seen earlier appeared from the kitchen and mewed at the front door. Mrs. Hayden seemed not to hear it. The cat mewed again, and I got up and let it out.

I turned back from the door and leaned against it with my arms folded. My side didn't seem to hurt quite as much if I stood that way.

"What about the girl?" I asked.

She shook her head.

"Look, Mrs. Hayden, you're in a box. You've got trouble you can't handle. There are people trying to kill your husband, the cops can't help because your husband is involved in a criminal act, you don't know what to do, and you just had hysterics to prove it. I'm all you've got. That may not make you happy, but there isn't any way around it. Asking your husband to go one-on-one with Joe Broz is like putting a guppy in the piranha pool. If we don't find him before Broz does, he'll be eaten alive."

Maybe it was the "we." Maybe it was my impeccable logic. Maybe it was desperation. But she said, "I'll take you to him."

Like that. No preamble.

I said, "Okay."

She went to the hall closet and put on a red quilted ski parka with a hood and brown knitted woolen gloves with imitation leather palms. She stepped out of the sandals and stuck her bare feet into green rubber boots with yellow laces. They were all laced and ready to go. She put on a white and brown knitted ski cap with a yellow tassle on the top and we went.

In my car I said, "Where?"

She said, "Boston, the Copley Plaza." And she didn't say another thing all the way back into town.

23

The Copley Plaza fronts on Copley Square, as do the Boston Public Library and Trinity Church. In the center of the square is a sunken brick piazza where in the summer a fountain plays. It is very nice there and a classy area to hide out in. The hotel itself is high ceilinged and deep carpeted. At four each afternoon they serve tea in the lobby. And if you want a drink you can go to the Merry-Go-Round Room and sit at a bar that revolves slowly. There is a good deal of gilt and there are a good many Grecian Revival columns, and the bellboys are very dignified in green uniforms with gold piping. I always felt I should lower my voice in the Copley Plaza, although my line of work didn't take me there with any regularity.

We went in the elevator, got off with another couple at the fourth floor, and walked down a corridor rather elegantly papered in pale beige. She knocked on the door of 411. The other couple passed us and went around the corner. They looked as if they might be on a honeymoon, or maybe they just worked in the same office and were on their lunch hour. Mrs. Hayden knocked again twice and then twice more. Christ, a secret code. Made you wish Ian Fleming had taken up music or something.

The door opened an inch on the chain. Hayden's voice emerged.

"What is it, Judy?" Judy? The name was bad; Mrs. Hayden wasn't a Judy. A Ruth, maybe, or an Elsie, but Judy?

"Let us in, Lowell."

"What's he doing here? Has he forced you, Judy? I told you never to bring anyone—"

Judy's voice got sharper. "Let us in, Lowell." And then more gently, "It's all right."

The door closed. The chain came off, and it opened again. In we went. It was a nice room with a big double bed, unmade now, and a window that looked out onto Dartmouth Street. The television was tuned to a game show. *The Boston Globe* was scattered around the room.

Hayden shut the door, put the chain lock back on, and put the bed between me and him.

"What do you want?" he said.

The game show host introduced their defending champion, "Mrs. Tyler Moorehouse from Grand Island, Nebraska." The audience cheered. I reached over and shut it off.

I said, "You owe me a favor."

Judy Hayden went over around the bed and stood beside her husband. She was at least three inches taller.

"I don't owe you anything, Spenser. You just stay away from me."

He was a consistent sonova bitch.

"If I hadn't happened along last night, Hayden, you would now be enriching the soil in the area of Jamaica Pond. And if you don't help me now, that time will come again."

"They were supposed to kill you." He seemed to be repeating some kind of litany—by rote, as if, like ritual, the repetition of it, if done just right, would save him.

"They are not going to kill me, Hayden. They are going to kill you. Here's why. They want this case closed and forgotten. I keep nosing around in it, and it is you that I've nosed up into the light. If they kill me that'll cause some more nosing around, by other people who know I'm nosing around you. You're the key, Hayden. You're the one who knows the stuff that Broz doesn't want known. If they kill me you are still the one who knows and you are still around and someone, like say a homicide cop named Quirk, might take hold of you and begin to shake you until what you know falls out. But"—Mrs. Hayden had put an arm around her husband's shoulder, maternal—"but if they kill you there isn't anyone around who knows what Broz doesn't want known and Quirk and I can shake each other till we turn to butter and no information is going to fall out because we don't have it. How's that sound to you?"

Hayden just looked at me. I plowed ahead.

"I figure that you and Powell were involved in pushing dope at the university. Maybe for money, maybe because you wanted to turn on the sons of the middle class, maybe because you're a screwball and Tim Leary is your idol. Why doesn't matter so much for now; you can tell us that later. Broz supplied you. For him the university was a nice new market for some goods he had on hand, and as long as you could deliver the market he could use you. But you and Powell had to get fancy. You stole that manuscript and held it for ransom. That was dumb, because that got the university police and me involved. No big threat, maybe, but there's no advantage to having legal types sniffing around. But what was dumber was that you and Powell had a falling out. About what, I don't know. You can tell me that, too. But it was you he was arguing with on the phone, and it was you who set him up for the mob hit. It had to be you because you're the only one around who could have supplied Terry Orchard's gun. You got it through Cathy Connelly."

Judy Hayden's arm tightened around Hayden's shoulder. He seemed to be resisting her, pulling against the arm pressure, like maybe he didn't want to be hugged as much as she wanted to hug him.

"She'd been Terry's roommate, and she knew about the gun. She was also your girl friend, and it had to be she who told you about it. So it was done and you were clean and all was well and then I showed up. And I talked to you about it, and you panicked. You must have called Broz the minute I left your office that day because he sent his people out to talk to me right after that. And the manuscript was returned the next day. But I kept it up and you panicked worse. Cathy Connelly could tie you to the murder. What if you broke up? What if your wife heard about her and blew the whistle on your girl friend and your girl friend talked for spite? She was the only one who knew about you and Broz. Other people maybe could tie you to SCACE, but the worst that would mean is a no decision at tenure time. The university wasn't pressing charges on the Godwulf Manuscript. If you could get rid of Cathy Connelly, you and Broz could recruit a new pusher to replace Dennis Powell and things would be going just as swell and nice as they had before. So you went and killed her. That was maybe the dumbest thing of all, because it's not your line of work and you did a terrible job. If Broz hadn't put a lot of pressure on someone you'd be sitting around in a small room at Walpole right now. And when I kept after you and you called Broz about it again, Broz must have had enough. So you thought he'd kill me, but he thought he'd kill you. And he will. You got one chance and that is to take away his reason. Tell me, tell the cops, maybe we can get Broz, but whether or not we do we can keep him from getting you . . . I think."

"She helped me," he said.

Judy Hayden said, "Lowell . . ." in a choked voice.

"It was her idea to kill Cathy. She went with me; she held Cathy when I hit her on the head. She said to make it look as if Cathy drowned in the tub."

Her arm dropped away from his shoulder and hung straight down by her side. She didn't look at him, or me.

Hayden went on with no animation, like a recording. "I don't use drugs, but many people need them to liberate their consciousness, to elevate their perceptions and free them from the bondage of American hypocrisy. A drug culture is the first step to an open society. I was the man who got them from Joseph Broz. Dennis supplied them to the community. He didn't know where I got them, and I didn't know where he sold them. It was just right." He had a dreamy little half smile on his face now as he talked, and his eyes were concentrating on a point somewhere left of my shoulder.

"Then he spoiled it. He complained about the quality. Said the heroin was cut too much. I said I'd speak to my supplier. Joseph Broz said that the quality was fine and was going to remain the way it was. Dennis threatened to tell the police on me. He threatened to bring down everything we'd worked for, everything that SCACE stood for. Simply because he wanted the heroin stronger. He sacrificed his every ideal. He betrayed the movement. He had to be executed. Miss Connelly and I discussed it and she suggested the gun. I discussed it with a representative of Joseph Broz and he said if we would give him the gun, he would manage the rest. Miss Connelly went there to visit and took the gun. It is too bad Miss Orchard has to suffer; she is a member of the movement and we bear her no ill will."

He paused. Still looking past my shoulder. The smile was a full smile now and his eyes were shiny. In a minute he'd start addressing me as "my fellow Americans."

The smile faded. "So now you know," he said.

"Will you tell it all to the police?" I said.

He shook his head. "I'll die without speaking," he said. Ronald Colman, Major André, Nathan Hale, the Christian martyrs.

"You're not going to die," I said. "The death penalty is not legal at the moment. You will merely go to jail, unless you don't tell the cops. Then you will die without speaking like you almost did last night. Remember last night. You didn't seem so eager for silent martyrdom last night."

Judy Hayden put her hand on his shoulder. "Tell them, Lowell," she said.

He shrugged his shoulder away from her touch. "I've told him, and that's all I'm telling anyone. You brought him here. I wouldn't have had to tell him anything if you'd not brought him here. I trusted you and you betrayed me too. Can I trust no one? You've never cared about the movement. Dennis never cared about the movement. Cathy never cared about the movement."

"I care about you," she said. She was standing very stiff and very still. The palms of her hands appeared to press hard against her thighs.

"I am the movement," he said, and the dreamy smile was back and the eyes positively glistened. He was listening to the sound of a different drummer all right, and it was playing "God Save the King."

No one said anything. I didn't want to look at Mrs. Hayden. In the silence I heard a click like a key turning in the lock. I turned toward the door behind me, but I was wrong. It was the connecting door to the next room. It swung open suddenly and Phil stepped through it. In his hand was a gun with a silencer. He pointed it at me, and said in his rusty voice, "Time's up."

24

Phil closed the door.

"The couple in the elevator with us," I said. Phil nodded.

"You had Mrs. Hayden staked out," I said. Phil nodded again.

"I am a horse's ass," I said.

"We used five people," Phil said. "It's hard to spot."

The gun in his hand was an Army issue .45 automatic. It fired a slug about the size of a baseball and at close range would knock down a sex-crazed rhinoceros. Most people didn't use them because they were big and clumsy and uncomfortable to wear and they jumped in your hand a lot when you fired. In Phil's hand it looked natural and just right.

Hayden said, "Thank God you're here."

Phil made a movement with his lower jaw that might have been a smile. "Get over beside Spenser," he said. Hayden stared at him.

Phil's voice grated without inflection. "Move."

Hayden moved. Mrs. Hayden moved with him. Fred Astaire and Ginger Rogers. What the hell made me think of that?

"Take your gun out with two fingers of your left hand, Spenser, and drop it on the floor."

I did as he said. Since the gun was on my right hip I had to twist my body some, and that made my side hurt more. In a little while it wouldn't matter.

I felt shaky, like I'd had too much coffee, and apprehension tingled along my arms. I fumbled the gun out and dropped it on the floor.

"Kick it under the bed," Phil said. Every time he talked you wanted to clear your throat. I kicked the gun.

"You can't harm me," Hayden said. "If you do and Joseph Broz hears of it, you will be in very serious trouble."

Jesus, Alice in Wonderland. I was studying Phil. He was a puzzle, and that opaque white walleye didn't help any. It was hard to tell what he was looking at. He was dressed as he had been before—the coat buttoned up the neck, the pink-tinted glasses. I watched his hand on the gun; maybe at the instant I saw the finger tighten on the trigger, I could jump him. The hammer wasn't back. Phil probably always carried a round in the chamber. That would give me an extra hundredth of a second. I wished my side weren't sore and bandaged. I felt weak, and diving across the bed and taking the gun away from Phil was not the kind of work that the weak do well. It wasn't a very big chance, but standing still while he shot me in the face was an even smaller chance. He'd shoot me first, figuring I'd be the one to give him trouble.

Hayden kept talking in a singsong voice that rose in pitch as he spoke. "Do you have any idea whom you're dealing with? Do you know how many people are in the movement? If anything happens to me they'll never rest till I'm avenged. They'll track you down and harry you out, however well hidden you may think you are. And Joseph Broz will be very angry with you."

Phil seemed interested. He'd probably never seen anything like Hayden before.

"And you know how angry Joseph Broz can be. I'm on your side. I want to change all of this. I want a world where you won't have to work outside the law. I'm not your enemy. Shoot them. He's your enemy and she is, too, she betrayed me. She led him here. She led you here. Kill her. Don't kill me. Please don't. Please don't."

His legs went out from beneath him, and he dropped to his knees and back onto his heels. "Please don't. Please don't. Please don't."

Phil liked it. He cackled to himself.

"What are you going to do to my husband?" Mrs. Hayden asked.

Phil cackled again. "I'm going to shoot him."

Mrs. Hayden jumped at him. The gun made a muffled thud as Phil fired. It must have hit her, but it didn't stop her. She got hold of his gun arm with both hands and bit into his wrist. She was making a sound that was somewhere between a moan and a growl. The gun thudded again. I went over the bed at Phil. With his left forearm he cuffed me across the face. It was like running into a tree branch. I sprawled on the bed, rolled onto the floor, and came up for him again. Mrs. Hayden had her teeth sunk in his arm. He was pounding the side of her head with his left hand, and trying to get his right loose to use the gun. I got on his back this time and got my right arm around his neck. He moved away from the bed and I rode his back like a kid, wrapping my legs around his middle. I was trying to get my left hand against the back of his head and lock my right hand against my left forearm. If I could do that, I could strangle him.

It was not easy to do. Phil kept his chin tucked down and I couldn't get my forearm against his windpipe. He reached backward with his left hand and got hold of my hair. He bowed his back and tried to flip me over forward. He couldn't, because I had my legs scissored around his middle. But the effort tumbled him forward and all three of us went down in a pile. Mrs. Hayden was beneath us, her teeth still sunk into Phil's forearm, her hands still clutching the gun. Phil let go of my hair with his left hand and his thumb felt for my eye. I pressed my face against his back to protect it. He had a sweaty, rancid smell. I got the fingers of my left hand hooked under his nostrils and pulled. He grunted and his chin came up an inch. It was enough. My right forearm slipped in against his Adam's apple. I put the right hand on the left forearm and made a pivot of it, bringing my left hand up behind his head. Then I squeezed.

I could feel the muscles in his neck bulge. It was like trying to strangle a hydrant. He gurgled, and I squeezed harder. He was incredibly strong. He heaved himself up, carrying me on his back and dragging Mrs. Hayden up too. The gun thudded three more times. He tried to break the hold by lunging back against the wall and knocking me loose, but he couldn't. He clawed left-handed at my forearm, then with his fingernails. The gun thudded again and again until all eight rounds were gone. I had no idea what they were hitting. I was concentrating everything I had on strangling Phil. My whole life was invested in the pressure of my forearm on his throat.

He gurgled again, and I could feel his chest heaving in the struggle to breathe. He was scratching at my forearm like he was digging for the bone. I squeezed. The blood pounded in my ears from the effort and I couldn't see anything but a dance of dust motes where my face stayed pressed against his shoulder. Phil made a noise like a crow cawing, turned very slowly in a complete turn, and fell over backward on top of me. He stopped clawing at my arm. He made no noise. He was inert. Mrs. Hayden was inert on top of both of us, her teeth still in his arm. I kept squeezing, unable to see with his back pressed against my face, unable to feel anything but the strain of my arm against his neck. I squeezed. I don't know how long I squeezed, but it was surely for a long time after it made any difference.

When I let go I could barely open my hand. I was slippery with sweat and too tired to move right away. I lay there panting with the weight of Phil and Judy Hayden on me. When the dancing motes began to dissipate I dragged myself out from under the body.

Phil was dead. I realized that Phil and the floor and my leg were sticky with blood—Mrs. Hayden's blood. I touched her and she didn't move. I felt for her pulse. She had none. She'd bled to death hanging on to Phil's arm. Her teeth were still bitten into it. Phil had emptied his gun in desperation. There was no way to tell how many had hit her. I didn't want to know. I stood up. The room was a shambles. Blood was smeared everywhere. The night stand was tipped over. So was the television set. The bed was broken. I was aware that my side hurt. There was some blood staining my shirt. The wound had opened again.

I remembered Hayden. I looked around. I didn't see him. He was going to get a few merit badges for *semper fidelis.* I started for the door. The chain lock was still on it. The door that Phil had come through locked from the other side. I went over to the bathroom. It was locked.

I said, "Hayden."

No answer. I banged on the door. Nothing. I felt crazy and hot. I backed up three steps and ran right through the door. It was thin and tore from its hinges. No Hayden. I pulled the shower curtain aside and there he was. In the tub, sitting down with his knees drawn up to his chest.

He looked at me and said, "Please don't."

I reached down, took the front of his shirt in both hands, and yanked him up out of the tub. There was a peculiar smell about him and I realized he'd wet himself. I was revolted. I swung him around, the way a trackman throws the hammer, and slung him into the bedroom. He stumbled, almost fell, and stopped, looking down at his wife. I came beside him. I took his chin in my hand and raised his head. I put my face up against his, so that our noses touched. I could barely speak, and my body was shivering. I said, "I have killed three people to save your miserable goddamn ass. Your wife took about six slugs in the stomach and bled to death in great agony to save your miserable goddamn ass. I will call up Martin Quirk in a minute, and he will come here to arrest you. You will tell him everything that you know and everything that I want you to tell him and everything that he asks you. If you do not, I will get Quirk to put us alone together in a cell in the cellar, and I will beat you to death. I promise you that I will."

He said, "Yes, sir." When I let him go he didn't move—just stood there looking down at his wife with his hands clasped behind his back. I went to the phone and dialed a number I knew too well.

25

The room was busy. The people from the coroner's office had come and taken Phil away, and Mrs. Hayden. The hotel doctor had come and rebandaged my side and told me to go in to outpatient this afternoon and have some new stitches in the wound. Beside the broken TV set Frank Belson stood in front of Lowell Hayden, who sat in the only chair in the room. Hayden was talking and Belson was writing things down as he talked. Quirk was there and three uniformed cops and a couple of plainclothes types were standing around looking shrewd and keeping an eye out for clues. The occupant of the next room had been whacked on the head and locked in a closet and was now planning to sue the hotel. The house man was trying to persuade him not to.

Quirk was as immaculate and dapper as ever. He had on a belted tweed topcoat, pale pigskin gloves.

"Not bad," he said. "He had a gun and you didn't and you took him? Not bad at all. Sometimes you amaze me, Spenser."

"We took him," I said. "Me and Mrs. Hayden."

"Either way," Quirk said.

"How about the kid?" I said.

"Orchard? I already called. They're processing her out now. She'll be on the street by the time we get through here."

"Yates?"

Quirk smiled with his mouth shut. "Captain Yates is at this moment telling the people in the pressroom about another triumph for truth, justice, and the American way."

"He's got all the moves, hasn't he?" I said.

One of the plainclothes dicks snickered, and Quirk looked at him hard enough to hurt.

"How about Joe Broz?"

Quirk shrugged. "We got a pickup order out on him. How long we can keep him when we get him, you can guess as well as I can. In the last fifteen years we've arrested him eight times and made one charge stick—loitering. It will help if Hayden sticks to his story."

I looked at Hayden, sitting in the chair. He was talking now in his deep, phony voice. Lecturing Belson. Explaining in detail every aspect of the case and explaining its connection with the movement, drawing inference, elaborating implications, demonstrating significance, and suggesting symbolic meaning. Belson looked as if he had a headache. Hayden was enjoying himself very much.

"He'll stick," I said. "Imagine him lecturing a jury. Your only problem will be getting him to stop."

The phone rang. One of the plainclothes cops answered and held it out to Quirk.

"For you, Lieutenant."

Quirk answered, listened, said "Okay," and hung up.

"Orchard's parents can't be located, Spenser. She says she wants you to come down and pick her up. How's your side?"

"It only hurts when I laugh."

"Okay, beat it. We'll be in touch about the coroner's inquest."

I looked at Hayden again. He was still talking to Belson, his rich voice rolling out and filling the room. For him, a big, homely, masculine woman had taken six .45 slugs in the stomach. The press arrived and a photographer in what looked like a leather trench coat was snapping Hayden's picture. Hayden looked positively triumphant. *Le mouvement, c'est moi.* Jesus!

Outside the room the corridor was crowded with people. Two

uniformed cops kept them at bay. As I shoved through, someone asked what had happened in there.

"It was a lover's quarrel," I said, "with the world."

I wondered what I meant. I didn't even remember where I got the phrase. Downstairs the lobby was as refined and ornate as ever. I went through it into the midafternoon sunshine. The hotel was dwarfed by the enormous insurance building that rose behind it. The sides of the skyscraper were reflecting glass, and the sun off the glass was dazzling. Tallest building in Boston. Excelsior, I thought. Tower of Babel, I thought. My car was parked in front of the library. I got in and drove the short block to police headquarters. I parked out front by the yellow curb on Berkeley Street. It's the only place in the area where there are always parking spaces.

I got out of the car arthritically. When I straightened up she was outside the building, on the top step. Squinting against the light, she was wearing a dapple gray suede coat with white fur trim at collar, cuffs, hem, and down the front where it buttoned. Her hands were thrust deep in her pockets and a shoulder purse hung against her left side. She was wearing black boots with three-inch heels, and looking up at her from street level, she looked a lot taller than I knew she was. Her hair was loose and dark against the high white fur collar.

Neither of us moved for a minute. We stood in silence in the bright afternoon and looked at each other. Then she came down the steps.

I said, "Hi."

She said, "Hi."

I went around and opened the door to my car on her side. She got in, tucking the skirt of her long coat modestly under as she slid in. I went around and got in my side.

She said, "Do you have a cigarette?"

I said, "No. But I can stop and pick some up. There's a Liggett's on the corner."

She said, "If you would. I'd like to buy some make-up too."

I pulled over and parked in the alley between the parking garage and the drugstore at the corner of Berkeley and Boylston streets. As we got out she said, "I don't have any money, can you lend me some?"

I nodded. We went into the drugstore. It was a big one—a soda fountain down one side, bottles of almost everything on the other three walls, three wide aisles with shelves selling heating pads and baby strollers, paperback books and candy and Christmas lights. Terry bought a package of Eve cigarettes, opened it, took one out, lit it, and inhaled half of it. She let the smoke out slowly through her nose. I paid. Then we went to the make-up counter. She bought eye liner, eye shadow, make-up base, rouge, lipstick, and face powder. I paid.

I said, "Would you like an ice cream cone?"

She nodded and I bought us two ice cream cones. Vanilla for me, butter pecan for her. Two scoops. We went back out to my car and got in.

"Could we drive around for a little while?" she asked.

"Sure."

I drove on down Berkeley Street and onto Storrow Drive. At Leverett Circle I went over the dam to the Cambridge side and drove back up along the river on Memorial Drive. When we got to Magazine Beach we parked. She used the rearview mirror to put on some of the makeup. I looked across the gray river at the railroad yards. Behind them, half-hidden by the elevated extension of the Mass Turnpike, was Boston University Field, with high-rise dorms built up around the stadium. When I was a kid it had been Braves Field until the Braves moved to Milwaukee and B.U. bought the field. I remembered going there with my father, the excitement building as we went past the ticket taker and up from the dark under stands into the bright green presence of the diamond. The Dodgers and the Giants used to come here then. Dixie Walker, Clint Hartung, Sibbi Sisti, and Tommy Holmes. I wondered if they were still alive.

Terry Orchard finished her makeup and stowed it all away in her shoulder purse.

"Spenser?"

"Yeah?"

"What can I say? Thank you seems pretty silly."

"Don't say anything, kid. You know and I know. Let it be."

She leaned forward and held my face in her hands and kissed me hard on the mouth and held it for a long time. The fresh make-up was sweet smelling. When she finished, her lipstick was badly smeared.

"Gotcha," I said. "Let's go home."

We drove on out Soldier's Field Road toward Newton. She slid over in the seat beside me and put her head against my shoulder while I drove, and smoked another cigarette. There was a maroon car in the driveway of her house when we got there.

"My father," she said. "The police must have reached him." As I pulled up to the curb the front door opened and Terry's mother and father appeared on the porch.

"Shit," she said.

"I'll let you out here and keep going, love," I said. "This is family business."

"Spenser, when am I going to see you again?"

"I don't know. We don't live in the same neighborhood, love. But I'm around. Maybe I'll come by sometime and take you to lunch."

"Or buy me an ice cream," she said.

"Yeah, that too."

She stared at me and her eyes filled up.

She said, "Thank you," and got out of the car and walked up toward her house. I drove back to town, got my side stitched at Boston City by the same doctor, and went home.

It was dark when I got there, and I sat down in my living room and drank bourbon from the bottle without turning on the lights. They'd given me two pills at the hospital and combined with the bourbon they seemed to kill the pain pretty well.

I looked at the luminous dial of my wristwatch. 6:45.

I felt as if I'd wrung out, and was drip-drying. I also felt that spending the night alone would have me screaming incoherently by 3 A.M.

I looked at my watch again. 6:55.

I turned the light on and took off the watch. Inside, it still said Brenda Loring, 555-3676.

I dialed the number. She answered.

I said, "Hello, my name is Spenser; do you remember me?"

She laughed, a terrific laugh, a high-class laugh. "With the shoulders, and the nice eyes, yeah, I remember." And she laughed again. A good laugh, full of promise. A hell of a laugh when you thought about it.

GOD SAVE THE CHILD

This is for my
Mother & Father

1

If you leaned way back in the chair and cranked your neck hard over, you could see the sky from my office window, delft-blue and cloudless and so bright it looked solid. It was September after Labor Day, and somewhere the corn was probably as high as an elephant's eye, the kind of weather when a wino could sleep warm in a doorway.

"Mr. Spenser, are you listening to us?"

I straightened my head up and looked back at Roger and Margery Bartlett.

"Yes, ma'am," I said. "You were just saying about how you never dealt with a private detective before, but this was an extreme case and there seemed no other avenue. Everybody who comes in here tends to say about that same thing to me."

"Well it's true." She was probably older than she looked and not as heavy. Her legs were very slim, the kind women admire and men don't. They made her plumpish upper body look heavier. Her face had a bland, spoiled, pretty look, carefully made up with eye shadow and pancake makeup and false eyelashes. She looked as though if she cried she'd erode. Her hair, freshly blond, was cut close around her face. Gaminelike, I bet her hairdresser said. Mia Farrow, I bet he said. She was wearing a paisley caftan slit up the side and black, ankle-strapped platform shoes with three-inch soles and heels. Sitting opposite me, she had crossed her legs carefully so that the caftan fell away above the knee. I wanted to say, don't, your legs are too thin. But I knew she wouldn't believe me. She thought they were wonderful.

Just below her rib cage I could see the little bulge where her girdle stopped and the compressed flesh spilled over the top. She was wearing huge lavender sunglasses and lavender-dyed wooden beads on a leather thong. Authentic folk art, picked them up in Morocco on our last long weekend, the naiveté is charming, don't you think?

"We want you to find our son," she said.

"Okay."

"He's been gone a week. He ran away."

"Do you know where he might have run?" I asked.

"No," her husband answered. "I looked everywhere I could think of—friends, relatives, places he might hang out. I've asked everyone I know that knows him. He's gone."

"Have you notified the police?"

They both nodded. Mr. Bartlett said, "I talked to the chief myself. He says they'll do what they can, but of course it's a small force and there isn't much . . ."

He let his voice trail off and sat still and uncomfortable looking at me. He looked ill at ease in a shirt and tie. He was dressed in what must have been his wife's idea of the contemporary look. You can usually tell when a guy's wife buys his clothes. He had on baggy white cuffed flares, a solid scarlet shirt with long collar points, a wide pink tie, and a red and white plaid seersucker jacket with wide lapels and the waist nipped. A prefolded handkerchief in his breast pocket matched the tie. He had on black and white saddle shoes and looked as happy as a hound in a doggie sweater. He should have been wearing coveralls and steel-toed work shoes. His hands looked strong and calloused, the nails were broken, and there was grime imbedded that the shower wouldn't touch.

"Why did he run away?" I asked.

"I don't know," Mrs. Bartlett answered. "He isn't a happy boy; he's going through some adolescent phase, I guess. Stays in his room most of the time. His grades are falling off. He used to get very good grades. He's very bright, you know."

"Why are you sure he ran away?" I didn't like asking the question.

Mr. Bartlett answered, "He took his guinea pig with him. Apparently he came home from school to get it and left."

"Did anyone see him leave?"

"No."

"Was anyone home when he came home?"

"No. I was at work and she was at her acting lessons."

"I take my acting lessons twice a week. In the afternoons. It's the only time I can get them. I'm a very creative person, you know, and I have to express myself."

Her husband said something that sounded like "umph."

"Besides," she said, "what has that got to do with anything? Are you saying if I'd been home he wouldn't have run off? Because that simply isn't so. Roger is hardly perfect, you know."

"I was asking because I was trying to find out if he snuck in and out or not. It might suggest whether he intended to run off when he came home."

"If I didn't express myself, I couldn't be as good a mother and wife. I do it for my family, mainly."

Roger looked like he'd just bitten his tongue.

"Okay," I said.

"Creative people simply must create. If you're not a creative person, you wouldn't understand."

"I know," I said. "I have the same damned problem. Right now for instance, I'm trying to create some information, and, for heaven's sake, I'm not getting anywhere at all."

Her husband said, "Yeah, will you for crissake, Marge, stop talking about yourself?"

She looked a little puzzled, but she shut up.

"Did the boy take anything besides the guinea pig?" I asked.

"No."

"Has he ever run away before?"

There was a long pause while they looked at each other. Then, like the punch line in a Frick-and-Frack routine, she said yes and he said no.

"That covers most of the possibilities," I said.

"He didn't really run away," Bartlett said. "He just slept over a friend's house without telling us. Any kid'll do that."

"He did not; he ran away," his wife said. She was intense and forgot about displaying her legs—the skirt slid over as she leaned forward and covered them entirely. "We called everywhere the next day, and Jimmy Houser's mother told us he'd been there. If you hadn't gone and got him at school, I don't think he'd have come back."

"Aw Marge, you make everything sound like a goddamned drama."

"Roger, there's something wrong with that kid, and you won't admit it. If you'd gone along with it when I wanted him looked at—but no, you were so worried about the money. 'Where am I going to get the money, Marge, do you think I've got a money tree in back, Marge?' If you'd let me take him someplace, he'd be home now."

The mimicry sounded true. Bartlett's tan face got darker.

"You bitch," he said. "I told you, take the money out of your goddamned acting lessons and your goddamned pottery classes and your goddamned sculpturing supplies and your goddamned clothes. You got twenty years of psychology payments hanging in your goddamned closet. . . ."

I was going to get a chance to check my erosion theory. Tears began to well up in her eyes, and I found I didn't want to check my theory nor did I want to see her erode. I put my fingers in my ears and waited.

They stopped.

"Good," I said. "Now, let us establish some ground rules. One, I am not on the Parent-of-the-Year committee. I am not interested in assessing your performance. Yell at each other when I'm not around. Second, I am a simple person. If I'm looking for a lost kid, that's what I do. I don't referee marriages; I don't act as creative consultant to the Rog and Margie show. I just keep looking for the kid until I find him. Third, I charge one hundred dollars a day plus whatever expenses I incur. Fourth, I need five hundred dollars as a retainer."

They were silent, embarrassed at the spillover I'd witnessed.

Bartlett said, "Yeah, sure, that's okay, I mean hey, it's only money, right? I'll give you a check now; I brought one with me, in case, you know?"

He hunched the chair forward and wrote a check on the edge of my desk with a translucent ballpoint pen. Bartlett Construction was imprinted in the upper left corner of the check—I was going to be a business expense. Deductible. One keg of 8d nails, 500 feet of 2 × 4 utility grade, one gumshoe, 100 gallons of creosote stain. I took the check without looking at it and slipped it folded into my shirt pocket, casual, like I got them all the time and it was just something to pass along to my broker. Or maybe I'd buy some orchids with it.

"What is your first step?" Mrs. Bartlett said.

"I'll drive up to Smithfield after lunch and look at your house and look at his room and talk to teachers and the local fuzz and like that."

"But the police have done that. What can you do that they can't?" I wondered if I was cutting into her modern dance lessons.

"I can't do anything they can't, but I can do it full time. They have to arrest drunks and flag down speeders and break up fights at the high school and keep the kids from planting pot in the village watering trough. I don't. All I have to do is look for your kid. Also, maybe I'm smarter than they are."

"But can you find him?"

"I can find him; he's somewhere. I'll keep looking till I do."

They didn't look reassured. Maybe it was my office. If I was so good at finding things, how come I couldn't find a better office? Maybe I wasn't all that good? Maybe nobody is. I stood up.

"I'll see you this afternoon," I said. They agreed and left. I watched them from my window as they left the building and headed up Stuart Street toward the parking lot next to Jake Wirth's. An old drunk man with a long overcoat buttoned to his chin said something to them. They stared rigidly past him without answering and disappeared into the parking lot. Well, I thought, the rents are low. The old man stumbled on toward the corner of Tremont. He stopped and spoke to two hookers in hot pants and fancy hats. One of them gave him something, and he shuffled along. A blue Dodge Club van pulled out of the parking lot and headed down Stuart toward Kneeland Street and the expressway. On the side it said BARTLETT CONSTRUCTION. I could see one arm in the sleeve of a paisley caftan on the window as it went by.

2

I drove north out of Boston over the Mystic River Bridge with the top down on my car. On the right was Old Ironsides at berth in the Navy Yard and to the left of the bridge the Bunker Hill Monument. Between them stretch three-decker tenements alternating with modular urban renewal units. One of the real triumphs of prefab design is to create a sense of nostalgia for slums. At the top of the bridge I paid my toll to a man who took pride in his work. There was a kind of precise flourish to the way he took my quarter and gave me back a dime with the same hand.

Out to the right now was the harbor and the harbor islands and the long curving waterfront. The steeple of the Old North Church poked up among the warehouses and lofts. On the East Boston side of the harbor was Logan Airport and beyond, northeast, the contours of the coast. The brick and asphalt and neon were blurred by distance and sunshine, and beneath it I got a sense of the land as it once must have been. The silent midsummer buzz of it and copper-colored near-naked men moving along a narrow trail.

The bridge dipped down into Chelsea and the Northeast Expressway. Across the other lane beyond a football field was a Colonel Sanders' fast-food restaurant. The brick and asphalt and neon were no longer blurred, and the sense of the land went away. The expressway connects in Saugus to Route 1 and for the next ten miles is a plastic canyon of sub-sandwich shops, discount houses, gas stations, supermarkets, neocolonial furniture shops (vinyl siding and chintz curtains), fried chicken, big beef sandwiches, hot dogs cooked in beer, quarter-pound hamburgers, pizzas, storm doors, Sears, Roebuck and Co., doughnut shops, stockade fencing—preassembled sections, restaurants that look like log cabins, restaurants that look like sailing ships, restaurants that look like Moorish town houses, restaurants that look like car washes, car washes, shopping centers, a fish market, a skimobile shop, an automotive accessory shop, liquor stores, a delicatessen in three clashing colors, a motel with an in-room steam bath, a motel with a relaxing vibrator bed, a car dealer, an indoor skating rink attractively done in brick and corrugated plastic, a trailer park, another motel composed of individual cabins, an automobile dealership attractively done in glass and corrugated plastic, an enormous steak house with life-sized plastic cows grazing out front in the shadow of a six-story neon cactus, a seat cover store, a discount clothing warehouse, an Italian restaurant with a leaning tower attached to it. Overpasses punctuate Route 1, tying together the north suburban towns that line it like culverts over a sewer of commerce. Maybe Squanto had made a mistake.

A sign said Entering Smithfield, and the land reappeared. There was grass along the highway and maple trees behind it and glimpes of lake through the trees. I turned off at an exit marked Smithfield and drove toward the center of town beneath a tunnel of elm trees that were as old as the town. They bordered the broad street and interlaced thirty feet above it so that the sun shone through in mottled patterns on the street. Bordering the street behind big lawns and flowering shrubs were spacious old houses in shingle or clapboard, often with slate roofs, occasionally with small barns that had been converted to garages. Stone walls, rose bushes, red doors with bull's-eye glass windows, a lot of station wagons, most of them with the fake wood on the sides. I was more aware than I had been of the big dent on the side of my car and the tear in the upholstery that I had patched with gray tape.

In the center of town was a common with a two-story white clapboard meeting house in the middle. The date on it was 1681. Across the street was a white spired church with a big church hall attached and next to that a new white clapboard library designed in harmony with the meeting house and church. On a stone wall across from the common six teenage kids, four boys and two girls, sat swinging their bare feet and smoking. They were long-haired and T-shirted and tan. I turned right onto Main Street at the end of the common and then left. A discreet white sign with black printing on it was set in a low curving brick wall. It said Apple Knoll.

It was a development. Flossy and fancy and a hundred thousand a house, but a development. Some of the trees had been left and the streets curved gently and the lawns were well landscaped, but all the homes were the same age and bore the mark of a central intelligence. They were big colonial houses, some garrisoned, some with breezeways, some with peaked and some with gambrel roofs, but basically the same house. Eight or ten rooms, they looked to be, on an acre of land. Behind the houses on my right the land sloped down to a lake that brightened through the trees here and there where the road bent closer.

The Bartletts' home was yellow with dark green shutters and a hip roof. The roof was slate, and there were A-shaped dormers protruding from it to suggest a third floor that was more than attic. Doubtless for the servants: they don't mind the heat under the eaves; they're used to it.

A brick walk led up to a wide green front door with sidelights. The brick driveway went parallel to the house and curved right, ending in a turnaround before a small barn designed like the house and done in the same colors. The blue van was there and a Ford Country Squire and a red Mustang convertible with a white roof and a black Chevrolet sedan with a buggy-whip antenna and no markings on the side.

The barn doors were open and swallows flew in and out in sharp, graceful sweeps. Behind the house was a square swimming pool surrounded by a brick patio. The blue lining of the pool made the water look artificial. Beyond the pool a young girl was operating a ride-around lawn mower. I parked next to the black Chevy, up against the hydrangea bushes that lined the turnaround and concealed it from the street. Black and yellow bumblebees buzzed frantically at the flowers. As I approached the house, a Labrador retriever looked at me without raising his head from his paws, and I had to walk around him to get to the back door. Somewhere out of sight I could hear an air conditioner droning, and I was conscious of how my shirt stuck to my back under my coat. I was wearing a white linen sport coat in honor of my trip to the subs, and I wished I could take it off. But since I'd made some people in the mob mad at me, I'd taken to wearing a gun everywhere, and Smithfield didn't seem like the kind of place where you flashed it around.

Besides the white linen jacket, I had on a red checkered sport shirt, dark blue slacks, and white loafers. Me and Betsy Ross. I was neat, clean, alert, and going to the back door. I rang the bell. Ding-dong, private eye calling.

Roger Bartlett came to the door looking more comfortable but no happier than when I'd last seen him. He had on blue sneakers and Bermuda shorts and a white sleeveless undershirt. He had a glass of what looked like gin and tonic in his hand and, from the smell of his breath, several more in his stomach.

"C'mon in, c'mon in," he said. "How about something to fight the heat, maybe a cold one or two, a little schnapps? Hey, why not?" He made a two-inch measuring gesture with his thumb and forefinger as he backed into the kitchen, and I followed. It was a huge kitchen with a big maple-stained trestle table in the bay of the back windows. A cop was sitting at the table with Margery Bartlett, drinking a sixteen-ounce can of Narragansett beer. He had a lot of gold braid on his shoulders and sleeves and more on the visored cap that lay beside him on the table. He had a pearl-handled forty-five in a black holster on a Sam Browne belt. The belt made a gully in his big stomach and the short-sleeved dark blue uniform shirt stretched very tight across his back. It was soaked with sweat around the armpits and along the spine. His bare arms were sunburned and almost hairless, and his big round face was fiery red with pale circles around his eyes where his sunglasses protected him. He'd recently had a haircut, and a white line circled each ear. His eyes were very pale blue and quite small, and he had hardly any neck, his head seeming to grow out of his shoulders. He took a long pull on the beer and belched softly.

"I'll take a can of beer," I said.

Bartlett got one from the big poppy-red refrigerator. "Want a glass?"

"No, thank you."

The kitchen was paneled in pale gray boards, the counter tops were three-inch maple chopping blocks, the cabinets were red and so were the appliances. The wall opposite the big bow window was brick, and the appliances were built into it. An enormous copper hood spread out over the stove, and on the brick wall hung copper pans which bore no marks of use.

The floor was square flagstone, gray and red, and a handbraided blue and red oval rug covered much of it. There were captain's chairs around the table and some reddish maple barstools along the counter. I sat on one and popped open the beer.

Margery Bartlett said, "Mr. Spenser, this is Chief Trask of our police force. He's been working on the case." Her voice was a little loud, and as she spoke she held her empty glass out toward her husband. Trask nodded at me. Bartlett filled his wife's glass from a half-gallon bottle of Beefeater gin on the counter, added a slice of lime, some ice, and some Schweppes tonic, and put it down in front of her.

Trask said, "I'd like to get a few things out in the open early, Spenser."

"Candor," I said, "complete candor. It's the only way."

He stared at me without speaking for a long while. Then he said, "Is that a wise remark, boy?" At thirty-seven I wasn't too used to being called boy.

"No, sir," I said. "Anyone who knows me will tell you that I'm really into candor. Only don't give me that hard look anymore; it makes it hard to swallow my beer."

"Keep it up, Spenser, and you'll see how hard things can get. Understand?"

I drank some more beer. It's one of the things I'm outstanding at. I said, "Okay, what was it you wanted to get out in the open?"

He kept the hard stare on me. "I did some checking with a few people I know in the AG's office, after Rog told me he'd hired you. And I found out some things I don't like hearing."

"I'll bet," I said.

"Among them is that you think you're kind of fancy and act like you're kind of special. You don't always cooperate with local authorities, they said."

"Jesus, I was hoping that wouldn't get out," I said.

"Well, let me tell you something right now, Mister; out here in Smithfield you'll cooperate. You'll keep in close touch with my department, and you'll be under the supervision of my people, or you'll be hauling your ass—excuse me, Marge—right back into Boston. You got that?"

"How long you been working on that stare?" I said.

"Huh?"

"I mean, do you work out with it every morning in the mirror? Or is it something that once you've mastered it you never forget, like, say, riding a bicycle?"

Trask brought his open hand down hard on the tabletop. The ice in Margery Bartlett's glass jingled. She said, "George, please."

"This isn't getting us nowhere, you know? This isn't getting us nowhere at all," Roger Bartlett said. Outside I could hear the low murmur of the power mower as it trimmed up the far side of the acre.

Trask took a deep forbearing breath and said, "Gimme another beer, will you, Rog?"

Bartlett did and put down another can by me, although I wasn't halfway through the first one.

I said, "What have you got, Chief?"

"Everything there is to get; we've covered everything. The kid has run off and there's no way to find him. I say he's probably in New York or maybe California by now."

"Why do you say that?"

"Because he's not around here. If he was we'd have found him." Trask drank again from the can.

"What did he take when he left?"

"Just a pet whatchamacallit," Margery Bartlett said. "Guinea pig."

"Yeah," Trask said, "guinea pig. He took that and what he was wearing and nothing else. Haven't the Bartletts told you all this?"

"What was he wearing?"

"Blue short-sleeved shirt, tan pants, white sneakers."

"Did he take any food for the guinea pig?"

Trask looked at me as if I were crazy. "Food?"

"Yeah. Food. Did he take any for the guinea pig?"

Trask looked at Margery Bartlett. She said, "I don't know. I had nothing to do with the guinea pig." She shivered. "Dirty little things. I hate them."

I looked at her husband. He shook his head. "I don't know."

"What goddamned difference does that make? We ain't worrying about the whatchamacallit; we're after a missing kid. I don't care if the whatchamacallit eats well or not."

"Well," I said, "if the kid cared enough about the guinea pig to come home and get it before taking off, he wouldn't have left without food for it, would he? How about a carrying case or a box or something?"

All three of them looked blank.

"Did the shirt he was wearing have a big pocket, big enough for a guinea pig?"

Roger Bartlett said, "No, I put it through the wash the day before he left, and I noticed there were no pockets. I always go through the pockets before I put things in the wash, ya know, because the kids are always sticking things in their pockets and then forgetting them and they get ruined in the machine. So I checked and I noticed, ya know?"

"Okay," I said, "let's see if we can figure out whether he took any food or anything to carry the guinea pig. If you're going to New York or California, you probably don't want to carry a guinea pig in your hand the whole way. You can't put him in your pants pocket, and you probably don't buy him a cheeseburger and a Ho-Jo at Howard Johnson's."

Roger Bartlett nodded and said, "Come on."

We went up through a center hall off the kitchen to the front stairs. The stairs were wide enough to drive a jeep up. Where they turned and formed a landing, a floor-to-ceiling window looked out over the bright blue pool. There was a trumpet vine fringing the window, and its big bugle-shaped red flowers obscured a couple of the window lights.

The boy's room was second floor front, looking out over the broad front lawn and the quiet curving street beyond it. The bed was against the far wall, a low, headboardless affair that the stores insist on calling a Hollywood bed. It was covered with a red and black spread. There was a matching plaid rug on the floor and drapes of the same material as the spread on the windows. To the left of the door as we entered the room was a built-in counter that covered the entire wall. Beneath it were bureau drawers, and atop it were books and paper and some pencils and a modular animal cage of clear plastic with an orange plastic base. There was a water bottle still nearly full in its slot and some food in the dish. The perforated metal cover was open, and the cage was empty. Beside the cage was a cardboard box with the cover on. Bartlett opened the box. Inside was a package of guinea pig food pellets, a package of Guinea Pig Treat, and a blue cardboard box with a carry handle and a yellow picture of a satisfied-looking guinea pig on the outside.

Bartlett said, "That box is what they give you at the pet store to bring them home in. Kevin kept it to carry him around in."

The two packages of food, both open, and the carry box occupied all the space in the shoe box.

I said, "Can you tell if there's any food missing?"

"I don't think so. This is where he kept it, and it's still there."

I stared around the room. It was very neat. A pair of brown loafers was lined up under the bed, and a pair of blue canvas bedroom slippers beside them, geometrically parallel. The bedside table had a reading lamp and a small red portable radio and nothing else. At the far end of the counter top was a brown and beige portable TV set. Neatly on top, one edge squared with the edge of the television, was a current *TV Guide.* I opened the closet door. The clothes were hung in precise order, each item on its hanger, each shirt buttoned up on the hanger, the pants each neatly creased on a pants hanger; a pair of Frye boots was the only thing on the floor.

"Who does his room?" I asked.

"He does," his father said. "Isn't he neat? Never saw a kid as neat as he is. Neat as a bastard, ya know?"

I nodded and began to look through the bureau drawers. They were as neat as the rest of the room. Folded underwear, rolled socks, six polo shirts of different colors with the sleeves neatly folded under. Two of the drawers were entirely empty.

"What was in these drawers?" I asked.

"Nothing, I think. I don't think he ever kept anything in there."

"Are you sure?"

"No. Like I say, he kept care of his own room, mostly."

"How about your wife; would she know?"

"No."

"Okay." I looked around the room in case there was a secret panel or a note written in code and scratched on the window with the edge of a diamond. I saw neither. In fact there was nothing else in the room. No pictures on the wall, no nude pictures, no pot, no baseballs autographed by Carl Yastrzemski. It was like the sample rooms that furniture departments put up in big department stores: neat, symmetrical, color-coordinated, and empty.

"What are you looking for?" Bartlett asked me.

"Whatever's here," I said. "I don't know until I see it."

"Well, you through?"

"Yeah," I said, and we went back downstairs.

When we came back to the kitchen, Trask was at the counter mixing another gin and tonic for Marge Bartlett. There were two more empty half-quart cans before his empty chair at the table, and Marge Bartlett's voice had gotten louder.

"Well, we put it on in front of a group of young high school kids out in Bolton," she was saying, "and the reception was fantastic. If you give children a chance to see creative drama, they'll respond."

Trask belched, less softly than he had the last time. " 'Scuse *me,* Marge," he said.

"Lotta gas in that 'Gansett," Roger Bartlett said. "It's a real gassy beer. I don't know why I buy it; it's really gassy, ya know?"

Bartlett made himself another gin and tonic as he spoke. I opened my second can of beer and swallowed a little. Gassy, I thought.

Marge Bartlett got up and bumped her hip against the table as she did. She crossed the kitchen toward me with an unlighted cigarette in her mouth and said quite close to my face, "Gotta match?"

I said, "No." She was leaning her thighs against me as I sat on the barstool, and the smell of gin was quite strong. I wondered if the gin was gassy too. She looked at me out of the corners of her eyes with her eyelids dropped down so her eyes were just slits and spoke to her husband.

"Why don't you have shoulders like Mr. Spenser, Rog? I bet he looks great with his shirt off. Do you look great with your shirt off, Mr. Spenser?" Her unlighted cigarette bobbed up and down in her mouth as she talked.

"Yeah, but I usually wear one because my tommy gun tends to cut into my skin when I don't."

She looked puzzled for a minute, but then Trask held a flaming Zippo lighter at her, and she got her cigarette going, took a big inhale and exhale through her nose without taking the cigarette out. She squeezed my upper arm with her right hand and said, "Oooooh." I said, "Seen many Marlene Dietrich movies lately?"

That puzzled look again. She stepped back and picked up her drink. "I have to wee wee," she said. And made what I guess was a seductive move toward the bathroom. I finished my beer.

"You spot anything, Sherlock Holmes?" Trask said.

I shook my head.

Trask looked pleased. "I didn't think you would," he said. "We're not a big force, but we're trained in modern techniques and we're highly disciplined."

"I think the kid's local, though," I said. "Or he went with someone."

"The hell you say."

"He wouldn't set out for a long trip with a guinea pig in his hand and no food, no carry case, not even a spacious pocket. He might run in from a waiting car and grab the guinea pig and run out again. He'd go a short ride carrying the guinea pig, but not a long one. He's a neat kid; everything is laid out in squares and angles. He wouldn't be so unneat as to forget food and lodging for the guinea pig."

"Hey, that's right," Bartlett said. "He would never have done that; Kevin wasn't like that; he'd never have gone off like that unless he was going like you say, Spenser. He'd never do that."

Somewhere off the kitchen a toilet flushed and a door opened and a minute later Marge Bartlett reappeared.

"Spenser thinks Kevin's around here somewhere," Bartlett said to her. "That he wouldn't have gone far without taking stuff for the guinea pig and some clothes and things."

She drained the rest of her drink and gestured the glass indiscriminately at the room. Trask jumped up. "I'll get it, Marge. Sit still, Rog, I got it."

"How does that sound to you, Mrs. Bartlett?" I asked. "Is Kevin the kind of kid to go off that way without preparation?"

"Marge," she said. "Call me Marge."

Trask gave her a fresh drink and helped himself to another beer from the refrigerator.

Bartlett said, "Jeez, I better slice up some more limes; gin and tonic without limes is like a kiss without a squeeze, right? I mean without a goddamned lime it's like a kiss without a squeeze."

Marge Bartlett popped another cigarette into her mouth. It had floral designs on it. Trask leaned over with his Zippo and lit it. The

Zippo had a Marine Corps world and anchor emblem on it. I bet he hadn't had the stomach thirty years ago at Parris Island.

"Is he, Marge?" I asked.

"Is he what?" she said.

"Is he the kind of kid that would go off without making any provisions for anything? His room doesn't look like the room of that kind of person."

"That's right. He's just like his damned father. So careful, so neat. Everything has to be the same. Not like me at all; I'm spontaneous. 'Spontaneous Me.' Ever read that poem? By Whittier?"

"Whitman," I said.

"Yes, excuse me, Whitman, of course. Anyway, I'm spontaneous, spur-of-the-moment, zip-zap, go anywhere, do anything. Most creative people are like that, I guess, but not Kevin; a stick-in-the-mud just like old Roger Stick-in-the-mud. Supper's got to be at six, plain food, roast beef, baked beans. I'd cook if they'd eat something creative, Julia Child, that kind of thing, but it's got to be the same old stew, steak, hamburg. The hell with them; let them cook it themselves. Now if they would eat veal steak in wine with cherries . . ."

"My ass," Bartlett said. "You're not creative, you're lazy. You haven't cooked a goddamned meal around here in five years. Veal with my ass."

"Hey, Rog," Trask said. "Now there's no way to talk. Marge has put out a wonderful feed at parties and stuff."

"Yeah, catered from the goddamned deli for half my freaking profits for the month."

"Oh, you sonova bitch," Marge said. "That's all you think about is your money. If you think I can take acting lessons and modern dance and sculpting all day long and try to keep myself young and interesting for you and the children and then come home and prepare a party that you'll be proud of . . ."

"Balls," Bartlett said, his face very red now. "You don't give a rat's ass about me or anybody else."

"Hold on now," Trask said. "Goddamn it, just hold on."

I got off my barstool and took another can of beer out of the refrigerator. You don't see red refrigerators much. I went to the back door and opened it and went out. The retriever still lay there on the back steps with his tongue out, and I sat down beside him and opened the beer. The door behind me was on a pneumatic closer, and as it shut I heard Marge Bartlett say "shit" in a very loud voice.

I drank a small swallow of the beer and scratched the dog's ear. His tail thumped on the porch. The sound of the lawn mower stopped, and a minute later a young girl came out of the barn and walked toward the house. She didn't look at me sitting on the back steps but detoured toward the front of the house, and a minute later I heard the front door open and close.

I drank some more beer. In the middle of the front lawn, past the hydrangea, was a huge flowering crab. It was too late for blossoms, but the leaves were still reddish fading into green, and there were small green crab apples beginning to form. Some robins and some sparrows and a Baltimore oriole swarmed in and out of the branches with considerable chatter. After the green fruit, I supposed. I hadn't seen a Baltimore oriole since I was a kid.

I heard the front door open and close again, and the girl came around the corner of the house wearing a bikini bathing suit and carrying a towel. She must have been thirteen or fourteen and was just beginning to get a figure. I was very careful not to lech at her. There has to be a line you won't cross, and my lower limit is arbitrarily set at sixteen. As she walked by she looked at the ground and said nothing. I watched her as she went around the corner of the house toward the pool. The retriever got up as she passed and followed her. They were out of sight, and then I heard two splashes in the pool. And the sound of swimming. My beer was gone. I looked at my watch; nearly four thirty. I put the beer can on the railing of the porch, walked across the driveway, got in my car, and drove back to Boston.

3

At eight the next morning I was out jogging along the Charles. From the concert shell on the Esplanade to the BU Bridge was two miles, and I always tried to make the round trip in about forty minutes. It was never fun, but this morning was tougher than usual because it was raining like hell. Usually there were other joggers, but this morning I was alone. I had on sweat pants and a hooded nylon shell, but the rain soaked my sneakers and needled at my face as I ran. Walking back up Arlington Street to my apartment on Marlborough, I could feel the sweat collect in the small of my back, trapped there by the waterproof parka.

Before I'd left I'd put the coffee on, and it was ready when I came back. But I didn't drink it yet. First a shower. A long time under the shower, a lot of soap, a lot of shampoo. I shaved very carefully, standing in the shower—I'd put a mirror in the stall just so I could do that—and rinsed off thoroughly. I put on a pair of light gray slacks and black over-the-ankle boots and went to the kitchen.

I sliced two green tomatoes, sprinkled them with black pepper and rosemary, shook them in flour, and put them in about a half-inch of olive oil to fry. I put a small porterhouse steak under the broiler and got a loaf of unleavened Syrian bread out of the refrigerator. While the steak and tomatoes cooked, I drank my first cup of coffee, cream, two sugars, and ate a bowl of blackberries I'd bought at a farm stand coming back from the Cape with a girl I knew. When it was ready, I ate my breakfast, put the dishes in the washer, washed my hands and face, clipped my gun on over my right hip pocket, put on a washed blue denim shirt with short sleeves, and let it hang outside to cover the gun. I was ready, exercised, washed, fed, and armed—alert for the slightest sign of a dragon. I had a white trench coat given me once by a friend. She said it made me look taller. I put it on now and headed for my car.

The rain was hard as I pulled out onto Storrow Drive and headed for Smithfield. The wipers were only barely able to stay ahead of it, and some of the storm culverts were flooded and backing up in the underpasses.

I stopped at a white colonial liquor store in Smithfield Center and got directions to the high school. It was a little out from the center of town in a neighborhood of expensive homes with a football field behind it and some tennis courts beyond that. A sign said VISITORS' PARKING, and I slid in between an orange Volvo and a blue Pinto station wagon. I turned the collar up on my trench coat, got out of the car, and sprinted for the front doorway.

Inside was an open lobby with display cases on the walls containing graphics done by students. To the left was a glassed-in room with a sign on the door saying ADMINISTRATION and a smaller sign beneath saying RECEPTION. I went in and spoke to a plump middle-aged lady with a tight permanent. I asked to see the principal.

"He's at conference this morning," she said. "Perhaps the assistant principal, Mr. Moriarty, can help you."

I said that Mr. Moriarty would be fine. She asked my name and disappeared into another office. She returned in a moment and gestured me in.

Mr. Moriarty was red-faced, swag-bellied, thick-necked Irish. He was wearing a dark blue sharkskin suit with natural shoulders and narrow lapels, a white shirt with button-down collar, and a thin black knit tie.

Cordovan shoes, I thought, not wing tips; plain-toed cordovan shoes and white socks. I wished there were someone there to bet with. He stood up behind his desk as I came in and put out his hand.

"I'm Mr. Moriarty, the assistant principal," he said. We shook hands.

His hair was brown and surprisingly long, cut square in a kind of Dutch-boy bob across the forehead, completely covering his ears, and waving over his shirt collar. Modish. I gave him my card. He read it and raised his eyebrows.

"Private investigator. Hey, I was an MP, you know. In Germany after the war, stationed in Stuttgart," he said.

I said, "I'm looking into the disappearance of one of your students, Kevin Bartlett. I was wondering if you could tell me anything about him that might help."

Moriarty frowned. "We've been through all that with Chief Trask," he said. "I don't know what I could add to what I told him."

"Let's go over what you told him," I said. "Sometimes a fresh slant can help."

"Does Chief Trask know you are here? I mean, I don't want to get into some conflict of ethics on this. Chief Trask is, after all, the —um—well—the chief."

"He knows, and I won't ask you to compromise your ethics. Just tell me about the kid."

"Well, he's quite a bright student. Good family, father runs a successful contracting firm. Good family, been in town a long time, beautiful home up in Apple Knoll."

"I know," I said. "I've been there, but I'm more interested in information about the kid. What kind of kid was he? Was he any kind of behavior problem? Did he have many friends? Who were they? What were they like? Was he using drugs? Did he drink? Did he have a girl friend? Was there a teacher he was close to? Why would he run off? That sort of thing. I'm glad he was from a good family, you understand; I'd just like to see about getting him back to it."

"Well, that's a big order," Moriarty said. "And I question whether or not I'm authorized to discuss these matters with you."

"Just 'whether,' " I said.

"I beg your pardon?" he said.

" 'Whether' implies 'or not,' " I said.

His professional manner slipped a little. "Listen," he said, "I don't need my grammar corrected by some damned gumshoe. And I don't have to tell you anything at all. You think I've got all day to sit around and talk, you got another think coming."

"You've got a real way with the language," I said. "But, never mind, I'm not here to fight with you. I'm looking for help. Was the kid ever in trouble?"

"Well, sometimes he got a little insolent, especially with the women teachers. He has only been up here a year. This is just the start of his second year here, and we don't have a lot of experience with him. You might want to talk with Mr. Lee down at the junior high." He looked at his watch. "Or perhaps while you're here you might want to talk with Mrs. Silverman of our guidance department. She might be able to tell you something."

Good going, Spenser. Insult the guy's grammar so he sulks at you and won't talk. Maybe I ought to watch my mouth as people keep telling me. Moriarty was up from his desk and walking me to the door. I glanced down. Right! Plain-toed cordovans. Not shined. White socks too. Perfect.

"Mrs. Silverman's office is third door down this corridor on the right. The door says Guidance on it, and you can't miss it."

I said thank you and went where he pointed me. There were lockers along the right-hand wall and doors with frosted-glass windows in them on my left. On the third one was lettered GUIDANCE. I went in. It was like the waiting room at a doctor's office. Low table in the center, a rack for periodicals on one wall, a receptionist opposite, and three doors on the left wall like examining rooms. The periodical rack was filled with college catalogues, and the low table had literature about careers and health on it. The receptionist was a great improvement on Moriarty's. She had red hair and a dark tan and a lot of good-sized bosom showing over and around a lime-green sleeveless blouse. I told her Mr. Moriarty had sent me down to talk with Mrs. Silverman.

"She has a student with her now. Could you wait a moment please?"

I picked up some of the career leaflets on the table. Nursing, Air Force, G.E. Apprentice Training; I wondered if they had one for Private Eye. I looked. They didn't. The door to Mrs. Silverman's office opened, and a thin boy with shoulder-length hair and acne came out.

He mumbled, "Thank you, Mrs. Silverman," and hustled out of the office.

The secretary and her bosom got up and went into the office. In a moment they came out, and she said, "Mrs. Silverman will see you now."

I put down my copy of *Opportunities in Civil Service* and went in. Susan Silverman wasn't beautiful, but there was a tangibility about her, a physical reality, that made the secretary with the lime-green bosom seem insubstantial. She had shoulder-length black hair and a thin dark Jewish face with prominent cheekbones. Tall, maybe five seven, with black eyes. It was hard to tell her age, but there was a sense about her of intelligent maturity which put her on my side of thirty.

She said, "Come in, Mr. Spenser. I'm Susan Silverman," and came around the desk to shake hands. She was wearing a black silk blouse with belled sleeves and white slacks. The blouse was open at the throat, and there was a thin silver chain around her neck. Her breasts were good, her thighs were terrific. When she shook hands with me, I felt something click down back of my solar plexus.

I said hello without stammering and sat down.

"Why don't you take off your coat?" she said.

"Well, it's supposed to make me look taller," I said.

"Sitting down?"

"No, I guess not," I said and stood up and took it off. She took it from me and hung it on a rack beside hers. Hers was white too, and the two coats overlapped on the rack. It wasn't much, but it was a start.

"I don't think you need to look taller, Mr. Spenser," she said. When she smiled the color of her face seemed to heighten. "How tall are you?"

"Six one," I said.

"Really? That's surprising. I must admit you don't look that tall."

"Even with the raincoat?" I said.

"Even with that," she said. "You're so wide. Do you work with weights?"

"Yeah, some. How could you tell? Your husband lift?"

"Ex-husband," she said. "Yes, he played tackle for Harvard and stayed with the weights afterward."

Ex-husband! I felt the click again. She wasn't wearing a wedding ring. She had red polish on her fingernails and a thin silver bracelet around her left wrist. Small coiled earrings matched the bracelet and necklace. Her eyes had a dusting of blue shadow, and her lipstick matched the nail polish. Her teeth were very even and white, slightly prominent. Her hair was shiny and done in what we called a pageboy when I was in high school. There was just the slightest suggestion of laugh lines around her mouth.

"What can I do for you, Mr. Spenser?" she asked, and I realized I'd been staring at her.

"I'm trying to find Kevin Bartlett," I said and handed her one of my cards. "Mr. Moriarty suggested you might be able to tell me something about him."

"Have you talked to Mr. Moriarty already?" she said.

"In a manner of speaking. He seemed a little cautious."

"Yes, he is. Public school administrators are often cautious. What did he tell you about Kevin?"

"That he came from a good family and lived in a nice house."

"That's all?"

"Yeah. I think I offended him."

"Why?"

"Because he pouted and stamped his foot and sent me down here."

She laughed. Her laugh sounded like I'd always imagined the taste of mead. It was resonant.

"You must have teased him," she said.

"Well, a little."

"Arthur does not respond well to teasing. But, about Kevin," she said. "Do you want to ask me questions, or do you want me to hold forth on what I know and think?"

"You hold forth," I said.

"Have you met Kevin's parents? You must have."

"Yes."

"What do you think?"

"Bad. Role identity is screwed up, no real communication. Probably a lot more than that, but I only met them twice. I think they probably drink too much."

"Okay. I've met them several times and we agree. Kevin's a product of that. He's a very intelligent kid, but he too has his roles tangled. And, at fifteen, going through adolescence, he still hasn't resolved his Oedipal conflicts. He's got some problems, I think, with gender identification, and strong problems of hostility toward both parents for different reasons."

"Are you suggesting he's homosexual?" I asked.

"No, not necessarily, but I think he could go that way. A dominant, but largely absent mother, a successful, but essentially passive father. Strength seems associated with femininity, resentful submission with masculinity, and love, perhaps, with neither."

"I have the feeling I'm only getting a piece of what you're saying," I said. "Is it too much of an oversimplification for me to say that because his parents are as they are, he's not sure whether he'd prefer to be like his mother or like his father when he gets to be an adult?"

She smiled a luminous smile and said, "That will do. One thing, though; this is only an opinion and one based on not enough data. I think I'm right, but I have a master's degree in guidance; I am not a psychiatrist."

"Okay, go ahead. What else can you tell me?"

"He moves with a really damaging group for a boy like him."

"Troublemakers?"

"No, not in the usual sense. Dropouts would be a better word. He has few friends in school. He spends most of his time with a group who have dropped out of school. Their approach to life is asocial if not antisocial, and for a boy with unresolved Oedipal hostilities it seems the worst possible choice of companions."

"Do you think he might be with one of this group?"

"Yes."

"Do you have an idea which?"

"No. That I can't be sure of. Kevin is not very talkative. He's been to see me a couple of times. He has difficulties with the women teachers. Nothing that is easily explained, but a kind of nagging hostility that is difficult to deal with."

"For instance?"

"Oh, telling one of the younger teachers she looks sexy. If she reprimands him he'll say, okay, you don't look sexy. That sort of thing. There's nothing really you can discipline him for, and indeed, to do so makes you look more ridiculous. He's very clever that way."

"Okay, can you give me an idea of this group he hangs with?"

"Well, as I say, he's not communicative, and he's very clever. When I've talked with him, I've learned that he has friends among the local dissidents, I suppose you'd call them, and he seems particularly friendly with someone named Vic Harroway. But who or where he is I don't know. I'm not close to the situation. Kevin is only one of maybe twenty kids a day I talk with."

"All with problems?"

"No, not emotional ones. Some of them just want advice on where to go to college, or when to take the college boards, or how to get a job as a bulldozer operator. But four or five a day are emotional problems, and there isn't time, nor have I sufficient training, really, to help them. The best I can do is recommend help at one or another guidance clinic and give the name of some psychotherapists I trust."

"Did you suggest that to Kevin's parents?"

"Well, I asked them to come and talk with me, but they never came. And I didn't want to just send them a letter suggesting it. So I did not make any recommendation."

"How did you ask them? I mean, did you write a letter or see them at PTA or send a note home with Kevin? Or what?"

"I called Mrs. Bartlett and asked if she and her husband could come in. She said yes and we made an appointment, but they never came. Why do you want to know?"

"Because it's there. Because it's better to know than not to know in my line of work."

She smiled, her teeth very white in her dark face.

"Maybe in all lines of work," she said. And I was proud that I'd said a smart thing.

4

The rain had stopped when I left Susan Silverman and headed back for the Bartletts' house. I wanted to see what they could tell me about their son's social circle. If there was a group like that around, it would be a fair bet he'd go to it. Smithfield didn't look like the spot for a commune. But then, I wasn't quite sure what a spot for a commune looked like.

When I pulled into the Bartlett driveway, the chief's car was there again along with three others. One was a cream-colored Thunderbird with a black vinyl roof. One was a blue Ford station wagon with SMITHFIELD POLICE lettered in black on the sides and the emergency number 555-3434 across the back. The third was a two-tone powder-blue and dark blue Massachusetts State Police cruiser. A state cop with a uniform that matched the cruiser and a gray campaign hat was leaning against it with his arms folded. The short-sleeved blue shirt was pressed with military creases; the black shoes were spit-shined. The campaign hat was tipped forward over the bridge of his nose like a Parris Island DI's. He had a big-handled Magnum .357 on a shiny black belt. He looked at me with no expression on his tanned and healthy face as I got out of my car.

"May I have your name, sir?" he said.

"Spenser," I said. "I'm working for the Bartletts. What's going on?"

"Do you have any identification, please," he said.

I fumbled under my sport coat for my wallet, and as I brought it out, the Magnum .357 was suddenly right up against my neck, and the cop said very seriously, "Put both hands on the top of the car, you sonova bitch." I put my hands, the wallet still clutched in the left one, on the top of my car and leaned.

"What's the matter," I said. "Don't you like my name?"

With his left hand he reached under my jacket and took my gun from the holster.

"Not bad," I said. "You must have gotten just a flash of it when I took out my wallet."

"Now the wallet," he said.

I handed it to him without ceasing to lean on the car.

"I've got a license for that gun," I said.

"So I see," he said. The gun barrel still pressed under my left ear. "Got a private cop license too. Stay right where you are." He backed two steps to the cruiser and, reaching through the window, honked the horn twice. The Magnum stared stolidly at my stomach.

A Smithfield cop came to the back steps. "Hey, Paul, ask Mr. Bartlett if he knows this guy," the state cop said. Paul disappeared and returned in a minute with Bartlett. Bartlett said, "He's okay. He's a private detective. I hired him to find Kevin. He's okay. Let him come in."

The state cop put the gun away with a nice neat movement, gave me back my own gun, and nodded me toward the house. I went in.

We were in the kitchen again. Margery Bartlett, her face streaked and teary, Bartlett, Trask, the Smithfield cop, and two men I didn't know.

Margery Bartlett said, "Kevin's been kidnapped."

Her husband said, "We got a ransom note today."

One of the men I didn't know said, "I'm Earl Maguire, Spenser," and put out his hand. "I'm Rog's attorney. And this is Lieutenant Healy of the State Police. I think you know Chief Trask." I nodded.

Maguire was small. His grip was hard when he took my hand,

and he shook it vigorously. He was dark-skinned with longish black hair carefully layered with a razor cut. Six bucks easy, I thought, for that kind of haircut. I bet the barber wore a black silk coat. He was wearing a form-fitting pale blue denim suit with black stitching along the lapels, blunt-toed, thick-soled black shoes with two-inch heels, a black shirt, and a pale blue figured tie. It must have been his T-Bird outside. BC Law School. Not Harvard, maybe BU, but most likely BC.

"Where'd you go to school?" I said.

"BC," he said. "Why?"

Ah, Spenser, you can do it all, kid. "No reason," I said. "Just wondered."

Healy I knew of. He was chief investigator for the Essex County DA's office. There were at least two first-run racketeers I knew who stayed out of Essex County because they didn't want any truck with him.

Healy said, "Didn't you work for the Suffolk County DA once?"

I said, "Yes."

"Didn't they fire you for hotdogging?"

"I like to call it inner-directed behavior," I said.

"I'll bet you do," Healy said.

He was a medium tall man, maybe five ten, slim, with very square shoulders. His gray hair was cut in a close crew cut, the sideburns trimmed at the top of the ears. The skin on his face looked tight, finely veined on the cheekbones, and his close-shaved cheeks had the faint bluish tinge of heavy beard. He had on a tan seersucker suit and a white shirt and a brown and yellow striped tie. A short-crowned, snap-brimmed straw hat with a flowery hatband lay on the table before him. His hands were folded perfectly still in his lap as he sat with his chair tilted back slightly. He wore a plain gold wedding ring on his left hand.

"What's hotdogging?" Marge Bartlett said.

"He's not too good about regulations," Healy answered.

Margery Bartlett said, "Can you get my child back, Mr. Spenser?" She was leaning forward, biting down on her lower lip with her upper teeth. Her eyes were wide and fixed on me. Her right hand was open on her breast, approximately above her heart. There were tears on her cheeks. Donna Reed in *Ransom,* MGM, 1956. "I don't care about the money; I just want my baby back."

Trask leaned over and patted her hand.

"Don't worry, Marge, we'll get him back for you. You got my word on it." John Wayne, *The Searchers,* Warner Bros., 1956.

I looked at Healy. He was carefully examining the backs of his hands, his lips pursed, whistling silently to himself. The Smithfield cop named Paul was looking closely at the copper switchplate on the wall by the back door.

"What have you got?" I asked Healy.

He handed me a sheet of paper inside a transparent plastic folder. It was a ransom note in the form of a comic strip. The figures were hand-drawn with a red ballpoint pen and showed some skill, like competent graffiti, say. They featured a voluptuous woman in a miniskirt seated on a barstool, leaning on the bar, speaking in voice balloons. "We have your son," she said in the first panel, "and if you don't give us $50,000 you'll never see him again." In the second panel she was taking a drink and saying nothing. In the third panel she said, "Follow the instructions on the next page exactly or it's all over." In the next panel she was lighting a cigarette. In the fifth panel she was full face to the reader and saying, "Be careful." In the sixth and last panel she had turned back to the bar and only her back was visible. I handed it back to Healy. He gave me the second page, similarly enclosed in clear plastic. It was typewritten, single-spaced, by someone who was inexpert at typing.

"Why the hell did they draw the picture?" Roger Bartlett said. "Why did they have to draw pictures? That don't make any sense."

"Take it easy, Rog," Earl Maguire said.

I started to read the typewritten sheet.

"Way to conceal their identity," said Trask. "That's why they're drawing pictures. Right, Healy?"

"Too early to say," Healy said.

It was hot and moist in the kitchen. Outside, the rain had started again. I read the instructions.

> There is a riding stable on route I. In front of it is a driveway. Have Margery Bartlett stand on the curb at the right hand corner of the driveway at High Noon, Sept. 10. Have the money in a green book bag. Have her hold it out in front of her. Have her do that till someone comes along and takes it. If anyone is around or any cops at all or anything goes wrong and you try some funny stuff. Then your kid gets the ax and we mean it. we will cut off his head and send it to you so Don't screw up. AFter we get the

money we will tell you where to go and get your kid. So. do what we say and stand by for further instructions.

I gave the paper back to Healy and raised my eyebrows.

"Yeah," Healy said. "I know."

"Know what? What do you mean by that?" Marge Bartlett said.

"It's an odd note and an odd set of instructions," I said. "Can you get the fifty?"

Bartlett nodded. "Murray Raymond, down the bank, will gimme the dough. I can put the business up as collateral. I already talked to him, and he's getting me the money from Boston."

"What's funny about the instructions?" Marge Bartlett said. "Why do I have to be there?"

Healy answered her. "I don't know why you have to be there except what they said, maybe to keep some kid from finding the bag and taking it home. The instructions are complicated in the wrong ways. For instance, they obviously want the bag to be where they can grab it on the move, but why there? And why no instructions about the kinds of money and the denominations of the bills? Why give us two days lead time like that to set up a stake?"

"But they needed to give Rog time to get the money," Trask said.

"Yeah, but they didn't need to tell us where they were going to pick it up," I said.

"Right," Healy said. "A call five minutes beforehand would have done that, and left us nothing to do but sit around and wonder."

"And why the mail?" I said.

"What's wrong with the mail?" Roger Bartlett said.

"That's one reason they had to give you lead time," Healy said. "They can't be sure when you'll get the letter, so they have to give themselves away several days ahead."

"What do you mean a stake?" Marge Bartlett asked.

"That's the stakeout," Trask answered. "We conceal ourselves in the adjacent area so's to be in a position to apprehend the kidnappers when they come for the ransom."

"Apprehend," Healy said, and whistled admiringly.

I said, "Adjacent isn't bad either, Lieutenant."

"What's wrong with you guys?" Trask said.

"You talk terrific," I said, "but I'm not sure you want to apprehend the culprits in the adjacent area. Maybe you might want to place them under close surveillance until they lead you to the victim. You know?"

"I don't want anything like that," Margery Bartlett said. And she shook her head. "I want nothing like that at all. They might get mad if they saw you. And they said—about his head—I couldn't stand that."

"I don't want that either," Roger Bartlett said. "I mean, it's only money, you know. I want to do what they say, and when it's over then you can catch them. I mean, it's only money, you know?"

Trask put his hand on Margery Bartlett's again. "We'll do just as you ask, Marge, just as you ask."

Healy shook his head. "A mistake," he said. "Your odds are better on getting the kid back if you let us in on it."

Margery Bartlett looked at me. "What does he mean?"

I took a deep breath. "He means that your best chance to get Kevin back okay is to have us find him. He means they might take the ransom and kill him anyway, or they might not. There's no way to tell. The statistics are slightly in favor of the cops. More kidnap victims survive the kidnapping when rescued by the police than when turned loose by the kidnappers. Not many more; I'd say it's about fifty-five percent to forty-five percent."

Healy said, "Maybe a little closer. But what else have you got?"

Roger Bartlett said, "I don't want him hurt."

Margery Bartlett put her face down in her hands and began to wail.

Her husband put one arm around her shoulder. She shrugged it away and cried louder. "Marge," he said. "Jesus, Marge, we gotta do something. Spenser, what should we do?" Tears formed in his eyes and began to slide down his face.

I said, "We'll stake it out."

"But . . ."

"We'll stake it out," I said again. "We'll be cool about it. We got two days to set it up."

Trask said, "Now just hold on, Spenser. This is my town, and I decide whether or not we do any surveillance."

Healy let the front legs of his chair down slowly to the floor, put his folded hands on the tabletop, leaned forward slightly, and with no inflection in his voice said, "George, please keep your trap shut until we are finished talking." Trask flushed. He opened his mouth and closed it. He looked hard at Healy for a minute, and then his eyes shifted away.

"Now," Healy continued. "George, here's what I want you to do. I want you to go down to the town hall and get some maps of that area from the surveyor's office and bring them back. And together we will go over them." He turned toward the Smithfield patrolman named Paul. "Marsh, I want you to take these two items into Ten-ten Commonwealth and have the crime lab go over them. You know people in there?"

Paul said, "Yessir, I been in there before."

Healy handed him the two envelopes. Paul started to leave, looked uncertainly at Trask, then at Healy. Healy nodded. Paul left, holding the two envelopes under his raincoat. Trask sat looking at his knuckles. The muscles at his jaw hinge were clenched. There was a tic in his left eyelid.

"The maps, George," Healy said. Their eyes locked again, briefly. Then Trask got up, put on a yellow slicker, and went out. He slammed the door. In the kitchen it was quiet except for Margery Bartlett's sobbing. Her husband stood about three feet from her, his arms hanging straight down as if he didn't know what to do with them.

Earl Maguire said, "We'd better get a doctor over here. He can give her something. Who's your doctor, Rog? I'll call him for you."

"It's there by the phone," Bartlett said. "Croft, Doctor Croft. Have him come over. Tell him what happened. Tell him she needs something. That's a good idea. Tell him to come over and give her something."

Healy stood up, took off his coat, hung it over the back of his chair, loosened his tie, and sat back down. He nodded toward the chair Trask had left. "Sit down, Spenser," he said. "We got some work to do."

5

Margery Bartlett had gone upstairs to lie down, Dr. Croft had come over and given her a shot. Roger Bartlett had gone to a neighbor's house to pick up his daughter. Trask had brought back the maps, and he and Healy and I were looking at them spread out on the kitchen table. A small slick-haired state cop in plainclothes and rimless glasses had hooked a tape recorder to the phone in the den off the kitchen and sat next to it with earphones, reading a copy of *Playboy* he'd found in the magazine rack. He turned it sideways to look at the centerfold.

"Sonova bitch," he said, "hair and all. You see this, Lieutenant?"

Healy didn't look up. "If you gotta read that garbage, read it, but don't narrate it."

The little cop held the magazine out at arm's length. "Sonova bitch," he said.

Healy said, "What's up here, back of the riding stable?"

"Nothing," Trask said, "just woods. It's the west end of the Lynn Woods. Runs for miles back on into Lynn."

"Hills?"

"Yeah, low ones; it slopes up back of the stable riding ring."

"Can we put someone up there with glasses?"

"Sure, the woods are thick. He could climb a tree if he wanted."

"You know the people at the stable?"

"Sure."

"Can we put somebody in there?"

"In the stable?"

Healy said, "I don't mean inside the stable. Can we have someone posing as an employee?"

"Oh yeah, sure. I'll set it up."

Healy made some notes on a small notepad he'd taken from inside his coat. He used a big red fountain pen that looked like one my father had used when I was small.

"If they pick up the money here," I said, "that's northbound. Where's the first place they can get onto Route 1 north?"

"Saugus," Healy said. "Here, by the shopping center."

"And the first place they can get off?"

"Here, about two hundred yards up, at this intersection. Otherwise they could dip down through the underpass here and head up Route 1 or turn off here at 128. We can put a couple of people at each place."

"And a walkie-talkie up on the hill with the glasses?"

Healy nodded. "We'll put an unmarked car here." He put a cross on the map at the intersection of Route 1 and Salem Street. "Here, here, he could U-turn at the lights. So here, southbound." Healy marked out eleven positions on the map.

"That's a lot of cars," Trask said.

"I know. We'll have your people use their own cars and supply them with walkie-talkies. How many people can you give me?"

"Everybody; twelve men. But who's going to pay them per diem?"

Healy looked at him. "Per diem?"

"For the cars. They're supposed to get a per diem mileage allowance for the use of their own cars on official business. This could mount up if all of them do it. And I have to answer to a town meeting every year."

I said, "Do you accept Master Charge?"

Trask said, "It's not funny. You've never had to answer to a town meeting. They're a bunch of unreasonable bastards at those things."

Healy said, "The state will rent the cars. I'll sign a voucher. But if you screw this up, you'll learn what an unreasonable bastard really is."

"There won't be any screw-up. I'll be right on top of every move my people make."

"Yeah," Healy said.

"Who you going to put into the stable?" I asked Healy.

"You want to do it? You're the least likely to be recognized."

"Yeah."

"You know anything about horses?"

"Only what I read in the green sheet."

"It doesn't matter. We'll go up and look around."

Healy put on his coat, tightened his tie, put the snap-brimmed straw hat squarely on his head, and we went out. The rain had started again. Healy ignored it. "We'll go in your car," he said. "No need to have them looking at the radio car parked up there. Stick here, Miles," he said to the cop leaning against the cruiser. He had on a yellow rain slicker now. "I'll be back."

"Yes, sir," Miles said.

I backed out, pulling the car up on the grass to get around the state cruiser.

"Your roof leaks," Healy said.

"Maybe I can get the state to give me per diem payment for a new one," I said.

Healy said nothing. The stable was about ten minutes from the Bartletts' home. We drove there in silence. I pulled into the parking lot in front of the stable, parked, and shut off the motor. The stable was maybe one hundred yards in from the road. The access to it was between a restaurant and a liquor store. The restaurant was roadside colonial: brick, dark wood and white plastic, flat-roofed. In front was an enormous incongruous red and yellow sign that advertised home cooking and family-style dining and cocktails. The store was glass-fronted; the rest was artificial fieldstone. It too had a flat room rimmed in white plastic. In the window was an inflated panda with a sign around his neck advertising a summer cooler. Across the top of the store was a sign that said PACKAGE STORE in pink neon. Two of the letters were out. The parking lot narrowed to a driveway near the stable.

The stable looked like someplace you'd go to rent a donkey. It was a one-story building with faded maroon siding, the kind that goes on in four-by-eight pregrooved panels. The trim was white, and the nails had bled through so that it was rust streaked. The roof was shingled partly in red and partly in black. Through it poked three tin chimneys. Next to it was a riding ring of unpainted boards and the trailer part of a tractor trailer rig, rusted and tireless on cinder blocks. In front of the stable parked among the weeds were five horse trailers, an old green dump truck with V-8 on the front, an aqua-colored '65 Chevy hardtop, a new Cadillac convertible, and a tan '62 Chevy wagon. A sign, SOLID FILL WANTED, stood at the edge of the road, and a pile of old asphalt, bricks, paving stones, tree stumps, gravel, crushed stone, sewer pipe, a rusting hot water tank, three railroad ties, and a bicycle frame settled into the marshy ground behind it. Marlboro country.

Healy looked at it all without speaking. Carefully. A sea gull lit on the containerized garbage back of the restaurant and began working on a chunk of something I couldn't identify through the rain.

"Let's get out," Healy said. We did. The rain was steady and warm and vertical. No wind slanted it. Healy had on no raincoat but seemed not to notice. I turned the collar up on my raincoat. We walked down toward the stable. The bare earth around it had been softened into a swamp of mud, and it became hard to walk. On the other side of the riding ring a handmade sign said BRIDLE PATH, and an arrow pointed to a narrow trail that led into the woods. We walked back out to the parking lot and stood at the edge of Route 1 at the spot where Mrs. Bartlett was to stand. Cars rushed past in a hiss of wet pavement. To the left the road curved out of sight beyond a hill. To the right it dipped into a tunnel with a service road branching off to the right and parallel. Two hundred yards down was a light on the service road and a cross street.

Healy turned and headed back toward the stable. I followed. Healy seemed to assume I would. I walked a little faster so I'd be beside him, not behind him. I was beginning to feel like a trainee.

At the far end of the stable was a door marked Office. The torn screen door was shut, but the wooden door inside was open and a television set was tuned to a talk show. "Were you first into transcendental meditation before or after you made this picture?" "During, actually. We were in location in Spain . . ." Healy rapped on the door, and a dark-haired man answered. He was wearing black Levi's jeans and a white T-shirt that was too small for him. His stomach spilled over his belt and showed bare where the T-shirt gapped. His skin was dark and moist-looking, and his face sank into several layers of carelessly shaved chin. He went perfectly with the stable. He also smelled strongly of garlic and beer.

"Yeah?"

I said, "I'd like to rent a high-spirited palomino stallion with a hand-tooled Spanish leather saddle and silver-studded bridle, please." The man looked at me with his eyes squinting, as if the light were too bright.

"A what?" he said.

"Shut up, Spenser," Healy said and showed his badge to the fat man. "May we come in, please?"

The fat man stepped back from the door. "Sure, sure, come on in; I'm just having lunch."

We went in. The television was on top of a rolltop desk. The actress was saying to the talk show hostess, "Sylvia, I never pay any attention to the critics." On the writing surface of the desk were a big wedge of cheese and a salami on the white butcher's paper in which they'd been wrapped. There was also a half-empty quart bottle of Pickwick ale, an open pocketknife, and a jar of pickled sweet peppers. The fat man belched as he waved us to a seat. Or waved Healy to a seat. There was only a straight-backed chair by the desk and a sprung swivel chair with a torn cushion on it. The fat man sat in the swivel chair, Healy took the straight chair, and I stood. "The critics I care about, Sylvia, are those people out there. If I can make them happy, I feel that I'm . . ." Healy reached over and shut off the television.

"What's up?" the fat man said.

"My name is Healy. I'm a detective lieutenant with the Massachusetts State Police. I want to have this man spend the next two days here as if he were an employee, and I don't want to tell you why."

A dirty white cat jumped up on the desk and began to chew on a scrap of salami. The fat man ignored it and cut a piece of cheese off the wedge. He speared it with the jackknife and popped it into his mouth. With the other hand he fished a pickled pepper out of the jar and ate it. Then he drank most of the rest of the ale from the bottle, belched again, and said, "Well, for crissake, Lieutenant, I got a right to know what's happening. I mean, for crying out loud, I don't want to screw up my business, you know. I got a right."

Healy said, "You gotta right to discuss with the building inspector the code violations he and I are going to spot in this manure bin if you give me any trouble."

The fat man blinked a minute at Healy and then said, "Yeah, sure, okay. Look, always glad to help out. I was just curious, you know. I don't want no trouble. Be glad to have this fellow around."

Healy said, "Thank you. He'll be here tomorrow morning dressed for work, and he'll hang around here for the next couple of days. I don't want you to say anything about this to anyone. It is a matter of life and death, and if anyone starts talking about this, it could be fatal. Kind of fatal for you too. Got me?"

"You can trust me, Lieutenant. I won't say nothing to nobody. Don't worry about it." He looked at me. "You're welcome to stay around all you want. My name's Vinnie. What's yours?"

"Nick Charles," I said. He grabbed my hand.

"Good to meet you, Nick. Anything you need, just holler. Want a piece of cheese or salami, anything?"

"No, thanks." Vinnie looked at Healy. Healy shook his head.

"Remember, Vinnie, keep your mouth shut about this. It matters."

"Right, Lieutenant. Mum's the word. Wild horses . . ."

"Yeah, okay. Just remember." Healy left. I followed.

6

I spent two days hanging around the riding stable and learned only that horses are not smart. Vinnie spent most of his time in with the TV and the Pickwick. And assorted kids, more girls than boys, in scraggly Levi's jeans and scuffed riding boots and white T-shirts that hung outside the jeans fed the horses and exercised them in the oozy ring and occasionally rented one to someone, usually a kid, who would ride it off into the bridle trail. I looked good in a plaid shirt with the sleeves cut off and a pair of jeans and high-laced tan work shoes. I had a gun stuck in the waistband under the shirt, and it dug into my stomach all day. For a prop I had a big wooden rake, and I spent the days moving horse manure around with it while I whistled "Home on the Range."

Pickup day was beautiful, eighty-two degrees, mild breeze, cloudless sunshine. A day for looking at a ball game or walking along with a girl and a jug of apple wine or casting for a smallmouth black bass where an elm tree hung out over the Ipswich River. That kind of a day. A day for collecting ransom, I supposed, if that was your style. I straightened up and stretched and looked around. Healy should have everyone in place by now. I saw nothing. The hill behind the stable culminated in a water tower; up in a tree near it there was supposed to be a guy with glasses and a walkie-talkie. I looked for sun flash on the lenses. I didn't see any. Healy would see that there was no lens flash. Just as he'd see that the two guys in Palm Beach suits he had in the window booth of the restaurant wouldn't be oiling their blackjacks. I looked at my watch—quarter to twelve. Marge Bartlett was supposed to arrive at noon. High noon, the letter had said. I wondered if there was a low noon. No one would make an appointment for it if there was.

I went back to the manure. In the woods behind the riding ring cicadas droned steadily in pleasant monotony. Now and then in the stable a horse would snort, or rattle a hoof against the stall. Several sea gulls were doing a good business in the garbage container back of the restaurant. I checked the parking lot again out of the corner of my eye. Marge Bartlett was there. Just getting out of her red Mustang. She went to the edge of the driveway carrying the green canvas book bag full of money and stood. She was dressed for a bullfight. Tight gold toreador pants with a row of buttons along the wide flare. A ruffled red shirt, a bronze-colored leather vest that reached to her thighs and closed with two big leather thongs across the stomach, high-heeled bronze boots with lacings, a bronze wide-brimmed vaquero hat, bronze leather gloves. I'd always wondered what to wear to a ransom payment. Traffic went by. Usually cars, now and then a truck downshifting as it came up the hill beyond the curve. Occasionally a motorcycle loud and whining. Noisy bastards. My hands were sweaty on the rake handle. My neck and shoulder muscles felt tight. I kept shrugging my shoulders, but they didn't loosen. I stood the rake against the stable and went and sat on a bale of straw against the wall. I'd brought lunch in a paper bag so I could be sitting and eating and looking when the pickup was made. A big refrigerator truck lumbered by on the highway. Marge Bartlett stood rigid and still, looking straight ahead with the bag held at her side. The sea gulls rustled away at the garbage. Somewhere in the woods a dog barked. Down the highway another motorcycle snarled. It appeared around the curve. A big one, three-fifty probably, high-rise handlebars, rearview mirror, small front wheel, sissy bar behind. My favorite kind. It swung into the parking lot, and without stopping the rider took the bag from Marge Bartlett, took one turn around the mirror support with the straps, and headed straight across the parking lot toward the stable.

Bridle path, I thought as he went by me. The license plates were covered. I got one flash of Levi's jeans and engineer's boots and field jacket and red plastic helmet with blue plastic face shield, and he was behind the riding ring into the bridle path and gone in the woods. I could hear the roar of the bike dwindle, and then I couldn't hear it, and all there was was the drone of the cicadas. And the traffic. Bridle path. Sonova bitch. A lot of per diem shot to hell.

Marge Bartlett got back in her Mustang and drove away. I threw my sandwich at the sea gulls, and they flared up and then came down on it and tore it apart. I stood up and took the rake from against the wall and broke the handle across my knee and dropped the two parts on the ground and started for my car. Then I stopped and took a ten-dollar bill out of my wallet and went back and folded it around one of the rake tines and left it there. Vinnie didn't look as if he could afford my temper tantrum. With the profits he'd shown in the two days I'd spent there, he couldn't buy a pocket comb.

Healy and Trask were sitting in the front seat of Trask's cruiser in the parking lot of the Catholic church four blocks from the stable. There was a map spread out against the dashboard in front of them. I pulled up beside them and shut off the engine.

"Your man in the tree spot them?" I asked.

"Nope, lost him as soon as he went into the woods. The trees overhang the trail."

Trask said, "The goddamned trail splits and runs off in all different directions. There's no real way to tell where it comes out. Some of the people riding have made new trails. He could have come out in Lynn, in Saugus, in Smithfield past the roadblock. He's gone."

Healy's face was stiff and the bones showed. He said, "Two days, two goddamned days looking at that place, looking at that goddamned bridle path sign, listening to motorcycles going by on Route 1. Two days. And we stood there with our thumb in our butt. For crissake, Spenser, you were there, you saw people riding into that path; why the hell didn't you put it together? You're supposed to be a goddamned hotshot."

"I'm not a big intellect like you state dicks. I was overextended raking the manure."

Healy took the map of the woods he'd been looking at and began to wad it into a ball, packing it in his thin freckled hands the way we used to make snowballs when I was a kid. The radio in Trask's car crackled, and the dispatcher said something I couldn't understand. Trask responded.

"This is Trask."

Again the radio in its crackly mechanical voice. And Trask. "Roger, out." Jiminy, just like in the movies. "Aren't you supposed to say 'Ten Four'?" I said.

Trask turned his big red face at me. "Look, you screwed this thing up, and you feel like a horse's ass now. Don't take it out on me." He looked at Healy. "Did you get that on the radio?" Healy nodded. I said, "What was it?"

"The Bartletts got a phone call from the kidnappers telling them where to get the kid." He put the car in gear and backed out of the parking lot. I followed. Maybe they'll give him back, I thought. Maybe.

7

The call had come perhaps ten minutes after the money had been picked up. The little slick-haired cop had recorded it, and he played it back for Trask and Healy and me. Roger Bartlett said, "Hello." There was a brief scrap of music and a voice said, "Howdy all you kidnapping freaks," in the affected southern drawl that is required of everyone who is under thirty and cool. "This is your old buddy the kidnapper speaking, and we gotta big treat for you all out there in kidnap land. The big prizewinners in our pay-the-ransom contest are Mr. and Mrs. Roger Bartlett of Smithfield." The music came up again and then faded, and several male voices sang a jingle:

Behind a school in old Smithfield
First prize your ransom it did yield,
So in that direction you should be steering,
From us no longer you'll be hearing.

Then the music came up and faded out with some giggles behind it. Roger Bartlett said to us, "He's gotta be behind one of the schools. There's six: the four elementary, the junior high, the high school . . ." Trask said, "What about Our Lady's?" And Bartlett said, "Right, the Catholic school," and Healy said, "How about kindergartens? How many private kindergartens in town?"

Trask looked at Bartlett; Bartlett shook his head. Trask shrugged and said, "Hell, I don't know."

Healy said, "Okay, Trask, run it down; get your people checking behind and around all the schools in town. And don't miss anything like a dog school or a driving school. These are odd people."

Trask went out to his car and got on the radio. Bartlett went with him. I said to Healy, "What in Christ have we got here?"

Healy shook his head. "I don't know. I don't remember anything like this anywhere. Do you realize the trouble they went to, to rig up that tape recording?"

"Yeah," I said, "and it's not just to conceal voices. There's something else going on. Something personal in this thing. The ransom note, this call—there's something wrong."

Margery Bartlett came in with Earl Maguire. "What's wrong?" she said. "Is something wrong? Have you found Kevin?"

"Nothing's wrong, ma'am," Healy said. "Spenser was talking about something else. Chief Trask is directing the search for Kevin now. I'm sure there will be good news soon."

But Healy didn't believe it and I knew he didn't and he knew I knew. He looked very steadily at me after he'd said it. I looked away. Maguire said, "Sit down, Marge, no sense tiring yourself." She sat at the kitchen table. Maguire sat opposite her. Healy looked out the back door at Trask. I leaned against the counter. The big Lab that I'd seen my first visit wandered into the kitchen and lapped water noisily from his dish.

Marge Bartlett said, "Punkin, you naughty dog, don't be so noisy." Punkin? The dog was big enough to pull a beer wagon. He stopped drinking and flopped down on his side in the middle of the floor. No one said anything. The dog heaved a big sigh, and his stomach rolled.

Marge Bartlett said again, "Punkin! You should be ashamed." He paid her no attention. "I apologize for my dog," she said. "But dogs are good. They don't demand much of you; they just love you for what you are. Just accept you. I'm doing a sculpture of Punkin in clay. I want to capture that trusting and undemanding quality."

I saw Healy's shoulders straighten, heard Trask's car door slam, and Trask pushed into the kitchen with Roger Bartlett.

Trask said to Healy, "Junior high school, come on." Healy went. I went after them. Trask already had the car in gear as I jumped into the backseat. He spun gravel out of the driveway, and the siren was whoop-whooping by the time he was in third gear.

It was maybe three minutes to the junior high school. Trask wrenched the cruiser into the big semicircular driveway in front of it with a screech of rubber and brakes and spun off that and onto the hot-top parking surface to the left of the school and on around behind it. He loved the noise and the siren. I bet he'd been dying to do that since the case began. There were maybe two dozen cars parked against the back of the two-story brick building. Most of them were small cars, suitable for junior high school teachers. On the end of the second row of cars was an old Cadillac hearse. The back door was open, and a group of kids stood around it, held back by two prowl car cops in short sleeves and sunglasses. The patrol car, blue light still turning, was parked beside the hearse. In the school windows most of the other kids were leaning out and some were yelling. The teachers were not having much luck with them. Most weren't trying but craned out the windows with the kids.

Trask jammed on the brakes and was out of the car while it was still lurching. He left the door open behind him and strode to the hearse. Healy got out, closed his door, and followed. I sat in the backseat a minute and looked at the hearse. I felt a little sick. I didn't want to look inside. I wanted to go home. There was a case of Amstel beer home in the refrigerator. I wanted to go home and drink it. I got out of the car and followed Healy.

Inside the hearse was a coffin made of scrap plywood. The plywood wasn't new, and the carpentry was not professional. It was padlocked. One of the prowl car cops got a tire iron, and Trask, squatting in the hearse, pried the hasp off. Healy lifted the lid. I bit down hard on my back teeth. A life-sized rag doll dummy sat bolt upright in the coffin and leered at us with its red Raggedy Andy lips. Still squatting, Trask started back with a yelp, lost his balance, and sat down awkwardly on the floor of the hearse. Healy never moved. The dummy flopped over sideways, and I could see a rusty spring attached to its back. I realized that my right hand was on the gun butt under my shirt. I took it away and rubbed it on my pants leg. The crowd was absolutely still. I said, "Trick or treat."

Healy said, "Get that thing out of there."

The two patrolmen lifted it out of the hearse and set it on the ground. Healy and I squatted down beside it.

"Shirt and pants stuffed with newspaper," Healy said. "Head seems to be made out of a pillowcase stuffed with cotton batting. Features drawn on with Magic Marker. Spring looks like it came from an easy chair."

He stood up. "Trask," he said, "keep people away from this area. I'll have some technicians come down and assist your people on the fingerprints and all."

Trask nodded. "Okay," he snapped to the crowd, "back it up. We've got to get lab specialists right on this." He spoke to the two prowlies. "Move 'em back, men. We'll seal this area off."

I wondered if he rode a white stallion in the Memorial Day parade.

Behind the school was an athletic field ringed with high evergreen woods. Healy walked out toward the trees; I walked along with him. He paused on the pitcher's mound and picked up some clay and rolled it in his right hand. He looked down at the pitching rubber. And then at home plate. He took his hat off and wiped his forearm across his forehead. He put his hat back on tipped low forward, shading his eyes, and looked out toward center field and the trees beyond it. He put his hands in his back pockets and rocked silently on the mound, his back toward home plate, staring out at the trees behind center field.

"Ever play ball, Spenser?"

"Some."

"I was a pitcher. All-State at Winthrop High School. Had a tryout with the Phillies. Coulda signed but the war was on. When I got out of the army, I was married, had two kids already. Had to get a steady job. Went with the state cops instead."

I didn't say anything. Healy continued to look at center field, his head tipped back a little to see out under the brim of his hat.

"Almost thirty years."

I didn't answer. He wasn't really talking to me, anyway.

"Got any kids, Spenser?"

"Nope."

"I got five. The little one is fifteen now; only one left at home. Plays for St. John's. He's a pitcher."

Healy stopped talking. The wind moved the pine branches in the woods. The trees had a strong smell in the September heat. Some starlings hopped about the infield near second base, pecking at the grass. Behind us the police radio squawked.

"Sonova goddamned bitch!" he said.

I nodded. "Me too," I said.

8

State and local cops swarmed over the hearse like ants on a marshmallow and learned nothing. It had been stolen six months before from two brothers in Revere who had bought it at a sheriff's sale and were going to fix it up as a camper. There were no fingerprints that meant anything to anyone. There was no opium stashed in the spare tire well, no hardcore porn taped to the chassis, no automatic weapons being smuggled to the counterculture. There were no laundry marks in the shirt and pants. The newspapers used to stuff the dummy were recent issues of *The Boston Globe* obtainable at any newsstand. The plywood and the hardware from which the coffin had been made were standard and could have come from any lumberyard in the country. There were no lube stickers or antifreeze tags anywhere on the vehicle to tell us anything. In short, the hearse was as blank and meaningless as a Styrofoam coffee cup.

Marge Bartlett was under sedation again. Roger Bartlett was

mad, scared, and mournful. It was the mad that showed. As I left he was yelling at Healy and at Trask. He'd already yelled at me.

"Goddamn it! What's going on? You people have found nothing. What's going on? Where's my son? I did what you said, and I get the bullshit with the funny coffin. You people have found nothing . . ." The door closed behind me. I didn't blame him for yelling. I looked at my watch—four fifteen. Time to go home.

When I got home the Amstel beer was still there in the refrigerator, a gift from a girl who knew the way to my heart. I popped the cap off a bottle and drank half of it. Jesus, the Dutch knew how to live. I remembered a café in a hotel in Amsterdam where Amstel was the house beer. I finished the beer, opened another, drank some while I got undressed, put it on the sink while I took a shower, finished it while I toweled off.

I went to the kitchen in my shorts, opened a third bottle, picked up the phone, and called information. I got Susan Silverman's number and called her. Her voice sounded very educated on the phone. She said, "Hello."

I said, "Help."

She said, "I beg your pardon?"

I said, "I am in desperate need of guidance. Do you make house calls?"

She said, "Who is this?"

I said, "How quickly they forget. Spenser. You remember . . . proud carriage, clear blue eyes that never waver, intrepid chin, white raincoat that makes me look taller?"

And she said, "Oh, that Spenser."

"I know it's late," I said, "but I'm about to cook a pork tenderloin *en croûte* and wondered if you would be willing to eat some of it while we talk more about Kevin Bartlett." She was silent. "I'm a hell of a cook," I said. "Not much of a detective, have some trouble locating my own Adam's apple, don't have much success with kidnapping victims, but I'm a hell of a cook."

"Mr. Spenser, it's five thirty. I was just about to put my own supper in the oven."

"I'll come out and get you if you wish," I said. "If you'd rather, I'll buy you dinner."

"No," she said. I could almost hear her make up her mind. "I'll come in. What is your address?"

"Do you know where Marlborough Street is?" I asked.

"Yes."

"Okay, I'm in the last block before you get to the Public Garden." I gave her the number. "It's on the left-hand side. How long will it take you?"

"Would seven thirty be all right?"

"Just right," I said. "I'll look for you then."

She said good-bye and we hung up. "Ha!" I said out loud. I drank down the rest of my beer to celebrate. Still got the old sex appeal, kid, still got all the old moves. She couldn't resist me. Or maybe she just liked pork tenderloin *en croûte.*

I turned on the oven to preheat, took the pork out of the meatkeeper to warm up, and set about making the crust. I opened another Amstel. Better watch it, though; didn't want to be drunk when she got here. It was, after all, business, or partly business. I made a very short crust and laid the tenderloin across it. I sprinkled in some thyme, some black pepper, and a dust of dill. I rolled the crust carefully around it and put it on a roasting pan. I brushed a little egg white on the top to glaze it and put it in a medium oven.

I peeled and sliced three green apples, some carrots, and some red onions. I added a lump of butter and put them to simmer in about an inch of cider in a tightly covered sauce pan. I made a Cumberland sauce for the pork. Then I went to get dressed. I decided against a gold lamé smoking jacket and white silk scarf. Instead I put on a black polo shirt and white trousers with a modest flare. I put on my black loafers, still shined, and walked up Arlington Street two blocks to Boylston and bought two loaves of hot French bread from a bake shop. Then I walked back to my apartment and put a bottle of red wine in the wine bucket, opened it to let it breathe, and packed it in ice. I knew that was bad—I was supposed to roll it on my palate at room temperature, but once a hick, always a hick, I guess. I liked it cold.

9

At seven fifteen I took the pork out of the oven and put it on the counter to rest. I took the lid off the vegetables, turned up the heat, and boiled away the moisture while I shook the pan gently. It made them glaze slightly. I put them in a covered chafing dish over a low blue flame. I put the French bread into the still warm oven. I had stopped on the way back from Smithfield and bought a dozen native tomatoes at a farm stand. Each was the size of a softball. I sliced two of them about a half-inch thick and sprinkled them lightly with sugar and arranged them slightly overlapping on a bed of Boston lettuce on a platter and put them beside the roast to warm up. Tomatoes are much better at room temperature.

I had just finished washing my hands and face when the doorbell rang. Everything was ready. Ah, Spenser, what a touch. Everything was just right except that I couldn't seem to find a missing child. Well, nobody's perfect. I pushed the release button and opened my apartment door. I was wrong. Susan Silverman was perfect.

It took nearly forty years of savoir faire to keep from saying "Golly." She had on black pants and a knit yellow scoop-necked, short-sleeved sweater that gaped fractionally above the black pants, showing a fine and only occasional line of tan skin. The sleeves were short and had a scalloped frill, and her black and yellow platform shoes made her damned near my height. Her black and yellow earrings were cubed pendants. Her black hair glistened, her teeth were bright in her tan face when she smiled and put out her hand.

"Come in," I said. Very smooth. I didn't scuff my foot; I didn't mumble. I stood right up straight when I said it. I don't think I blushed.

"This is a very nice apartment," she said as she stepped into the living room. I said thank you. She walked across and looked at the wood carving on the server. "Isn't this the statue of the Indian in front of the museum?"

"Yes."

"It's lovely. Where did you get it?"

This time I think I did blush. "Aw hell," I said.

"Did you do it?"

"Yes."

"Oh, it's very good." She ran her hands over the wood. "What kind of wood is it?"

"Hard pine," I said.

"How did you get the wood so smooth?"

"I rubbed it down with powdered pumice and a little mineral oil."

"It is very lovely," she said. "Did you do all these wood carvings?" I nodded. She looked at me and shook her head. "And you cook too?"

I nodded again.

"Amazing," she said.

"Can I get you a drink?" I said.

"I'd love one."

"Would you take a vodka gimlet?"

"That would be splendid," she said. Splendid. In her mouth it sounded just right. Anyone else who said "splendid" would have sounded like the wrong end of a horse.

I put five parts of vodka and one part Rose's lime juice in a pitcher, stirred it with ice, and strained some into two short glasses.

"Would you care to sit on a stool and drink it while I make last-minute motions in the kitchen?"

"I'll do better than that, I'll help set the table while I'm drinking my drink."

"Okay."

The kitchen area was separated from the living-dining area by a waist-high partition and some lathe-turned risers extending to the ceiling. As I poured oil and vinegar over the tomatoes, I watched her through the partition. She was probably between thirty-five and forty. Her body was strong, and as she bent over the table placing the silverware her thighs were firm and smooth and her back and waist graceful and resilient where the blouse gapped. She moved surely, and I bet myself she played good tennis.

I sliced half the pork *en croûte* in quarter-inch slices and arranged them on the serving platter. I put the chafing dish of vegetables on the table, put the tomatoes and roast out also. Susan Silverman's glass was empty, and I filled it. My head was feeling a little thick from five beers and a large gimlet. Some would say a thickness of head was my normal condition.

"Candles too hokey?" I said.

She laughed and said, "I think so."

"Shall we finish our drinks before we eat?" I asked.

"If you wish."

She sat at the end of the couch and leaned back slightly against the arm, took a grown-up sip of her gimlet, and looked at me over the glass as she did so.

"What ever happened to your nose, Mr. Spenser?"

"A very good heavyweight boxer hit it several times with his left fist."

"Why didn't you ask him not to do that?"

"It's considered bad form. I was hoping for the referee."

"You don't seem to choose the easiest professions," she said.

"I don't know. The real pain, I think, would be nine to five at a desk processing insurance claims. I'd rather get my nose broken weekly."

Her glass was empty. I filled it from the pitcher and freshened mine. Don't want to get drunk on duty. Don't want to make a damned fool of myself in front of Susan Silverman, either.

She smiled her thanks at me. "So, sticking your nose into things and getting it broken allows you to live life on your own terms, perhaps."

"Jesus, I wish I'd said that," I said. "Want to eat?"

"I think we'd better; I'm beginning to feel the gimlets."

"In that case, my dear, let me get you another." I raised my eyebrows and flicked an imaginary cigar.

"Oh, do the funny walk, Groucho," she said.

"I haven't got that down yet," I said. I gestured toward the pitcher, and she shook her head. "No thank you, really."

I held her chair as she sat down, sat down opposite her, and poured some wine in her glass.

"A self-effacing little domestic red," I said, "with just a hint of presumption."

She took a sip. "Oh, good," she said, "it's cold. I hate it at room temperature, don't you?"

I said, "Let's elope."

"Just like that," she said. "Because I like cold wine?"

"Well, there are other factors," I said.

"Let's eat first," she said.

We ate. Largely in silence. There are people with whom silence is not strained. Very few of them are women. But Susan Silverman was one. She didn't make conversation. Or if she was making conversation she was so good at it that I didn't notice. She ate with pleasure and impeccable style. Me too.

She accepted another slice of the roast and put sauce on it from the gravy boat.

"The sauce is super," she said. "What is it?"

"Cumberland sauce," I said. "It is also terrific with duck."

She didn't ask for the recipe. Style. I hate people who ask for recipes.

"Well, it is certainly terrific with pork."

"Jesus Christ," I said.

"What's the matter?"

"You're Jewish."

"Yes?"

"You're not Orthodox?"

"No."

"Serving a pork roast on your first date with a Jewish lady is not always considered a slick move."

She laughed. "I didn't even think of that. You poor thing. Of course it is not a slick move. But is this a date? I thought I was going to be questioned."

"Yeah. That's right. I'm just softening you up now. After dessert and brandy I break out the strappado."

She held out her wineglass. "Well then, I'd better fortify myself as best I can."

I poured her more wine.

"What about Kevin Bartlett? Where do you think he is?"

She shrugged. "I don't know. How could I? Haven't you got any clues at all?"

"Oh yeah, we got clues. We got lots of clues. But they don't lead us to anything. What they tell us is that we're into something weird. It's freak-land again."

"Again?"

"That's just nostalgia, I guess. Used to be when you got a kidnapping you assumed the motive to be greed and you could count on that and work with it. You ran into a murder and you could figure lust or profit as a starter. Now you gotta wonder if it's political, religious, or merely idiosyncratic. You know, for the hell of it. Because it's there."

"And you yearn for the simple crimes like Leopold-Loeb?"

"Yeah," I grinned. "Or Ruth Judd, the ax murderess. Okay, so maybe there was always freaky crime. It just seems more prevalent. Or maybe I grow old."

"Maybe we all do," she said.

"Yeah, but I'd like to find Kevin Bartlett before I get senile. You know about the kidnapping note and the hearse and the dummy?"

"Some. The story was all over the school system when they found the hearse behind the junior high. But I don't know details."

"Okay," I said, "here they are." I told her. "Now," I said, and gestured with the wine bottle toward her glass.

"Half a glass," she said. I poured. "That's good."

"Now," I said again, "do you think he was kidnapped? And if he was kidnapped, was it just for money?"

"In order," she said, "I don't know, and no."

"Yeah, that's about where I am," I said. "Tell me about this group he ran with."

"As I said when you saw me the other day in my office, I really know very little about them. I've heard that there is a group of disaffected young people who have formed a commune of some sort.

Commune may be too strong a word. There is a group, and I only know this from gossip in the high school, that chooses to live together. I don't want to stereotype them. They are mostly, I've heard, school- and college-age people who do not go to school or work in the traditional sense. I've heard that they have a house somewhere around Smithfield."

"Who owns the house?"

"I don't know, but there is a kind of leader, an older man, maybe thirty or so, this Vic Harroway. I would think he'd be the owner."

"And Kevin was hanging around with this group?"

"With some of them. Or at least with some kids who were said to be associated with this group. I'd see him now and then sitting on the cemetery wall across from the common with several kids from the group. Or *maybe* from the group. I'm making this sound a good deal more positive than it is. I'm not sure of any of this or even of the existence of such a group. Although I'm inclined to think there is a group like that."

"Who would know?"

She frowned. "I don't know. Chief Trask, I suppose."

"How bizarre is this group?"

"Bizarre? I don't know. I hadn't heard anything very bizarre about them. I imagine there's grass smoked there, although not many of us find that bizarre anymore. Other than that I can't think of anything particularly bizarre. What kind of bizarre do you mean?"

The wine was gone, and I was looking a little wistfully at the empty bottle. It was hard concentrating on business. I was also looking a little wistfully at Susan Silverman. Neither rain nor sleet nor snow nor dark of night maybe, but red wine and a handsome woman—that was something else.

She said, "What kind of bizarre are you looking for?"

"Any kind at all. The kind of bizarre that would be capable of that dummy trick in the coffin, the kind of bizarre that would make a singing commercial out of the telephone call. The kind of bizarre that would do the ransom note in a comic strip. Would you like some brandy?"

"One small glass."

"Let's take it to the living room."

She sat where she had before, at one end of the couch. I gave her some Calvados and sat on the coffee table near her.

"I don't know anything bizarre about the group. I have the impression that there is something unusual about Vic Harroway, but I don't know quite what it is."

"Think about it. Who said he was odd? What context was his oddness in?"

She frowned again. "No, just an idea that he's unusual."

"Is he unusual in appearance?"

"I don't know."

"Size?"

"Really, I can't recall."

"Is he unusual in his sex habits?"

She shrugged and spread her hands, palms up.

"Religious zealot?"

She shook her head.

"Unusual family connections?"

"Damn it, Spenser, I don't know. If I knew, I'd tell you."

"Try picturing the circumstances when you got the impression he was unusual. Who said it? Where were you?"

She laughed. "Spenser, I can't do it. I don't remember. You're like a hammer after a nail."

"Sorry, I tend to get caught up in my work."

"I guess you do. You're a very interesting man. One might misjudge you. One might even underrate you, and I think that might be a very bad error."

"Underrate? Me?"

"Well, here you are a big guy with sort of a classy broken nose and clever patter. It would be easy to assume you were getting by on that. That maybe you were a little cynical and a little shallow. I half figured you got me in here just to make a pass at me. But I just saw you at work, and I would not want to be somebody you were really after."

"Now you're making me feel funny," I said. "Because half the reason I invited you in here was to make a pass at you."

"Maybe," she said and smiled. "But first you would work."

"Okay," I said. "I worked. I am a sleuth, and being a sleuth I can add two and two, blue eyes. If you half expected me to make a pass and you came anyway, then you must have half wanted me to do so . . . sweetheart."

"My eyes are brown."

"I know, but I can't do Bogart saying 'brown eyes.' And don't change the subject."

She took the final sip from her brandy glass and put it on the coffee table. When she did she was close to my face. "See?" she said looking at me steadily. "See how brown they are?"

"Black, I'd say. Closer to black."

I put my hands on either side of her face and kissed her on the mouth. She kissed me back. It was a long kiss, and when it ended I still held her face in my hands.

"Maybe you're right," she said. "Maybe they are more black than brown. Perhaps if you were to sit on the couch you might be able to see better."

I moved over. "Yes," I said, "this confirms my suspicion. Your eyes are black rather than brown."

She leaned forward and kissed me. I put my arms around her. She turned across my lap so I was holding her in my arms and put her arms around my neck. The kiss lasted longer than the first one and had some body English on it. I ran my hand under her sweater up along the depression of her spine, feeling the smooth muscles that ran parallel. We were lying now on the couch, and her mouth was open. I slid my hand back down along her spine and under the waistband of her pants. She groaned and arched her body against me, turning slightly as I moved my hand along the waistband toward the front zipper. I reached it and fumbled at it. Old surgeon's hands. She pulled back from the kiss, reached down, and took my hand away. I let her. We were gasping.

"No, Spenser," she managed. "Not the first time. Not in your apartment."

I didn't say anything. I couldn't think of anything to say, and I was concentrating on breathing.

"I know it's silly. But I can't get rid of upbringing; I can't get rid of Momma saying that only dirty girls did it on the first date. I come from a different time."

"I know," I said. "I come from the same time." My voice was very hoarse. I cleared my throat. We continued to lie on the couch, my arm around her.

"There will be other times. Perhaps you'd like to try my cooking. In my house. I'm not cold, Spenser, and I would have been hurt if you hadn't tried, but not the first time. I just wouldn't like myself. Next time . . ."

"Yeah," I said. Clearing my throat hadn't helped, but I was getting my breathing under control. "I know. I'd love to try your cooking. What say we hop in the car and drive right out to your place now for a snack?"

She laughed. "You're not a quitter, are you."

"It's just that I may be suffering from terminal tumescence," I said.

She laughed again and sat up.

I said, "How about dinner together next week? That way you won't feel quite so hustled, maybe?"

She sat and looked down at me for some time. Her black hair falling forward around her face. Her lipstick smeared around her mouth. "You're quite nice, Spenser." She put her hand against my cheek for a moment. "Will you come and have dinner with me at my home next Tuesday evening at eight?"

"I will be very pleased to," I said.

We stood up. She put her hand out. I shook it. I walked to the door with her. She said, "Good night, Spenser."

I said, "Good night, Susan."

I opened the door for her, and she went out. I closed it. I breathed as much air as I could get into my lungs and let it out very slowly. Next time, I thought. Tuesday night. Dinner at her house. Hot dog.

10

Susan Silverman called me at my office at nine thirty the next morning.

"I've found out about that commune," she said.

"Tell me," I said.

"It's an old house in the woods back from Lowell Street near the Smithfield-Reading line."

"Can you tell me how to get there?"

"I'll take you."

"I was hoping you would. I'll be out in an hour."

"Come to my office," she said.

"At the school?" I said.

"Yes, what's wrong?"

"Mr. Moriarty might assault me with a ruler. I don't want to start up with no assistant principal."

"He probably won't recognize you without your white raincoat," she said. "The sun's out."

"Okay," I said, "I'll run the risk."

It was sunny, and the first hint of a New England fall murmured behind the sunshine. Warm enough for the top down on my convertible. Cold enough for a pale denim jacket. I drank a large paper cup of black coffee on the way and finished it just before I got to the Smithfield cutoff.

I found a space in the high school parking lot and went in.

The receptionist in the guidance office was in brown knit today and displaying a lot of cleavage. I admired it. She wasn't Susan Silverman, but she wasn't Lassie either, and there was little to be gained in elitist thinking.

Susan Silverman came out of her office with a red, blue, and green striped blazer on.

"I'll be back in about half an hour, Carla," she said to the redhead, and to me, "Why don't we take my car? It'll be easier than giving you directions."

I said, "Okay," and we went out of the office and down a school corridor I hadn't walked before. But it was a school corridor. The smell of it and the long rows of lockers and the tone of repressed energy were like they always were. The guidance setup was different, though. Guidance counseling in my school meant the football coach banged your head against a locker and told you to shape up.

Susan Silverman said, "Were you looking down the front of my secretary's dress when I came out?"

"I was looking for clues," I said. "I'm a professional investigator."

She said, "Mmmm."

We went out a side door to the parking lot. Behind it the lawn stretched green to a football field ringed with new-looking bleachers and past that a line of trees. There was a group of girls in blue gym shorts and gold T-shirts playing field hockey under the eye of a lean tan woman in blue warm-up pants and a white polo shirt with a whistle in her mouth.

"Gym class?" I asked.

"Yes."

Susan's car was a two-year-old Nova. I opened the door for her, and she slipped into the seat, tucking her blue skirt under her.

We drove out of the parking lot, turned left toward the center of town, and then right on Main Street and headed north.

"How'd you locate this place so quickly?"

"I collected a favor," she said, "from a girl in school."

We turned left off Main Street and headed east. The road was narrow, and the houses became sparser. Most of the road was through woods, and it seemed incredible that we were but fifteen miles from Boston and in the northern reaches of a megalopolis that stretched south through Richmond, Virginia. On my right was a pasture with black and white Ayrshire cows grazing behind a stone wall piled without benefit of mortar. Then more woods, mostly elm trees with birch trees gleaming through occasionally and a smattering of white pine.

"It's along here somewhere," she said.

"What are we looking for?"

"A dirt road on the left about a half mile past the cow pasture."

"There," I said, "just before the red maple."

She nodded and turned in. It was a narrow road, rocky and humpbacked beneath the wheel ruts. Tree branches scraped the sides and roof of the car as we drove. Dogberry bushes clustered along the edge of the path. A lot of rust-colored rock outcroppings showed among the greenery, and waxy-looking green vines grew among them in the shade, putting forth tiny blue flowers. All that waxy green effort for that reticent little flower.

We pulled around a bend about two hundred yards in and stopped. The land before us was cleared and might once have been a lawn. Now it was an expanse of gravel spattered with an occasional clump of weeds, some of which, coarse and sparse-leafed, looked waist-high. Behind one clump was a discarded bicycle on its back, its wheelless forks pointing up. The scavenged shell of a 1937 Hudson Terraplane rusted quietly at the far edge of the clearing. The remnants of a sidewalk, big squares of cracked cement, heaved and buckled by frost, led up to a one-story house. Once, when it was newly built, an enthusiastic real estate broker might have listed it as a contemporary bungalow. It was a low ranch built on a slab. The siding was asphalt shingle faded now to a pale green. A peak over the front door had been vertically paneled with natural planks, and a scalloped molding, showing traces of pink paint, ran across the front. Attached to the house was a disproportionate cinder block carport, partly enclosed, as if the owner had given up and moved out in mid-mortar. From the carport came the steady whine of a gasoline engine. Not a car, maybe a generator. I saw no utility wires running in from the road.

A narrow mongrel bitch, about knee-high, with pendulous dugs, burrowed in an overturned trash barrel near the front door. A plump brown-haired girl of maybe fourteen sat on the front steps. She had big dark eyes that looked even bigger and darker in contrast with her white, doughy face. She had on a white T-shirt, blue dungarees with a huge flare at the bottom, and no shoes. She was eating a Twinkie and in her right hand held an open can of Coke and a burning filter tip cigarette. She looked at us without expression as we got out of the car and started up the walk.

"I don't like it here," Susan Silverman said.

"That's the trouble with you urban intellectuals," I said. "You have no sense of nature's subtle rhythms."

The girl finished her Twinkie as we reached her and washed it down with the rest of the Coke.

"Good morning," I said.

She looked at me without expression, inhaled most of her filter tip cigarette, and without taking it from her mouth, let the smoke out through her nose. Then she yelled, "Vic."

The screen door behind her scraped open—one hinge was loose—and out he came. Susan Silverman put her hand on my arm.

"You were right," I said. "He is unusual, isn't he?"

Vic Harroway was perhaps five ten, three inches shorter than I, and twenty pounds heavier. Say, 215. He was a body builder, but a body builder gone mad. He embodied every excess of body building that an adolescent fantasy could concoct. His hair was a bright cheap blond, cut straight across the forehead in a Julius Caesar shag. The muscles in his neck and chest were so swollen his skin looked as if it would burst over them. There were stretch marks pale against his dark tan where the deltoid muscles drape over the shoulder and stretch marks over his biceps and in the rigid valley between his pectoral muscles. His abdominal muscles looked like cobblestones. The white shorts were slit up the side to accommodate his thigh muscles. They too showed stretch marks. My stomach contracted at the amount of effort he'd expended, the number of weights he'd lifted to get himself in this state.

He said, "What do you turds want?" Down home hospitality.

I said, "We're looking for Walden Pond, you glib devil you."

"Well there ain't no Walden Pond around here, so screw."

"I just love the way your eyes snap when you're angry," I said.

"If you came out here looking for trouble, you're gonna find it,

Jack. Take your slut and get your ass out of here, or I'll bend you into an earring."

I looked at Susan Silverman. "Slut?" I said.

Harroway said, "That's right. You don't like it? You want to make something out of it?" He jumped lightly off the steps and landed in front of me, maybe four feet away, slightly crouched. I could feel Susan Silverman lean back, but she didn't step back. A point for her. A point for me too, because as Harroway landed I brought my gun out, and as he went into his crouch he found himself staring into its barrel. I held it straight out in front of me, level with his face.

"Let's not be angry with each other, Vic. Let us reason together," I said.

"What the hell is this? What do you want?"

"I am looking for a boy named Kevin Bartlett. I came out here to ask if you'd seen him."

"I don't know anybody named Kevin Bartlett."

"How about the young lady," I asked, still looking at Harroway. "Do you know Kevin Bartlett?"

"No." I heard a match strike and smelled the cigarette smoke as she lit up. Imperturbable.

The generator in the garage whined on. The dog had found a bone and was crunching on it vigorously. There was color on Harroway's cheekbones; he looked as if he had a fever. I was stymied. I wanted to search the place, but I didn't want to turn my back on Harroway. I didn't want to have to herd him and the girl around with me. I didn't want Susan out of my sight. I was trespassing, which bothered me a bit. And I had no reason not to believe them. I didn't know who might be in the house or behind it or in the garage.

"If at first you don't succeed," I said to Susan Silverman, "the hell with it. Come on."

We backed down the sidewalk to her car and got in. Harroway never took his eyes off me as we went. Susan U-turned on the lawn, and we drove away. Another point for Susan. She didn't spin gravel getting out of there.

She didn't say anything, but I noticed her knuckles were white on the steering wheel. When we got back to Main Street, she pulled over to the side of the road and stopped.

"I feel sick," she said. She kept her hands on the wheel and stared straight ahead. She was shivering as if it were cold. "My God, what a revolting creature he was. My God! Like a . . . like a rhinoceros or something. A kind of impenetrable brutality."

I put a hand on her shoulder and didn't say anything.

We sat maybe two minutes that way. Then she put the car in gear again. "I'm okay," she said.

"I'll say."

"What do you think?" she said. "Did you learn anything?"

I shrugged. "I learned where that place is and what Vic Harroway is like. I don't know if Kevin is there or not."

"It seemed like an unpleasant experience for nothing," she said.

"Well, that's my line of work. I go look at things and see what happens. If they were lying, maybe they will do some things because I went there today. Maybe they will make a mistake. The worst thing in any case is when nothing is happening. It's like playing tennis: you just keep returning the ball until somebody makes a mistake. Then you see."

She shook her head. "What if you hadn't had a gun?"

"I usually have a gun."

"But, my God, if you hadn't, or you hadn't reached it in time?"

"I don't know," I said. "It depends on how good Harroway really is. He looks good. But guys that look like that often don't have to fight. Who's going to start up with them? There's a lot to being strong, but there's a lot to knowing how. Maybe someday we'll find out if Harroway knows how."

She looked at me and frowned. "You want to, don't you? You want to fight him. You want to see if you can beat him."

"I didn't like that 'slut' remark."

"Jesus Christ," she said. "You adolescent, you. Do you think it matters to me if someone like Vic Harroway calls me a slut? Next thing you'll challenge him to a duel." She wheeled the car into the high school parking lot and braked sharply.

I grinned at her boyishly, or maybe adolescently.

She put her hand on my forearm. "Don't mess with him, Spenser," she said. "You looked . . ." she searched for a word, "frail beside him."

"Well, anyway," I said, "I'm sorry you had to go. If I'd known, I'd have left you home."

She smiled at me, her even white teeth bright in her tan face. "Spenser," she said, "you are a goddamned fool."

"You think so too, huh?" I said and got out.

11

That afternoon I was in the ID section of the Boston Police Department trying to find out if Vic Harroway had a record. If he did, the Boston cops didn't know about it. Neither did I.

It was almost five o'clock when I left police headquarters on Berkeley Street and drove to my office. The commuters were out, and the traffic was heavy. It took me fifteen minutes, and my office wasn't worth it. It was stale and hot when I unlocked the door. The mail had accumulated in a pile under the mail slot in the door. I stepped over it and went across the room to open the window. A spider had spun a symmetrical web across one corner of the window recess. I was careful not to disturb it. Every man needs a pet. I picked up the mail and sat at my desk to read it. Mostly bills and junk mail. No letter announcing my election to the Hawkshaw Hall of Fame. No invitation to play tennis with Bobby Riggs in the Astrodome. There was a note on pale violet stationery from a girl named Brenda Loring suggesting a weekend in Provincetown in the late fall when the tourists had gone home. I put that aside to answer later.

I called my answering service. They reported five calls from Margery Bartlett during the afternoon. I said thank you, hung up, and dialed the Bartlett number.

"Where on earth have you been?" Margery Bartlett said when I told her who I was. "I've been trying to get you all afternoon."

"I was up to the Boston Athenaeum browsing through the collected works of Faith Baldwin," I said.

"Well, we need you out here, right away. My life has been threatened."

"Cops there?"

"Yes, there's a patrolman here now. But we want you here right away. Someone has threatened my life. Threatened to kill me. You get right out here, Spenser, right away."

"Yes, ma'am," I said, "right away."

I hung up, looked at my watch—five twenty—got up, closed the window, and headed for Smithfield. It was six fifteen when I got there. A Smithfield police cruiser was parked facing the street in the driveway. Paul Marsh, the patrolman I'd met before, was sitting in it, his head tipped back against the headrest, his cap tilted forward. The barrel end of a pump-action shotgun showed through the windshield held upright by a clip lock on the dashboard. I could hear the soft rush of open air on the police radio in the car as I stopped at the open side window near the driver.

"What's happening?" I asked.

He shook his head. "Phone call. Mrs. Bartlett answered and was threatened. Something about evening the score. I didn't talk to her. Trask did. He knows the details. I don't. This was my day off."

"You eaten?"

"No, but one of the guys'll bring me down something in a while."

"I'll be here if you want to shoot out and get something."

Marsh shook his head again. "Naw, Trask would have my ass. I think he's hot for Mrs. Bartlett."

"Okay," I said. "I'll go in and see what she can tell me. Her husband home?"

"Nope. He's still working. I guess. Just her and her daughter and the lawyer, Maguire."

They were in the kitchen. Maguire, small, neat, and worried, let me in. Marge Bartlett in a green crepe pants suit and white shirt with ruffled cuffs was standing against the kitchen counter turning a highball glass in her hands. She was very carefully made-up. At the kitchen table was the same young girl I'd seen going for a swim on my first visit. The Bartletts' daughter, I assumed. She was eating a macaroni and cheese TV dinner and drinking a can of Tab. Her bones were small, her face was delicate and impassive. Her black hair was long and straight. She was wearing a faded yellow sweat shirt that said MAKE LOVE NOT WAR in black letters across the front. The Lab sat on the floor by her chair and watched every mouthful as it moved from the foil container to her mouth.

Marge Bartlett said, "Spenser, where the hell were you?"

"You already asked me that," I said.

Maguire said, "Glad you got here, Spenser."

Marge Bartlett said, "They threatened me. They said they'd . . ." She glanced at her daughter. "Dolly, why don't you finish your supper and go watch TV in the den?"

"Oh, Ma . . . I know what they said. I heard you talking about it with Mr. Trask this afternoon." She drank some Tab.

"Well you shouldn't have. You shouldn't be hearing that sort of thing."

"Oh, Ma."

"What exactly happened, Mrs. Bartlett?" I asked.

"They called about noon," she said.

"Did you record it?"

Maguire said, "No. They took the recorder off this morning about three hours before the call."

"Okay," I said, "what did they say? Be careful and get it as exact as possible."

Dolly said, "Ma, is there any dessert?"

"I don't know. Look in the cupboard and don't interrupt." She turned toward me. "The call came about noon. I was in the study running over my lines. I'm playing Desdemona in a production of *Othello* we're putting on in town. And the phone rang and I answered it. Hoping it might be about Kevin, and a girl's voice said, 'We got Kevin, now we're going to even it up with you. We're going to shoot you in the . . .' and she used a dirty word. It refers to the female sex area. Do you know which one I mean? It starts with *c*." She glanced at her daughter.

"Yeah, I know the word. Anything else?"

"No. She just said that and hung up. Why would she say that?"

I shrugged. Dolly Bartlett got a package of Nutter Butter cookies from the cabinet and another Tab from the refrigerator and sat back down at the table.

"And you didn't recognize the voice?"

"No."

Maguire poured a stiff shot into the glass, added ice and soda, and gave it to Marge Bartlett.

"When you say girl's voice, how old a girl?"

"Oh, a girl. You know, not a woman, a teenager."

Dolly Bartlett said, "Ma, why don't you ever get Coke. I hate Tab."

"Dolly, damn it, will you not interrupt me? Don't you realize that I'm under great stress? You might have a little consideration. The Tab has almost no calories. Don't you care that I'm in danger? Great danger?" Tears began to form, and her lower lip began to quiver. "Oh, goddamn you," she said and hustled out of the room without spilling her drink.

Maguire said, "Aw, Marge, c'mon," rolled his eyeballs at me, and hustled out after her. Dolly Bartlett continued to eat her Nutter Butter cookies.

"My name is Spenser," I said. "I gather you're Dolly."

"Yes," she said. "My name is really Delilah. Isn't that a dumb name?"

"Yeah," I said, "Delilah is kind of dumb."

"Want a cookie?"

I took one. "Thank you."

"You're welcome. Want any Tab?"

"No, thank you." The cookie tasted like a peanut-flavored matchbook.

"She lied to you, you know," Dolly said.

"Your mother?"

"Yes."

"How do you know?"

"I listened upstairs on the other phone. I do it all the time. If you pick it up before she does, she never notices. She's really dumb."

"What did the girl really say when she called?"

"She said they were going to punish my mother for screwing her ass off all over town," Dolly said. She offered Punkin a Nutter Butter cookie. He sniffed it and refused. My respect for him increased. "Then the girl said that about shooting her down there. Isn't that gross?"

"Gross," I said.

"Don't tell my mother I told you."

"I won't. Did the girl say anything else?"

"No."

"Do you think what she said about your mother was true?" That was a nice touch; grill the kid about her mother's sex habits. Nice line of work you're in, Spenser.

"Oh sure. Everybody knows about my mother except maybe Daddy. She screws with everybody. She screws with Mr. Trask, I know."

I wanted to know who else but couldn't bring myself to ask. Instead I said, "Does it bother you?"

"Yeah, of course, but," she shrugged, "you get used to it, you know?"

"I guess you would, wouldn't you."

"Used to drive Kevin crazy, though. I don't know if he ever got used to it like I did."

"It's harder for boys to get used to, maybe," I said. It wasn't too easy for me to get used to. Maybe I should become a florist.

She shrugged again.

Her mother came back into the kitchen, her eyes puffy, with fresh makeup around them. Earl Maguire came with her. Was she screwing with him? Screwing with Mr. Trask? Christ.

Marge Bartlett said, "Dolly, go in the den and watch TV, please, darling. Mommy is upset. It will be better for you to go in there now." She kissed her daughter on top of her head. Dolly picked up the package of cookies. "Come on, Punkin," she said, and the dog followed her out of the kitchen.

"Well, Mr. Spenser, I see you've met my Dolly. Did you and she have a nice talk?"

"Yep."

"Good. Chief Trask has left a patrolman here to guard the house. But I'd feel much safer if you'd stay too."

Earl Maguire said, "We'd expect to pay you extra, of course. Mrs. Bartlett has already talked to her husband, and Rog has authorized payment to you."

"What can I do the cops can't?"

"You can stay close to me," Mrs. Bartlett said. "You can go with me when I shop and go to parties and play rehearsal and things. You can be right here in the house."

"We'd be employing you as a bodyguard," Maguire said.

"While I'm guarding your body, I can't be looking for your kid," I said.

"Just for a little while," she said. "Please? For me?"

"Okay. I'll have to go home and pack a suitcase. You'll be all right with Marsh here. Just stay close till I come back. This may just be a crank call, you know. Kidnappings and disappearances bring out a lot of crank calls."

12

One of the good parts of living alone is when you move out no one minds. It's also one of the bad parts. I went home, packed, and was back at the Bartletts' in an hour and a half.

Roger Bartlett was home from work, and he installed me in a bedroom on the second floor. It was a big pleasant room, paneled in pine planking stained an ice blue. The ceiling was beamed in a crisscross pattern; there was a wide-board floor and a big closet with folding louvered doors and a bureau built in behind them. There was a double bed with a Hitchcock headboard and a patchwork quilt, a pine Governor Winthrop desk, and a wooden rocker with arms and a rush seat that had been done in an antique blue and stenciled in gold. There was a blue and red braided rug on the floor, and the drapes on the windows were a red and blue print featuring Revolutionary War scenes. Very nice.

"You eat supper yet?" Roger Bartlett asked.

"No."

"Me either. Come on down and we'll rustle up a little grub. Gotta eat to live, right?" I nodded.

"Gotta eat to live," he repeated and headed downstairs.

A portable TV on the kitchen counter was showing a ball game. The Sox were playing the Angels, and neither was a contender. It was nearly the end of the season, and the announcers and the crowd noise reflected that fact. There is nothing quite like the sound of a pointless ball game late in the season. It is a very nostalgic sound. Sunday afternoon, early fall, car radio, beach traffic.

Bartlett handed me a can of beer, and I sipped it looking at the ball game. Order and pattern, discernible goals strenuously sought within rigidly defined rules. A lot of pressure and a lot of grace, but no tragedy. The Summer Game.

"What do you think about this stuff, Spenser? What's going on?" Bartlett was cutting slices of breast meat from a roast turkey. "I mean, where's my kid? Why does someone want to kill my wife? What the hell have I ever done to anybody?"

"I was going to ask you," I said.

"What do you mean?"

"I mean this whole thing smells of revenge. It smells of harassment. It just doesn't feel right as a kidnapping. The time between the disappearance and the ransom demand. The peculiar note. The peculiar phone call. The trick with the coffin—someone put a lotta work into that. Now the threatening phone call—if it's not just a crank. Someone doesn't like you or your wife or both."

"But who the hell . . ." Marge Bartlett came in carrying the highball glass. Her lipstick was fresh and her hair was combed and her eye shadow looked newly applied. She poked the glass at her husband. "Fill 'er up," she said and giggled. "Fill 'er up. Or is there a fuel shortage?"

"Why don't you slow down, Marge?" Bartlett said. He took the glass.

"Slow down. Slow down. That's all you can say. Slow down. Well I'm not going to slow down. Live fast, die young, and have a good-looking corpse. That's my motto." She did a pirouette and bumped against the counter. "Everything is slow down with you, Roger. Old slow-down-Roger, that's you."

Bartlett gave her a new drink.

"You want mayonnaise?" he asked me.

"Please," I said. He put a plate of sliced turkey, a jar of mayonnaise, some bread-and-butter pickles, and a loaf of oatmeal bread on the table. "Help yourself," he said.

"My God, Roger," Marge Bartlett said. "Is that how you're going to feed him? No plate? No napkins? Can't you even make a salad? We have those nice mugs for beer that Dolly and I bought you."

"It's a lot better than the way you're feeding him," Bartlett answered. "Or me."

"Oh, certainly. I should be cooking a big meal when my very life has been threatened. I should be keeping your supper warm in the oven when you won't even come home from work to protect me."

"Christ! Trask was here and Paul Marsh and Earl. I was way the hell and gone out past Worcester on a job."

"Well, why don't you work closer to home, anyway? You're never around when I need you."

"I can't find enough work close to home to pay for all the goddamned Scotch you drink."

"You bastard," she said and threw her drink at him. A little Scotch spattered on my turkey sandwich. Not a bad combination.

"Oh, stop showing off for Spenser," Bartlett said. He got a paper towel and wiped up the moisture on the table. She made a new drink.

"I'm sorry, Mr. Spenser. It's just that I'm under great strain, as you might imagine. I'm an artist. I'm volatile; I'm quick to anger."

"Yeah," I said, "both those things. You got a lousy arm, though. You got Scotch on my sandwich."

She drank half her drink. Not only her face but her whole body seemed to get progressively slacker as she drank. Her voice got harsher, while her language got more affected. I wondered if the progress continued until she sank to the floor screaming nonsense. I didn't think I'd find out. I was pretty sure I'd crack first.

"Can you think of any connection between this death threat and Kevin's disappearance?" Slick how smoothly I changed the subject.

"I think someone is out to get us," she said. Oddly, I agreed with her. It made me nervous.

"Who the hell would be out to get us?" Bartlett said. "We haven't got any enemies."

"How about in business? Got anyone mad at you there? Fire anyone? Out-shrewd someone?"

He shook his head. His wife said, "Not good old Rog. Everybody likes good old Rog. Everyone thinks he's so terrific. Everyone feels sorry for him married to a bitch. But I know him. The bastard."

"How about you?" I said to her. "Anyone you can think of that has reason to hate you? Or hates you without reason?" She looked at me blankly. The booze was weaving its magic spell. "Any old boyfriends, disappointed lovers?"

"No"—she shook her head angrily—"of course not."

"Can either of you think of anyone at all who hates you enough to give you this kind of trouble?" Blank stares. "There must be someone. Maybe hate is too strong a word. Who dislikes you the most of anyone you know?"

In a voice thick and furry with booze she said, "Kevin."

Bartlett said, "Marge, for God's sake."

"It's true," she said. "The little sonova bitch hates us."

"Marge, goddamn you. You leave my kid alone. He didn't kidnap himself."

"The little sonova bitch." She was mumbling now.

"She's drunk as a goddamned skunk, Spenser. I'm putting her to bed. Drunk as a skunk." He took her arm, and she sagged protestingly away from him. "Sonova bitch." She began to giggle. "He's the little sonova bitch, and you're the big sonova bitch." She sat down on the floor still giggling. I got up.

"You need any help?" I said.

He shook his head. "I've done this before."

"Okay, then I'll go to bed. Thanks for supper." As I went out of the kitchen I saw Dolly Bartlett scuttle up the stairs ahead of me and into her room. Pleasant dreams, kid.

13

The next morning, Saturday, Kevin's guinea pig turned up. I was sitting at the kitchen table reading the *Globe* when I heard Marge Bartlett scream in the front hall. A short startled scream and then a long steady one. When I got there the front door was ajar, and she was holding an open package about the size of a shoe box. I took it from her. Inside was a dead guinea pig on its back, its short legs sticking stiffly up. I looked out the door. A young Smithfield cop I didn't know came bustling around the corner of the house with a shotgun at high port.

"It's okay," I said. Marge Bartlett continued to scream steadily. Now that I was holding the package her hands were free, and she put both of them over her face. The cop came in holding the shotgun down along the side of his leg, the muzzle pointing at the floor. He looked in the box and made a face. "Jesus Christ," he said.

"It came in the mail," I said. "I suppose it's the same one the kid took with him when he disappeared."

Marge Bartlett stopped screaming. She nodded without taking her hands from her face. The cop said, "I'll call Trask," and headed back for the cruiser in the driveway. I took the box and wrapping paper and dead guinea pig into the kitchen and sat down at the table and looked at them. There was nothing to suggest what killed the guinea pig. The box said THOM MCAN on the cover, and the brown paper in which it had been wrapped looked like all the other brown paper wrapping in the world. The box had been mailed in Boston, addressed to Mrs. Margery Bartlett. There was no return address. They're too smart for me, I thought.

"What does it mean, Spenser?" Marge Bartlett asked.

"I don't know. Just more of the same. I'd guess the guinea pig died, and someone thought it would be a good idea to send it to you. It doesn't look as if it's been killed. That might suggest that Kevin is well."

"Why?"

"Well, a kidnapper or a murderer is not likely to bother keeping a guinea pig, right?"

She nodded. I heard a car spin gravel into the driveway and slam to a stop. I bet myself it was Trask. I won. He came in without knocking.

"Oh, George," Marge Bartlett said, "I can't stand much more."

He crossed to where she was standing and put an arm around her shoulder. "Marge, we're doing what we can. We're working on it around the clock." He looked at me. "Where's the evidence?"

I nodded at the box on the table.

"You been messing with it?" Trask said. Tough as nails.

"Not me, Chief. I've been keeping it under close surveillance. I think the guinea pig is faking."

"Move aside," he said and picked up the box. He looked at the guinea pig and shook his head. "Sick," he said. "Sickest goddamned thing I ever been involved in. Hey, Silveria." The young cop appeared at the back door. He had a round moon face and bushy black hair. His uniform cap seemed too small for his head.

"Take this stuff down to the station and hold it for me. I'll be down in a while to examine it. Send Marsh back here to relieve you."

Silveria departed. Trask took a ball-point pen and a notebook out of his shirt pocket. "Okay, Marge," he said, "let's have it all. When did the package arrive?" I didn't need to dance that circle with them. "Excuse me," I said and went out the back door. The day was new and sunny. All it needed to be September Morn was a nude bathing in the pool. I looked, just to be sure, but there wasn't any. A scarlet tanager flashed across the lawn from the crab apple tree to the barn and disappeared into an open loft where the fake post for a hay hoist that never existed jutted out over the door.

I walked over to the barn. Inside was a collection of power mowers, hedge trimmers, electric clippers, rollers, lawn sweepers, barrels, paint cans, posthole diggers, shovels, rakes, bicycle parts, several kegs of eight-penny nails, some folding lawn chairs, a hose, snow tires, and a beach umbrella. To the right a set of stairs ascended to the loft. On the first step Dolly Bartlett was sitting listening to a portable radio through an earplug. She was eating Fritos from a plastic bag. The dog sat on the floor beside her with his mouth open and his tongue hanging out, panting.

"Good morning," I said.

"Hi." She offered the bag of Fritos to me. I took one and ate it. It wasn't as bad as some things I'd eaten. The Nutter Butter cookies, for instance.

"Had breakfast?" I really know how to talk to kids. After that I could ask her how she was doing in school, or maybe her age. Really get her on my side.

She shook her head and nodded at the Fritos.

"You'd be better off eating the bag," I said.

She giggled. "I bet I wouldn't," she said.

"Maybe not," I said. "Bags aren't nourishing anymore. Now when I was a boy . . ."

She made a face and stuck out her tongue. "Oh," I said, "you heard that line before?"

She nodded. I was competing with the top forty sounds in Boston playing loud in her earphone, and she was only half-listening to me. That was okay because I was only half-saying anything.

"You want to see Kevin's hideout?" she said, one ear still fastened to the radio.

"Yes," I said.

"Come on." She got up carrying the radio and headed up the stairs. Punkin and I scrambled for second position. I won. Still got the old reflexes.

The second floor of the barn was unfinished. Exposed beams, subflooring. At one end a small room had been studded off and

Sheetrock nailed up. Some carpenter tools lay on the floor near it, and a box of blue lathing nails had spilled on the floor. It looked like a project Roger Bartlett was going to do in his spare time, and he didn't have any spare time. There was scrap lumber and Sheetrock trimmings in a pile as if someone had swept them up and gone for a trash barrel and been waylaid. A number of four-by-eight plywood panels in a simulated wood-plank texture were leaning against a wall.

"In here," Dolly said. And disappeared into the studded-off room. I followed. It was probably going to be a bathroom from the size and the rough openings that looked to be for plumbing. A makeshift partition had been constructed out of some paneling and two sawhorses. Behind it was a steamer trunk and a low canvas lawn chair. The steamer trunk was locked with a padlock. The floor was covered with a rug that appeared to be a remnant of wall-to-wall carpeting. The window looked out over the pool and the back of the house. The wiring was in, and a bare light bulb was screwed into a porcelain receptacle. A string hung from it.

"What's in the trunk?" I asked.

"I don't know. Kevin always kept it locked up. He never let me in here."

"Do your mother and father know about this place?"

"I doubt it. My father hasn't worked up here since last summer, and my mother's never been up here. She says it should be fixed up so she can have it for a studio. But she hasn't ever come up. Just me and Kevin, and Kevin always kicked me out when he came up here. He didn't want anyone to know about his place."

"How come you're telling me?"

She shrugged. "You're a detective."

I nodded. I was glad she said that because I was beginning to have my doubts.

"You get along with Kevin?" I asked.

"He's creepy," she said, "but he's okay sometimes." She shrugged again. "He's my brother. I've known him all my life."

"Okay, Dolly, here's what I'm going to do. I'm going to break into that trunk. Maybe it won't have anything that will help, but maybe it will, and the only way to know is to look. I know it's not mine, but maybe it will help us find Kevin, all right?"

"Kevin will be mad."

"I won't tell him about your being here."

"Okay."

I found a pinch bar among the tools on the floor and pried the hasp off the trunk. Inside the cover of the trunk an eight-by-ten glossy was attached with adhesive tape, a publicity still of Vic Harroway in a body-building pose. In the trunk itself was a collection of body-building magazines, a scrapbook, a pair of handsprings that you squeezed to build up your grip, and two thirty-pound dumbbells.

Dolly did an exaggerated shudder. "Gross," she said.

"What?" I said.

"The guy in the picture. Ugh!"

"Do you know him?" I asked.

"No."

I sat down in the lawn chair and picked up the first magazine in the pile. Dolly said, "Are you going to read that?"

I said, "I'm going to read them all."

"Sick," she said.

"They're clues. That's what I'm supposed to do—study clues and after studying enough of them I'm supposed to solve a mystery and . . ."

"Are you going to tell?" she said.

I knew what she meant. Kevin had hidden this stuff from his parents, for whatever reason.

"No," I said. "Are you?"

"No."

I opened a copy of *Strength and Health.* On the inside cover and spilling over onto page 1, there was an ad for high-protein health food and pictures of hugely muscled people who apparently ate it. There were badly laid-out ads for strength-training booklets, weight-lifting equipment, and choker bathing suits; and pictures of weight lifters and Mr. America contestants. On page 39 was a sepia-tone picture of Vic Harroway. He had on a white bikini and was posed on a beach in front of a low shelf of rock that kicked spray up as the sea hit it. His right arm was flexed to show the biceps. His left hand was clamped behind his neck, and he was flexed forward with his right knee bent and the toes of his left leg barely touching the ground. The sun glistened on his features, and his narrowed eyes were fixed on something high and distant and doubtless grand behind the camera. Beauty is its own excuse for being. The caption said, "Vic Harroway, Mr. Northeastern America, Combines Weight

Lifting and Yoga." I read the story. It said the same thing in supermasculine prose that made me want to run out and uproot a tree.

While I read, Dolly Bartlett sat down against the wall with her knees drawn up to her chest and listened to her radio.

I went through all the strength magazines. They dated back five years, and each of them had a story on Vic Harroway. I learned how Vic trained down for "that polished look." I learned Vic's diet-supplement secrets for gaining "ten to fifteen pounds of solid muscles." I learned Vic's technique for developing "sinewy and shapely underpinnings." I didn't learn much about Vic's theories on kidnapping and harassment or if he might know where Kevin Bartlett was.

I looked at the scrapbook. It was what I thought it would be. Clippings of Vic Harroway's triumphs in body-building contests. Ads announcing the opening of a new health spa where Vic Harroway would be the supervisor of physical conditioning. Fifteen-year-old newspaper clippings of Vic Harroway as a high school football hero in Everett. Snapshots of Vic and one of Vic and Kevin with Vic's arm around Kevin's shoulder. Harroway was smiling. Kevin looked very serious.

"Did Kevin lift weights?" I asked Dolly.

"No. I remember he wanted to buy a set once, but my mother wouldn't let him."

"Why not?"

"I don't know. She said it would make him big and beefy and stuff, you know?"

I nodded.

"They had a big fight about it."

I nodded again.

"Would it?"

"Would it what?"

"Would it make him big and beefy?"

"Not if he did it right," I said. I took the publicity shot of Harroway, put the magazines and the scrapbook back in the trunk, and closed it. Dolly and the dog and I went downstairs. The dog edged me out on the way down, and I was last. In the driveway Marge Bartlett was standing looking impatiently into the open barn. She had on a pale violet pants suit with huge cuffed bell-bottoms and blunt-nosed black shoes poking out underneath. A big burlap purse with a crocheted design hung from her shoulder. She wore white lipstick, and her nails were polished in a pale lavender.

"Come on, Dolly, time to go to Aunt Betty's. Hop in the car."

"Aw, Ma, I don't want to go over there again."

"Come on now, no arguing. Hop in the car. I've got a lot of shopping to do. The party is tonight, and I don't want you in the way. You know how nervous I get when I'm having a big party. And while I'm at the shopping center I don't want you here alone. It's too dangerous."

I went to my car and put the photo in the glove compartment.

"Well, lemme stay with Mr. Spenser."

Marge Bartlett shook her head firmly. "Not on your life. Mr. Spenser is my bodyguard, and he'll have to go with me to the shopping center." She clapped her hands once, sharply. "In the car."

Dolly climbed into the backseat of the red Mustang. Marge Bartlett got in behind the wheel, and I sat beside her. The dog stood in front of the car with his ears back and stared at us.

"Can I bring Punkin?" Dolly asked.

"Absolutely not. I don't want him getting the car all muddy, and Aunt Betty can't stand dogs anyway."

"He's not muddy," Dolly said.

The cop in the Smithfield cruiser poked his head out the side window and said, "Where you going?"

"It's all right. Mr. Spenser is with me. We'll be gone most of the day, shopping."

"Whoopee," I said. "All day."

The cop nodded. "Okay, Mrs. Bartlett. I'm going to take off then. You let us know when you're back, and Chief'll send someone up."

He started the cruiser and headed down the drive. We followed. He turned left. We turned right.

14

The north shore shopping center was on high ground north off Route 128 in Peabody. Red brick, symmetrical evergreens, and parking for eight thousand cars. I discovered that Marge Bartlett was a member of the shopping center the way some people belong to a country club. Between ten fifteen and one twenty she charged $375 worth of clothes. I spent that time watching her, nodding approval when she asked my opinion, keeping a weather eye out for assailants, and trying not to look like a pervert as I stood around outside a series of ladies' dressing rooms. I was glad I hadn't worn my white raincoat. There were a lot of very well-shaped suburban ladies shopping in the same stores. Suburban ladies tended to wear their clothes quite snug, I noticed. I was alert for concealed weapons.

We got back to Smithfield at about a quarter of two. The house was still. Roger Bartlett worked Saturdays, and Dolly was going to spend the night with Aunt Betty. Punkin lay placidly in a hollow under some bushes to the right of the back door. Marge Bartlett held the door for me as I carried in the shopping bags. The dog came in behind us.

"Put them on the couch in the living room," she said. "I want to call the caterer."

There was a corpse in the living room. On the floor, face down, with its head at a funny angle. I dropped the shopping bags and went back to the kitchen with my gun out.

Marge Bartlett was still on the phone with her back to me. No one was in sight. The back door was closed. The dog had settled under the kitchen table. I turned back to the living room and stood in the center, beside the corpse, and held my breath and listened. Except for Marge Bartlett talking with animation about a jellied salad, there was no sound.

I put the gun back in the hip holster and squatted down beside the corpse and looked at its face. It had been Earl Maguire. That's it for the law practice, Earl. I picked up one hand and bent the forefinger back and forth. He was cold and getting stiff. I put the hand down. All the college and all the law school and all the cramming for the bar, and someone snaps your neck for you when you're not much more than thirty. I looked around the room. A glass-topped rug was bunched toward Maguire's body. A fireplace poker lay maybe two feet beyond Maguire's outflung hand. An abstract oil painting was on the floor beneath a picture hook on the wall as if it had fallen.

I duck-walked over to the poker and looked at it without touching it. There was no sign of blood on it. I stood up and went to the front door. The lock button in the middle of the knob was in. The door was locked. I'd seen Marge Bartlett unlock the back door. I opened the front door. No sign of it being jimmied. There'd been no sign of jimmying on the back door. I'd have noticed when we came in. There weren't any other doors. I walked across the front hall to the dining room. It was undisturbed except that the door to the liquor cabinet was open. There was a lot of booze inside. It didn't look as if any was missing.

I heard Marge Bartlett hang up. I headed for the kitchen and cut her off before she got to the door.

"Stay here," I said.

"Why?"

"Earl Maguire is dead in your living room."

"My God, the party's in six hours."

"Inconsiderate bastard, wasn't he," I said.

She opened her mouth and then put both hands over it and pressed and didn't say anything. "Sit there," I said and steered her to a kitchen chair. She kept her hands over her mouth and watched me minutely while I called the cops. When she heard me say Maguire's neck was broken, she made a muffled squeak.

Five minutes later Trask arrived with a bald, fat old geezer who carried a black bag like the ones doctors used to carry when they made house calls. He eased himself down on his knees beside the body and looked at it. He was too fat to squat.

"When'd he die, Doc?" Trask had a notebook out and held a yellow Bic Banana pen poised over it to record the answer.

The doctor was strained for breath, kneeling down like that; it didn't help his temperament. "Before we got here," he said.

Trask got a little redder. "I know that, goddamn it. What I want to know is how long before we got here?"

"How the hell do I know, George? I don't even know what killed him, yet. His neck looks broken." The doctor picked up Maguire's head and turned it back and forth. A dark bruise ran along his cheek from the earlobe to the corner of his mouth. "Yep, neck's broken."

"What time you find him, Spenser?" Trask decided to question me. It wasn't going well with the doctor.

"Quarter of two."

"Exactly?"

"Approximately."

"Well, goddamn it, can't you be more exact? You're supposed to be some kind of hot stuff. I want to know the exact time of the discovery of the deceased. It could be vital."

"Only in the movies, Trask."

Trask looked past me and said, "Hello, Lieutenant." I turned and it was Healy. He had on the same straw hat with the big headband that I'd seen him in before. His jacket was gray tweed with a muted red line forming squares in it. Gray slacks, white shirt with a button-down collar, and a narrow black knit tie. Tan suede desert boots. He had his hands in his hip pockets, and his face was without expression as he looked down at the body.

"Worse and worse," he said.

Trask said, "This is Doc Woodson, Lieutenant. He was just saying that Maguire died of a broken neck."

"No, I didn't, George. I said his neck was broken. I didn't say it killed him."

"Well, it didn't help him none. That's for damned certain," Trask said.

Healy said, "When can you give me a report on him, Doctor Woodson?"

"We'll take him down Union Hospital now, and I can have something for you by, say, suppertime." He looked at me. "Gimme a hand up, young fella; you look strong enough." I helped him up. The effort left him red-faced, and there was sweat on his forehead. "Don't get the exercise I should," he said.

"Who found the body?" Healy asked.

Trask said, "Spenser," and jerked his head in my direction. I got the feeling he wished I were the body.

"Okay, tell me about it." Healy squatted down on his heels beside the corpse and looked at it while I told him.

"Doors locked when you got here?"

"Yep, both of them. Mrs. Bartlett opened the back door with a key, and the front door was locked. I checked it."

"Let's check again," Healy said. We walked to the front door. Healy opened it, went outside, shut it behind him, and tried the knob. Locked. I opened it for him from the inside. We went to the back door. Healy did the same thing. Same result. I let him in. We walked around looking at the windows. Most of them were closed and locked. Those that weren't locked were screened. There was no sign they'd been tampered with. The screens were aluminum, part of screen and storm combinations.

"Someone could have gone out, reached back in, released the catches, and lowered the screen," I said, "to make it look like it was inside business."

Healy nodded absently. "Yeah," he said, "but why would someone do that?"

"Misdirect the cops," I said.

"Maybe," Healy said.

" 'Course with Chief Trask on the track," I said, "you probably don't need too much misdirection."

Healy separated a peppermint Life Saver from the roll and popped it into his mouth. He didn't offer me one. "Well, he's just a hick cop. Not a high-powered fast gun in from the city. Couldn't even solve a simple missing person squeal." He sucked on the Life Saver. "You find the kid yet?"

"Nope."

Healy said, "Oh."

We went back to the living room. The photographs had been taken. The measurements made. The corpse was wrapped in a blanket and lying on a stretcher. Trask looked at Healy. Healy nodded and Trask said, "Okay, let's get him out of here."

Two Smithfield cops picked up the stretcher and went out the front door.

"Union Hospital," Trask yelled after them. "And tell 'em it's for Doc Woodson when you get there."

"Anything missing, Trask?" Healy asked.

"Mrs. Bartlett says no. She don't see anything gone. Liquor cabinet was open but nothing missing."

Marge Bartlett was sitting with her knees pressed together on the couch. The lines around her mouth seemed to have deepened. She needed to freshen her makeup.

"What was he doing here, Mrs. Bartlett?" Healy said.

"Who?"

"Maguire. What was Maguire doing in your house while you were away?"

"Oh, Earl has his own key. He's an old and dear friend. He often lets himself in. We're having a party tonight, and he said he'd come out early and help me set up the bar and things because Roger wouldn't be able to get home till after supper. Almost time for . . . My God"—she looked at her watch—"it's after four. My company is coming in three and a half hours. I've got to get ready. Spenser, you're going to have to help me."

I nodded. Healy said, "Do you have any idea, Mrs. Bartlett, who might have done this?"

"To Earl? I don't know. He was a lawyer; perhaps he made enemies." She shrugged. "I don't know. Lieutenant, I simply must get ready. I'm having sixty-five people here tonight. And I'm already very late." She was on her feet moving toward the hall as she spoke.

Healy looked at her with a puzzled expression. "It's grief, Lieutenant," I said. "She's hiding her grief and carrying on."

Healy snorted. Trask said, "Well, she is. She's being damned brave."

"Brave," Healy said.

"I'll question her later on," Trask said, "when she's gotten herself together more. Ya know."

"Yeah," Healy said, "you do that."

Trask said, "Got any theories, Lieutenant?"

"I'd guess someone was in here expecting no one to be home, and Maguire came in and surprised him. There was a fight, Maguire went for the poker, and whoever it was hit him with something else and broke his neck. Then he got out of here."

"From the way the rug's bunched up and the body's lying, I figure he came at him from the dining room," I said.

Healy said, "Maybe."

Trask said, "How'd he get in?"

"That's a problem. Maybe one of the screens was unlocked or the door was ajar. Maybe somebody had a key."

Trask looked shocked. "Wait a minute, who the hell would have a key except the family?"

Healy shrugged. "Maybe the lock was picked," Trask said.

"How long you been chief here?" Healy asked.

"Seven years," Trask said. "Before that I was a sergeant."

"How many people have you run into out here that can pick that kind of a lock?" I said.

"There's always a first time."

"We'll wait and see what the doctor can give us," Healy said. "If I was you, Trask, I'd put a man here."

"I had one, but when Mrs. Bartlett went off with Spenser, I took him off. She was supposed to call when she came back. I only got twelve goddamned men, Healy."

"I know. Spenser, you hanging in here?"

"Yeah. I'm staying in the guest room. If you get a chance, let me know what the doctor says about cause of death."

"Oh, of course," Healy said. "Want I should iron your shirts for you or anything while I'm here?"

I let that pass. "Well," I said, "time to dig out the old gold lamé tux and freshen up for the party."

Both Trask and Healy looked very sourly at me. I knew how they felt. I felt the same way.

15

Helping Margery Bartlett overcome her grief involved a lot of housework. The caterer arrived about twenty minutes after they'd hauled Maguire away in a blanket. He had two eight-foot tables in his truck and enough food to cover both of them. It was warm and I had my coat off. The caterer's assistant stared covertly at the gun on my hip but made no comment. I helped them set up the tables and carry in the food.

Marge Bartlett was hustling about in a passion of haste, directing me where to put the cold ham and what kind of silverware needed to go beside the schmaltz herring. Roger Bartlett got home about six o'clock and was told to set up the bar before he was told about Earl Maguire.

"Sonova bitch," he said, "sonova bitch." He kept shaking his head as he lined the bottles up on the counter in the kitchen. At six thirty Marge Bartlett retired to her room to begin getting ready, and Roger Bartlett went down to the store for soda. I called Susan

Silverman. It was late on a Saturday, but there was no harm trying, and if I had to stand around at a cocktail party in the subs, I might as well have a date. She answered on the second ring.

"Mrs. Silverman, I'm calling to tell you that you've won the Jackie Susann look-alike contest. First prize is an evening with a sophisticated sleuth at the Bartletts' cocktail party tonight."

"And second prize is two evenings," she said.

"Well, I'm doing guard duty here, and I wondered if you wanted to come along and carry my ammo."

"Seriously?"

"Seriously."

"Okay. What is anyone wearing?"

"I would say it's dress-up stuff. You know, sixty-five people. The food catered. A punch bowl. Ice sculpture. White linen tablecloth. Real silver. Mrs. Bartlett has started getting ready, and the guests don't come till eight."

"All right, I'll dress accordingly. Will you pick me up?"

"No, I'm sorry, I can't. There was a murder here today and Mrs. Bartlett's been threatened and I can't leave her. Can you drive yourself over okay?"

"A murder? Who?"

"The Bartletts' lawyer, Earl Maguire. I'll tell you about it tonight."

"What time do I arrive?"

"Eight o'clock."

"See you then."

I said good-bye. There was a pause at the other end, then she said, "Jackie Susann?"

"Maybe it was Jackie O.," I said.

She said, "Well, it's better than Jackie Coogan, I suppose," and hung up.

Bartlett came back in the house with a case of club soda and put it on the floor beside the refrigerator.

"I'm going to take a shower," I told him. "Lock the door and don't let anyone in till I'm back down here. Okay?" I was much jumpier about the threats to Marge Bartlett since Maguire had turned up dead.

"Well, don't be long," he said. "I gotta get ready too."

"Ten minutes," I said.

"Right."

"Oh, by the way, I've invited a woman I know, Mrs. Silverman from the high school. I hope you don't mind."

"Mind? Hell no. A man needs some female companionship, long as he doesn't get carried away and end up married. You know? Don't need to be married to have fun. Right? Don't need that."

"Sure don't," I said, heading up the stairs.

I stuck to my word and was out of the shower in four minutes and dressed in another five. I put on a dark blue two-button suit with wide lapels and a shaped waist, a blue and white checked shirt, and a wide red tie striped blue and black. I didn't have any shoe polish, but I managed to freshen up my black boots with some Kleenex. I clipped my gun on and went back downstairs. I hoped there'd be no gunplay tonight. My hip holster was brown, and it didn't go with my outfit.

At eight the first guests began to arrive. Marge Bartlett was still getting ready, but her husband was there at the door dressed fit to kill. He had on a green and gold paisley-print jacket that was loose-fitting around the collar, a yellow shirt with long collar points, a narrow green and red paisley tie, brown flared slacks with cuffs, and black and brown blunt-toed stacked-heel shoes that made him walk a little awkwardly. His tailor looked to be Robert of Hall. How he must have yearned for a blue work shirt and khaki pants.

I stood around the hall with a can of beer in my hand as Bartlett let the guests in. He kept saying "Say hello to old Spenser here; he's a detective," which produced a lot of warm handshakes. I felt like a weed at a flower show.

Susan Silverman showed up at eight thirty, and a lot of people, mostly but not exclusively men, turned and looked at her. She was wearing a full-length backless dress with red and black flowers against a white background. The top tied in two thin strings around her neck. Her arms and back were still tanned from summer, and her black hair glistened. She had red earrings and fingernails to match. I introduced her to Bartlett.

"Hey," he said, "aren't you down the high school?"

"Yes, I'm a guidance counselor."

"Boy, they didn't look like you when I was in high school. Hey, Spenser? I bet they didn't look like that in your high school, huh?"

"No," I said, "nothing like that."

Marge Bartlett appeared. She was carrying a dark Scotch and water in one hand and seemed the ultimate triumph of Elizabeth

Arden. No hint of flesh showed through the uninterrupted gleam of her makeup. She wore a violet lavender top with long puffy sleeves and a deep neckline that showed a lot of cleavage. The kind of cleavage that required artifice. There were false eyelashes and pale lipstick and lavender nail polish the color of the eye shadow. Her lower half was covered in black crepe that dragged on the floor. I could never tell if it was a skirt or pants, and I forgot to ask Susan. Small black beads, maybe obsidian, hung in several coils from her neck, and black and lavender earrings swayed like exotic fruit from her ears. Her lavender shoes were open-toed with very high black heels. Her toenails were painted the same color as her fingernails.

Everything fitted very snugly, and one got a sense of Latex stretched, of pressures tightly contained. Her bright blond hair was artfully tousled over her forehead and doubtless sprayed in place. She embraced one of the men, a short, fat guy with a long crew cut and a guardsman mustache, holding her head back so's not to mess her hair and turning away as he tried to kiss her so's not to mess the makeup.

"Vaughn, you gorgeous hunk," she cried, "if your wife weren't such a good friend of mine—"

Two more couples arrived, and she turned toward them, leaving Vaughn with his mouth half-open. The wives, one tall and handsome with early gray salting her black hair, the other small, blond, and pretty, stopped to talk with Marge Bartlett; the husbands headed directly for the buffet spread in the dining room. I watched them go. One was middle height and muscular with rounded shoulders and the kind of rolling walk associated normally with sailors and gorillas. His buddy was shorter and wider with the body of a Turkish wrestler and the haircut of a monk.

"Beer," I said to Susan. "And I'll bet they never leave the buffet."

"The taller one's the hockey coach at the high school," she said.

"How about the other guy?"

"I don't know him; maybe he's a violinist."

"Yeah," I said, "or an elephant tamer."

Marge Bartlett moved into the living room, where the noise and smoke were already thickening. I said to Susan, "Come on. Whither she goest you and I goest as well. Or at least I do."

"Whither thou goest . . ." she said.

"How about whither I liest?" I said.

"I'm going to get us a drink. You want one?"

"Beer," I said. "I'm sorry it's self-service, but I'm working."

"I know."

She left me and returned shortly with a can of beer and a Scotch on the rocks. She gave me the beer. Marge Bartlett had settled herself carefully on one arm of the living room sofa, not far from where Earl Maguire had gotten his neck broken. She was talking with three businessy-looking guys and inhaling her wine-dark Scotch and water.

"What happened here today?" Susan Silverman asked. We stood in the archway that separated the living room from the front hall, and she rested one hand lightly on my upper arm. I restrained the urge to flex it.

"Somebody hit a lawyer named Earl Maguire on the side of the head so hard it broke his neck and he died. Or that's probably what happened. I found him here dead with his neck broken and a large bruise on the side of his face."

"Do you have any idea who?"

"Nope, nor why. There had been a threatening phone call directed at Mrs. Bartlett that seemed as bizarre and disjointed as everything else going on here. That's why I'm doing my centurion routine."

"And she's going on with the party just like this?" Susan shook her head. "I don't know if that's courage or obsession or madness."

"I don't either," I said, "but courage doesn't seem the most likely choice."

A middle-sized handsome man stopped in front of us. "A real blast, huh?" he said.

"Yeah," I said. "Fake ones are better than none, though."

"You bet your ass," he said. He slurred the *s*'s, and I realized he was drunk already. "Marge and Rog really know how to throw a blast. What you do?"

"I'm a grape stomper at a winery. I stopped by here to get my feet bleached."

Susan Silverman giggled at my elbow. I said, "It's an old George Gobel line." The handsome man said, "I'm into confidence training myself. If you believe in your product, then, by God, you can sell it, ya know? And the greatest product ya got to sell is yourself. Right?"

"I don't know," I said. "I'm not sure I'm for sale."

"Oh, yeah. Look, you wouldn't believe the change a confidence seminar can make in your whole approach to living. I mean, it's like getting psyched up for a football game, ya know? I'm going all over the state having these confidence seminars, and the results are fantastic, fan-tastic."

"How about not giving one right now though; my ears are beginning to smart."

"You got some terrific sense of humor. What did you say your name was?"

"Spenser."

"Well, Spence, you got some terrific sense of humor. I like that. This the little woman?"

Susan Silverman looked as if she were carsick.

He went on, "I was into losing, ya know? And so I took this confidence seminar and they showed me how I wasn't using all my potential and now I'm part of the team and running the seminars myself. What'd you say you did?"

"I said I was a grape crusher at a winery, but I was only kidding."

"Yeah, I got that. What's your real job? I mean, maybe I could help you or your people, ya know? Maybe you could use a little confidence."

Susan Silverman said, "Do you have a program for overconfidence?"

He frowned. "No. But you know, there might be a market there. You got a pretty good head for business for a lady. By God, I never thought of that." He moved off.

Marge Bartlett said something to one of the businessy types and stood up. He gave her a slap on the rear end, and all three men on the couch laughed. Marge Bartlett moved away and headed for the kitchen. I moved along after her. Susan said, "I'll be along. I think I'll sample the buffet before those two guys finish it."

As I passed the dining room, I noticed the coach and his buddy still at the buffet. A colony of beer cans had sprung up on the highboy beside them. In the kitchen Roger Bartlett was mixing drinks at the counter from half-gallons of booze. A plastic trash can was filled with chopped ice and beer cans, and a whole ham garnished with fruit was being readied for the buffet table. I wondered if the two gourmets in the corner had already polished off the first one. It would be fun to join them and comment on the broads and make wisecracks about the other guests and eat and drink till it became self-destructive and have your wife drive home. That would be more fun than finding a guy with his neck snapped, or going one-on-one with a weight lifter. Or following Marge Bartlett around all evening. I looked around for Mr. Confidence. I needed a booster shot.

Bartlett poured a glass near full of Scotch, added an ice cube and a teardrop's worth of water, and gave it to his wife. She took a big drink and said, "Whoooo, that's strong. You want me to get drunk so you can take advantage of me."

"Dear, by the time I get to the bedroom tonight, you'll be snoring like a hog."

"Roger!" she said and turned away. She saw me standing in the doorway and came over.

"My God, Spenser, you're a big handsome brute," she said and leaned against me with her right arm around me.

I said, "You're really into words, aren't you?"

"He's my bodyguard," Marge Bartlett said to a woman with bags under her eyes and a pouty mouth. "Don't you think I ought to keep my body very close to him so he can guard it?" She made snuggling motions at me. Pressed against me, she felt tightly cased and ready to burst, like a knockwurst.

The woman with the baggy eyes said, "Someone should guard your body, sweetie, that's for sure."

I said, "You're leaning on my gun arm."

She put her mouth up close to my ear and said, "I could lean on something else, if you were nice."

"It wouldn't carry the weight," I said.

"You're awful," she said and stepped away from me.

I said, "All us big handsome brutes are like that."

Baggy-eyes snickered, and Marge Bartlett spotted Mr. Confidence across the kitchen and went after him.

"Are you really a bodyguard?" Baggy-eyes said.

"Yep."

"Do you have a gun?"

"No," I said. "I have this mysterious power I acquired in the Orient to cloud men's minds so they cannot see me."

Susan appeared with an assorted platter from the buffet table and offered me some. "I have two forks," she said. Baggy-eyes moved off. Marge Bartlett and Mr. Confidence were in close proximity across the kitchen. I wondered if she had called him a big handsome brute.

"Having a nice time?" Susan asked.

"It's better than getting bitten by a great white shark," I said.

"Oh, it's not that bad. In fact, you kind of like it. I've been watching you. You look at everything; you listen to everybody. I bet you know what everyone in the kitchen is talking about and what they look like. They fascinate you."

"Yeah," I said, "I'm into people."

"Oh, you're such a big tough guy, and you think you're funny, but I'll bet if that fool with the confidence courses got in trouble, you'd get him out of it."

"A catcher in the rye," I said.

"You're being smart, I know, but that's right. That's exactly what you are. You are exactly that sentimental."

The wall phone in the kitchen rang. A thin woman said, "Oh, Christ, that's my kid, I'll bet anything." And a tall white-haired man with a red face and a green polka-dot bow tie answered. "Duffy's Tavern, Archie the manager speaking." He listened and then he said, "Anybody here named Spenser?" The thin woman said, "Whew." I took the phone and said hello.

"Mr. Spenser? This is Mary Riordan at the State Police. Lieutenant Healy asked me to call you and tell you that Earl Maguire died of a broken neck, apparently the result of being struck on the side of the face with a solid blunt object."

"Son of a gun," I said. "Thank you."

She hung up. Susan looked at me and raised her eyebrows.

"Nothing," I said. "Just a confirmation on the cause of death. I asked Healy to let me know, and he did. I didn't think he would."

"Who's Healy?" she asked.

"State cop."

I looked across the kitchen and was suddenly aware that I didn't know where Marge Bartlett was. "Where'd Marge Bartlett go?" I said to Susan.

"I don't know. Just a minute ago she was over there talking to a fat guy with a mustache."

I walked through the kitchen to the dining room. And on into the living room. No sign. I felt the first small tug of anxiety in my stomach. Atta boy, lose your goddamned assignment in her own house. On either side of the fireplace in the living room were French doors, thinly curtained. One was slightly ajar, and I walked toward it. Outside I heard someone say in a half scream, "Don't, don't." The little tug in my solar plexus darted up to my throat, and I jumped through the door. I was on a screened porch that ran the whole side of the house. In the dim light I could see a man and a woman struggling. The man had his back to me, but I could see the woman's face across his shoulder, white in the dimness. It was Marge Bartlett. She wrenched away from him as I came onto the porch. I took one step with my left foot, planted it, turned sideways, and drove my right foot into the small of the man's back. He said, "Ungh," and went headfirst through the screen and into a mass of forsythia. I went after him. Marge Bartlett was screaming. The man was sluggishly trying to get out of the forsythia. I got his right arm bent up behind him and my left hand clamped under his chin and dragged him back onto the porch.

He was protesting, but not coherently. The porch light snapped on. People were crowding out on the porch. The guy I had hold of was Vaughn, the fat man with the crew cut and the big mustache who had been one of the first to arrive.

"Goddamned tease," he was yelling now. "She got me out here; I didn't do anything. Goddamned stinking tease. Get you hot and then scream when you touch her. Bastard. Bitch." There were scratches on his face where he went through the screen. There was lipstick on his face too. I looked at Marge Bartlett; her lipstick was smudged. The deep V-neck of her blouse was torn, and some of a black longline bra showed.

"Let him go, Spenser. Are you crazy? We were just talking. For God's sake, haven't you ever been to a party? We were just talking, and I guess he got the wrong idea. You know how men are." Dimly visible through her makeup her face seemed to be red. "They always get the wrong idea. I was just surprised. I could have handled this. Look at my screen. Look . . ." I let the man go.

"Goddamned liar. You got me out here and started playing goddamned kissy-face with me and rubbing your boobs up against me and when I get serious you start screaming and yelling and your goddamned gorilla comes charging out and hits me from behind."

"Gorilla?" I said.

Susan Silverman had come up beside me. "*Goddamned* gorilla," she said.

16

It was two thirty-five in the morning. The noise was dense and tangible in the living room. Marge Bartlett had changed from a lavender to a yellow top, and the lavender trimmings she still wore glared more brusquely than ever. Vaughn, his back sore but unbroken, had collected his very silent and thin-mouthed wife and departed. The stereo was playing, and Billie Holiday's remarkable voice cut through the coarse air. ". . . *Papa may have, but God bless the child that's got his own* . . ." I edged a little closer so I could listen.

Two women, one red-haired, one brunette, both wearing pants suits a little tighter than they should be, were talking between me and the speakers.

"Do you think she'll pass out?"

"Why should this party be different?"

"She's got to be drunk out of her mind to be wearing that top with those earrings. She'd never do that sober. One thing you can always say for Margie, her taste in clothes is terrific."

"It's a little wild for her age."

Across the room Susan was talking with a tall, thin dark-faced man with flaring nostrils that gave him the look of an Arabian horse. It was Dr. Croft. His hair was short and slicked straight back. His sideburns, thin and barbered, came to his jawline. He patted her hip. I squeezed past the fashion commentary and came up beside Susan and put my hand on her shoulder.

"Oh, Spenser," she said, "I'd like you to meet Doctor Croft."

I said, "We met briefly. How are you, Doctor Croft?"

He smiled and put out his hand. "Ray," he said. "Good to see you again."

We shook hands. His fingers were very long and showed the marks of a manicurist. They thickened at the ends.

"What's your specialty?" I asked.

"General practice." Again the big brilliant smile. When he smiled, the lines around his mouth became very pronounced. "I'm a specialist in general practice. It's what medicine is about, I believe. People to people. Is Mrs. Silverman here with you?"

"Yes." I phrased a remark about hip touchers but thought it would be immature to make it. So I didn't.

"I understand you're a detective."

"Yes."

"I understand you kicked Vaughn Meadows through a screen a little while ago." His wide mouth was almost lipless, and when he smiled he looked less like an Arabian horse and more like a shark.

"Mistaken identity," I said.

"That's okay," he said. "Vaughn Meadows would be a far better person if someone would give him a kick in the ass about weekly." His smile shut off, and a serious frown replaced it. "It's a terrible sequence of things that has befallen this family."

I nodded. Susan said, "Isn't it? The Bartletts seem so resilient, though. They keep bearing up."

"How about the boy?" Croft asked. "Is there any trace of him?"

I shook my head. "Haven't been able to look for him lately. I've had to stick around his mom."

Croft rattled the ice cubes in his glass. "Looks like I'm empty," he said. "Excuse me while I fix myself a new one. Getting through one of these parties sober is more than I could do." He bared his brilliant shark smile again and then closed it off like a trap shutting and went to the kitchen.

"He appeared to be patting you on the hip," I said.

"That's why you came over." Susan smiled and shook her head. "Were you prepared to defend my virtue?"

"I'm in pursuit of it myself, and I don't like poachers."

"He's a very big man in this town," Susan said. "Board of Selectmen, Conservation Commission, adviser to the Board of Health, used to be Planning Board chairman. All the best people have him when they're sick."

"He's a hip patter," I said.

"Very wealthy," she said. "Very big house."

"Pushy bastard," I said.

"I wonder what it is in women," she said. "Whenever they find a big strong guy with a wide adolescent streak running through him, they get a powerful urge to hold his head in their laps."

"Right here?" I said.

"About now I think we could probably marry and raise a family here without anyone noticing."

She was right. It looked like a Busby Berkeley production of Dante's *Inferno.* To my left in the dining room the food was scattered on the table and floor. The platters were nearly empty, and the tablecloth was stained and littered with potato salad, cole slaw, miniature meatballs, tomato sauce, mustard, ham scraps, ring tabs, ashes, and things unrecognizable. The detritus of jollity.

The hockey coach had departed, but his buddy remained, red-eyed and nearly motionless, in his oversized right hand a can of beer, and a platoon, perhaps a company, of its dead companions in silent formation on the highboy beside him. His wife was speaking sharply to him with no effect.

Marge Bartlett was back on the couch between two of the business types in the razor-styled haircuts and the double knit suits. She was talking thickly, her mouth loose and wet, an iceless drink in her right hand, her left rubbing the thigh of one of the men. As she talked, the two men exchanged grins behind her head, and one of them rolled his eyes upward and stuck his tongue out of the left corner of his mouth.

"I'm a very nice person," she was saying. It came out "nishe pershon."

"Hey Marge," one of the business types said, "you know the definition of a nice girl?"

"One who puts it in for you," I murmured to Susan.

"I know," she said. "It's a very old joke."

"One that puts it in for you," the business type answered his own question, and both men laughed very loudly.

Marge Bartlett looked puzzled, a look I'd seen before. She took a slug from her glass.

Roger Bartlett had gone to bed. The good-looking guy who ran confidence courses seemed to be running one in the oversize chair in the corner with a woman I hadn't seen before. There was a flash of bare thigh and lingerie as they moved about.

"Maybe I *will* take that guy's confidence seminar," I said to Susan.

She looked and glanced away quickly. "Jesus," she said, "I think I'm shocked."

"I guess you don't want to make reservations for the chair later on then?"

She shook her head. "That poor kid," she said. "No wonder he's gone."

"Kevin?"

She nodded.

"You think he ran away?"

"Wouldn't you," she said, "if you lived here?"

"I've been thinking about it," I said.

17

Marge Bartlett got to bed about four. I helped her up the stairs, and she stumbled into her bedroom in a kind of stupefied silence. The lights were on. Roger Bartlett was sleeping on his back with his mouth open. On the bureau a small color TV set flickered silently, the screen empty, a small barren buzz coming from it. Marge Bartlett moved painfully toward her twin bed. I closed the door, went to the guest room, undressed, and flopped on the bed. If I lived here, I might run away. The room was warm, and some of the smoke from downstairs had drifted up. But if the kid ran away, why the merry prankster kidnap gig? Why all that childish crap with the coffin? Maybe that was it. Childish. It was the kind of thing a kid would do. Why? "The little sonova bitch hates us," Marge Bartlett had said. But Maguire, that wasn't the kind of thing a kid would do. Or could do. Somebody had hit Maguire very hard. Where would the kid go if he ran away? Harroway's place? He had something for Harroway, obviously. Harroway could hit somebody very hard. I fell asleep.

When I woke up it was ten o'clock. No one else was up. I stood for a long time under the shower before I got dressed. Downstairs looked like the rape of Nanking. Everywhere there was the smell of stale cigarettes and booze and degenerating shrimp salad. Punkin appeared very pleased to see me and capered around my legs as I let him out the back door. The Smithfield police cruiser was parked in the driveway again. Ever vigilant. I found an electric percolator and made coffee. I brought a cup out to the cop in the driveway.

I hadn't seen him before. He had freckles and looked about twenty-one. He was glad to get the coffee.

"You going to be here all day?" I asked.

"I'm on till three this afternoon, then someone else comes on."

"Okay. I'm going to be gone for a while, so stay close. If they're looking for me, tell them I'm working. Don't let her go out alone, either."

"If I have to take a leak, is it okay if I close the door?"

"Why don't you wait till you're off duty," I said.

"Why don't you go screw an onion," he said.

There seemed little to say to that, so I moved off. The morning was glorious, or maybe it just seemed so in contrast to the situation indoors. The sky was a high bright blue with no clouds. The sun was bright, and the leaves had begun to turn. Some of the sugar maples scattered along Lowell Street were bright red already. There weren't many cars out. Church or hangover, I thought. I found the turn for Harroway's house, drove about a hundred yards beyond it, and pulled off on the side of the road.

If my mental map was right, I could cut across the woods and get a look at the house and grounds from a hill to the right of the road we'd driven in. It had been a while since I took a walk in the woods, and the sense of it, alone and permanent, was strong as I moved through the fallen leaves as quietly as I could. I was dressed for stalking: Adidas sneakers, Levi's jeans, a black turtleneck sweater, blue nylon warm-up jacket, thirty-eight caliber Smith and Wesson. Kit Carson.

A swarm of starlings rose before me and swooped off to another part of the woods. Two sparrows chased a blue jay from a tree. High up a 747 heaved up toward California, drowning out the protests of the jay. There was low growth of white pine beneath the higher elms and maples, and thick tangles of thorny vines growing over a carpet of leaf mold that must have been two feet thick.

The land rose slowly but steadily enough so that I began to feel it in the tops of my thighs as I reached the crest. The hill down was considerably steeper, and the house was below in a kind of punch-bowl valley, a shabby building in a cleared patch of gravel and weeds among the encroaching trees.

The engine noise had been a generator. I could see it from here. There were five-gallon gasoline cans clustered around it, but it was silent at the moment. Conserving energy? Out of gas? A late model two-toned pink and gray Dodge Charger was parked, sleek and incongruous, behind the house. I looked at my watch. Twelve minutes past ten in the morning. Probably sleeping late out here on nature's bosom. I sat down and leaned against the base of a maple tree and watched. In the next two hours six more planes flew over. Then about twelve fifteen the young girl I'd seen before came out with a big cardboard box, jammed it into a rusty perforated barrel, and set it ablaze. She had on, as far as I could tell, exactly what she'd been wearing before. White too-big T-shirt, wide-flared jeans, no shoes. Maybe she had ten outfits all the same. She paused to light a cigarette from the blaze and then went back inside. At twelve thirty the mongrel bitch came out and nosed around near the burning trash till she found a scrap of bone that hadn't made it to the incinerator. She rolled on it several times, then took it to the corner of the house and buried it.

At one twenty-two Kevin Bartlett came out of the house with Vic Harroway. The boy's arm was around Harroway's waist and Harroway's arm was around the boy's shoulder. Like lovers. They walked to the Charger, separated. The boy got in the passenger's side, Harroway got in the driver's side, and they drove away. Just like that. They drove away, and I sat on my butt under the maple tree and watched them. We never sleep. We just sit and watch.

I sat and watched for the rest of the day and into the night. They didn't come back. I was beginning to hallucinate about cheeseburgers and cashew nuts by the time I gave up. It was after eleven when I headed back through the woods, stumbling more in the dark. Visions of pepper steaks danced in my head. When I got really hungry, I never thought about coq au vin or steak Diane. I wondered why that was, but I had trouble concentrating because I kept thinking about the American chop suey my mother used to make and how I felt after I had eaten it. It was a lot better than thinking how I'd found Kevin Bartlett and lost him in the space of say, fifteen seconds. By the time I got to my car, I had a long scratch across the back of one hand from the thorny vines, and one eye was tearing from a twig. That time of night is cold in September north of Boston, and I turned on the heater. I found a place to eat that advertised itself as a "pub." I think I was the only person there to eat. I jammed in at a stool at the bar and ordered three hamburgers and a beer. The beer came in a big stein that must have held half a quart. I drank two before the hamburgers arrived with two slices of kosher dill pickle and a handful of potato chips on an oval platter. It was a little hard to distinguish the hamburg from the bun, but I didn't mind; I was busy trying not to break into a sweat as I ate. The place was obviously a singles spot or pickup bar. The sound system was up full blast and featured high velocity hard rock music without interruption. All the booths and tables were filled, with people, mostly subthirty, standing together in between them and moving but barely on a very small dance floor. It was dim and very smoky. The décor was standard: dark panels, red carpet, pseudo-barn. I was jostled often as I ate, once while drinking, and the beer dribbled down my chin and soaked through my stalking sweater. A bartender in a red Ike jacket and a mod blond haircut put a bowl of peanuts in front of me and refilled my beer glass.

I sipped at it now that the beast within had been pacified. At least I knew that Kevin's stay with Harroway was voluntary. They liked each other. Maybe stronger. That was apparent from the hillside. Almost like lovers. His parents would be relieved at least that he was safe. But that didn't do anything for explanation. Or maybe it did. Maybe it made the explanation worse. Maybe Kevin was in on all that stuff. Maybe he was in on the death threats. Maybe he was in on Maguire's death. Good news and bad news, Mr. and Mrs. Bartlett, your kid's not dead. He's a murderer. Which is the good news you say? How the hell do I know? If I knew that kind of stuff, would I be sitting alone in a singles bar in a strange suburb at twelve thirty-five on a Sunday night? I'm a detective; I just find out things. I don't solve things. Well no, I don't know where your boy is right this minute, ma'am. Yes, sir, they drove away while I was up on the hill watching. I watched closely, though. Balls. The next guy that jostled me while I was drinking beer I was going to level. Trouble was the place was so crowded if I swung at someone, I'd hit three people. I got up and shoved my way out of the pub. I couldn't stand the thought of going back to the Bartletts'. I drove on into Boston and went to bed in my own apartment. I took the phone off the hook, went right to sleep, and didn't dream.

18

I woke up about twenty minutes of ten within the bright tangible silence of my bedroom. I was glad to be there. I got up and went to the kitchen. The cleaning woman had been there yesterday, and the place gleamed. I squeezed a big glass of orange juice and drank it while I put the coffee on to perk. Then I took a shower and shaved very carefully. When I was through, the coffee was ready, and I drank a cup while I made breakfast. I took two egg rolls from the freezer and put them in the oven, sliced two pieces of Williamsburg ham, a thick slice from a wedge of Swiss cheese, added a paper-thin slice of red onion, and arranged them on a plate with some tomato quarters. When the egg rolls were heated, I split them and put them on the plate too. I put out a saucer of sour cream, then I poured a new cup of coffee and sat down on a stool at the counter to eat, and read the *Globe.*

It was eleven when I left the apartment, full of stomach and clear of eye. I drove over to the Harbor Health Club, the second floor of an old building on Atlantic Avenue. Until the new high-rise apartments had started going in along the waterfront, it had been the Harbor Gym, and once, when I'd thought I was a boxer, I'd trained there. I still went in sometimes to hit the speed bag and work on the heavy bag and maybe do some bench presses, but mostly I went to the Y. The Harbor Gym had become upwardly mobile. Now it had steam rooms and inhalant rooms and exercise devices that jiggled your body while you leaned on them and chrome plating on the barbells and carpeting in the weight room.

I asked a receptionist in a toga where Henry Cimoli was, and she sent me to the Roman bath room. Henry was in there talking with two fat, hairy men who sat in a circular pool of hot water. Henry looked like an overdeveloped jockey. He was about five four in a snow-white T-shirt and maroon warm-up pants. The muscles in his arms bulged against the tight sleeve of the T-shirt, and his neck was thick and muscular with a prominent Adam's apple. There was scar tissue around his eyes. His thick black hair was cut close to his head and brushed forward.

"Spenser," he said when he saw me, "want a free go on the irons?"

"Not today, Henry. I want to talk."

"Sure." He spoke to the fat men in the hot water, "Excuse me, I gotta talk with this guy."

We walked back toward the cubbyhole office beyond the weight room.

"You still lifting?" Cimoli asked.

"Yeah," I said, "some. Too bad about how you're letting yourself go."

"Hey, I gotta work at it all the time. Guy my height, man, you let it go and you look like a fat broad in about two weeks."

"Yeah, after I go you better go sit in the tub with those two guys, get a real workout."

Cimoli shrugged. "Aw, you gotta offer that shit. They come in and sit in the steam room and soak in the pool and go home and tell everybody how they're getting in shape. But we got the real stuff too. You remember."

I nodded. "I'm looking for a guy, Henry." I showed him the picture of Vic Harroway. He took it and looked at it. "One of those guys, huh?" He shook his head. "Assholes," he said. I nodded again. Cimoli studied the picture. Then he broke into a big grin.

"Yeah," he said. "Yeah, I know this bastard. That's Vic Harroway. I'll be goddamned, old Vicki Harroway, la *de* da."

"What do you mean, la *de* da?" I said.

"He's a fag. He's building himself up for the boys down the beach, you know?"

"Do you know that or do you just think it?"

"Well, hell, I mean he never made no pass at me, but everybody knows about Vicki. I mean, all the lifters know Vic, you know? He's queer as a square doughnut."

"He work out here?"

"Naw, he used to be the pro at a health club in one of the big hotels, but I heard he got canned for fooling around. I ain't heard of him in about a year or so."

"Any place he hangs out?"

Cimoli shook his head and shrugged. "Beats me," he said.

"Friends? People who knew him?"

"Christ, I don't know. I barely knew the guy. I seen him in a couple contests I had to judge—it's hokey, but it's good PR for the club—and you hear talk, but I don't know the guy myself. Why?"

"He's my weight-lifting idol. I want to find him so he can autograph this picture."

"Yeah, me too," Cimoli said. "Well, look, if I hear anything I'll give you a buzz, okay? Still in the same crummy dump?"

"I have not relocated my office," I said. "Better check the boys in the pool. Don't want them exhausting themselves first time out."

"Yeah, I better. They tend to get short of wind just climbing in."

When I got back out on the street, the bright day had turned dark. The city and the sky were the same shade of gray, and they seemed to merge so that there was no horizon. Vicki Harroway? Goddamn.

I drove back up onto the expressway, around Storrow Drive, off at Arlington Street, and parked in a tow zone by the Ritz a block from Boylston Street. The gray sky was spitting a little rain now, just enough to mist on my windows. Enough to make me turn the collar up on my sport coat as I headed up Newbury Street.

Halfway up the block, past the Ritz, on the same side was a five-story brick building with a windowed, five-story, pentagonal bay and a canopied entry. The bay window on the third floor said RACE'S FACES across it in black script outlined with gold.

I took the open-mesh black iron elevator up. It let me out right in the waiting room. Gold burlap wallpaper, gold love seat, gold glass-topped coffee table, gold wall-to-wall carpet, and a blond receptionist with centerfold boobs, in a lime-green chiffon dress, sitting at a lime-green plastic desk. On the walls were black and white photographs of women with lots of fancy-focus blurring and light glinting on their hair. To the right of the receptionist was a lime-green door with a black-lettered gold-trimmed script sign that said STUDIO.

The receptionist pointed her chest at me and said, "May I help you?"

"Yes, you may," I said, "but it would involve wrinkling your dress."

"Did you wish to make an appointment with Mr. Witherspoon, sir?"

"Doesn't he mind wrinkling his dress?"

She said, "I beg your pardon."

I said, "Never mind. I would, in fact, like to see Mr. Witherspoon."

"Did you have an appointment?"

"No, but if you'd tell him Spenser is here, I bet he'd see me."

"What is it you wish to see him about?"

"I'm posing for the centerfold in the December *Jack and Jill* and wondered if Race would be willing to handle the photography."

She picked up the phone and pressed the intercom button. "Mr. Witherspoon? I'm sorry to bother you, but there's a man here who says his name is Spenser. He said something about posing for some pictures in *Jack and Jill.* I'm not familiar with it. Yes sir." She hung up and said to me, "Mr. Witherspoon says to come in. He's right through that door."

"Jack and Jill," I said, "is a magazine that celebrates the heterosexual experience."

She looked at me without expression and said, "Why don't you shove *Jack and Jill* magazine up your ass."

"Class will out," I said and went into the Studio.

It was white: floor, ceiling, walls, rugs, except one wall which was covered in uninterrupted black velvet. Opposite the door the room bellied out into the pentagonal bay I'd seen from the street. There were black velvet drapes gathered at each side of the windows. On a Victorian-looking black sofa a very thin girl reclined with her head propped on one elbow and a rose in her teeth. She was wearing a billowy diaphanous white gown, very red lipstick, and nail polish.

Her black hair was very long and very straight. Surrounding her was a cluster of light poles and bounce lighting. Extension cords tangled around the floor near the sofa. Around her moved a graceful man with a Hasselblad camera.

Race Witherspoon was six feet tall, slim, tanned, and entirely bald. I never did know whether he was naturally bald or if he shaved his head. His eyebrows were black and symmetrical, and a blue shadow of closely shaved beard darkened his jaw and cheeks. He had on tight black velvet pants that rode low on his hips and tucked into white leather cowboy boots. His shirt was white silk, open almost to his belt. The sleeves were belled. His tanned chest was as tight-skinned and hairless as his head, and a big silver medallion hung on a silver chain against his sternum. Susan had an outfit like it. But Race's was more daring. He moved fluidly around the model with the Hasselblad, snapping pictures and cranking the film ahead.

"I'll be with you in a minute, old Spenser, my friend." He spoke while he shot. He wore a large onyx ring on his right index finger, and a black silk kerchief was knotted around his throat. Outside the bright bath of the photography lights, the room was dim, and the misting rain that had begun while I walked up Newbury Street had become a hard rain that rattled on the windows. I sat on the edge of an ebony free-form structure that I took to be a desk.

"All right, Denise, take a break while I talk to the man."

The model got up off the couch without any visible effort, like a snake leaving a rock, and slunk off through a door behind the velvet hangings on the far wall. Witherspoon walked over to me and put the camera down beside me on the desk.

"What is it I can do for you, Chickie?" he said.

"I've come for one last try, Race," I said. "I've got to know. What is your name, really?"

"Why do you doubt me?"

I shook my head. "No one is named Race Witherspoon."

"Someone is named anything."

I took out my photo of Vic Harroway and handed it to Witherspoon.

"I'd like to locate this guy, Race. Know him?"

"Hmm, fine-looking figure of a man. What makes you think I might know him?"

"I heard he was gay."

"Well, for crissake, Spenser, I don't know every queer in the country. It's one thing to come out of the damned closet. It's quite another to run a gay data bank."

"You know him, Race?"

"I've seen him about. What's your interest? Want me to fix you up; maybe you could go dancing at Nutting's on the Charles?"

"Naw, he'd want to lead. I think I'll just stay home and wash my hair and listen to my old Phil Brito albums. What do you know about Harroway?"

"Not much, but I want to know the rap on him before I say anything. I owe you some stuff, but, you know, I don't owe you everything I am."

"Yeah," I said. "You don't. Okay, there's a missing boy, about fifteen. I saw him with Harroway. I want the kid back, and I would like to ask Harroway about a murder."

Witherspoon's thick eyebrows raised evenly. "Heavy," he said. "Very heavy. A fifteen-year-old kid, huh? Harroway was always a damned baby-raper, anyway."

"He's got no record," I said.

"I know. I didn't mean literally. He's the kind of guy who likes young kids. If he were straight, he'd be queer for virgins, you know."

"He is gay, then?"

"Oh hell, yes."

"Where's he hang out?"

"I see him at a gay bar over in Bay Village, The Odds' End. Isn't that precious? I don't go there much. It attracts a kinkier crowd than I like."

"Know what he does for a living?"

"No. I thought he lifted weights all the time. I know he was fired from a health club a year or so ago, and as far as I know he never got another job. He's around with a lot of bread, though. Fancy restaurants, clothes, new car. That kind of thing."

"Think he might kill someone?"

"He's a mean bitch, you know. He's a fag that doesn't like fags. He likes to shove people around. One of those I'm-gay-but-I'm-no-fairy types."

"Anything else you know that could help? Friends, lovers, anything?"

Witherspoon shook his head. "No, I don't know him all that well, only seen him around. He's not my type."

"Okay," I said. "Thank you."

"Now, on the other hand," Witherspoon said, "you are."

"Not with someone who won't give his real name," I said.

"Well, how about Denise then?"

"Not till you feed her," I said. "Your secretary, however, is another matter."

Witherspoon gave me a big smile. "Sorry, old Spenser, she's hot for Denise."

I said, "I think I'll go look for Harroway before I find myself mating with a floor lamp," and I left.

19

The Odds' End was on a side street off Broadway in the Bay Village section of Boston. The neighborhood was restored red-brick three-story town houses with neat front steps and an occasional pane of stained glass in the windows. The bar itself had a big fake lantern with Schlitz written on it hanging over the entrance and the name THE ODDS' END in nineteenth-century lettering across the big glass front.

I got a crumpled-up white poplin rain hat with a red and white band out of the glove compartment and put it on. I put on my sunglasses and tipped the rain hat forward over my eyes. Harroway had seen me only once, and then briefly; I didn't think he'd recognize me. I looked at myself in the rearview mirror and adjusted the hat down a little. Rakish. I turned up the collar on my tweed jacket. Irresistible. I got out of the car and went into The Odds' End.

It was dark inside, and it seemed darker with sunglasses. There was a bar along the left wall, tables in the middle, a jukebox, high-backed booths along the right wall, and an assortment of what looked like Aubrey Beardsley drawings framed above the booths and on either side of the jukebox.

A thin black man in pointed patent leather shoes and a green corduroy dungaree suit was nursing a brandy glass at the near end of the bar. His hair was patterned in dozens of small braids tight against his scalp. He looked at me as I came in, then went back to his brandy. On the bar in front of him was an open package of Eve cigarettes.

I sat at the far end of the bar, and the bartender moved down toward me. He was middle-sized and square with curly black hair cut close and a long strong nose. There were acne scars on his cheeks. He had on a blue oxford button-down shirt with the collar open and the cuffs rolled back. His hands were square and strong-looking. The nails were clean.

"Yes, sir," he said, looking at a point about two inches left of my face.

"Got draft beer?" I said.

"Miller's and Löwenbräu."

"Miller's is okay."

He put a cardboard coaster on the bar in front of me and a half-pint schooner on the coaster.

"I might be here awhile," I said. "Want to run a tab on me?"

"On the house," he said.

I widened my eyes and raised my eyebrows.

"I haven't seen you before, and I know most of the guys from Station Four. You from Vice?"

"Oh," I said, "that's why it's free."

"Sure, I spotted you the minute you walked in," he said.

Spenser, man of a thousand faces, master of disguise. "I'm not a cop," I said. "I just came in to kill a rainy afternoon. Honest."

The bartender put a tray of crackers and a crock of orange cheese in front of me.

"Yeah, sure, whatever you say, man," he said. "I'll run a tab on you if you want."

"Please," I said. "Actually, I'm kind of flattered that you thought I was a cop. Do I look tough to you?"

"Sure," he said, "tough," and moved down the bar to wait on a new customer. Maybe I should have worn my jade earrings.

The new customer probably wasn't a cop. He did have earrings.

But they weren't jade. They were big gold rings. He was a middle-aged white man with gray hair pulled up into a topknot. He had on a red and gold figured dashiki that was too big for him and woven leather sandals. His fingernails were an inch beyond the ends of his fingers. He had come in at a sort of shuffling quickstep, his head still, his eyes looking left and right, like a kid about to soap a window. He was at the bar about halfway between the black guy at one end and me at the other.

"I'll have a glass of port, Tom," he said to the bartender in a soft raspy mumble.

"Got the bread, Ahmed?"

Ahmed reached inside the dashiki and came out with a handful of silver. It clattered loudly on the bar.

The bartender put a pony of wine on the bar in front of him and slid ninety cents out of the small pile of change. Ahmed chuga-lugged it and put the glass down on the bar. Tom filled it again, took the rest of the change, and moved away. Ahmed nursed the second one. He looked from me to the black guy in the green corduroy. Then he moved down near me.

"Hi," he whispered. He sounded like Rod McKuen doing the Godfather.

"Where'd you leave your spear?" I said.

"My spear?"

Close up Ahmed smelled stale, and the long fingernails were dirty.

"My, you're a big one," he said. "What's your name?"

"Bulldog Turner," I said.

"Hey, that's kind of a cute name, Bulldog." He squeezed my left bicep. "I bet you're awfully strong."

The bartender stood polishing shot glasses, watching us with no expression of any kind.

"But oh so gentle," I said.

"You gotta quarter for the jukebox?" He was rubbing his flat hand up and down the back of my arm. Close up there was a gray stubble of beard showing, maybe two days' worth. I gave him a quarter. "I'll be right back," he said and scuttled across to the jukebox. He played an old Platters record, "My Prayer," and hurried back to his stool beside me. He never straightened fully up. There was a hunched quality to him, like a dog that's just wet on the rug. He drank the rest of his wine.

"Wanna buy me a drink?" he asked. His breath was sour.

"Ahmed," I said, "I'll buy you two drinks if you'll take them down the other end of the bar. I think you're a fantastic looker, but I'm spoken for."

Ahmed hissed at me, "Mother sucker," and scooted down the bar.

I motioned the bartender. "Give him two drinks, on me," I said.

20

It was five more draft beers and two passes later that Harroway showed. It was about four thirty now, and The Odds' End had filled up. The jukebox was playing "Boogie-Woogie Bugle Boy of Company B," and two guys were doing the Funky Chicken in a small open area in front of it.

Harroway came in shrugging his shoulders to shake off the rain. He had an Aussie campaign hat on over his blond hair—probably didn't want the color to run—and a rust-colored wraparound leather overcoat with black epaulets, a black belt, and black trim at the collar, cuffs, and along the skirt. Slick. He scanned the bar while he took off the coat. His eyes ran over me with no hesitation and kept going. He hung the coat and hat on a rack at one of the booths and sat down. His back to me. I noticed his white shirt was a see-through model. Be still my heart.

The guy he sat down with was a fat Oriental-looking Italian man in a blue chesterfield overcoat with velvet lapels. He kept the coat buttoned up to the neck. The bartender came out from behind the bar and put two highball glasses down on their table and went back behind the bar. When he got back I paid my bill.

Harroway talked with the fat man for fifteen minutes, finished his second drink, and stood up. He put on his leather coat and Aussie campaign hat, said something to the fat man, and went out into the rain, hunching his shoulders automatically as he opened the door.

I went after him. When I reached the street, he was already turning the corner toward Park Square. I hurried along, crossed to the other side of the street, and hung back about a half block behind him. It was raining hard and soaked through my tweed jacket in less than two blocks. Tailing a guy alone is mostly luck, and if he's being careful, it can't be done. Harroway, however, didn't seem worried about a tail. He never looked around. It was twenty past five on a Monday night, and the city was crowded with commuters. That made it easier. We crossed Park Square past the grateful statue of a freed slave. "Lawzy me, Marse Whitey, Ah'm pow'ful obliged fo' ma freedom." Balls.

We crossed Boylston and headed past the big United Fund sign up across the Common. The trees still had most of their leaves, and it cut the rain a little but not enough. We went up hill to the round bandstand. Harroway stopped there and looked around. I kept going with my head down and passed him. He ignored me and stood against the bandstand with his hands in his pockets, his collar up.

I went twenty yards further and stopped at a bench. I swayed a little, put one hand on the back of the bench, and stood half-bent-over as if I might be sick. Two old ladies with umbrellas went by. One of them said, "Sober up, sonny, and go home." With my head hanging like this, I could look back and see him standing in the dark; he hadn't moved. I eased myself onto the bench and lay down with my knees pulled up to my chest and my head resting on one arm. I could stare right at Harroway through the wet sunglasses. I hoped a cop didn't come by and run me off. On a night like this I had the feeling the cops were checking for crime down at the Hayes-Bickford cafeteria and making sure no one tried sneaking in the Park Street subway without paying.

It was cold and getting colder. The rain fell steadily on the exposed half of my face and got under my collar and ran down my neck. My gun was pressing into my hip, but since I was supposed to be passed out, I didn't dare shift to adjust it. A guy adjusting a holster looks like a guy adjusting a holster. I lay still and let the rain soak through my clothes.

Harroway shifted from one foot to the other, his hands jammed into the pockets of his leather coat, his campaign hat tilted forward over his face. Two sailors went by with a fat barelegged girl between them. One of the sailors said something I couldn't hear and slapped the girl on the fanny. Both sailors laughed. The girl said, "Oh, piss on you," and they went by. Ah, to be young and in love. Or even just upright and dry. A bum shuffled around the bandstand and spoke to Harroway. Harroway put one hand on the bum's shoulder, turning him around. Placed his foot against the bum's backside and shoved him sprawling into the mud. The bum picked himself up and shuffled away.

The cold rain had collected in my left ear. The whole left side of my face was beginning to feel glazed over, as if the rain were freezing. If something didn't happen pretty soon, I'd look like a gumshoe aspic. A lean man with a big black umbrella walked up past me from the direction of Tremont Street. He stopped beside Harroway. His right hand held the umbrella. In his left was a briefcase. I couldn't see his face, or even the upper half of his body, because he had the umbrella canted toward me against the drive of the rain. His lower half was in dark trousers and raincoat. He wore rubbers. A clandestine meeting in the rain and you wear your rubbers: Romance is dead. Harroway took out an envelope from inside his coat. The Umbrella Man handed him the briefcase and moved off down the hill away from me in his rubbers toward Charles Street. Harroway came past me toward Tremont carrying the briefcase. I had a very quick choice to make. I was pretty sure I could pick Harroway up again at The Odds' End or the ranch house. It looked as if Harroway had bought something covertly from the Umbrella Man. I wanted a look at him. I stumbled up off the bench and followed the black umbrella down the hill. I staggered legitimately now—my legs felt like two duckpins and my feet were numb. At the foot of the hill there was a lighted entry to the underground garage. The Umbrella Man stopped in front of it and closed the umbrella. It was Dr. Croft. He headed down the stairs to the garage. I didn't have a car there and saw no point in going too.

I turned back up the hill and ran as hard as I could back across the Common. I got to Tremont Street by the information booth with my chest heaving and sweat mixing with the rain on my face.

No sign of Harroway. I turned right, down Tremont across Boylston. No sign of Harroway. I turned right on Stuart back toward The Odds' End. I passed my car. There was a soaked parking ticket under the wiper on the passenger side. I went into The Odds' End. No Harroway. I ordered a double cognac and sat at the bar to drink it. I think it saved my life. By the time I finished it, it was nearly midnight. Harroway hadn't returned. I had another cognac. My head felt a little light. I paid and headed out of the place. If I was going to pass out, I wanted it to be someplace where there wouldn't be mouth-to-mouth resuscitation. Driving back to my apartment, I tried to sort out what I'd bumped into today, but I was too cold and too tired and too wet. Images of steam rising from my shower stall kept getting in the way.

21

At ten thirty the next day, showered, shaved, warmed, and dried, with nine hours' sleep behind me and hot corn muffins nicely balancing cold vealwurst in my stomach, I headed back for Smithfield. I'd called my service before I left that morning and found that there were nine calls recorded from Marge Bartlett. I ignored them. I wanted Harroway and the kid. I didn't think Marge Bartlett was in all that much danger. I wanted the kid. At five after eleven I was parked along the side of the street just down from the corner of the road that led into Harroway's sylvan retreat. I didn't want to get left standing on a hill this time while they drove away. The road was the only way in or out. I'd settle in here. I watched for eight hours. Nobody went in. Nobody came out.

At seven fifteen Harroway's pink and gray Charger nosed out of the leafy road and turned right, away from me toward Smithfield. It was dusk, and I couldn't see if Kevin was in the car, but Harroway's big blond head was clear enough. I followed. We drove through Smithfield and straight up Lowell Street into Peabody to Route 1. On Route 1 we headed south back toward Smithfield. I drifted back a little on Route 1. Let two cars in between us so he wouldn't spot me. He pulled into the parking lot of a big new motel with an illuminated sign outside: YES! WE HAVE WATER BEDS! I pulled in after him and drove on past behind the motel, parked near the kitchen entrance, and hustled back toward the lobby. It was dark out now and bright inside. Harroway was at the desk apparently registering. A girl was with him. She was young, high school age. Her hair was blond and cut short and square. She was wearing harlequin glasses with blue rims and a high-necked white blouse with a small black bow tie. Ah, Dorothy Collins, I thought, where are you now?

The clerk pulled a key out of one of the mail boxes in back of the desk: first row, fifth from the left. He pointed down a corridor to the left of the desk, and the two of them went on down it, turned another left, and disappeared. I went in, got close enough to check the number on the box the key had come from—112—bought a newspaper at the cigar counter, and sat down behind it in a leather chair in the lobby. Now what? I could go knock on the door. "Hi, I'm Snooky Lamson. Is Dorothy Collins in there?" I was punchy from sitting and doing nothing for eight hours. Checking into a motel with a girl didn't seem to fit Harroway's reputation. At seven thirty in came the man who ran confidence courses.

"Mr. Victor's room, please," he said.

Holy Christ, I thought, something's happening. I might actually find out if I keep sitting long enough and don't run my mouth.

Mr. Confidence went the same way Harroway and escort had gone, and ten minutes later Harroway appeared. He went across the lobby and into the dining room. Got himself a table, ordered a drink, and looked at the menu. I went back to the cigar counter, bought two Baby Ruths, sat down again, and munched them behind my newspaper. By the time Harroway had finished his steak, I had read the obituaries, the office equipment for sale classified, the ads for Arizona real estate, and was going back to the funnies for a second run-through on my favorite, "Broom Hilda."

Harroway had pie and two cups of coffee. I looked at my watch—nine fifteen. We'd been there an hour and forty-five minutes. I read "Broom Hilda" again. Harroway had a brandy. At nine forty-five the girl came on down the corridor and joined Harroway. He paid the bill, and they got up and left. I let them. As soon as they were out the door, I headed down the corridor toward Room 112. I figured the Confidence Man would wait a bit before he left, and if I could catch him there in the room, I might get a handle on the case, or I might get a free introductory trial offer on a confidence course. One never knows.

The door was locked. I knocked. There was no answer. I knocked again, trying to get that Motel Manager sound in it, firm but friendly. A voice said, "Who is it?" The voice was not confident.

I said, "It's me, Vic."

The lock turned and the door opened a crack. I put my shoulder into it, and in we went. He said, "Hey." I shut the door behind me. The force of my charge made him back into the bed and sit on it. He said, "What do you want?" with absolutely no confidence at all.

I said, "Don't you remember me? We met at the Bartletts' party."

He opened his mouth and closed it. He remembered. "You're the detective," he said.

"Right, and I'm detecting at this very moment." He was wearing jockey shorts and black socks. The bed he sat on was rumpled. There were lipstick smears on the sheet. On the dresser beside the color TV were two empty bottles of Taylor pink champagne and two empty glasses, one with a lipstick half moon on the rim. "You have just shacked up," I said. "And I have caught you."

"What are you talking about? You're crazy. You get out of my room right now."

"Aw, come on, sir. What is your name, by the way?"

"I'm not telling you. I don't have to tell you anything." His pants were draped over the back of a leatherette chair. I reached over and took his wallet out of the pocket. He said "Hey" again but stayed on the bed. I was out of his weight class anyway, but it is always hard to feel tough in your underwear. I found his driver's license: Fraser W. Robinson. I put the license back in the wallet and the wallet back in the pants.

"Now, Fraser, let us talk. I was sitting in the lobby when Harroway checked in with the jailbait. I was there when you came in and he came out. And I am here now. And I've got you. But I'll make a trade."

Fraser Robinson was looking at the door and at the window and at the four corners of the room, and nowhere did he see a way out.

"What kind of trade?"

"You tell me a lot of stuff about Harroway and the girl and the commune. And I tell no one anything about Harroway the girl and the commune and you. How's that for swaps?"

"What if I just call the manager and have you arrested for breaking into my room?"

"It's not your room. It's Mr. Victor's room. And I'd have to arrest you on suspicion of violating the Mann Act, possible statutory rape, contributing to the delinquency of a minor child, and resisting arrest. In fact, I think you'd probably get hurt resisting arrest."

"Look, if you want dough, I could get you some. I mean I haven't got much on me but . . ."

"Unh-unh," I said. "I want information." I took my gun out, flipped open the cylinder, checked the load, and flipped it shut. "You going to resist arrest," I said, "or are you going to tell me things?" I looked at him hard, as I'd seen Lee Marvin do in the movies.

"What do you want to know?" he said.

I put the gun back. "I want to know what Harroway is running over there. This setup was obviously arranged and obviously routine. Harroway's got a movable whorehouse going, and I want to know details and I want to know what else he has going."

"He's got everything else," Robinson said.

"Tell me."

"Drugs, dirty movies, sex shows, gang bangs, still photos, fetish stuff—you know, like if chains turn you on or leather bras and stuff."

"What kind of drugs?"

"I don't know. Everything, I guess. I'm not into drugs. I heard he didn't deal heroin. One of the girls was talking about Quads, but I don't really know."

"Where's he get the drugs?"

"I don't know. I told you I'm not into drugs."

"Yeah, that's right." I looked at the empty bottles. "You're into New York State champagne. I forgot. How did you get in touch with Harroway?"

"Doctor Croft. Gave me a little card with the phone number. Said if I was looking for anything, to call and say what I wanted."

"How'd he happen to do that?"

"I was having some trouble with my wife, you know. I mean she wasn't interested much in sex, and I thought maybe I was doing something wrong; you know, technique. So I went to Doctor Croft, and he said maybe I could find a release if I wanted to and it would make our marriage better and he gave me this card. Here, gimme my pants. It's still in my wallet." Robinson dug it out. A calling card cheaply printed with only a phone number.

Wise old Doc Croft. Save your marriage, son; get out and screw a groupie. "Your wife ever go to Doc Croft?" I said.

"No, why?"

"Never mind. Okay, what's the connection between Croft and Harroway?"

"I don't know. Neither one of them ever mentioned it. Croft never said another word about it after that time he gave me the card. I never brought it up to him. I mean, it's not the kind of thing you want to talk about, you know. I mean, how your wife is frigid and you have to go to others." He'd found the basis for his actions as he talked. It was all his wife's doing anyway, the bitch.

"How much does it cost?" I said.

"A hundred for a regular shack. That's all night, if you want, but I can't stay out all night. I mean, my wife won't even go to bed till I come home, you know? If you want something special, the price goes up from there."

The telling was building its own momentum, as if he'd had no one to tell about all this till now. He was getting excited. "Like sometimes I go for a nineteen-fifties' look, like little prim broads with high necks and wide skirts, sort of cute and high-class like, like ah, oh, you know, some of those broads on TV in the fifties, like . . ."

"Dorothy Collins," I said.

"Yeah, yeah, like her, and June Allyson in that movie about the ball player with one leg, like that. Well anyway. For a hundred and a half I get a chick like that, you know, dressed up and everything."

"Isn't that something," I said.

"And they'll cater parties too. You know, stag parties. Like I was at one down the Legion Hall one night they had five broads and a goat. And reefers for anyone that wanted them and a lot of other stuff I don't know about. Jesus, you should see the equipment on that goat."

"Sorry I missed it," I said. "Where's Harroway get the girls?"

"I don't know, but they're all young, and they live with him out somewhere on a farm or something. You know like Charles Manson, a commune or whatever. And I guess they'll do anything he says."

"Okay, Fraser," I said, "you're off the hook. But I know who you are and where you live and what your hobbies are. I'll keep in touch."

"Look, I told you whatever you wanted, right? I mean you got no reason to bring me into anything, have you? I mean if Harroway ever found out I told . . ."

"Mum's the word, Fraser. Put on your pants." I looked at the empty champagne bottles. "A hundred and a half," I said, "and you get domestic champagne." I went out and closed the door.

In the lobby I looked at my watch—ten fifteen; I was missing the Tuesday night movie again. Then it hit me. Tuesday night I was supposed to be having dinner with Susan Silverman, with maybe a surprise treat afterward. I was two hours and fifteen minutes late.

I called her from a pay phone. "Susan," I said, "I'm being held captive by the West Peabody Republican Women's Club which wishes to exploit me sexually. If I overpower my captors and escape, is it too late?"

There was silence. Then she said, "Almost," and hung up.

As I left the phone booth I saw Fraser Robinson walk out of the lobby and toward the parking lot. Five girls, I thought, and a goat? Jesus Christ.

22

I stopped to buy a bottle of Dom Perignon and still made it to Susan Silverman's by ten thirty-five. Susan let me in without comment. I held the wine out to her. "They were out of Annie Greenspring," I said.

She took it. "Thank you," she said. She had on a chocolate satin shirt with an oversize collar and copper-colored pants. "Do you want some now?"

"Yes."

"Then come out in the kitchen and open it. I have trouble with champagne corks."

The house was a small Cape with some Early American antiques around. A small dining room ran between the living room and the kitchen. There was a miniature harvest table set for two with white china and crystal wineglasses. Gulp!

The kitchen was walnut-paneled and rust-carpeted with a wagon wheel ceiling fixture hanging over a chopping-block table. She put the champagne on the table and got two glasses out of the cabinet. I twisted the cork out, poured, and handed her a glass.

"I'm sorry as hell, Susan," I said.

"Where were you?"

"Mostly sitting in the lobby at the Hideaway Inn reading 'Broom Hilda' and eating a Baby Ruth."

She picked up the champagne bottle and said, "Come on. We may as well sit by what's left of the fire." I followed her into the living room. She sat in a black Boston rocker with walnut arms, and I sat on the couch. There was a cheese ball and some rye crackers on the coffee table, and I sampled them. The cheese ball had pineapple and green pepper in it and chopped walnuts on the outside.

"This is even better than a Baby Ruth," I said.

"That's nice," she said.

I picked up the champagne bottle from where she'd set it on the coffee table. "Want some more?" I said. "No, thank you," she said. I poured some in my glass and leaned back. The fire hissed softly, and a log shifted with a little shower of sparks. The living room was papered in royal blue, with the woodwork white and a big print of *Guernica* over the fireplace.

"Look, Suze," I said. "I work funny hours. I get into places and onto things that I can't stop, and I can't call and I gotta be late. There's no way out of that, you know?"

"I know," she said. "I knew all the two and one half hours I was walking around here worrying about you and calling you a bastard."

"Is the dinner ruined?" I said.

"No, I made a cassoulet. It probably improves with age."

"That's good."

She was looking at me now, quite hard. "Spenser, what the hell happened to you? What were you doing?"

I told her. Halfway through she got up and poured herself some more champagne and refilled my glass. When I finished she said, "But where's Kevin?"

"I don't know. I figure that Harroway's got him stashed somewhere else. In Boston, maybe. He must have gotten nervous after we were out to his house."

"And Harroway's running a whole, what, vice ring? Right here in town? How can he get away with it? I mean, this isn't a big town. How can the police not know?"

"Maybe they do know."

"You mean bribery?"

"Maybe, or maybe Harroway has friends in high places. Remember Doctor Croft was the one who shilled old Fraser Robinson onto Vicki's scam."

"But to corrupt the police . . ."

"Cops are public employees, like teachers and guidance counselors. They tend to give a community what it wants, not always what it should have. I mean, if you happen to go for an evening out with five broads and a goat, and you are a man of some influence, maybe the cops won't prevent it. Maybe they'll try to contain it and keep everybody happy."

The bottle of Dom Perignon was empty. Susan said, "I bought some too," and went to the kitchen to get it. I got another log out of the hammered-brass wood bucket on the hearth and settled it on top of the fire. Susan returned with the champagne. Mumm. Good. I was more than a domestic champagne date. Next time, she'd said. Tuesday, at my house. Hot-diggity. She sat down on the couch beside me and handed me the bottle. I twisted the cork out and poured.

"I always thought you had to pop it and make a mark in the ceiling and spill some on the rug," she said.

"That's for tourists," I said.

"Where are you now, Spenser? What do you make of everything?"

"Well, I know that Kevin is with Vic voluntarily. I know Vic is a homosexual."

"You don't *know* that."

"I haven't proved it, but I know it. I heard it from people I trust. I don't need to prove it."

"That's an advantage you have on the police, isn't it?"

"Yeah, one. Okay, so Harroway's gay and Kevin's staying with him. You told me that Kevin had unresolved sexual identity problems . . ."

"I said he might have . . ."

"Right, he might have sexual identity problems, so the relationship between them might be romantic. Agree?"

"Spenser, you can't just say things like that; there's so much more that goes into that kind of diagnosis. I'm not qualified . . ."

"I know, I'm hypothesizing. I don't have the luxury of waiting to be sure."

"I guess you don't, do you?"

"I figure Vic and Kevin are living together, and he finds in Harroway a combination of qualities he misses in his parents. I figure the kid ran off with Harroway and then afterward, out of hatred or perversity or boyish exuberance, they decided to put on the straights and make some money to boot. So they rigged the kidnapping, and they sent the notes and made the phone calls and shipped the guinea pig after it died. Then they went, maybe to get some things of Kevin's, maybe to steal the old man's booze, maybe to play a new trick, and broke into the house. Actually Kevin probably had a key. And Earl Maguire caught them and they panicked, or Harroway did, and he killed Maguire. You saw Harroway; you can imagine how he could hit someone too hard, and if he did he could make it permanent."

"But what do you suppose Doctor Croft has to do with all this?"

"Maybe nothing, maybe just doing a favor for his buddy, Fraser Robinson. Maybe he's no more than a satisfied customer. Or maybe he's a convenient source of drugs. An M.D. has a better shot than most people at getting hold of narcotics. I can't see the mob doing business with the likes of Harroway."

"What are you going to do?"

"Well, I was thinking of putting my hand on your leg and quoting a few lines from Baudelaire."

"No, dummy, I mean what are you going to do about Vic Harroway and Doctor Croft and Kevin?"

"One thing I'll do right now. Where's your phone?"

"In the kitchen."

I got up and called Boston Homicide. "Lieutenant Quirk, please." Susan came out with me and looked at the cassoulet in the oven.

"Who's calling?"

"My name's Spenser."

"One moment." The line went dead and then a voice came on.

"Spenser, Frank Belson. Quirk's home asleep."

"I need a favor, Frank."

"Oh, good, me and the Lieutenant spent most of today hanging around thinking what could we do to be nice to you. And now you call. Hey, what a treat."

"I want to know anything you can find out about a medical doctor named Raymond Croft, present address . . ." I thumbed through the Smithfield phone book on the shelf below the phone, "Eighteen Crestview Road, Smithfield, Mass. Specializing in internal medicine. I don't know his previous address. Call me here when you can tell me something." I gave him Susan's number. "If I'm not here leave a message."

"You're sure you don't want me to hand-carry it out there?"

"Maybe I can do you a favor sometime, Frank."

"Oh, yeah, you could do everybody a favor sometime, Spenser."

The conversation wasn't going my way, so I let it go and hung up. "How's the cassoulet?" I said.

"On warm," she said. "It'll keep. I think we need more wine."

"Yes," I said, "I believe we do."

We went back into the living room and sat on the couch and drank some more. My head felt expanded, and I felt very clever and adorable.

"Darling," I said, leaning toward Susan, *"je vous aime beaucoup, je ne sais pas* what to do."

"Ah, Spenser, you romantic fool," she said and looked at me over the rim of her champagne glass while she drank. "Are you really a detective, or are you perhaps a poet after all?"

"Enough with the love talk," I said, "off with the clothes."

She put the champagne glass down and looked at me full face and said, "Be serious, now, please. Just for now." My throat got tight, and I swallowed audibly.

"I am serious," I said.

She smiled. "I know you are. It's funny, isn't it? Two sophisticated adult people who want to make love with each other, and we don't know how to make the transition to the bedroom. I haven't felt this awkward since college."

I said, "May I kiss you?" and my voice was hoarse.

She said, "Yes, but not here. We'll go in the bedroom."

I followed her down a short corridor and into her bedroom. There was a spool bed with a gold-patterned spread. An air conditioner hummed softly in the far window. The walls were covered in a beige burlap paper, and there was a pine sea chest at the foot of the bed.

She turned toward me and began to unbutton her blouse. "Would you turn the spread down, please?" she said. I did. The sheets were gold with a pattern of coral flowers. As I undressed I looked at Susan Silverman on the other side of the bed. She unhooked her bra. There is something enormously female in that movement. I stopped with my shirt off and my belt unbuckled to watch her. She saw me and smiled at me and let the bra drop. I took a deep inhale and finished undressing. We were naked together then, on opposite sides of the bed. I could see the pulse in her throat. She lay down on her side of the bed and said, "Now you may kiss me."

I did. With my eyes closed, for a long time. Then I opened my eyes and discovered that she had hers open too and we were looking at each other from a half inch away. With her eyes wide open she darted her tongue into my mouth and then giggled, a rich bubbling half-smothered giggle that I caught. We lay there pressed together kissing and giggling with our eyes open. It was a different beginning, but a very good one. Then we closed our eyes again, and the giggling stopped.

23

We ate cassoulet and drank Beaujolais at two fifteen in the morning in the dining room with candles and didn't get to sleep till four. In the morning she called in sick, and we stayed in bed till almost noon. We had a cup of coffee together and cleaned up the dining room and kitchen. It was two o'clock in the afternoon before I was back to work.

Dr. Croft had an office in a medical building on one side of a small shopping center in the middle of Smithfield. Two stories, brick, pastel plywood panels, a flat roof, and maybe ten offices. Inside there was the cool smell of air-conditioned money. There were four people in Croft's office, three women and a man. Well, you see, Doctor, I'm horny but my spouse thinks I'm a creep. Oh, yes, of course, I'll make an appointment for you with Doctor Harroway, my horniness consultant.

The office was paneled in light plywood and carpeted in beige. A dark-faced girl with an enormous bouffant hairdo and a starched white uniform eyed me from behind a counter in the far wall. I said, "I'd like to see the doctor, please."

She said, "Have you an appointment?"

I said, "No, but if you'll give him my card and tell him it's important, I think he'll see me." I gave her a card with just my name and address on it. The one with the crossed sabers on it might seem a little pushy, I thought.

"Have you ever been a patient of Doctor Croft's before?"

"No, ma'am."

"And what is your complaint?" She was pulling out a little yellow record card and rolling it into the typewriter.

"Functional curiosity about a guy named Fraser Robinson."

She stopped rolling the record form into the typewriter and looked at me. "I beg your pardon?"

"Look, ducks, why don't you just take the card to the doctor, tell him my ailment, and let him puzzle out the proper response."

She gazed at me with manifest disapproval for a long time. Then without a word got up and disappeared through a door behind the counter. In about thirty seconds she was back with her disapproval even more manifest and said icily, "The doctor will see you now." She was hoping for a prognosis of incurable. One of the ladies in the waiting room said something about the nerve of some people, and I slunk in through the doctor's door; no one likes a line bucker. Inside was a long corridor with examining rooms on either side. Croft stepped out of the last door on the right and said, "Come right in, Spenser. Good to see you again."

I went in and sat down in the patient's chair in front of Croft's big reassuring desk. On the wall was a big reassuring medical school diploma in Latin and several official-looking reassuring documents with state seals and such on them. Croft had a white medical coat over his wide-striped blue shirt and striped tie. He rested his elbows on the desk and cathedraled his hands in front of him with the tips of his fingers touching the bottom of his chin. He had a gold ring with a blue stone on the little finger of his left hand.

"How can I help you?" he asked and gave me his big predator's smile. Consoling. Reassuring. Phooey.

"Fraser Robinson tells me you are pimping for Vic Harroway." Croft didn't move except for the big smile. It went away. He said, "I beg your pardon?"

I said, "Knock it off, Croft. I've got you. I caught Robinson in a motel with an adolescent girl, and he confided in me. It doesn't have to be a long fall for you; I'm not with the AMA. Or the Vice Squad. You want to supplement your income by pimping while you heal, that's your doing. But I want to know everything you know about Harroway and Kevin Bartlett and how Earl Maguire got his neck broken and that kind of thing."

Croft reached over and pushed the intercom switch. "Joan," he said into it, "I can't be disturbed for at least a half hour. If an emergency comes up, switch it to Doctor LeBlac." He turned back toward me. "This is a mountain out of a molehill, Spenser."

"Yeah, I'll bet it is," I said.

"It is, in fact. Robinson is oversexed, and he's married to a woman who is undersexed. Nothing pathological, but it was making their marriage an armed camp. He came to me for help. You'd be surprised how many people come to their family doctor in time of trouble."

I said, "Cue the organ." Croft paid no attention.

"Fraser is not only a patient, he's a friend. Most of my patients are friends too. It's not all injections and take-these-pills-three-times-a-day. A lot of any family doctor's task is counseling, sometimes just being a guy that will listen."

"You may replace Rex Morgan as my medical idol, Doctor."

"I know, Spenser, you're a smart aleck, but the practice of medicine doesn't come out of a textbook. Fraser needed an outlet, a chance for sexual adventure, and I gave it to him. It has saved his marriage, and I would do it again in a moment."

"How'd you happen to know about Harroway, Doctor?"

"I'd heard about him in town. Being a doctor in a town this size, the word gets around; you hear things."

"You ever meet him?"

"Of course not. We hardly move in the same circles." Croft looked at me steadily.

Candid. A modern Hippocrates.

"How'd you happen to have a card with his phone number on it?"

Croft's eyes faltered, only for a minute. "Card? I've never had a card for Harroway." He dropped his hands toward the middle drawer of his desk, then caught himself and folded them in his lap and leaned back in his chair.

"Yeah you did, and you gave it to Robinson—a little white card with a phone number printed on it and nothing else." I got up and walked past the desk to look out the window. It afforded a nice view of Route 128. Two small kids were sliding down the grassy embankment away from the highway using big pieces of cardboard for sleds. I turned around suddenly and pulled the middle drawer open. He tried to jam it shut, but I was stronger. In one corner was a neat stack of little white cards just like the one Robinson had given me. I took one out and stepped back away from the desk and sat down. Croft's face was red, and two deep lines ran from his Arabian nostrils to the corners of his mouth. I held the card in my right hand and snapped the edge of it with the ball of my thumb. It was very noisy in the quiet office.

He regrouped. "Well, naturally, it's not the kind of thing you admit. But I ran into Harroway once or twice at a pub on the highway and one thing led to another and I spent an evening with one of the girls from his house. Afterward, Harroway asked me to take a few of these cards and give them to any of my patients who might be in, ah, the situation that Fraser was in."

"Croft," I said, "I am getting sort of mad. You are bullshitting me. A little discreet business card, printed up with just a phone number on it, for the sexually dysfunctional? Harroway? Harroway's idea of a subtle pander would be to stand on the corner near the Fargo Building yelling, *'Hey sailor, you want to get laid?'* You thought of this, and you're in it like an olive in a martini."

"You can't prove that."

"I can prove that. The point is you don't want me to. If I have to prove it, you'll be giving enemas at Walpole for the next five to ten. Now we can get around that, but not till you've spoken to me the words I'm longing to hear."

"What do you want?" Croft said. "What do you want me to tell you?"

"Where's Kevin Bartlett?"

"He's with Vic, in Boston. Vic's got an apartment in there on the Fenway."

"Address?"

"I don't know."

"You supply Harroway with drugs?"

"Absolutely not." He wasn't admitting what I hadn't proved.

"He ever give you money?"

"Never." The firmness of his denials seemed to give him confidence. He denied it again. "Never."

"Silly old me. I thought two nights ago by the bandstand on the Boston Common that you gave him a briefcase full of Quads and he gave you an envelope full of money." Croft looked as if his stomach hurt. "Probably not that at all though, huh? Probably buying your collection of Kay Kayser records so he and the gang out at the house could have a sock hop. That what it was?"

Croft looked at the window and then the door and then at me. None of us helped him. He opened his mouth and closed it again. He rubbed both hands, palms down, along the arms of his chair. "I want a lawyer," he said. The words came out in a half croak.

"Now that's dumb," I said. "I mean, I might let you off the hook on this if you help me find the kid. But if you get a lawyer, then all this is going to come out, and maybe you'll end up being accessory to murder. You know how that'll cut into a guy's practice."

"I told you everything I know about the boy. He's with Vic in Boston."

"I need an address, and you have one. You're too much involved with Harroway not to know. You give me the address and maybe I can keep you out of the rest."

"On the Fenway. One-thirty-six Park Drive, apartment three."

I reached across the desk, picked up Croft's phone, and dialed. His eyes widened. "What are you going to do?" he said.

"I'm going to keep you on ice for a while." A voice answered, "Essex County Court House." I said, "Lieutenant Healy, please."

Croft started up from his seat. I reached over and pushed him back down with my hand on his shoulder. "Be cool," I said. "I can't trust you not to warn Harroway. If I get the kid back okay, I'll spring you."

Healy came on. I said, "This is Spenser. I got a suspect on the Bartlett kidnapping, or whatever."

Healy said, "Or whatever."

"And I want to put a lid on him for the afternoon so I can find the kid."

Healy said, "What's his name?"

"John Doe."

"Oh," Healy said. "Him."

"He gave me a lead on the kid, Lieutenant, and I've got to be sure he doesn't tip him off before I get there."

"I gather he didn't volunteer the lead."

"We practiced the art of compromise."

"And you want me to bury him someplace without a charge till you get the Bartlett kid, is that right?"

"Yeah."

"That is unconstitutional."

"Yeah."

"You think you'll lose the kid if you turn your back on John Doe?"

"Yeah." Croft was sitting perfectly still now, not looking at anything. There was a pause at Healy's end of the line. Then he said, "Okay. Where are you? I'll have one of the road patrols in your area pick him up."

"We'll be parked in the northbound lane of 128 under the Route 1 overpass. Red nineteen-sixty-eight Chevy convertible. Mass. plates seven-one-two-dash-two-three-four. If you need to contact me, call me here." I gave him Susan's number.

Healy said, "If this backfires, Spenser, I'll have your license and your ass," and hung up.

I said, "Okay, Doc. You get the picture. Let's go."

"How long will they hold me?"

"Till I get the kid. When he's home I'll come by and get you out."

"How will you know where I am?"

"Healy will know."

"Who is Healy?"

"State cop, works out of the Essex County DA's office. Don't offer him money. He will deviate your septum if you do."

Croft called his girl again on the intercom, told her there was an emergency and he'd be gone for the day. We went out the back door of the office building and were parked under the Route 1 overpass when a blue State Police cruiser pulled up behind us and a tall red-haired state cop with big ears got out and came around to the driver's side of my car.

"You Spenser?" he said.

"Yep."

"I'm supposed to pick up a Mr. Doe," he said with no expression on his face.

I nodded at Croft. The trooper went around and opened the door. Croft got out. The trooper closed the door. I drove away.

24

The light blue Smithfield cruiser was still parked in the Bartletts' driveway, and Silveria, the bushy-haired cop, was reading a copy of *Sports Illustrated* in the front seat.

I parked beside him in the turnaround, and he looked at me over the top of the magazine as I got out. "Better not park that thing on the street on trash day," he said.

"Don't your lips get tired when you read?" I said.

"Your ears are gonna be tired when Mrs. Bartlett gets talking to you. She's been calling you things I don't understand."

"I gather no one tried to do her in."

"I think her husband might, and I wouldn't blame him. Jesus, what a mouth on that broad."

"Watch me soothe her with my silver tongue," I said.

Silveria said, "Good luck."

Marge Bartlett opened the back door and said, "Spenser, where in hell have you been, you rotten bastard?"

Silveria said, "Good, you've already got her half won over."

At the door I said to her, "I know where your son is."

She said, "We're paying you to protect me and you run off on your damned own."

I said, "I know where your son is, and I want your husband and you to come with me to get him."

She said, "It's lucky I'm alive."

I pushed past her into the house and said, "Where's your husband? Working today?"

She said, "Damn you, Spenser, aren't you going to explain yourself."

I went to the sink, filled a glass with water, turned back to her. She said, "I want a goddamned explanation." I poured the water on her head. She screamed and stepped back. She opened her mouth but nothing came out. The relief was wonderful.

"Now," I said. "I want you to listen to me, or I will get you so wet your skin will wrinkle." She pulled a paper towel from its roller under a cabinet and dried her hair. "I know where Kevin is. I want you and your husband to come with me to Boston and get him back."

"Can't you get him? I mean, won't there be trouble? I'm not even dressed. My hair's a mess. Mightn't it be better if you got him and brought him here? I mean, with me there he might make a scene."

"No," I said. "I'll locate him. And I'll take care of any trouble. But he's your kid. You bring him home. I won't drag him home for you. You owe him that."

"My husband is working in town—Arden Estates—he's putting up half a dozen houses near the Wakefield line on Salem Street. We can stop for him on the way."

"Okay," I said, "let's go. We'll take my car."

"I have to change," she said, "and put on my face and do something with my hair. I can't go out like this." She had on jeans and sneakers and a man's white shirt. The curls on each side of her face were held in place by Scotch Tape.

"We are not going out dancing to the syncopated rhythms of Blue Barron," I said.

She said, "I can't leave the house looking like this," and went upstairs. Twenty minutes later she descended in a double-breasted blue pinstripe pants suit with a blue and white polka-dot shirt and three-inch blue platform shoes. She had on lipstick, rouge, eye makeup, earrings, and doubtless much more that I didn't recognize. Her hair was stiff with spray. She put on big round blue-colored sunglasses, got her purse from the table in the front hall, and said she was ready.

I said, "I hope you got on clean underwear so if we get in an accident." She didn't answer me. And I left it at that. As long as she was quiet, I didn't want to press my luck.

When we found him at the construction trailer, Roger Bartlett was wearing green twill work clothes and carrying a clipboard.

"Hey," he said when I told him, "hey, that's great. Wait a minute, I'll tell the foreman and I'll be with you. Hey, that's okay." He went across the bulldozed road to a half-framed house and yelled up to one of the men on a scaffold. Then he put the clipboard down on the subfloor of the house and came to my car.

"Get in back, Roger, would you? It's hard for me without wrinkling my suit."

She leaned forward and held the seat, and he slid into the back.

On the ride in I told them a little of what I knew. I didn't mention Croft or Fraser Robinson. I merely told them that I had an address in town where Kevin was staying, and I knew he was staying with Vic Harroway. Neither Bartlett nor his wife knew Harroway. "The sonova bitch," Bartlett said, "if he's hurt my kid, I'll kill him."

"No," I said. "You let me handle Harroway. He is not easy. You stay away from him."

"He's got my kid, not yours," Bartlett said.

"He hasn't harmed Kevin. They like one another. Kevin's with him by choice."

Bartlett said, "The sonova bitch."

We drove along Storrow Drive with the river on our right, took the Kenmore exit, went up over Commonwealth Avenue and onto Park Drive. On the right, apartment houses in red brick and yellow brick, most of them built probably before the war, some with courtyards, low buildings, no more than five stories. It was a neighborhood of graduate students and retired school teachers and middle-aged couples without children. On the left, following the curve of the muddy river, was the Fenway. In early fall it was still bright with flowers, the trees were still dominantly green, and the reeds along the river were higher than a man. Whenever I passed them, I expected Marlin Perkins to jump out and sell me some insurance.

Number 136 was three quarters of the way down Park Drive, across from the football field. At that point the drive was divided by a broad grass safety island, and I pulled my car up onto it and parked.

Marge Bartlett said, "It's not a bad neighborhood. Look, it's across the street from the museum. And there's a nice park."

"Breeding shows," I said. We went across the street and rang the bell marked SUPER. A fat middle-aged woman with no teeth and gray hair in loose disorganization around her head shuffled to the door. She was wearing fluffy pink slippers and a flowered housedress. When she opened the door, I showed her a badge that said SUBURBAN SECURITY SERVICE on it and said in a mean vice-squad voice, "Where's apartment three?"

She said, "Right there on the left, officer, first door. What's the trouble?"

"No trouble," I said, "just routine."

I knocked on the door with the Bartletts right behind me. No answer. I knocked again then put my ear against the panel. Silence. "Open it," I said to the super.

"I don't know," she said, "I mean the tenants get mad if . . ."

"Look, sweetheart," I said, "if I have to come back here with a warrant, I might bring along someone from the Building Inspector's office. And we might go over this roach farm very closely, you know."

"Okay, okay, no need to get mad. Here." She produced a key ring and opened the door. I went in with my hand on my gun. It was not a distinguished place. Two rooms, kitchen and bath off a central foyer that was painted a dull pink. The place was neat. The bed was made. There was a pound of frozen hamburg half-defrosted on the counter. In the bedroom there were twin beds. On each were some clothes.

Roger Bartlett looked at a pair of flared jeans and a pale blue polo shirt and said, "Those are Kevin's." On the other bed was a pair of Black Watch plaid trousers with deep cuffs, and a forest-green silk short-sleeved shirt with a button-down collar. A pair of stacked-heel black loafers was on the floor beside the bed. On the bureau there was a framed eight-by-ten color photo of Harroway and the boy. Harroway had an arm draped over the boy's shoulders, and they were both smiling.

Two spots of color showed on Roger Bartlett's face as he looked at the picture.

"This the guy?" he said.

"That's him."

"He's really quite nice-looking in a physical sort of way," Marge Bartlett said. "The apartment is quite neat too." Her husband looked at her, opened his mouth, and then closed it.

"Let's go," I said. And we trailed out. The super came last in line to make sure we didn't lift anything and closed the door behind her. I said, "Okay for now. If you run into Mr. Harroway, say nothing. This is official business, and it's to be kept still." I thought about invoking national security, but she might get suspicious.

"What now?" Bartlett said when we got outside again.

"We wait," I said. "Obviously they'll be coming back. Clothes laid out on the bed, hamburg defrosting for supper." We walked back toward my car when Marge Bartlett said, "My God, it's Kevin."

25

On the far side of the Fenway two figures were jogging. One big man, one small one. Vic and Kevin. Harroway was taking it easy, and the boy was obviously straining to stay with him. Cross streets made a natural circle of that part of the Fenway, and one complete lap around it, without crossing any streets, was about a mile. If we stayed where we were, Harroway and the boy would run right up to us. We walked across to the park and stood, partly shielded by a blue hydrangea, watching them. As they got closer, you could see Harroway talking, apparently encouragingly, to Kevin, who had his head down, jogging doggedly. Harroway had on a lavender net sleeveless shirt and blue sweat pants with zippers at the ankles and white stripes down the sides. Kevin had on a white T-shirt and gray sweat pants, a little big and obviously brand-new. The boy was breathing hard, and Harroway said, "Just to the edge of the stands, Kev; that's a mile. Then we'll walk a bit. You can make it. You're doing terrific." Behind us, along the near sideline of the football field, cement stands descended maybe twenty feet below street level to the field.

Roger Bartlett stepped forward and said, "Kevin." The boy saw him and without a word he veered left, jumped the low back of the grandstand, and ran down the cement stands. Bartlett went after him. Marge Bartlett began to scream after them, "Kevin, you come back here. Kevin." I was watching Harroway. He looked at me a long ten seconds, then looked after the boy. Bartlett was gaining on his son rapidly. The boy was bushed from jogging. Bartlett caught the boy in midfield, and Harroway went after them. I said, "Stay here," to Marge Bartlett and went after Harroway. Bartlett had Kevin by the arm, and the boy was struggling and punching at his father with his free hand.

"Let me go, you sonova bitchin' bastard," Kevin said.

"Kevin, Kevin, I want us to go home," Bartlett said. He was crying.

Harroway got there ahead of me. He caught a handful of the back of Bartlett's work shirt and threw him sprawling toward the end zone.

"I want to stay with you, Vic." Kevin was crying too now, and behind me I could hear Marge Bartlett begin to wail. Jesus. Maybe I should get out of this line of work. Get into something simple and clean. Maybe a used-car salesman. Politics. Loan sharking.

Harroway said, "No one's taking you anywhere, Kev. No one."

Bartlett came up on his feet, the red spots on his cheekbones much brighter now. "Stay out of this, Spenser," he said. "That's my kid."

Harroway's arms and shoulders gleamed with sweat, and the afternoon sun made glistening highlights on the deltoid muscles that draped over his incredible shoulders.

"Bartlett," I said, "don't be crazy."

"Let him try it," Kevin said. "No one can beat Vic. All of you together can't beat Vic. Go ahead, Roger." The first name dripped with distaste. "Let's see you try to handle Vic."

Bartlett did. He must have been nearly fifty and probably hadn't had a fight since World War II. He was a wiry man and had worked with his hands all his life, but compared to Harroway he was one of the daughters of the poor. He ran at Harroway with his head down. Harroway caught him by the shirt front with his left hand and clubbed him across the face with his right. Twice. Then he let him go, and Bartlett fell. He tried to get up, couldn't, caught hold of Harroway's leg, and tried to pull him down. Harroway didn't move.

"Okay," I said and reached back for my gun, "that's . . ." and Marge Bartlett jumped at Harroway, still wailing, and swung at him with both clenched fists. He swatted her away from him with the back of his right hand, and she sprawled in the mud on her back. Told her to stay up there. There was blood showing from her nose. Kevin said, "Mama."

I had the gun out now and held it by my side. "Enough," I said. Bartlett was oblivious. All he had left was going into bending Harroway's leg, and he might as well have been working on a hydrant.

Harroway said, "Get him off me or I'll kick him into the river."

I stepped closer with the gun still at my side and pulled Bartlett away by the collar. Marge Bartlett was sitting on her heels with her head back trying to stop her nose from bleeding. Bartlett sat on the ground and looked at Harroway. Harroway had his arm around Kevin's shoulder.

"He's staying with me," Harroway said.

I held the gun up and said, "We'll have to see about that."

"No," Harroway said. "We won't see. He's staying with me. I don't care about your goddamned gun."

"That's the only way you can get me," Kevin said, "if you use a gun. You don't dare try and stop Vic by yourself. Nobody does. Nobody can. We're staying together. If you try to shoot him, you'll have to shoot me first." The kid moved between Harroway and me.

Marge Bartlett said, "Kevin, you stop that right now. You are coming home with us. Now don't be ridiculous."

Kevin didn't look at her. "You see what he did to Big Rog." I could feel the distaste like a force. I wondered how his father must feel. "He'll do that to anyone that bothers me. He takes care of me. We take care of each other." The kid had big dark eyes, and on his cheeks, just like his father's, two bright spots of color showed.

I flipped the cylinder open on my gun and, with the barrel pointing up, shook the bullets out into my left hand. I put the bullets in my pants pocket, put the gun in my holster. Then I took off my jacket, folded it, and put it on the ground. I unclipped my holster and put it on the jacket.

Kevin said, "What are you doing?"

I said, "I'm going to beat your man."

Marge Bartlett said, "Spenser," in a strained voice.

Harroway smiled.

"I'm going to beat your man, Kevin, so you'll know it can be done. Then I'm going to let you decide."

Marge Bartlett said, "He can't decide. He's not old enough." No one paid any attention. Harroway gently took Kevin's shoulders and moved him out of the way. "Watch this, Kev. It won't take long." He shrugged his shoulders forward, and the triceps swelled out at the back of his upper arms. "Come and get it, Spenser."

I wasn't paying attention to his arms. I was watching his feet. If he set up as if he knew what he was doing, I might be in some trouble. We both knew I couldn't outmuscle him. He stood with his feet spread, flat-footed in a slight crouch. Good. He didn't know what he was doing. Sometimes an iron freak will get hung up on karate and kung fu, or sometimes they're wrestlers. Harroway was none of those. If I could keep my concentration, and if he didn't get hold of me, I had him.

I shuffled toward him. The ground was dry and firm. I had a lot of room. We were in the middle of the football field. A few people had begun to gather in along the sidewalk and a couple in the stands. They were uneasy, looking at the trouble. We who are about to die salute you. I was dressed for the work; I had on sneakers and Levi's jeans, my stakeout clothes. I put a left jab on Harroway's nose. He grabbed at me, and I moved out. Float like a butterfly, sting like a bee. Come to think of it, he wasn't champ anymore, was he? Harroway swung on me with his right hand. Better and better. I let it go by, stepped in behind it, and drove two hard right-hand punches into his kidneys; hitting the muscle web of the latissimus dorsi under his rib cage was like hitting a chain link fence. I moved back away from him. He grazed me with his left fist, and I hit him in the nose again. It started to bleed. I hoped Marge Bartlett was pleased. The silence in the open field seemed thunderous. The sound of a helicopter, probably one of the traffic reporters, made the silence seem more thunderous by contrast. The helicopter bothered my concentration. Watch his middle, watch his feet, let peripheral vision take care of his fists, he can't fake with his middle. Stay away. Don't let him get hold of you. I tried a combination. Left jab, left hook, right cross. It worked. I scored on all three. But no one was counting. Harry Balleau wasn't going to jump into the ring at the end and raise my hand. If we clinched, Artie Donovan wasn't going to jump in and make sure we broke clean. There was a mouse starting under Harroway's right eye. I circled him counterclockwise. Moving my hands in front of me, shuffling, keeping my left foot forward. Don't get caught walking. Don't let him get you between steps. Shuffle, jab, one two, shuffle, jab, one two. Move in. Move out. I was way ahead on points. But Harroway didn't seem to be weakening. He lunged at me. I moved out of the way and got him with the side of my fist on the temple. Don't break your hand. Don't hit his head with your knuckles. Shuffle, move. Jab. The sweat began to slip down my chest and arms; it felt good. I was getting looser and quicker. Ought to warm up really. Should do some squat jumps and stretching exercises before you have a fight with a 215-pound body builder who probably killed a guy with his fist last week. Harroway was breathing a little short. I gave him a dip with my right shoulder, went left, and dug my left fist into his stomach. He grunted. He got hold of my shoulder with his left hand. I twisted in toward him and came up under his jaw with the heel of my right hand. His head jolted back. I hammered him in the Adam's apple with the edge of the same hand. He made a choking sound. I rolled on out away from him, breaking the grip on my shoulder as I did, and brought my left elbow back against his cheekbone with the full weight of my rolling 195 behind it. He went down. I heard Kevin gasp. Harroway was halfway up when I finished my roll and kicked him in the face. I sprawled him over on his side. He kept going, rolled over, and came up. Maybe I was just making him mad. There was a lot of blood on his face and shirt now. Besides his nose, there was a cut under the eye where the mouse had been. The eye was almost closed. The right side of his face where my elbow had caught him was beginning to puff. He seemed to have trouble breathing. I wondered if I'd broken something in the neck. He came at me. I went to work on the other eye. Two jabs, a left hook. Move away, circle. Concentrate. Don't let him grab you. Don't let him tag you. Concentrate. Move. Jab. He swung a right roundhouse, and I caught it on my forearm. The whole arm went numb, and I backpedaled out of range waiting for it to recover. Better not let that happen again. Harroway kept coming. His face was bloody. One eye was shut and the other closing. His breathing was hoarse and labored, but he kept coming on. I felt a tickle of fear in my stomach. What if I couldn't stop him? Never mind what if I couldn't. Think about jabbing and moving. Concentrate. Don't think things that don't help. Don't think at all. Concentrate. I jabbed the closing eye. Harroway grunted in pain. He was having trouble seeing. I hit the same eye again. There was a cut on the eyebrow, and the blood was blinding him. He stood still. Weaving a little. Like a buffalo, with his head lowered. I stepped away from him.

"Stop it, Harroway," I said.

He shook his head and lunged toward the sound of my voice. I moved away and hit him a left hook in the neck.

"Stop it, you goddamned fool," I said.

He came at me again. I stepped in toward him like a lineman on a pass rush and came up against the side of his head with my forearm, my whole body behind it, driving off my legs. Harroway straightened up and fell over on his back without a sound. The shock of the impact tingled the length of my arm and up into my shoulder. No one said anything. Kevin stood by himself opposite his mother and father, with Harroway between them lying on his back in the sun.

Kevin said, "Don't, Vic. Get up. Don't quit. Don't let him beat you. Don't quit."

"He didn't quit, kid, he's hurt. Anybody can be hurt."

"He let you beat him."

"No. He couldn't stop me. But there's no shame in that. It's just something I know how to do better than he does. He's a man, kid. I think he's a no-good sonova bitch. But he didn't quit. He went as far as he could, for you. In fact he went a lot farther than he could, for you. So did your mother and father."

Now that it was over I was shaky. My shirt was soaked with sweat. My arms trembled and my legs felt weak. I took the bullets out of my pants pocket and reloaded the gun while I talked. "How far have you gone for anybody lately?"

The boy still looked at Harroway. In the distance I heard a siren. Somebody had called for the buzzers, and here they came. Kevin started to cry. He stood looking at Harroway and cried with his hands straight down by his side.

"I don't know what to do," he said. Roger Bartlett got his feet under him and stood up. He put out his hand and helped his wife up. He fumbled a handkerchief out of his hip pocket and gave it to her, and she held it against her still-leaky nose. The two of them stood looking at Kevin who stood crying. Then Marge Bartlett said, "Oh, honey," and stepped over Harroway and put her arms around the kid and cried too. Then Bartlett got his arms around both of them and held on for dear life. Harroway sat up, painfully, and hugged his knees and looked at me with his one slightly open eye.

"Slut?" I said. He looked at me without comprehension. I said, "A couple of days ago you called Susan Silverman a slut." He still looked blank. "Never mind," I said.

26

It was suppertime before we got things cleaned up with the Boston cops and I got back to Smithfield. Boston would hold Harroway on an assault charge until they straightened out with Healy and Trask the kidnapping, murder, extortion, contributing to the delinquency of a minor, and procuring charges that seemed likely. Kevin went home with his mother and father, and I went to Susan Silverman's house to see if there was any cassoulet or champagne or whatever left around and to soak my hands in ice water. She gave me bourbon on the rocks with a dash of bitters in a big glass. We sat on her couch.

"And was it Vic Harroway all along?" she said.

"Nope, not entirely. According to Harroway it was actually Croft that ran things. He got them drugs, set up the prostitution customers, kept things cool with the local fuzz."

"Chief Trask?"

"Maybe. Harroway says he doesn't know. He knows only that Croft said the cops wouldn't bother him."

"Did he kill Maguire?"

"Yeah. Harroway says it was an accident. He and Kevin were going to get some of Kevin's things. Harroway was lifting some booze while they were at it, and Maguire caught them. Maguire panicked, grabbed for the poker, and Harroway hit him too hard."

"And the kidnapping and the sick jokes and everything?"

"That's not too clear. Harroway seemed to have two reasons. First, practical: he thought that they could finance 'a new life together'—that's what he called it—by putting the arm on the old man for the ransom money. And he says then he thought once they got the dough that they'd have a little sport with the straight world. Kevin says it was his idea, but Harroway says no, it was all his own doing. He also says that Kevin was upstairs in his room when Maguire got killed, but Kevin says he was there. Harroway seems to be protecting him, and Kevin's not entirely coherent. You can imagine. He's torn apart. He found out he still had some feelings for his mother and father he didn't realize he had, and it's all over for Harroway, and the kid knows it."

Susan said, "I wonder if it was good or bad for him to see Harroway beaten."

"I thought it would be good. I hope I was right. Harroway represented something solid and safe and indestructible; you know, a kind of fantasy superhero to insulate Kevin from the world, to be everything his father wasn't and his mother wouldn't let him or his father be."

"Maybe," she said. "Or maybe it's a glib generalization that won't hold. I guess we'll have to wait awhile and see how therapy works. Psychological truth usually isn't that neat."

"Yeah," I said, "but I didn't have time to wait and see out there in the field."

She said, "I know. You do what you have to. And besides, he insulted us once, didn't he?"

"Yeah," I said, "there's that."

I rattled the empty glass at her, and she got up and refilled it. The bourbon made a spread of warmth in my stomach. I took my left hand out of the ice water and put my right one in. I put my feet up on the coffee table and rested my head on the back of her couch. Susan came back with the second drink.

"You know," I said, "he was a nasty, brutish, mean sonova bitch. But he loved that kid."

"They all do," Susan Silverman said.

"You mean his mother and father?" She nodded. "Yeah, you're right," I said, "they do. You should have seen that henpecked, browbeaten bastard try to go up against Harroway. You've seen what Harroway looks like, and Bartlett tried to take him. And so did she. Amazing." I took my right hand out of the ice water and switched my glass to it and put my left arm around Susan's shoulder.

She said, "How did Croft and Harroway get mixed up together?"

"Harroway says that Croft looked him up. Harroway was doing a little bit of small-time pimping, and he says Croft told him he knew all about it and had an idea for them to get a much bigger and more profitable operation. He'd supply the drugs, get the word around, and Harroway would do the on-the-spot managerial duties."

"And they split?"

"No, that's the interesting part. Harroway says Croft had a silent partner. Harroway never knew who it was. One third of the take was a lot more dough than Harroway ever dreamed of, and he didn't complain."

"Do we know the silent partner?"

I shook my head. "I imagine Healy will get that out of Croft in a while."

"Oh, speaking of Healy, there's a message here for you from him. And one from some policeman in Boston." She went to the kitchen and came back with an envelope that said New England Telephone in the return address space. She looked at it and said, "A woman called—I didn't get her name—and said she was from Lieutenant Healy's office, and the Lieutenant wanted you to know that the package you gave him to keep is being stored at the Smithfield Police Station. You can pick it up when you need it, but it better be soon."

"That's Croft," I said. "They must have gotten nervous riding him around and figured to let Trask bear the brunt of a false arrest suit."

"And," she said, "I have a message that you should call either a Sergeant Belson or a Lieutenant Quirk when you came in. They said you knew the number."

"Do I ever," he said. "Okay. I'll do that now." I hated to get up, and I was beginning to get stiff. Ten years ago I didn't get stiff this soon. I let my feet down off the coffee table and drank most of the second bourbon and got myself upright. I felt as if I needed a lube job. A few more bourbons and I'd be oiled. Ah, Spenser, your wit's as keen as ever. I dialed Boston Homicide and got Quirk.

"I got the information on your man," he said. No salutation, no golly, Spenser, it's swell to hear your voice. Sometimes I wasn't sure how fond Quirk was of me.

"Okay," I said.

"He's got a record. Wanted in Tacoma, Washington, for performing an illegal abortion. Got himself disbarred or delicensed or whatever the hell they do with doctors that screw up. That was about seven years ago. Now he could probably do it legal in half the country, but then it was still a big unh-unh."

"And he's still wanted?"

"Yeah, he skipped bail and disappeared. The AG's office out there has an outstanding warrant on him, but it's not international intrigue. I don't think there are a lot of people working on it these days."

"Anything else?"

"Nothing much. Seems the guy had a good practice before this happened. I met the homicide commander out there once, and I gave him a call. Says this Croft was well thought of. Probably did the abortion as a kindness, not for dough. Didn't want to be quoted, but said he thought it was kind of a shafting. Girl's old man made a goddamned crusade of it, you know?"

"Yeah."

"One thing, though," Quirk said.

"What's that?"

"Yours isn't the first inquiry on him. Chief Trask of the Smithfield Police checked on him six years ago. There's a Xerox copy of Trask's request and a Xerox copy of the report the ID Bureau sent him."

"Six years ago?" I said. Something bad was nudging at me.

"Yeah, what's going on out there? Nice to see you're in close touch with the local law enforcement agencies."

I said, "Jesus Christ."

Quirk said, "What?"

I said, "I'll get back to you," and hung up.

Susan said, "What's the matter?"

I said, "I'll be back," and headed for my car. It was about five minutes from Susan's house to the Smithfield jail. "Trask," I said out loud, "that sonova bitch." I slammed the car into the parking lot in front of the town hall and ran for the police station. Fire, police, and town hall were connected in a brick-faced white-spired town hall complex. The police station was in the middle between the double-doored fire station and the church-fronted town hall. Like a breezeway, I thought as I went in.

Trask was at the desk. I didn't like that. The chief shouldn't do desk duty. He looked up as I came in. "Well, Spenser," he said, "solve everything?"

I said, "Where's Croft?"

Trask jerked his head toward a door behind the desk. "Down there in a cell, safe and sound."

"I want to see him."

Trask was friendly, positively jolly. My stomach felt tight. I didn't want to go down and see Croft. "Sure," Trask said. He swiveled his chair around and snapped the bolt back on the door. "Third cell," he said. And opened the door.

There was a short corridor with three barred cells along the left side and a blank cinder block wall along the right. The first two cells were empty. In the third one Dr. Croft was hanging from the highest bar with his swollen tongue sticking out and his blank eyes popped way out. He was dead. I felt the nausea start up my throat, and it took me about thirty seconds to swallow it back. His striped necktie was knotted around his neck and around the top cross member in the barred door. I knew he was dead even before I reached my hand through to feel his pulse. I also knew I had something to do with it. I went back down the corridor and closed the door behind me. Trask had his feet up on an open desk drawer and was reading a mimeographed sheet of paper. He was wearing glasses. His thick red neck was smoothly shaved where his crew cut ended. He looked up as I closed the door.

"Everything okay down there?" he said. The glasses distorted his small pale eyes when he looked at me.

I said, "How come you're doing desk duty, Chief?"

"Aw, hell, you know how a small department is. I mean, we only got twelve men. I like to give some of the kids a break. You know. I mean it ain't like I'm commissioner in Boston or something." He smiled at me, a big friendly hick smile. He'd never liked me this well before.

There was a table along the wall to the left of the cell block door. It had chrome legs and a maple-colored Formica top. There was a coffee percolator plugged in on it and a half-empty box of paper cups. I took one and poured myself some coffee. Then I sat on the table facing Trask. The silent partner.

"Trask," I said, "I know you murdered Croft."

He never blinked. "What the hell are you talking about?" he said.

"No crap now, there's just the two of us here. You went down that corridor and tied that tie around his neck and hoisted him up there and let him strangle because he was the only link between you and Harroway and with him dead no one would have any way of finding out what you were into."

Trask looked straight at me and said, "What was I into?"

"You were into prostitution and narcotics and sex shows and probably can be arraigned for abusing a goat."

"You can't prove any of that."

"Not right now, I can't. But I know some things and I'm going to tell them to Healy and he's going to prove it."

"What do you know?"

"I know that you know that Croft is wanted in Tacoma, and that you knew it six years ago. Now that's not much for starters. But I bet if we start pulling on that little loose end, after a while there may be a whole weave we can ravel out. You learned that little bit of business, and you used it to blackmail Croft. Maybe you got suspicious of the way he just drifted in here; maybe he confided in you; I don't know. But I'll bet you had the whole cesspool all worked out in your head and were just waiting for a middleman. And plop, into your lap dropped Croft. So he dealt with Harroway and you dealt with him. And nobody else knew anything about it. Until Harroway got a crush on a goddamned runaway and screwed up the whole thing."

Trask was still looking straight at me.

"And then you get Croft right in your own jail. Merry Christmas, from me and Healy. And you figured, okay, this is the only way they can get me. If he's gone, I'm safe. Did it bother you to strangle him like that with the necktie? Did he croak and kick trying to breathe? How you going to explain not taking his tie away from him?"

Trask kept looking without a word.

"I feel mean about it. I think Croft wasn't that bad a guy and he made a mistake that was motivated by a decent impulse and it destroyed him, and you used it to make him a goddamned pimp and then you killed him. I feel really mean about that part, you cold-blooded sonova bitch. Because I delivered him to you. And Healy will feel mean about it because he did too. And we will nail your ass for it. You can believe that. We only know a little, and we'll have to guess a lot, but we will have you for it."

Trask said, "Not if you don't tell anybody. It's a sweet setup. Or it was. I could pass on a few of the profits to you. Maybe you could even recruit a new manager for the girls and take Croft's job yourself. Or maybe we could cut out the middleman; you could combine the jobs. Maybe you don't have the drug contacts, but the girls are better revenue in this town anyway."

I leaned forward a little and spit in his face. He flushed red and the pearl-handled General Patton forty-five came out. "All right, smart guy. If you don't want coin, maybe there's another way." He wiped my saliva away with the back of his hand. His sun-bleached blond eyebrows looked white against his red face. "You came in here, tried to spring Croft, pulled a gun, I shot you in self-defense, and Croft sees it's no use hoping anymore and hangs himself."

I laughed. "Oh, good, even though the state cop who put him here told you to hold Croft for me. Even though I'm here five minutes after a Boston dick named Quirk tells me about your request for info on Croft six years ago. What a mammoth intellect you are, Trask. How the hell did you figure out this hustle by yourself anyway?"

Trask said, "Yeah, you think you're so goddamned smart; you'll be dead and I'll be gone and we'll see who's so goddamned smart then."

I threw the cup of coffee in his face and kicked the gun out of his hand. It went over the counter and skidded along the floor. Trask started to get up, and I was on my feet in front of him. "Go for it," I said. "Get up and try and get by me and go for the gun, you piece of garbage." He half rose from the chair and then sat down. "I'm not moving," he said.

I turned and walked away from him. At the door I picked up his gun. A Colt, single-action, six-inch barrel. I threw it through the glass front window.

"I'll be in touch with Healy," I said. "And he'll be in touch with you. Start running, you sonova bitch."

I walked out and left the door open behind me.

MORTAL STAKES

This too is for
Joan, David, and Daniel

1

It was summertime, and the living was easy for the Red Sox because Marty Rabb was throwing the ball past the New York Yankees in a style to which he'd become accustomed. I was there. In the skyview seats, drinking Miller High Life from a big paper cup, eating peanuts and having a very nice time. I wasn't supposed to be having a nice time. I was supposed to be working. But now and then you can do both.

For serious looking at baseball there are few places better than Fenway Park. The stands are close to the playing field, the fences are a hopeful green, and the young men in their white uniforms are working on real grass, the authentic natural article; under the actual sky in the temperature as it really is. No Tartan Turf. No Astrodome. No air conditioning. Not too many pennants over the years, but no Texans either. Life is adjustment. And I loved the beer.

The best pitcher I ever saw was Sandy Koufax, and the next best was Marty Rabb. Rabb was left-handed like Koufax, but bigger, and he had a hard slider that waited for you to commit yourself before it broke. While I shelled the last peanut in the bag he laid the slider vigorously on Thurman Munson and the Yankees were out in the eighth. While the sides changed I went for another bag of peanuts and another beer.

The skyviews were originally built in 1946, when the Red Sox had won their next-to-last pennant and had to have additional press facilities for the World Series. They were built on the roof of the grandstand between first and third. Since the World Series was not an annual ritual in Boston the press facilities were converted to box seats. You reached them over boardwalks laid on the tar and gravel roof of the grandstand, and there was a booth up there for peanuts, beer, hot dogs, and programs and another for toilet facilities. All connected with boardwalks. Leisurely, no crowds. I got back to my seat just as the Sox were coming to bat and settled back with my feet up on the railing. Late June, sun, warmth, baseball, beer, and peanuts. Ah, wilderness. The only flaw was that the gun on my right hip kept digging into my back. I adjusted.

Looking at a ball game is like looking through a stereopticon. Everything seems heightened. The grass is greener. The uniform whites are brighter than they should be. Maybe it's the containment. The narrowing of focus. On the other hand, maybe it's the tendency to drink six or eight beers in the early innings. Whatever—Alex Montoya, the Red Sox center fielder, hit a home run in the last of the eighth. Rabb fell upon the Yankee hitters in the ninth like a cleaver upon a lamb chop, and the game was over.

It was a Wednesday, and the crowd was moderate. No pushing and trampling. I strolled on down past them under the stands to the lower level. Down there it was dark and littered. A hundred programs rolled and dropped on the floor. The guys in the concession booths were already rolling down the steel curtains that closed them off like a bunch of rolltop desks. There were a lot of fathers and kids going out. And a lot of old guys with short cigars and plowed Irish faces that seemed in no hurry to leave. Peanut shells crunched underfoot.

Out on Jersey Street I turned right. Next door to the park is an office building with an advance sale ticket office behind plate glass and a small door that says BOSTON AMERICAN LEAGUE BASEBALL CLUB. I went in. There was a flight of stairs, dark wood, the walls a pale green latex. At the top another door. Inside were a foyer in the same green latex with a dark green carpet and a receptionist with stiff blue hair. I said to the receptionist, "My name is Spenser. To see Harold Erskine." I tried to look like a short-relief prospect just in from Pawtucket. I don't think I fooled her.

She said, "Do you have an appointment?"

I said, "Yes."

She spoke into the intercom, listened to the answer, and said, "Go in."

Harold Erskine's office was small and plain. There were two green file cabinets side by side in a corner, a yellow deal desk opposite the door, a small conference table, two straight chairs, and a window that looked out on Brookline Ave. Erskine was as unpretentious as his office. He was a small plump man, bald on top. The gray that remained was cut close to his head. His face was round and red-cheeked, his hands pudgy. I'd read somewhere that he'd been a minor-league shortstop and hit .327 one year at Pueblo. That had been a while ago; now he looked like a defrocked Santa.

"Come in, Mr. Spenser, enjoy the game?"

"Yeah, thanks for the pass." I sat in one of the straight chairs.

"My pleasure. Marty's something else, isn't he?"

I nodded. Erskine leaned back in his chair and cleaned the corners of his mouth with the thumb and forefinger of his left hand, drawing them together along his lower lip. "My attorney says I can trust you."

I nodded again. I didn't know his attorney.

Erskine rubbed his lip again. "Can I?"

"Depends on what you want to trust me to do."

"Can you guarantee that what we say will be confidential, no matter what you decide?"

"Yes." Erskine kept working on his lower lip. It looked clean enough to me.

"What did my lawyer tell you when he called?"

"He said you'd like to see me after today's game and there'd be a pass waiting for me at the press entrance on Jersey Street if I wanted to watch the game first."

"What do you charge?"

"A hundred a day and expenses. But I'm running a special this week; at no extra charge I teach you how to wave a blackjack."

Erskine said, "I heard you were a wit." I wasn't sure he believed it.

"Your lawyer tell you that too?" I asked.

"Yes. He discussed you with a state police detective named Healy. I think Healy's sister married my lawyer's wife's brother."

"Well, hell, Erskine. You know all you really can know about me. The only way you can find out if you can trust me is to try it. I'm a licensed private detective. I've never been to jail. And I have an open, honest face. I'm willing to sit here and let you look at me for a while, I owe you for the free ball game, but eventually you'll have to tell me what you want or ask me to leave."

Erskine stared at me some more. His cheeks seemed a little redder, and he was beginning to develop callus tissue on his lower lip. He brought his left hand down flat on the top of the desk. "Okay," he said. "You're right. I got no choice."

"It's nice to be wanted," I said.

"I want you to see if Marty Rabb's got gambling connections."

"Rabb," I said. Snappy comebacks are one of my specialties.

"That's right, Rabb. There's a rumor, no, not even that, a whisper, a faint, pale hint, that Rabb might be shading a game now and then."

"Marty Rabb?" I said. When I've got a good line, I like to stick with it.

"I know. It's hard to believe. I don't believe it, in fact. But it's possible and it's got to be checked. You know what even the rumor of a fix means to baseball."

I nodded. "If you did have Rabb in your teacup, you could make a buck, couldn't you?"

Just hearing me say it made Erskine swallow hard. He leaned forward over the desk. "That's right," he said. "You can get good odds against the Sox anytime Marty pitches. If you could get that extra percentage by having Rabb on your end of the bet, you could make a lot of money."

"He doesn't lose much," I said. "What was he last year, twenty-five and six?"

"Yeah, but when he does lose, you could make a bundle. And even if he doesn't lose, what if you've got money bet on the biggest inning? Marty could ease up a little at the right time. We don't score much. We're all pitching and defense and speed. Marty wouldn't have to give up many runs to lose, or many runs to make a big inning. If you bet right he wouldn't have to do it very often."

"Okay, I agree, it would be a wise investment for someone to get Rabb's cooperation. But what makes you think someone has?"

"I don't quite know. You hear things that don't mean anything by themselves. You see stuff that doesn't mean anything by itself. You know, Marty grooving one to Reggie Jackson at the wrong time. Could happen to anyone. Cy Young probably did it too. But after a while you get that funny feeling. And I've got it. I'm probably wrong. I got nothing hard. But I have to know. It's not just the club, it's Marty. He's a terrific kid. If other people started to get the funny feeling it would destroy him. He'd be gone and no one would even have to prove it. He wouldn't be able to pitch for the Yokohama Giants."

"Hiring a private cop to investigate him isn't the best way to keep it quiet," I said.

"I know, you've got to work undercover. Even if you proved him innocent the damage would be done."

"There's another question there too. What if he's guilty?"

"If he's guilty I'll hound him out of baseball. The minute people don't trust the integrity of the final score, the whole system goes right down the tube. But I've got to know first, and I'm betting there's nothing to it. I've got to have absolute proof. And it's got to be confidential."

"I've got to talk to people. I've got to be around the club. I can't find out the truth without asking questions and watching."

"I know. We'll have to come up with a story to cover that. I don't suppose you play ball?"

"I was the second leading hitter on the Vine Street Hawks in nineteen forty-six."

"Yeah, you ever stood up at the plate and had someone throw you a major-league curve ball?"

I shook my head.

"I have. Nineteen fifty-two I went to spring training with the Dodgers and Clem Labine threw about ten of them at me the first intersquad game. It helped get me into the front office. Besides, you're too old."

"I didn't think it showed," I said.

"Well, I mean, for a ballplayer, starting out."

"How about a writer?" I said.

"The guys know all the writers."

"Not a sports reporter, a writer. A guy doing a book on baseball—you know, *The Boys of Summer, The Summer Game,* that stuff."

Erskine thought about it. "Not bad," he said. "Not bad. You don't look much like a writer, but hell, what's a writer look like? Right? Why not? I'll take you down, tell them you're doing a book and you're going to be hanging around the club and asking questions. It's perfect. You know anything about writing?"

"I've read some," I said.

"I mean, can you sound like a writer? You look like the bouncer at a health club."

"I can keep from sounding as stupid as I look," I said.

"Yeah, okay, it sounds good to me. I see no problem. But you gotta be, for crissake, discreet. I mean dis-goddamn-creet. Right?"

"I am, as we writers say, the very soul of discretion. I'll need a press pass or whatever credentials you people issue. And it is probably smart if you take me down and introduce me around."

"Yeah, I'll take care of that." He looked at me and started working on his lip again. "This is between you and me," he said. "No one else knows. Not the manager, not the owners, not the players, nobody."

"How about your lawyer?" I asked.

"He is my own lawyer, not the club's. He thinks I wanted you for personal business."

"Okay, when do I meet the team?"

Erskine looked at his watch. "Too late today, half of them are showered and gone. How about tomorrow? We'll go in before the game and I'll introduce you around."

"I'll show up here about noon tomorrow then."

"Yeah," he said. "That'll be good. You got a title for this book you're supposed to be writing?"

"I'm looking for sales appeal," I said. "How about *The Sensuous Baseball*?"

Erskine said he didn't like that title. I went home to think of another one.

2

I got up early the next morning and jogged along the river. There were sparrows and grackles mixed in among the pigeons on the esplanade, and I saw two chickadees in the sandpit of one of the play areas. A couple of rowers were on the river, a girl in jeans tucked into high brown boots was walking two Welsh corgis, and there were some other joggers.

Near the lagoon, past the concert shell, a bum in an old blue sharkskin suit was sleeping on a newspaper, and along Storrow Drive the commuter traffic was just beginning. I was still living at the bottom of Marlborough Street and the run up to the BU footbridge took about ten minutes. I crossed the footbridge over Storrow Drive and went in the side door of the BU gym. I knew a guy in the athletic department and they let me use the weight room. I spent forty-five minutes on the irons and another half hour on the heavy bag. By that time some coeds were passing by on their way to class and I finished up with a big flourish on the speed bag. They didn't seem impressed.

I jogged back downriver with the sun much warmer now and the dew gone from the grass and the commuter traffic in full cry. I was back in my apartment at five of nine, glistening with sweat, and reeking of good circulation, and throbbing with appetite.

I squeezed some orange juice and drank it, plugged in the coffee, and went for a shower. At quarter past nine I was back in the kitchen again in my red and white terry-cloth robe that Susan Silverman had given me on my last birthday. It had short sleeves and a golf umbrella on the breast pocket and the label said JACK NICKLAUS. Every time I put it on I wanted to yell "Fore."

I drank my first cup of coffee while I made a mushroom omelet with sherry, and my second cup of coffee while I ate the omelet, along with a warm loaf of unleavened Arab bread, and read the morning *Globe.* When I finished, I put the dishes in the dishwasher, made the bed, and got dressed. Gray socks, gray slacks, black loafers, and an eggshell-colored stretch knit shirt with small red hexagons all over it. I clipped my holster on over the belt on my right hip. The blue steel revolver was nicely color-coordinated with the black holster and the gray slacks. It clashed badly when I wore brown. To cover the gun I wore a gray denim jacket with red stitching along the pockets and lapels. I checked myself in the mirror. Adorable. Lucky it wasn't ladies' day. I'd get molested at the park.

The temperature was in the mid-eighties and the sun was bright when I got out onto Marlborough Street. I walked a block over to Commonwealth and strolled up the mall toward Fenway Park. It was still too early for the crowd to start gathering, but the early signs of a game were there. The old guy that sells peanuts from a pushcart was pushing it along toward Kenmore Square, an old canvas over the peanuts. A middle-aged couple had parked a maroon Chevy by a hydrant near Kenmore Square and were setting up to sell balloons from the trunk. The trunk lid was up, an air tank leaned against the rear bumper, and the husband, wearing a blue and red tennis visor, was opening a large cardboard box in the trunk. Near the corner of Brookline Ave, outside the subway kiosk, a young man with shoulder-length blond hair was selling small pennants that said RED SOX in red script against a blue background. I looked at my watch: 11:40. You couldn't see the park from Kenmore Square, but the light standards loomed up over the buildings and you knew it was close. As I turned down Brookline Ave toward the park I felt the old feeling. My father and I used to go this early to watch the teams take infield.

I walked the two blocks down Brookline Ave, turned the corner at Jersey Street, and went up the stairs to Erskine's office. He was in, reading what looked like a legal document, his chair tilted back and one foot on the open bottom drawer. I closed the door.

"You think of a new title for that book yet, Spenser?" he said.

An air conditioner set in one of the side windows was humming.

"How about *Valley of the Bat Boys*?"

"Goddamn it, Spenser, this isn't funny. You gotta have some kind of answer if someone asks you."

"The Balls of Summer?"

Erskine took a deep breath, let it out, shook his head, as if there were a horsefly on it, kicked the drawer shut, and stood up. "Never mind," he said. "Let's go."

As we went down the stairs, he handed me a press pass. "Keep it in your wallet," he said. "It'll let you in anywhere."

A blue-capped usher at Gate A said, "How's it going, Harold?" as we went past him. Vendors were starting to set up. A man in a green twill work uniform was unloading cases of beer onto a dolly. We went into the locker room.

My first reaction was disappointment. It looked like most other locker rooms. Open lockers with a shelf at the top, stools in front of them, nameplates above. To the right the training area with whirlpool, rubbing table, medical-looking cabinet with an assortment of tape and liniment behind the glass doors at the top. A man in a white T-shirt and white cotton pants was taping the left ankle of a burly black man who sat on the table in his shorts, smoking a cigar.

The players were dressing. One of them, a squat red-haired kid, was yelling to someone out of sight behind the lockers.

"Hey, Ray, can I be in the pen again today? There's a broad out there gives me a beaver shot every time we're home."

A voice from behind the lockers said, "Were you looking for her in Detroit last week when you dropped that foul?"

"Ah come on, Ray, Bill Dickey used to drop them once in a while. I seen you drop one once when I was a little kid and you was my idol."

A tall, lean man came around the lockers with his hands in his back pockets. He was maybe forty-five, with black hair cut short and parted on the left. There were no sideburns, and you knew he went to a barber who did most of his work with the electric clippers. His face was dark-tanned, and a sprinkle of gray showed in his hair. He wore no sweat shirt under his uniform blouse, and the veins were prominent in his arms. Erskine gestured him toward us. "Ray," he said, "I want you to meet Mr. Spenser. Spenser, Ray Farrell, the manager." We shook hands. "Spenser's a writer, doing a book on baseball, and I've arranged for him to be around the club for a while, interview some players, that sort of thing."

Farrell nodded. "What's the name of the book, Spenser?" he said.

"The Summer Season," I said. Erskine looked relieved.

"That's nice." Farrell turned toward the locker room. "Okay, listen up. This guy's name is Spenser. He's writing a book and he'll be around talking with you and probably taking some notes. I want everyone to cooperate." He turned back toward me. "Nice meeting you, Spenser. You want me to have someone introduce you around?"

"No, that's okay, I'll introduce myself as we go," I said.

"Okay, nice meeting you. Anything I can do, feel free." He walked away.

Erskine said, "Well, you're on your own now. Keep in touch," and left me.

The black man on the training table yelled over to the redhead, "Hey, Billy, you better start watching your mouth about beaver. This guy'll be writing you up in a book, and Sally will have your ass when she reads it." His voice was high and squeaky.

"Naw, she wouldn't believe it anyway." The redhead came over and put out his hand. "Billy Carter," he said. "I catch when Fats has got a hangover." He nodded at the black man who had climbed off the table and started toward us. He was short and very wide and the smooth tan coating of fat over his body didn't conceal the thick elastic muscles underneath.

I shook hands with Carter. "Collect all your bubble-gum cards," I said. I turned toward the black man. "You're West, aren't you?"

He nodded. "You seen me play?" he said.

"No," I said, "I remember you from a Brut commercial."

He laughed, a high giggle. "Never without, man, put it on between innings." He did a small Flip Wilson impression and snapped his fingers.

From down the line of lockers a voice said, "Hey, Holly, everybody in the league says you smell like a fairy."

"Not to my face," West squeaked.

Most of the players were dressed and heading out to the field. A short, thin man in a pale blue seersucker suit and dark hornrimmed glasses came into the locker room. He spotted me and came over. "Spenser?" he said. I nodded. "Jack Little," he said. "I do PR for the Sox. Hal Erskine told me I'd find you here."

I said, "Glad to meet you."

He said, "Anything I can do to help, I'd be delighted. That's my job."

"Do you have biog sheets on the players?" I said.

"You bet. I've got a press book on every player. Stop by my office and I'll have my gal give you the whole packet."

"How old is your gal?" I said.

"Millie? Oh, Christ, I don't know. She's been with the club a long time. I don't ask a lady her age, Spenser. Get in trouble that way. Am I right?"

"Right," I said. "You're right."

"C'mon," he said, "I'll take you out to the dugout, point out some of the players, get you what you might call acclimated, okay?"

I nodded. "Acclimated," I said.

3

I sat in the dugout and watched the players take batting practice. Little sat beside me and chain-smoked Chesterfield Kings.

"That's Montoya," he said. "Alex Montoya was the player of the year at Pawtucket in 'sixty-eight. Hit two ninety-three last year, twenty-five homers."

I nodded. Marty Rabb was shagging in the outfield. Catching fly balls vest-pocket style like Willie Mays and lobbing the ball back to the infield underhanded.

"That's Johnny Tabor. He switch-hits. Look at the size of him, huh? Doesn't look like he could get the bat around. Am I right or wrong?"

"Thin," I said. "Doesn't look like he could get the bat around."

"Well, you know. We pay him for his glove. Strong up the middle, that's what Ray's always said. And Tabor's got the leather. Right?"

"Right."

The crowd was beginning to fill the stands and the noise level rose. The Yankees came out and took infield in their gray road uniforms. Most of them were kids. Long hair under the caps, bubble gum. Much younger than I was. Whatever happened to Johnny Lindell?

Rabb came into the dugout, wearing his warm-up jacket.

"That's Marty Rabb, with the clipboard," Little said. "He pitched yesterday, so today he charts the pitches."

I nodded. "He's a great one," Little said. "Nicest kid you ever want to see. No temperament, you know, no ego. Loves the game. I mean a lot of these kids nowadays are in it for the big buck, you know, but Marty. Nicest kid you ever want to meet. Loves the game."

A man with several chins came out of the alleyway to the clubhouse and stood on the top step of the dugout, looking over the diamond. His fading blond hair was long and very contemporary. It showed the touch of a ten-dollar barber. He was fat, with a sharp, beaked nose jutting from the red dumpling face. A red-checked shirt, the top two buttons open, hung over the mass of his stomach like the flag of his appetite. His slacks were textured navy blue with a wide flare, and he had on shiny white shoes with brass buckles on them.

"Who's that?" I asked Little.

"Don't you know him? Hell, that's Bucky Maynard. Only the best play by play in the business, that's all. Don't let him know you didn't recognize him. Man, he'll crucify you."

"I gather he doesn't work out a lot with the team," I said. Maynard took out a pale green cigar and lit it carefully, turning it as he puffed to get it burning evenly.

"Jesus, don't comment on his weight either," Little said. "He'll eat you alive."

"Is it okay if I clear my throat while he's in the park?"

"You can kid around, but if Bucky Maynard doesn't like you, you got a lot of trouble. I mean, he can destroy you on the air. And he will."

"I thought he worked for the club," I said.

"He does. But he's so popular that we couldn't get rid of him if we wanted. God knows there have been times." Little stopped. His eyes shifted up and down the dugout. I wondered if he was worried about a bug. "Don't get me wrong, now. Buck's a great guy; he's just got a lot of pride, and it don't help to get on the wrong side of him. Course it don't pay to get on the wrong side of anybody. Am I right or wrong?"

"Right as rain," I said. Little liked the phrase. I bet he'd use it within the day. I'm really into language.

Maynard came toward us, and Little stood up. "Hey, Buck, how's it going?"

Maynard looked at Little without speaking. Little swallowed and said, "Like to have you say hello to Mr. Spenser here, doing a book about the Sox."

Maynard nodded at me. "Spenser," he said. His southern accent stretched out the last syllable and dropped the *r*.

"Nice to meet you," I said. I hoped he wasn't offended.

"He'll be wanting to talk to you, Buck, I know. No book about the Sox would be worth much if Old Buck wasn't in it. Am I right, Spenser, or am I right?"

"Right," I said. Little lit a new Chesterfield King from the butt of the old one.

Maynard said, "Why don't y'all come on up the booth later on and watch some of the game? Get a chance to see how a broadcast team works."

"Thanks," I said, "I'd like to."

"Just remember you're not going to get any predigested Pablum up there. In mah booth by God we call the game the way it is played. No press release bullshit; if a guy's doggin' it, by God we say he's doggin' it. You follow?"

"I can follow that okay."

Maynard's eyes narrowed as he looked at me. They were pale and small and flat, like two Necco wafers. "You better believe it 'cause anyone who knows me knows it's true. Isn't that right, Jack?"

Little answered before Maynard finished asking. "Absolutely, Buck, anybody knows that. Bucky tells it like it is, Spenser. That's why the fans love him."

"C'mon up, Spenser, anytime. Jack'll show you the way." Maynard rolled the green cigar about in the center of his mouth, winked, and moved out onto the field toward the Yankee dugout.

Billy Carter from the end of the dugout yelled, "Whale, ho," and then stared out toward the right-field stands as Maynard whirled and looked into the dugout. Ray Farrell had come out of the dressing room and was posting the lineup at the far end of the dugout. He ignored Carter and Maynard. Maynard looked for maybe a minute into the dugout while Carter observed the right-field foul line from under the brim of his cap, his feet cocked up against one of the dugout supports. He was whistling "Turkey in the Straw." Maynard turned and continued toward the Yankee dugout.

Little blew out his breath. "That goddamned Carter is going to get in real trouble someday. Always the wisecracks. Always the goddamned hot dog. He ain't that good. I mean, he catches maybe thirty games a year. You'd think he'd be a little humble, but always the big mouth." Little spilled some ashes onto his shirtfront and brushed them off vigorously.

"I was thinking about some Moby-Dick humor myself when Maynard was standing there blotting out the sun."

"You screw around with Bucky and you'll never get your book written, I'll tell you that straight out, Spenser. That's no shit." Little looked as if he was in pain, his small-featured face contorted with sincerity. Farrell went up the steps of the dugout and out toward home plate with his lineup card. The Yankee manager came out toward home plate from the other side, and, for the first time, I saw the umpires. Older than the players, and bulkier.

"I think I'll go up in the broadcast booth," I said. "If Maynard turns on me and truths me to death, I want you to write my mom."

Little didn't even want to talk about it. He brought me up to the press entry, along the catwalk, under the roof toward Maynardville.

The broadcast booth was a warren of cable lash-up, television monitors, microphone cords, and one big color TV camera set up to point at a blank wall to the rear of the booth. For live commercials, I assumed. Give Bucky Maynard a chance to tell it like it is about somebody's bottled beer. There were two men in the booth already. One I recognized. Doc Wilson, who used to play first base for the Minnesota Twins and now did color commentary for the Sox games. He was a tall, angular man, with rimless glasses and short, wavy brown hair. He was sitting at the broadcast table, running through the stat book and drinking black coffee from a paper cup. The other man was young, maybe twenty-two, middle height and willowy with Dutch boy blond hair and an Oakland A's mustache. He had on a white safari hat with a wide leopard-skin band, pilot's sunglasses, a white silk shirt open to the waist, like Herb Jeffries, and white jeans tucked into the top of rust-colored Frye boots. There was a brass-studded rust-colored woven leather belt around his waist and a copper bracelet on his right wrist. He was slouched in a red canvas director's chair with his feet up on the broadcast counter, reading a copy of the *National Star* and chewing gum.

Wilson looked up as we came in. "Hey, Jack, howsa kid?"

"Doc, say hello to Spenser, here. He's a writer, doing a book on the Sox, and Bucky invited him up to the booth for a look-see."

Wilson reached around, and we shook hands. "Good deal," he said. "If Buck says go, it's go. Anything I can help with, just give a holler." The kid in the safari hat never looked up. He licked his thumb, turned a page of the *Star,* his jaws working smoothly, the muscles at the hinge swelling regularly as he chewed.

Little said, "This here's Lester Floyd. Lester, this is Mr. Spenser."

Lester gave a single upward jerk of his head, raised one finger without releasing the magazine, and kept reading. I said, "What's he do, sing 'Flamingo' at the station breaks?"

The kid looked up then. I couldn't see his eyes behind the amber lenses of his aviator shades. He blew a large pink bubble, popped it with his teeth, and slowly chewed it back into his mouth.

Little said, "Lester is Bucky's driver, Spenser. Spenser's going to be doing a book on the Sox and on Bucky, Lester."

Lester blew another big bubble and chewed it back in. "He's gonna be looking up his own asshole if he gets smart with me," he said. There was a red flush on his cheekbones.

"Guess he doesn't sing 'Flamingo,' " I said to Wilson.

"Aw now, Lester, Mr. Spenser's just kidding around." Little did a small nervous shuffle step. Wilson was staring out at the diamond. Lester was working harder on the gum.

"And I'm telling him not to," Lester said.

"Never mind, Lester." The voice came from behind me. It was Maynard. "Ah invited Mr. Spenser up here to listen to mah broadcast. He's mah guest."

"He said something smart about me singing, Bucky. I don't like that sorta talk."

"Ah know, Lester, ah don't blame you. Mr. Spenser, Ah'd appreciate it if you was to apologize to Lester here. He's a good boy, but he's very emotional. He's also got a black belt in tae kwon do. And ah wouldn't want to get your writing hand all messed up before you even start."

Waltzing with Lester in the broadcast booth wasn't going to tell me anything about Marty Rabb. If he was any good, it might tell me something about me, but that wasn't what I was getting paid for. Besides, I knew about me. And if I was a writer, I wasn't supposed to be roughing it up with black belts. Maybe box with José Torres on a talk show, but brawling at a ball game . . . ? "I'm sorry, Lester," I said. "Sometimes I try too hard to be funny."

Lester popped his gum at me again and went back to the *National Star*. Maynard smiled with his mouth only and moved to a big upholstered swivel chair at the broadcast table. He sat down, put on big padded earphones, and spoke into the mike. The small monitor built into the table to his right had flickered into life and displayed a picture of the batter's box below. There was a long mimeographed list in front of him on a clipboard, and he checked off the first two items as he spoke.

"Burt, ah want to open on Stabile warming up. Doc and me will do some business about the knuckler and how it flutters. Right? . . . Yup, soon's you run the opening cartridge."

Wilson looked over and said to me, "He's talking to the people outside in the truck." I nodded. Lester licked his thumb again and turned another page.

Little leaned over and whispered to me. "Gotta run, anything you need just let me know." I nodded again, and Little tiptoed out like a man leaving church early.

Maynard said to the people in the truck, "Ah got nothing to do live up here, right? . . . well, ah don't see nothing on the sheet . . . no, goddamn it, ah taped that yesterday afternoon . . . okay, well get it straight, boy."

A cartoon picture of a slightly loutish-looking baseball player in a Red Sox uniform appeared on the monitor. Maynard said, "Twenty seconds," to Wilson. Below and to our right along the first-base line a portly right-handed pitcher named Rick Stabile was warming up. He threw without effort, lobbing the ball toward the catcher.

Wilson said into his mike, "Good afternoon, everyone, from Fenway Park in Boston, where today the Red Sox go against the Yankees in the rubber game of a three-game series. This is Doc Wilson along with Bucky Maynard standing by to bring you all the action."

A beer commercial appeared on the monitor screen, and Wilson leaned back. "You gonna pick it up on Stabile, Buck?"

Maynard said, "Check." Wilson handed him the stat sheet and leaned forward as the beer company logo filled the monitor screen.

Lester was finished with the tabloid and settled down into his chair and apparently went to sleep. He looked like a peaceful serpent. Tae kwon do? Never tried somebody that did that. I gave him a hard look. He was motionless; the breath from his nostrils ruffled his mustache gently. He was probably paralyzed with fear. Maynard said, "Howdy, all you Red Soxers, this is the old Buckaroo and you're looking at Rick Stabile's butterfly . . ."

By the sixth inning the game was gone for Boston. Stabile's knuckler had apparently decked when it should have dived, and the Yankees led 11 to 1. I made two trips, one for beer and hot dogs and one for peanuts. Lester slept, and Maynard and Wilson tried to talk some excitement into a laugher.

"Stabile's got to get some of the lard off from around his middle, Doc."

"Well, he's a fine boy, Bucky, but he's been playing a little heavy this year."

"Tell it like it is, Doc. He came into spring training hog fat and he hasn't lost it. He's got the tools, but he's gotta learn to back off from the table or he'll eat himself right out of the league." Maynard checked off an item on his log sheet.

"Here's Graig Nettles, two for two today, including the downtowner in the first with Gotham on all the corners."

I got up and headed out of the booth. Wilson winked at me as I left.

I stopped by at Little's office to pick up the press kit on Marty Rabb and four others. Little's gal had dentures.

4

Steam from the showers drifted into the locker room and made the air moist. The final score was 14 to 3 and no one was pouring champagne on anyone. I sat down beside Marty Rabb. He was bent over, unlacing his spikes. When he straightened, I said, "My name's Spenser, I'm writing a book about the Sox, and I guess I oughta start with you."

Rabb smiled and put out his hand. "Hi, glad to help. How about you don't mention today, though, huh?" He shook his head. He was well above my six feet one—all flat planes and sharp angles. His short brown hair grew down over his forehead in a wedge. His head was square and long, like a square-bladed garden spade. His cheekbones were high and prominent, making the cheeks slightly hollow beneath them.

I said, "Bucky Maynard tells me Stabile's too fat and that's why he's having trouble."

"You ever see Lolich or Wilbur Wood?" Rabb said.

"Yeah," I said. "I've seen Maynard too."

Rabb smiled. "Ricky doesn't pitch with his stomach. The ball wasn't moving for him today, that's all."

"It was moving for you yesterday."

"Yeah, I had it grooved yesterday." Rabb undressed as he talked. He was long-muscled and bony, his body pale in contrast to the dark tan on his face, neck, and arms.

"Well," I said, "I'm really more interested in the human side of the game, Marty. Could we get together tonight and talk a little?"

Rabb was naked now, standing with a towel over his shoulder. In fact, most of the people in the dressing room were naked. I felt like a streaker in a nudist colony.

"Yeah, sure. Ah, lemme see, no, we're not doing anything tonight that I know of. Why don't you come over to the apartment, meet my wife, maybe have a drink? That okay with you?"

"Fine, what time?"

"Well, the kid goes to bed about seven—about seven thirty. Wanna do that?"

"Yes. Where?"

"Church Park. You know where that is?"

"Yeah."

"Apartment six twelve."

I looked at my watch: 4:35. "That's fine. I'll be there. Thanks very much."

"See you." Rabb headed for the showers. His body high and narrow, the left trapezius muscle overdeveloped, swelling out along the left side of his spine.

I left. Outside the dressing room there were two people sweeping. Other than that the place was empty. I walked up the ramp under the stands and looked out at the field. It was empty. I went down and hopped the railing of the box seats. There was no sound. I walked over to home plate. The wall in left seemed arm's length away and 300 cubits high. The sun was still bright and at that time of day slanted in over the third-base stands, and the shadows of the light towers looked like giant renderings by Dali. A pigeon flew down from the center-field bleachers and pecked at the warning track. I walked out to the pitcher's mound and stood with my right foot on the rubber, looking down into home plate. Traffic sounds drifted in from the city, but muffled. I put my right hand behind me and let it rest against my butt. Left hand relaxed on my left thigh. I squinted in toward the plate. Last of the ninth, two out, three on, Spenser checks the sign. One of the men who'd been sweeping came out of the passageway and yelled, "Hey, what the hell are you doing out there?"

"Striking out Tommy Henrich, you dumb bastard. Don't you know anything?"

"You ain't supposed to be out there."

"I know," I said. "I never was."

I walked back in through the stands and on out of the ball park. I looked at my watch. It was nearly five. I walked back down the Commonwealth Avenue mall to Massachusetts Avenue. If Commonwealth Ave is yin, then Mass Ave is yang. Steak houses that no one you knew had gone to, office buildings with dirty windows, fast food, a palm reader, a massage parlor. I crossed Mass Ave and went into the Yorktown Tavern. It had plate glass windows and brown linoleum, a high tin ceiling painted white, booths along the left, a bar along the right. In the back corner was a color TV carrying a bowling game called *Duckpins for Dollars.* No one was watching. All the barstools were taken, and most of the booths. No one was wearing a tie. No one was drinking a Harvey Wallbanger. The house special was a shot and a beer.

In the last booth on the left, alone, was a guy named Seltzer who always reminded me of a seal. He was sleek and plumpish, thin through the chest, thicker through the hips. His hair was shiny black, parted in the middle and slicked tight against his head. He had a thin mustache, a pointed nose, and a dark pin-striped suit that cost at least $300. His white shirt gleamed in contrast to the darkness of the suit and the dinginess of the bar. He was reading the *Herald American.* As I slid in opposite him, he turned the page and folded it neatly back. I could see the big diamond ring on his little finger and the diamond chips set in the massive silver cuff links. He smelled of cologne, and when he looked up at me and smiled, his white teeth were even, cap perfect in his small mouth.

I said, "Evening, Lennie."

He said, "You know, Spenser, little things break your balls. You ever notice that? I mean I used to read the *Record American,* right? Nice little tabloid size, easy to handle. Then they buy up the *Herald* and go the big format and it's like reading a freakin' road map. Now that busts my nuts, trying to fold this thing right. That kinda stuff bother you ever?"

"On slow days," I said.

"Want a drink?"

"Yeah, I'll have a brandy Alexander," I said.

Seltzer laughed. "Hey, Frank." He raised a finger at the bartender. "A shot and a beer, okay?"

The bartender brought them over, put the beer on a little paper coaster, and went back behind the bar. I drank the shot.

"Well," I said, "if I had worms, I guess they're taken care of."

"Yeah, Frank don't age that stuff all that long, does he?"

I sipped the beer. It was better than the whiskey. "Lennie, I need to know something without letting it get around that I'm asking." His skin was remarkable. Smooth and pale and unlined. The sun had rarely shone upon it. It made him look a lot younger than I knew he was.

"Yeah," he said. "Sure, kid. I never saw any advantage talking about things for no good reason. What do you want to know?" He sipped some beer, holding the glass in the tips of his fingers with the little finger sticking out. When he put the glass down, he took the handkerchief from his breast pocket and wiped his mouth carefully.

"I want to know if you've heard anything about Marty Rabb."

Seltzer was very careful putting the handkerchief back in his pocket. He got the three points arranged and stood half up in the booth to look across the bar into the mirror and make sure they were right.

"Like what?" he said.

"Like anything at all."

"You mean, does he occasionally place a wager? That kind of thing?"

"That, or anything else."

"Well, he never placed a bet with me," Seltzer said, "but I heard something peculiar about him. The odds seem to shift a little when he pitches. I mean, there's some funny money placed when he's scheduled to go. Nothing big, nothing I'd even think about if somebody like you didn't come around and ask about him."

"You think he's in the satchel?"

"Rabb? Hell, no, Spenser. Nothing that strong. There's just a whisper, just a ruffle, that not everything is entirely jake. I wouldn't hesitate taking money when Rabb's pitching. I don't know anyone that would. It's just . . ." He shrugged and spread his hands out palms up. "Want another drink?"

I shook my head. "The last one took the enamel off my front teeth," I said.

"Aw, Spenser." Seltzer shook his head. "You're going soft. I remember twenty years ago you was fighting prelims in the Arena, you thought that stuff was imported from France."

"In those days I don't remember you dressing like George Brent either," I said.

Seltzer nodded. "Yeah," he said, "things change. Now instead of a newspaper, they give you a freaking road map. You know?"

I left him refolding his paper and went to get something to eat. The bar whiskey was thrashing about in my stomach, and I thought maybe I could smother it with something.

5

I had two cheeseburgers and a chocolate shake at an antique brick McDonald's on Huntington, just down from Symphony Hall. The food throttled the whiskey okay, but I was furtive coming out. If anyone saw me, I could never eat at Locke-Ober's again. The guilty part was I liked the cheeseburgers.

It was a little after six and I had some time to kill. There seemed to be more of it and harder to kill as I got older. I strolled back down Mass Ave toward the river. The college kids were out on the esplanade in large numbers, and the air was colorful with Frisbees and sweet with the smell of grass. I sat on a bench near the Mass Ave Bridge and looked at the river and watched a boy and girl share a bottle of Ripple. Sailboats veered and drifted on the river, and an occasional powerboat left a rolling wake upstream. Across the river MIT loomed like a concrete temple to the Great God Brown. A six-foot black girl with red hot pants and platform sandals went by with a Lhasa apso on a short leash. I watched her out of sight around the bend westbound.

At seven fifteen I strolled back up Mass Ave toward Church Park. Church Park is a large, gray, cement urban development associated with the Christian Science church complex across the street. It replaced a large number of shabby brick buildings with a very long twelve-story cement one that had stores on the bottom floor and apartments above. The doorman made me wait while he called up.

When I came out of the elevator, Marty Rabb was at his door, looking down the corridor at me. There was something surrealistic about the way his head appeared to violate the fearful symmetry of the hall.

"Down this way, Spenser," he said. "Glad to see you."

The front door opened into the living room. To the right a bedroom, straight ahead a small kitchen. To the left the living room opened out toward the street and looked out at the dome of the Mother Church of Christ Scientist across the street. Traffic sound drifted up through the open windows. The living room was done in wall-to-wall beige carpet; the walls were eggshell white. There were framed mementos of Rabb's career scattered on the walls. The furniture was in browns and beiges, and the tone was modern. On the glass-topped coffee table near the couch were a tray of raw vegetables and a bowl of sour cream dip.

"Honey, this is Mr. Spenser that's writing the book," Rabb said. "Spenser, this is my wife, Linda."

We shook hands. She was small and black-haired. Her features were small and close together, and her eyes dominated her face. They were very round and dark, with long lashes. Her black hair was long down her back and pulled back at the nape of her neck with a dark wooden clip. She had on a salmon pink sleeveless shell and white jeans. Her makeup was so understated that at first I thought she wore none.

"Nice to meet you, Mr. Spenser. Why don't you have a seat here on the couch? It's closest to the dip." She smiled, and her teeth were small and rather sharp.

I said, "Thank you."

"Would you like a hard drink, Mr. Spenser, or beer?" Rabb said. "I got some nice ale from Canada, Labatt Fifty, you ever try it?"

"Tried and approved," I said. "I'll take the ale."

"Honey?"

"You know what I'd love, that we haven't had in a while, a Margarita. Have we got the stuff to make a Margarita, Marty?"

"Yeah, sure. We got about everything."

"Okay, and put a lot of salt on the rim," she said.

She sat on one of the big armchairs opposite the couch, kicked her sandals off, and tucked her feet up under her. "Tell me about this book you're writing, Mr. Spenser."

"Well, Mrs. Rabb—"

"Linda."

"Okay, Linda. I suppose you'd say it's along the lines of several others, looking at baseball as the institutionalized expression of human personality." She nodded and I wondered why. I didn't know what the hell I'd just said.

"Isn't that interesting," she said.

"I like to see sports as a kind of metaphor for human life, contained by rules, patterned by tradition." I was hot now, and rolling. Rabb came back with the Margarita in a lowball glass and the ale in Tiffany-designed goblets that said COCA-COLA. I thought Linda Rabb looked relieved. Maybe I wouldn't switch to the talk show circuit yet. Rabb passed out the drinks.

"What's patterned by tradition, Mr. Spenser?" he said.

"Sports. It's a way of imposing order on disorder."

Rabb nodded. "Yeah, right, that's certainly true," he said. He didn't know what the hell I had just said either. He drank some of the ale and put some dry-roasted cashews in his mouth, holding a handful and popping them in serially.

"But I'm here to talk about you, Marty, and Linda too. What is your feeling about the game?"

Rabb said, "I love it," at the same time that Linda said, "Marty loves it." They laughed.

"I'd play it for nothing," Rabb said. "Since I could walk, I been playing, and I want to do it all my life."

"Why?" I said.

"I don't know," Rabb said. "I never gave it any thought. When I was about five my father bought me a Frankie Gustine autograph glove. I can still remember it. It was too big for me and he had to buy me one of those little cheap ones made in Taiwan, you know, with a couple of little laces for webbing? And I used to oil that damn Frankie Gustine glove and bang my fist in the pocket and rub some more oil until I was about ten and I was big enough to play with it. I still got it somewhere."

"Play other sports?" I didn't know where I was going, but I was used to that.

"Oh yeah, matter of fact, I went to college on a basketball scholarship. Got drafted by the Lakers in the fifth round, but I never thought about doing anything else but baseball when I got out."

"Did you meet Linda in college?"

"No."

"How about you, Linda, how do you feel about baseball?"

"I never cared about it till I met Marty. I don't like the traveling part of it. Marty's away about eighty games a season. But other than that I think it's fine. Marty loves it. It makes him happy."

"Where'd you two meet?" I asked.

"It's there in the biog sheet, isn't it?" Rabb said.

"Yeah, I suppose so. But we both know about PR material."

Rabb said, "Yeah."

"Well, let's do this. Let's run through the press kit and maybe elaborate a little." Linda Rabb nodded.

Rabb said, "It's all in there."

"You were born in Lafayette, Indiana, in nineteen forty-four." Rabb nodded. "Went to Marquette, graduated nineteen sixty-five. Signed with the Sox that year, pitched a year in Charleston and a year at Pawtucket. Came up in nineteen sixty-eight. Been here ever since."

Rabb said, "That's about it."

I said, "Where'd you meet Linda?"

"Chicago," Rabb said. "At a White Sox game. She asked for my autograph, and I said, yeah, but she had to go out with me. She did. And bingo."

I look at my biog sheet. "That would have been in nineteen seventy?"

"Right." My glass was empty, and Rabb got up to refill it. I noticed his was less than half gone.

"We were married about six months later in Chicago." Linda Rabb smiled. "In the off-season."

"Best thing I ever did," Rabb said, and gave me a new bottle of ale. I poured it into the glass, ate some peanuts, and drank some ale.

"You from Chicago, Linda?"

"No, Arlington Heights, a little bit away from Chicago."

"What was your maiden name?"

Rabb said, "Oh for crissake, Spenser, why do you want to know that?"

"I don't know," I said. "You ever see one of those machines that grades apples, or oranges, or eggs, that sort of thing, by size? They dump all sizes in the hopper and the machine lets the various sizes drop into the right holes as it works down. That's how I am. I just ask questions and let it all go into the hopper and then sort it out later."

"Well, you're not sorting eggs now, for crissake."

"Oh, Marty, let him do his job. My maiden name was Hawkins, Mr. Spenser."

"Okay, Marty, let's go back to why you love baseball," I said. "I mean, think about it a little. Isn't it a game for kids? I mean, who finally cares whether a team beats another team?" It sounded like the kind of thing a writer would ask, and I wanted to get them talking. Much of what I do depends on knowing who I'm doing it with.

"Oh, Christ, I don't know, Spenser. I mean, what isn't a game for kids, you know? How about writing stories, is that something for grown-ups? It's something to do. I'm good at it, I like it, and I know the rules. You're one of twenty-five guys all working for something bigger than they are, and at the end of the year you know whether or not you got it. If you didn't get it, then you can start over next year. If you did, then you got a chance to do it again. Some old-timey ballplayer said something about you have to have a lot of little boy in you to play this game, but you gotta be a man too."

"Roy Campanella," I said.

"Yeah, right, Campanella. Anyway, it's a nice clean kind of work. You're important to a lot of kids. You got a chance to influence kids' lives maybe, by being an example to them. It's a lot better than selling cigarettes or making napalm. It's what I do, you know?"

"What about when you get too old?"

"Maybe I can coach. I'd be a good pitching coach. Maybe manage. Maybe do color. I'll stay around the game one way or another."

"What if you can't?"

"I'll still have Linda and the boy."

"And when the boy grows up?"

"I'll still have Linda."

I was getting caught up in the part. I'd started to lose track. I was interested. Maybe some of the questions were about me.

"Maybe I better finish up my Labatt Fifty and go home," I said. "I've taken enough of your time."

Linda Rabb said, "Oh no, don't go yet. Marty, get him another beer. We were just getting started."

I shook my head, drained my glass, and stood up. "No, thank you very much, Linda. We'll talk again."

"Marty, make him stay."

"Linda, for crissake, if he wants to go, let him go. She does this every time we have company, Spenser."

They both walked with me to the door. I left them standing together. He towered over her in the doorway. His right arm was around her shoulder, and she rested her left hand on it. I took a cab home and went to bed. I was working my way through Samuel Eliot Morison's *The Oxford History of the American People,* and I spent two hours on it before I went to sleep.

6

It was dead quiet in my bedroom when I woke up in the morning. The sun vibrated in the room and the hum of my air conditioner underlined the silence. I lay on my back with my hands behind my head for a while and thought about what was bothering me about Linda Rabb.

What was bothering me was that she'd said she knew nothing about baseball till she met Marty but that she'd met Marty at a ball game when she'd asked for his autograph. The two didn't go together. Nothing much, but it didn't fit. It was the only thing that didn't. The rest was whole cloth. Middle American jock-ethic-kid and his loving wife. In the off-season I bet he hunted and fished and took his little boy sliding. Would he be going into the tank? "It's what I do," he'd said. "I know the rules." I could understand that. I knew about the need for rules. I didn't believe he'd dump one. I never believed Nixon would be President either. I got up, did 100 push-ups, 100 sit-ups, took a shower, got dressed, and made the bed.

There's a restaurant in Portsmouth, New Hampshire, that makes whipped cream biscuits, and I got the recipe once while I was up there having dinner with Brenda Loring. I made some while the coffee perked, and while they baked I squeezed a pint of orange juice and drank it. I had the biscuits with fresh strawberries and sour cream and three cups of coffee.

It was nearly ten o'clock when I got out onto the street. There was a bright smell of summer outside my apartment house. Across Arlington Street the Public Garden was a sunny pleasure. I strolled on past the enormous Thomas Ball statue of Washington on horseback. The flower beds were rich with petunias and redolent of pansies against a flourish of scarlet snapdragons. The swan boats had begun to cruise the pond, pedaled by college kids in yachting caps and trailed by an orderly assemblage of hungry ducks that broke formation to dart at the peanuts the tourists threw. I crossed the bridge over the swan boat lake and headed toward the Common on the other side of Charles Street. At the crossing there was a guy selling popcorn from a pushcart and another selling ice cream and another selling balloons and little monkeys dangling from thin sticks and blue pennants that said BOSTON, MASS., in yellow script. I turned right, walked up Charles toward Boylston. At the corner was the old guy that takes candids with a big tripod camera; faded tan samples were displayed in a case on the tripod. I turned up Boylston toward Tremont and down Tremont toward Stuart. My office was on Stuart Street. It wasn't much of an office, but it suited the location. It would have been an ideal spot for a VD clinic or a public exterminator.

I opened the window as soon as I got in. I'd have to remember not to do push-ups on the days I had to open that window. I hung up my blue blazer, sat down at my desk, got my yellow pad out, and pulled the phone over. By one thirty I had pretty well confirmed Marty Rabb's biography as stated. The town clerk's office in Lafayette, Indiana, established that Marty Rabb had in fact lived there and that his parents still did. The office of the registrar at Marquette confirmed his attendance and graduation in 1965. I called a cop I knew in Providence and asked him if they had anything on Rabb when he was at Pawtucket. He called me back in forty minutes to say no. He promised me he'd keep his mouth shut about my question, and I half thought he would. He was as trustworthy as I was likely to find.

Linda Rabb was more of a problem. There was no record of her marriage to Rabb at the Chicago Hall of Records. As far as they knew, Marty Rabb hadn't married Linda Hawkins or anyone else in Chicago in 1970 or any other time. Maybe they got married by some JP in a suburb. I called Arlington Heights and talked with the city clerk himself. No record. How about any record of Linda Hawkins or Linda Rabb? None, no birth certificate, no marriage license. If I'd wait a minute, he'd check motor vehicles. I waited. It was more like ten minutes. The air blowing in from Stuart Street was hot and gritty. The sweat had soaked through my polo shirt and made it stick to my back. I looked at my watch: 3:15. I hadn't had lunch yet. I sniffed at the hot breeze. If the wind was right, I could catch the scent of sauerbraten wafting across the street from Jake Wirth's. It wasn't right. All I could smell was the uncontrolled emission of the traffic.

The Arlington Heights city clerk came back on the phone.

"Still there?"

"Yep."

"Got no record of a driver's license. No auto registration. There's four Hawkinses in the city directory but no Linda. Want the phone numbers?"

"Yes, and can you give me the number of the school administration department?"

"Yeah, one minute, I'll check it here."

He did and gave it to me. I called them. They had no record of Linda Rabb or Linda Hawkins. There had been eight children named Hawkins in the school system since 1960. Six were boys. The other two were named Doris and Olive.

I hung up. Very cooperative.

I called the first Hawkins number in Arlington Heights. No soap. Nor was there any soap at the next two. The fourth number didn't answer. But unless they were the ones when I finally got them, I was going to have to wonder about old Linda. I looked at my watch: 4:30. Three thirty in Illinois. I hadn't eaten since breakfast. I went over to Jake Wirth's, had some sauerbraten and dark beer, came back to the office at five forty-five, and called the fourth Hawkins again. A woman answered who had never heard of Linda Hawkins.

I swung my chair around and propped my feet on the windowsill and looked out at the top floor of the garment loft across the street. It was empty. Everyone had gone home. There are a lot of reasons why someone doesn't check out right off quick when you begin to look into her background. But most of them have to do with deceit, and most deceit is based on having something to hide. Two pigeons settled down onto the window ledge of the loft and looked at me looking at them. I looked at my watch: 6:10. After supper on a summer evening. Twilight softball leagues were getting under way at this hour. Kids were going out to hang out on the corner till dark. Men were watering their lawns, their wives sitting nearby in lawn chairs. I was looking at two pigeons.

Linda Rabb was not what she was supposed to be, and that bothered me, like it bothered me that she met Rabb at a ball game even though she wasn't interested in baseball till she married him. Little things, but they weren't right. The pigeons flew off. The traffic sounds were dwindling. I'd have to find out about Linda Rabb. The Sox had a night game tonight, which meant Rabb wouldn't be home. But Linda Rabb probably would be because of the kid. I called. She was.

"I wonder if I could drop by just for a minute," I said. "Just want to get the wife's angle on things. You know, what it's like to be home while the game's on, that sort of thing." What a writer I'd make, get the wife's angle. Slick. Probably should have said "little woman's angle."

"That's okay, Mr. Spenser, I'm just giving the baby his bath. If you drop around in an hour or so, I'll be watching the game on television, but we can talk."

I thanked her and hung up. I looked at the window ledge on the garment loft some more. My office door opened behind me. I swiveled the chair around. A short fat man in a Hawaiian shirt and a panama hat came in and left the door open behind him. The shirt hung outside his maroon double knit pants. He wore wraparound black-rimmed sunglasses and smoked a cigar. He looked around my office without saying anything. I put my feet up on my desk and looked at him. He stepped aside, and another man came in and sat down in front of my desk. He was wearing a tan suit, dark brown shirt, and a wide red-striped tie in browns, whites, and yellows. His tan loafers were gleaming; his hands were manicured; his face was tanned. His hair was bright gray and expensively barbered, curling over his collar in the back, falling in a single ringlet over his forehead. Despite the gray hair, his face was young and unlined. I knew him. His name was Frank Doerr.

"I'd like to talk with you, Spenser."

"Oh golly," I said, "you heard about my whipped cream biscuits and you were hoping I'd give you the recipe."

The fat guy in the panama hat had closed the door behind Doerr and was leaning against it with his arms folded. Akim Tamiroff.

Doerr said, "You know who I am, Spenser?"

"Aren't you Julia Child?" I said.

"My name's Doerr. I want to know what business you're doing with the Red Sox."

A master of disguise, the man of 1,000 faces. "Red Sox?" I said.

"Red Sox," he said.

"Jesus, I didn't think the word would get out that quickly. How'd you find out?"

"Never mind how I found out, I want answers."

"Sure, sure thing, Mr. Doerr. You any relation to Bobby?"

"Don't irritate me, Spenser. I am used to getting answers."

"Yeah, well, I didn't know you had anything against Bobby Doerr, I thought he was a hell of a second baseman."

Doerr said, "Wally," without looking around, and the fat man at the door brought a gun out from under his flowered shirt. "Now knock off the bullshit, Spenser. I haven't got a lot of time to spend in this roach hole."

I thought "roach hole" was a little unkind, but I thought the gun in Wally's hand was a little unkind too. "Okay," I said, "no need to get sore. I was a regional winner in the Leon Culberson look-alike contest, and the Sox wanted to talk to me about being a designated hitter."

Doerr and Wally looked at me. The silence got to be quite long. "You don't think I look like Leon Culberson?" I said.

Doerr leaned forward. "I asked around a little about you, Spenser. I heard you think you're a riot. I think you're a roach in a roach hole. I think you're a thirty-five-cent piece of hamburg, and I think you need to learn some manners."

The building was quiet; the traffic sounds were less frequent through the open window. Wally's gun pointed at me without moving. Wally sucked on one of his canine teeth. My stomach hurt a little.

Doerr went on. "You are hanging around Fenway Park, hanging around the broadcast booth, talking with people, pretending you're a writer, and not telling anyone at all that you're only a goddamned egg-sucking snoop, a nickel-and-dime cheapie. I want to know why, and I want to know right now or Wally will make you wish you'd never been born."

I took my feet off the desk, slowly, and put them on the floor. I put my hands, slowly, on the desk and stood up. When I was on my feet, I said, "Frank, baby, you're a gambling man, and I'll make a bet with you. In fact, I'll make two. First one is that you won't shoot because you want to know what's happening and what I'm into and it's lousy percentage to shoot a guy without being sure why. Second bet is that if your pet pork chop tries to hassle me, I can take away his piece and clean his teeth with it. Even money."

As far as Wally showed anything, I might have been talking about Sam Yorty or the Aga Khan. He didn't move. Neither did the gun. Doerr's sun-lamp face seemed to have gotten whiter. The lines from his nostrils to the corners of his mouth had gotten deeper, and his right eyelid tremored. My stomachache continued.

Another silence. If I weren't so tough, I would have thought maybe I was scared. Wally's gun was a Walther P.38. Nine-millimeter. Seven shots in the clip. Nice gun, the grip on a Walther was very comfortable, and the balance was good. Wally seemed happy with his. Below on Stuart Street somebody with a trick horn blew shave-and-a-haircut-two-bits. And some brakes squealed.

Doerr got up suddenly, turned on his heels, and walked out. Wally put the gun away, followed him out, and closed the door. I breathed in most of the air in the office through my nose and let it out again very slowly. My fingertips tingled. I sat down again, opened the bottom desk drawer, took out a bottle of bourbon, and drank from the neck. I coughed. I'd have to stop buying the house brand at Vito's Superette.

I looked around at the empty office. Green file cabinet, three Vermeer prints that Susan Silverman had given me for Christmas, the chair that Doerr had sat in. Didn't look so goddamned roachie to me.

7

I took a Polaroid camera with me when I visited Linda Rabb.

"I want to think about graphics, maybe a coffee table book," I told her. "Maybe a big format."

She was in blue jeans, barefoot, a ribbon in her hair, her makeup fresh. On a twenty-five-inch color console in the living room, Buck Maynard was calling the play by play. "Ah want to tell ya, Holly West could throw a lamb chop past a wolf pack, Doc. He gunned Amos Otis down by twenty feet."

"Great arm, Buck," Wilson said, "a real cannon back there."

I snapped some pictures of Linda and the living room from different angles.

"Do you get nervous watching Marty pitch, Linda?" I lay on the floor to get an exotic angle, shooting up through the glass top of the coffee table.

"No, not so much anymore. He's so good, you know—it's more, I'm surprised when he loses. But I don't worry."

"Does he bring it home or leave it at the park?"

"When he loses? He leaves it there. Unless you've been watching the game, you don't know if he won or lost when he comes in the door. He doesn't talk about it at all. Little Marty barely knows what his father does."

I placed the five color shots on the coffee table in front of Linda Rabb.

"Which one do you like best?" I said. "They're only idea shots; if the publishers decide to go the big picture format, we'll use a pro." I sounded like Arthur Author—it pays to listen to the Carson show.

She picked up the last one on the left and held it at an angle to the light.

"This is an interesting shot," she said. It was the one I'd taken from floor level. It was interesting. Casey Crime Photographer.

"Yeah, that's good," I said. "I like that one too." I took it from her and put it in an envelope. "How about the others?"

She looked at several more. "They're okay, but the one I gave you first is my favorite."

"Okay," I said. "We agree." I scooped the other four into a second envelope.

Bucky Maynard said, "We got us a real barn burner here, Doc. Both pitchers are hummin' it in there pretty good."

"You're absolutely right, Bucky. A couple of real fine arms out there tonight."

I stood up. "Thank you, Linda. I'm sorry to have barged in on you like this."

"That's okay. I enjoyed it. The only thing is, I don't know about pictures of me, or of the baby. Marty doesn't like to have his family brought into things. I mean, we're very private people. Marty may not want you to do pictures."

"I can understand that, Linda. Don't worry. There are lots of people on the team, and if we decide to go to visuals, we can use some of them if Marty objects."

She shook my hand at the door. It was a bony hand and cold.

Outside, it was dark now, and the traffic was infrequent. I walked up Mass Ave toward the river, crossing before I got to Boylston Street to look at the Spanish melons in the window of a gourmet food shop. Mingled with the smell of automobiles and commerce were the thin, damp smell of the river and the memory of trees and soil that the city supplanted. At Marlborough I turned right and strolled down toward my apartment. The small trees and the flowering shrubs in front of the brick and brownstone buildings enhanced the river smell.

It was nine fifteen when I got in my apartment. I called the Essex County DA's office on the chance that someone might be there late. Someone was, probably an assistant DA working up a loan proposal so he could open an office and go into private practice.

"Lieutenant Healy around?" I asked.

"Nope, he's working out of ten-ten Commonwealth, temporary duty, probably be there a couple of months. Can I do anything for you?"

I said no and hung up.

I called state police headquarters at 1010 Commonwealth Ave in Boston. Healy wasn't in. Call back in the morning. I hung up and turned on the TV. Boston had a two-run lead over Kansas City. I opened a bottle of Amstel beer, lay down on my couch, and watched the ball game. John Mayberry tied the game with a one-on home run in the top of the ninth, and I went through three more Amstels before Johnny Tabor scored from third on a Holly West sacrifice fly in the eleventh inning. While the news was on, I made a Westphalian ham sandwich on pumpernickel, ate it, and drank another bottle of Amstel. A man needs sustenance before bed. I might have an exciting dream. I didn't.

Next morning I drove over to 1010 Commonwealth. Healy was in his office, his coat off, the cuffs of his white shirt turned back, but the narrow black knit tie neat and tight around the short, pointed collar. He was medium height, slim, with a gray crew cut and pale blue eyes like Paul Newman. He looked like a career man in a discount shirt store. Five years ago he had gone into a candy store unarmed and rescued two hostages from a nervous junkie with a shotgun. The only person hurt was the junkie.

He said, "What do you want, Spenser?" I was always one of his favorites.

I said, "I'm selling copies of the *Police Gazette* and thought you might wish to keep abreast of the professional developments in your field."

"Knock off the horse crap, Spenser, what do you want?"

I took out the envelope containing my Polaroid picture of Marty Rabb's coffee table.

"There's a photograph in here with two sets of prints on it. One set is mine. I want to know who the other one belongs to. Can you run it through the FBI for me?"

"Why?"

"Would you buy, I'm getting married and want to run a credit check on my bride-to-be?"

"No."

"I didn't think so. Okay. It's confidential. I don't want to tell you if I don't have to. But I gotta know, and I'll give you the reasons if you insist."

"Where do you buy your clothes, Spenser?"

"Aha, bribery. You want the name of my tailor, because I'm your clothing idol."

"You dress like a goddamned hippie. Don't you own a tie?"

"One," I said. "So I can eat in the main dining room at the Ritz."

"Gimme the photo," Healy said. "I'll let you know what comes back."

I gave him the envelope. "Tell your people to try and not get grape jelly and marshmallow fluff all over the photo, okay?"

Healy ignored me. I left.

Going out, I got a look at myself in the glass doors. I had on a red and black paisley sport coat, a black polo shirt, black slacks, and shiny black loafers with a crinkle finish and gold buckles. Hippie? Healy's idea of aggressive fashion was French cuffs. I put on my sunglasses, got in my car, and headed down Commonwealth toward Kenmore Square. The top was down and the seat was quite hot. Not a single girl turned to stare at me as I went by.

8

I went over to Fenway and watched the Sox get ready for an afternoon game. I talked for a half hour with Holly West and a half hour with Alex Montoya to keep up my investigative-writer image, but I wondered how long that would last. Doerr knew I was there, which meant probably that someone there knew I was not a writer. Which also meant that there was a connection between Doerr and the Sox, a connection Doerr wanted to protect. He'd made an error coming to see me. But it's the kind of error guys like Doerr are always making. They get so used to having everyone say yes to them that they forget about the chance that someone will say no. People with a lot of power get like that. They think they're omnipotent. They screw up. Doerr was so surprised that I told him and Wally to take a walk that he didn't know what else to do, so he took a walk. But the cat was now out of the valise. I had a feeling I might hear from Doerr again. It was not a soothing feeling.

I was leaning against the railing of the box seats by the Red Sox dugout, watching batting practice, when Billy Carter said, "Hey, Spenser, want to take a few cuts?"

I did, but I couldn't take my coat off and show the gun. And I didn't want to swing with my coat on. I didn't need any handicaps. I shook my head.

"Why not? Sully's just lobbing them up," Carter said.

"I promised my mom when I took up the violin I'd never play baseball again."

"Violin? Are you shitting? You don't look like no violinist to me. How much you weigh?"

"One ninety-five, one ninety-seven, around there."

"Yeah? You work out or anything?"

"I lift a little. Run some."

"Yeah. I thought you did something. You didn't get that neck from playing no fiddle. What can you bench?"

"Two fifty."

"How many reps?"

"Fifteen."

"Hey, man, we oughta set up an arm wrestle between you and Holly. Wouldn't that be hot shit if you beat him? Man, Holly would turn blue if a goddamned writer beat him arm wrestling."

"Who's pitching today?" I asked.

"Marty," Carter said. "Who busted up your nose?"

"It's a long list," I said. "I used to fight once. How's Marty to catch?"

"A tit," Carter said. One of the coaches was hitting fungoes to the outfield from a circle to the right of the batting cage. The ball parabolaed out in what seemed slow motion against the high tangible sky. "A real tit. You just sit back there and put your glove on the back of the plate and Marty hits it. And you can call the game. You give a sign, Marty nods, and the pitch comes right there. He never shakes you off."

"Everything works, huh?"

"Yeah, I mean he's got the fast ball, slider, a big curve, and a change off all of them. And he can put them all up a gnat's ass at sixty feet six, you know. I mean, he's a tit to catch. If I could catch him every day, and the other guys didn't throw curves, I could be Hall of Fame, baby. Cooperstown."

"When do you think you'll catch a game, Billy?"

"Soon as Holly gets so he can't walk. Around there. Whoops . . . here comes the song of the South, old hush puppy."

Bucky Maynard had come out from under the stands and was behind the batting cage. With him was Lester, resplendent in a buckskin hunting shirt and a black cowboy hat with big silver conches on the band around the crown. Maynard had swapped his red-checked shirt for a white one with green ferns on it. His arms in the short sleeves were pink with sunburn. He had the look of someone who didn't tan.

"You don't seem too fond of Maynard," I said.

"Me? I love every ounce of his cuddly little lard-assed self."

"Okay to quote you?" I wanted to see Carter's reaction.

"Jesus, no. If sowbelly gets on your ass, you'll find yourself warming up relievers in the Sally League. No shit, Spenser, I think he's got more influence around here than Farrell."

"How come?"

"I don't know. I mean, the freakin' fans love him. They think he's giving them the real scoop, you know, all the hot gossip about the big-league stars, facts you don't get on the bubble-gum card."

"Is he?"

"No, not really. He's just nasty. If he hears any gossip, he spreads it. The goddamned yahoos eat it up. Tell-it-like-it-is Bucky. Shit."

"What's the real story on the lizard that trails behind him?"

"Lester?"

"Yeah."

Carter shrugged. "I dunno, he drives Bucky around. He keeps people away from him. He's some kind of karate freak or whatever."

"Tae kwon do," I said. "It's Korean karate."

"Yeah, whatever. I wouldn't mess much with him either. I guess he's a real bastard. I hear he did a real tune on some guy out in Anaheim. The guy was giving Maynard some crap in the hotel bar out there and Lester the Fester damn near killed him. Hey, I gotta take some swings. Catch you later."

Carter headed for the batting cage. Clyde Sullivan, the pitching coach, was pitching batting practice, and when Carter stepped in, he turned and waved the outfielders in. "Up yours, Sully," Carter said. Maynard left the batting cage and strolled over toward me. Lester moved along bonelessly behind him.

"How you doing, Mr. Spenser?" Maynard said.

"Fine," I said. "And yourself?"

"Oh, passable, for an older gentleman. That Carter's funny as a crutch, ain't he?"

I nodded.

"Ah just wish his arm was as good as his mouth," Maynard said. "He can't throw past the pitcher's mound."

"How's his bat?"

Maynard smiled. It was not a radiant smile; the lips pulled down over the teeth so that the smile was a toothless crescent in his red face with neither warmth nor humor suggested. "He's all right if the ball comes straight. Except the ball don't never come straight a course."

"Nice kid, though," I said. Lester had hooked both elbows over the railings and was standing with one booted foot against the wall and one foot flat on the ground. Gary Cooper. He spit a large amount of brown saliva toward the batter's cage, and I realized he was chewing tobacco. When he got into an outfit, he went all the way.

"Maybe," Maynard said, "but ah wouldn't pay much mind to what he says. He likes to run his mouth."

"Don't we all," I said. "Hell, writers and broadcasters get paid for it."

"Ah get paid for reporting what happens, Carter tends to make stuff up. There's a difference."

Maynard looked quite steadily at me, and I had the feeling we were talking about serious stuff. Lester spit another dollop of tobacco juice.

"Okay by me," I said. "I'm just here listening and thinking. I'm not making any judgments yet."

"What might you be making judgments about, Spenser?"

"What to include, what to leave out, what seems to be the truth, what seems to be fertilizer. Why do you ask?"

"Just interested. Ah like to know a man, and one way is to know how he does his job. Ah'm just lookin' into how you do yours."

"Fair enough," I said. "I'll be looking into how you do yours in a bit." Veiled innuendo, that's the ticket, Spenser. Subtle.

"Long as you don't interfere, ah'll be happy to help. Who'd you say was your publisher?"

"Subsidy," I said. "Subsidy Press, in New York."

Maynard looked at his watch. It was one of those that you press a button and the time is given as a digital readout, "Well, time for the Old Buckaroo to get on up to the booth. Nice talking to you, Spenser."

He waddled off, his feet splayed, the toes pointing out at forty-five-degree angles. Lester unhinged and slouched after him, eyes alert under the hatbrim for lurking rustlers. There never was a man like Shane. Tomorrow he'd probably be D'Artagnan.

There'd been some fencing going on there, more than there should have been. It was nearly one. I went down into the locker room and used the phone on Farrell's desk to call Brenda Loring at work.

"I have for you, my dear, a proposition," I said.

"I know," she said. "You make it every time I see you."

"Not that proposition," I said. "I have an additional one, though that previously referred to above should not be considered thereby inoperative."

"I beg your pardon?"

"I didn't understand that either," I said. "Look, here's my plan. If you can get the afternoon off, I will escort you to the baseball game, buy you some peanuts and Cracker Jacks, and you won't care if you ever come back."

"Do I get dinner afterward?"

"Certainly and afterward we can go to an all-night movie and neck. What do you say?"

"Oh, be still my heart," she said. "Shall I meet you at the park?"

"Yeah, Jersey Street entrance. You'll recognize me at once by the cluster of teenyboppers trying to get me to autograph their bras."

"I'll hurry," she said.

9

When Brenda Loring got out of a brown and white Boston cab, I was brushing off an old man in an army shirt and a flowered tie who wanted me to give him a quarter.

"Did you autograph his bra, sweetie?" she said.

"They were here," I said, "but I warned them about your jealous passion and they fled at your approach."

"Fled? That is quite fancy talk for a professional thug."

"That's another thing. Around here I'm supposed to be writing a book. My true identity must remain concealed. Reveal it to no one."

"A writer?"

"Yeah. I'm supposed to be doing a book on the Red Sox and baseball."

"Was that your agent you were talking with when I drove up?"

"No, a reader."

She shook her head. Her blond hair was cut short and shaped around her head. Her eyes were green. Her makeup was expert. She was wearing a short green dress with a small floral print and long sleeves. She was darkly tanned, and a small gold locket gleamed on a thin chain against her chest where the neckline of the dress formed a V. Across Jersey Street a guy selling souvenirs was staring at her. I was staring at her too. I always did. She was ten pounds on the right side of plump. "Voluptuous," I said.

"I beg your pardon."

"That's how we writers would describe you. Voluptuous with a saucy hint of deviltry lurking in the sparkling of the eyes and the impertinent cast of the mouth."

"Spenser, I want a hot dog and some beer and peanuts and a ball game. Could you please, please, please, pretty please, please with sugar on it knock off the writer bullshit and escort me through the gate?"

I shook my head. "Writers aren't understood much," I said, and we went in.

I was showing off for Brenda and took her up to the broadcast booth to watch the game. My presence didn't seem to be a spur to the Red Sox. They lost to Kansas City 5–2, with Freddie Patek driving in three runs on a bases-loaded fly ball that Alex Montoya played into a triple. Maynard ignored us, Wilson studied Brenda closely between innings, and Lester boned up on the *National Enquirer* through the whole afternoon. Thoughtful.

It was four ten when we got out onto Jersey Street again. Brenda said, "Who was the cute thing in the cowboy suit?"

"Never mind about him," I said. "I suppose you're not going to settle for the two hot dogs I bought you."

"For dinner? I'll wait right here for the cowboy."

"Where would you like to go? It's early, but we could stop for a drink."

We decided on a drink at the outdoor café by City Hall. I had draft beer, and Brenda a stinger on the rocks, under the colorful umbrellas across from the open brick piazza. The area was new, reclaimed from the miasma of Scollay Square where Winnie Garrett the Flaming Redhead used to take it all off on the first show Monday before the city censor decreed the G-string. Pinball parlors, and tattoo shops, the Old Howard and the Casino, winos, whores, sailors, barrooms, and novelty shops: an adolescent vision of Sodom and Gomorrah, all gone now, giving way to fountains and arcades and a sweep of open plaza.

"You know, it never really was Sodom and Gomorrah anyway," I said.

"What wasn't?"

"Scollay Square. It was pre-Vietnam sin. Burlesque dancers and barrooms where bleached blondes danced in G-strings and net stockings. Places that sold plastic dog turds and whoopee cushions."

"I never came here," she said. "My mother had me convinced that to step into Scollay Square was to be molested instantly."

"Naw. There were ten college kids here for every dirty old man. Compared to the Combat Zone, Scollay Square was the Goosie Gander Nursery School."

I ordered two more drinks. The tables were glass-topped and the café was carpeted in Astroturf. The waitress was attentive. Brenda Loring's nails were done in a bright red. Dark was still a long way off.

Brenda went to the ladies' room, and I called my answering service. There was a message to call Healy. He'd be in his office till six. I looked at my watch: 5:40. I called.

"This is Spenser, what have you got?"

"Prints belong to Donna Burlington." He spelled it. "Busted in Redford, Illinois, three-eighteen-sixty-six, for possession of a prohibited substance. That's when the prints got logged into the bureau files. No other arrests recorded."

"Thanks, Lieutenant."

"You owe me," Healy said and hung up. Mr. Warmth.

I was back at the table before Brenda.

At seven fifteen we strolled up Tremont Street to a French restaurant in the old City Hall and had rack of lamb for two and a chilled bottle of Traminer and strawberry tarts for dessert. It was nearly nine thirty when we finished and walked back up School Street to Tremont. It was dark now but still warm, a soft night, midsummer, and the Common seemed very gentle as we strolled across it. Brenda Loring held my hand as we walked. No one attempted to mug us all the way to Marlborough Street.

In my apartment I said to Brenda, "Want some brandy or would you like to get right to the necking?"

"Actually, cookie, I would like first to take a shower."

"A shower?"

"Uh-huh. You pour us two big snifters of brandy and hop into bed, and I'll come along in a few minutes."

"A shower?"

"Go on," she said. "I won't take long."

I went to the kitchen and got a bottle of Rémy Martin out of the kitchen cabinet. Did David Niven keep cognac in the kitchen? Not likely. I got two brandy snifters out and filled them half full and headed back toward the bedroom. I could hear the shower running. I put the two glasses down on the bureau and got undressed. The shower was still running. I went to the bathroom door. My bare feet made no noise at all on the wall-to-wall carpeting. I turned the handle and it opened. The room was steamy. Brenda's clothes were in a small pile on the floor under the sink. I noticed her lingerie matched her dress. Class. The steam was billowing up over the drawn shower curtain. I looked in. Brenda had her eyes closed, her head arched back, the water running down over her shiny brown body. Her buttocks were in white contrast to the rest of her. She was humming an old Billy Eckstine song. I got in behind her and put my arms around her.

"Jesus Christ, Spenser," she said. "What are you doing?"

"Cleanliness is next to godliness," I said. "Want me to wash your back?"

She handed me the soap and I lathered her back. When I was finished, she turned to rinse it off, and her breasts, as she faced me, were the same startling white that her buttocks had been.

"Want me to wash your front?" I said.

She laughed and put her arms around me. Her body was slick and wet. I kissed her. There is excitement in a new kiss, but there is a quality of memory and intimacy in kissing someone you've kissed often before. I liked the quality. Maybe continuity is better than change. With the shower still running we went towelless to bed.

10

Ten hours later I was in the coach section, window seat, aft of the wing, in an American Airlines 747, sipping coffee and chewing with little pleasure a preheated bun that tasted vaguely of adhesive tape. We were passing over Buffalo, which was a good idea, and heading for Chicago.

Beside me was a kid, maybe fifteen, and his brother, maybe eleven. They were discussing somebody named Ben, who might have been a dog, laughing like hell about it. Their mother and father across the aisle took turns giving them occasional warning glances when the laughter got raucous. Their mother looked like she might be a fashion designer or a lady lawyer; the old man looked like a stevedore, uncomfortable in a shirt and tie. Beauty and the beast.

We got into Chicago at eleven. I rented a car, got a road map from the girl at the rental agency counter, and drove southwest from Chicago toward Redford, Illinois. It took six and a half hours, and the great heartland of America was hot as hell. My green rental Dodge had air conditioning and I kept it at full blast all the way. About two thirty I stopped at a diner and had two cheeseburgers and a black coffee. There was a blackberry pie that the counterman claimed his wife made, and I ate two pieces. He had married well. About four thirty the highway bent south and I saw the river. I'd seen it before, but each time I felt the same tug. The Mississippi, Cartier and La Salle, Grant at Vicksburg and "it's lovely to live on a raft." A mile wide and "just keeps rolling." I pulled up onto the shoulder of the highway and looked at it for maybe five minutes. It was brown and placid.

I got to Redford at twenty of seven and checked into a two-story Holiday Inn just north of town that offered a view of the river and a swimming pool. The dining room was open and more than half empty. I ordered a draft beer and looked at the menu. The beer came in an enormous schooner. I ordered Wiener schnitzel and fresh garden vegetables and was startled to find when it came that it was excellent. I had finished two of the enormous schooners by then and perhaps my palate was insensitive to nuance. My compliments to the chef. Three stars for the Holiday Inn in Redford, Illinois. I signed the check and went to bed.

The next morning I went into town. Outside the air-conditioned motel the air was hot with a strong river smell. Cicadas hummed. The Holiday Inn and the Mississippi River were obviously Redford's high spots. It was a very small town, barely more than a cluster of shabby frame houses along the river. The yards were mostly bare dirt with an occasional clump of coarse and ratty-looking grass. The town's single main street contained a hardware and feed store, a Woolworth's five-and-ten, Scooter's Lunch, Bill and Betty's Market with two Phillips 66 pumps out front, and, fronting on a small square of dandelion-spattered grass, the yellow clapboard two-story town hall. There were two Greek Revival columns holding up the overhanging second floor and a bell tower that extended up perhaps two more stories to a thin spire with a weathervane at the tip. In the small square were a nineteenth-century cannon and a pyramid of cannonballs. Two kids were sitting astride the cannon as I pulled up in front of the town hall. In the parking area to the right of the town hall was a black and white Chevy with a whip antenna and POLICE lettered on the side. I went around to that side and down along the building. In the back was a screen door with a small blue light over it. I went in.

There was a head-high standing floor fan at the long end of a narrow room, and it blew a steady stream of hot air at me. To my right was a low mahogany dividing rail, and behind it a gray steel desk and matching swivel chair, a radio receiver-transmitter and a table mike on a maple table with claw and ball feet, a white rounded-edged refrigerator with gold trim, and some wanted posters fixed to the door with magnets. And a gray steel file cabinet.

A gray-haired man with rimless glasses and a screaming eagle emblem tattooed on his right forearm was sitting at the desk with his arms folded across his chest and his feet up. He had on a khaki uniform, obviously starched, and his black engineer boots gleamed with polish. A buff-colored campaign hat lay on the desk beside an open can of Dr Pepper. On a wheel-around stand next to the radio equipment a portable black-and-white television was showing *Hollywood Squares.* A nameplate on the desk said T. P. DONALDSON. A big silver star on his shirt said SHERIFF. A brown cardboard bakery box on the desk contained what looked like some lemon-filled doughnuts.

"My name's Spenser," I said, and showed the photostat of my license in its clear plastic coating. Germ-free. "I'm trying to backtrack a woman named Donna Burlington. According to the FBI records she was arrested here in nineteen sixty-six."

"Sheriff Donaldson," the gray-haired man said, and stood up to shake hands. He was tall and in shape with healthy color to his tan face, and oversize hands with prominent knuckles. His shirt was ironed in a military press and had been tailored down so that it was skintight.

"Hundred and First?" I said.

"The tattoo? Yeah. I was a kid then, you know. Fulla piss and vinegar, drunk in London, and three of us got it done. My wife's always telling me to get rid of it but . . ." He shrugged. "You airborne?"

"Nope, infantry and a different war. But I remember the Hundred and First. Were you at Bastogne?"

"Yep. Had a bad case of boils on my back. The medics said I ought to eat better food and wash more often." His face was solemn. "Krauts took care of it, though. I got a back full of shrapnel and the boils were gone."

"Medical science," I said.

He shook his head. "Christ, that was thirty years ago."

"It's one of the things you don't forget," I said.

"You don't for sure," he said. "Who was that you were after?"

"Burlington, Donna Burlington. A.k.a. Linda Hawkins, about twenty-six years old, five feet four, black hair, FBI records show she was fingerprinted here in nineteen sixty-six, at which time she would have been about eighteen. You here then?"

He nodded. "Yep, I been here since nineteen forty-six." He turned toward the file cabinet. A pair of handcuffs draped over his belt in the small of his back, and he wore an army .45 in a government-issue flap holster on his right hip. He rustled through the third file drawer down and came up with a manila folder. He opened it, his back still to me, and read through the contents, closed it, turned around, put the folder facedown on the desk, and sat down. "You want a Dr Pepper?" he said.

"No, thanks. You have Donna Burlington?"

"Could I see your license again, and maybe some other ID?"

I gave him the license and my driver's license. He looked at them carefully and turned them back to me. "Why do you want to know about Donna Burlington?"

"I don't want to tell you. I'm looking into something that might hurt a lot of people, who could turn out to be innocent, if the word got out."

"What's Donna Burlington got to do with it?"

"She lied to me about her name, where she lived, how she got married. I want to know why."

"You think she's committed a crime?"

"Not that I know of. I don't want her for anything. I just ran across a lie and I want to run it down. You know how it goes, people lie to you, you want to know why."

Donaldson nodded. He took a swig from his Dr Pepper, swallowed it, and began to suck on his upper lip.

"I don't want to stir up old troubles," I said. "She was eighteen when you busted her. Everyone is entitled to screw up when they're eighteen. I just want to know about her."

Donaldson kept sucking on his upper lip and looking at me.

"It'll be worse if I start asking around and get people wondering why some dick from the East is asking about Donna Burlington. I'll find out anyway. This isn't that big a place."

"I might not let you ask around," Donaldson said.

"Aw come on, Hondo," I said. "If you give me trouble, I'll go get the state cops and a court order and come on back and ask around and more people will notice and a bigger puff of smoke will go up and you'll be worse off than you are now. I'm making what you call your legitimate inquiry."

"Persistent sonovabitch, aren't you? Okay, I'll go along. I just don't like telling people's business to others without a pretty good reason."

"Me either," I said.

"Okay." He opened the folder and looked at it. "I arrested Donna Burlington for possession of three marijuana cigarettes. She was smoking with two boys from Buckston in a pickup truck back of Scooter's Lunch. It was a first offense, but we were a little jumpier about reefers around here in 'sixty-six than we are now. I booked her; she went to court and got a suspended sentence and a year's probation. Six weeks later she broke probation and went off to New York City with a local hellion. She never came back."

"What was the hellion's name?"

"Tony Reece. He was about seven or eight years older than Donna."

"What kind of kid was she?"

"It was a while ago," Donaldson said. "But kind of restless, not really happy, you know—nothing bad, but she had a reputation, hung out with the older hotshots. The first girl in class to smoke, the first to drink, the first one to try pot, the one the boys took out as soon as they dared while the other girls were still going to dancing school at the grange hall and blushing if someone talked dirty."

"Family still live in town?"

"Yeah, but they don't know where she is. After she took off, they were after me to locate her. But there's only me and two deputies, and one of them's part-time. When nothing came of that, they wrote her off. In a way they were probably glad she took off. They didn't know what to do with her. She was a late baby, you know? The Burlingtons never had any kids, and then, when Mrs. Burlington was going through the change, there came Donna. That's what my wife says anyway. Embarrassed hell out of both of them."

"How about Reece? He ever show up again?"

Donaldson shook his head. "Nope. I heard he got in some kind of jam in New York and he might be doing time. But he hasn't shown up around here anyway."

"Okay, any last known address?"

"Just the house here."

"Can you give me that? I'd like to talk to the parents."

"I'll drive you over. They'll be a little easier if I'm there. They're old and they get nervous."

"I'm not going to give them the third degree, Donaldson, I'm just going to talk to them and ask them if they know anything more than you do about Donna Burlington."

"I'll go along. They're sorta shiftless and crummy, but they're my people, you know? I like to look out for them."

I nodded. "Okay, let's go."

We got into Donaldson's black and white and drove back up the main street past the row of storefronts and the sparse yards. At the end of the street we turned left, down toward the river, and pulled up in front of a big shanty. Originally it had probably been a four-room bungalow backing onto the river. Over the years lean-tos and sagging additions had been scabbed onto it so that it was difficult to say how many rooms there were now. The area in front of the house was mud, and several dirty white chickens pecked in it. A brown and white pig had rooted itself out a hollow against the foundation and was sleeping in it. To the right of the front door, two big gas bottles of dull gray-green metal stood upright, and to the left the remnants of a vine were so bedraggled I couldn't recognize what kind it was. The land to the side and rear of the house sloped in a kind of eroded gully down to the river. There was a stack of old tires at the corner of one of the lean-tos, and beyond that the rusted frame of a forty-year-old pickup truck, a stack of empty vegetable crates, and on the flat mud margin where the river lapped at the land a bedspring, mossy and slick with river scum.

I thought of Linda Rabb in her Church Park apartment with the fresh jeans and her black hair gleaming.

"Come to where the flavor is," I said.

"Yeah, it's not much, is it? Don't much wonder that Donna took off as soon as she could." We got up and walked to the front door. There were the brown remains of a wreath hanging from a galvanized nail. The ghost of Christmas past. Maybe of a Christmas future for the Burlingtons.

An old woman answered Donaldson's knock. She was fat and

lumpy in a yellow housedress. Her legs were bare and mottled, her feet thrust into scuffed men's loafers. Her gray hair was short and straight around her head, the ends uneven, cut at home probably, with dull scissors. Her face was nearly without features, fat puffing around her eyes, making them seem small and squinty.

"Morning, Mrs. Burlington," Donaldson said. "Got a man here from Boston wants to talk with you about Donna."

She looked at me. "You seen Donna?" she said.

"May we come in?" I said.

She stood aside. "I guess so," she said. Her voice wasn't very old, but it was without variation, a tired monotone, as if there were nothing worth saying.

Donaldson took off his hat and went in. I followed. The room smelled of kerosene and dogs and things I didn't recognize. The clutter was dense. Donaldson and I found room on an old daybed and sat. Mrs. Burlington shuffled off down a corridor and returned in a moment with her husband. He was pallid and bald, a tall old man in a sleeveless undershirt and black worsted trousers with the fly open. His face had gray stubble on it, and some egg was dried in the corner of his mouth. The skin was loose on his thin white arms and wrinkled in the fold at the armpit. He poured a handful of Bond Street pipe tobacco from a can into the palm of his hand and slurped it into his mouth.

He nodded at Donaldson, who said, "Morning, Mr. Burlington." Mrs. Burlington stood, and they both looked at Donaldson and me without moving or speaking. American Gothic.

I said, "I'm a detective. I can't tell you where your daughter is, except that she's well and happy. But I need to learn a little about her background. I mean her no harm, and I'm trying to help her, but the whole situation is very confidential."

"What do you want to know?" Mrs. Burlington said.

"When is the last time you heard from her?"

Mrs. Burlington said, "We ain't. Not since she run off."

"No letter, no call, nothing. Not a word?"

Mrs. Burlington shook her head. The old man made no move, changed his expression not at all.

"Do you know where she went when she left here?"

"Left us a note saying she was going to New York with a fellow we never met, never heard nothing more."

"Didn't you look for her?"

Mrs. Burlington nodded at Donaldson. "Told T.P. here. He looked. Couldn't find her." A bony mongrel dog with short yellow fur and mismatched ears appeared behind Mr. Burlington. He growled at us, and Burlington turned and kicked him hard in the ribs. The dog yelped and disappeared.

"You ever hear from Tony Reece?" It was like talking to a post-operative lobotomy case. And compared to the old man, she was animated.

She shook her head. "Never seen him," she said. The old man squirted a long stream of tobacco juice at a cardboard box of sand behind the door. He missed.

And that was it. They didn't know anything about anything, and they didn't care. The old man never spoke while I was there and just nodded when Donaldson said good-bye.

In the car Donaldson said, "Where to now?"

"Let's just sit here a minute until I catch my breath."

"They been poor all their life," Donaldson said. "It tends to wear you out." I nodded.

"Okay, how about Tony Reece? He got any family here?"

"Nope. Folks are both dead." Donaldson started the engine and turned the car back toward the town hall. When we got there, he offered me his hand. "If I was you, Spenser, I'd try New York next."

"Fun City," I said.

11

It was sunset when the plane swung in over the water and landed at La Guardia Airport. I took the bus into the East Side terminal at Thirty-eighth Street and a cab from there to the Holiday Inn at West Fifty-seventh Street. The Wiener schnitzel had been so good in Redford, I thought I might as well stay with a winner.

The West Side hadn't gotten any more fashionable since I had been there last and the hotel looked as if it belonged where it was. The lobby was so discouraging that I didn't bother to check the dining room for Wiener schnitzel. Instead, I walked over to a Scandinavian restaurant on Fifty-eighth Street and ravaged its smorgasbord.

The next morning I made some phone calls to the New York Department of Social Services while I drank coffee in my room. When I finished I walked along Fifty-seventh Street to Fifth Avenue and headed downtown. I always walk in New York. In the window of F.A.O. Schwarz was an enormous stuffed giraffe, and Brentano's had a display of ethnic cookbooks in the window. I thought about going in and asking them if they were a branch of the Boston store but decided not to. They probably lacked my zesty sense of humor.

It was about nine forty-five when I reached Thirty-fourth Street and turned left. Four blocks east, between Third and Second avenues, was a three-story beige brick building that looked like a modified fire station. The brown metal entrance doors, up four stairs, were flanked with flagpoles at right angles to the building. A plaque under the right-hand flagpole said CITY OF NEW YORK, DEPARTMENT OF SOCIAL SERVICES, YORKVILLE INCOME MAINTENANCE CENTER. I went in.

It was a big open room, the color a predictable green; molded plastic chairs in red, green, and blue stood three rows deep to the right of the entrance. To the left a low counter. Behind the counter a big black woman with blue-framed glasses on a chain around her neck was telling an old woman in an ankle-length dress that her check would come next week and would not come sooner. The woman protested in broken English, and the woman behind the desk said it again, louder. At the end of the counter, sitting in a folding chair, was a New York City cop, a slim black woman with badge, gun, short hair, and enormous high platform shoes. Beyond the counter the room L'd to the left, and I could see office space partitioned off. There was no one else on the floor.

Behind me, to the right of the entry, a stair led up. A handprinted sign said FACE TO FACE UPSTAIRS with an arrow. I went up. The second floor had been warrened off into cubicles where face to face could go on in privacy. The first cubicle was busy; the second was not. I knocked on the frame of the open door and went in. It was little bigger than a confessional, just a desk, a file cabinet, and a chair for the face to face. The woman at the desk was lean and young, not long out of Vassar or Bennington. She had a tanned outdoor face, with small lines around the eyes that she wasn't supposed to get yet. She had on a white sleeveless blouse open at the neck. Her brown hair was cut short and she wore no makeup. Her face presented an expression of no-nonsense compassion that I suspected she was still working on. The sign on her desk said MS. HARRIS.

"Come in," she said, her hands resting on the neat desk in front of her. A pencil in the right one. I was dressed for New York in my wheat-colored summer suit, dark blue shirt, and a white tie with blue and gold stripes. Would she invite me to her apartment? Maybe she thought I was another welfare case. If so, I'd have to speak with my tailor. I gave her a card; she frowned down at it for about thirty seconds and then looked up and said, "Yes?"

"Do you think I ought to have a motto on it?" I said.

"I beg your pardon?"

"A motto," I said. "On the card. You know, like 'We never sleep' or maybe 'Trouble is my business.' Something like that."

"Mr."—she checked the card—"Spenser, I assume you're joking and there's nothing wrong with that, but I have a good deal to do and I wonder if you might tell me what you want directly?"

"Yes, ma'am. May I sit?"

"Please do."

"Okay, I'm looking for a young woman who might have showed up here and gone on welfare about eight years ago."

"Why do you want to find her?"

I shook my head. "It's a reasonable question, but I can't tell you."

She frowned at me the way she had frowned at my card. "Why do you think we'd have information about something that far back?"

"Because you are a government agency. Government agencies never throw anything away because someone someday might need something to cover himself in case a question of responsibility was raised. You got welfare records for Peter Stuyvesant."

The frown got more severe, making a groove between her eyebrows. "Why do you think this young woman was on welfare?"

"You shouldn't frown like that," I said. "You'll get little premature wrinkles in the corners of your eyes."

"I would prefer it, Mr. Spenser, if you did not attempt to personalize this contact. The condition of my eyes is not relevant to this discussion."

"Ah, but how they sparkle when you're angry," I said.

She almost smiled, caught herself, and got the frown back in place. "Answer my question, please."

"She was about eighteen; she ran away from a small midwestern town with the local bad kid, who probably ditched her after they got here. She's a good bet to have ended up on welfare or prostitution or both. I figured that you'd have better records than Diamond Nell's Parlor of Delight."

The pencil in her right hand went tap-tap-tap on the desk. Maybe six taps before she heard it and stopped. "The fact of someone's presence on welfare rolls has sometimes been used against them. Cruel as that may seem, it is a fact of life, and I hope you can understand my reticence in this matter."

"I'm on the girl's side," I said.

"But I have no way to know that."

"Just my word," I said.

"But I don't know if your word is good."

"That's true," I said. "You don't."

The pencil went tap-tap-tap again. She looked at the phone. Pass the buck? She looked away. Good for her. "What is the girl's name?"

"Donna Burlington." I could hear a typewriter in one of the other cubicles and footsteps down another corridor. "Go ahead," I said. "Do it. It will get done by someone. It's only a matter of who. Me? Cops? Courts? Your boss? His boss? Why not you? Less fuss."

She nodded her head. "Yes. You are probably right. Very well." She got up and left the room. She had very nice legs.

It took a while. I stood in the window of the cubicle and looked down on Thirty-fourth Street and watched the people coming and going from the welfare office. It wasn't as busy as I'd thought it would be. Nor were the people as shabby. Down the corridor a man swore rapidly in Spanish. The typewriter had stopped. The rest was silence.

Ms. Harris returned with a file folder. She sat, opened it on the desk, and read the papers in it. "Donna Burlington was on income maintenance at this office from August to November nineteen sixty-six. At the time her address was One Sixteen East Thirteenth Street. Her relationship with this office ended on November thirteenth, nineteen sixty-six, and I have no further knowledge of her." She closed the folder and folded her hands on top of it.

I said, "Thank you very much."

She said, "You're welcome."

I looked at my watch: 10:50. "Would you like to join me for an early lunch?" I said.

"No, thank you," she said. So much for the operator down from Boston.

"Would you like to see me do a one-hand push-up?" I said.

"Certainly not," she said. "If you have nothing more, Mr. Spenser, I have a good deal of work to do."

"Oh, sure, okay. Thanks very much for your trouble." She stood as I left the room. From the corridor I stuck my head back into the office and said, "Not everyone can do a one-hand push-up, you know?"

She seemed unimpressed and I left.

12

Thirteenth Street was a twenty-five-minute walk downtown and 116 was in the East Village between Second and Third. There was a group of men outside 116, leaning against the parked cars with their shirts unbuttoned, smoking cigarettes and drinking beer from quart bottles. They were speaking Spanish. One Sixteen was a four-story brick house, which had long ago been painted yellow and from which the paint peeled in myriad patches. Next to it was a six-story four-unit apartment building newly done in light gray paint with the door and window frames and the fire escapes and the railing along the front steps a bright red. The beer drinkers had a portable radio that played Spanish music very loudly.

I went up the four steps to number 116 and rang the bell marked CUSTODIAN. Nothing happened, and I rang it again.

One of the beer drinkers said, "Don't work, man. Who you want?"

"I want the manager."

"Inside, knock on the first door."

"Thanks."

In the entry was an empty bottle of Boone's Farm apple wine and a sneaker without laces. Stairs led up against the left wall ahead of me, and a brief corridor went back into the building to the right of the stairs. I knocked on the first door and a woman answered the first knock.

She was tall and strongly built, olive skin and short black hair. A gray streak ran through her hair from the forehead back. She had on a man's white shirt and cutoff jeans. Her feet were bare, and her toenails were painted a dark plum color. She looked about forty-five.

I said, "My name is Spenser. I'm a private detective from Boston, and I'm looking for a girl who lived here once about eight years ago."

She smiled and her teeth were very white and even. "Come in," she said. The room was large and square, and a lot of light came in through the high windows that faced out onto the street. The walls and ceiling were white, and there were red drapes at the windows and a red rug on the floor. In the middle of the room stood a big, square, thick-legged wooden table with a red linoleum top, a large bowl of fruit in the center and a high-backed wooden chair at either end. She gestured toward one of the chairs. "Coffee?" she said.

"Yes, thank you."

I sat at the table and looked about the room while she disappeared through a bead-curtained archway to make the coffee. There was a red plush round-back Victorian sofa with mahogany arms in front of the windows and an assortment of Velázquez prints on the wall. She came back in with a carafe of coffee and two white china mugs on a round red tray.

"Cream or sugar?"

I shook my head. She poured the coffee into the cups, gave me one, and sat down at the other end of the table.

"The coffee is wonderful," I said.

"I grind it myself," she said. "My name is Rose Estrada. How can I help you?" There was a very small trace of another language in her speech.

I took out the picture of Linda Rabb that I'd taken at her apartment. "This is a recent picture of a girl named Donna Burlington.

In nineteen sixty-six, from August to November, she lived at this address. Can you tell me anything about her?"

She thought aloud as she looked at the picture. "Nineteen sixty-six, my youngest would have been ten. . . . Yes, I remember her, Donna Burlington. She came from somewhere in the Midwest. She seemed very young to be alone in New York, far from home. She was with a boy for a little while, but he didn't stay."

"What happened to her when she left you, do you know?"

"No."

"No forwarding address?"

"None. I remember she had no money and was behind in her rent, and I sent her down to the welfare people on Thirty-fourth Street. And then one day she gave me all the back room rent in cash and moved out."

"Any idea where she got the money?"

"I think she was hustling."

"Prostitute?"

She nodded. "I can't be sure, but I know she was out often and she brought men home often and she used to spend time with a pimp named Violet."

"Is he still around?"

"Oh sure. People like Violet are around forever."

"Where do I find him?"

"He's usually on Third Avenue, in front of the Casa Grande near Fifteenth."

"What's his full name?"

She shrugged. "Just Violet," she said. "More coffee?"

"Thank you." I held my cup out, and she poured from the carafe. Her hands were strong and clean, the fingernails the same plum color as her toenails. No rings. Outside I could hear the portable radio playing and occasionally the voices of the men drinking beer.

"She was a very small, thin, little girl," Rose Estrada said. "Very scared. She didn't want to be here, but she didn't want to go home. She didn't know anything about makeup or clothes. She didn't know what to say to people. If she was turning tricks, it must have been very hard on her."

I finished my coffee and stood. "Thank you for the coffee and for the information," I said.

"Is she in trouble?"

"No, I don't think so," I said. "Nothing I can't get her out of."

We shook hands and I left. The street seemed hot and noisy after Rose Estrada's apartment. I walked the half block to Third Ave and turned uptown. At the corner of Fourteenth Street a man in a covert cloth overcoat was urinating against the brick wall of a variety store. He was having trouble standing and lurched against the wall, holding his coat around him with one hand. Modesty, I thought, if you're going to whiz on a wall, do it with modesty. A few feet downstream another man was lying on the sidewalk, knees bent, eyes closed. Drinking buddies. I looked at my watch, it was two thirty in the afternoon.

At the corner of Fifteenth Street was a bar with a fake fieldstone front below a plate glass window. The entry to the left of the window was imitation oak. A small neon sign said CASA GRANDE, BEER ON DRAFT. At the curb in front of the Casa Grande were a white Continental and a maroon Coupe de Ville with a white vinyl roof. Leaning against the Coupe de Ville was a man who'd seen too many *Superfly* movies. He was a black man probably six-three in his socks and about six-seven in the open-toed red platform shoes he was wearing. He was also wearing red-and-black argyle socks, black knickers, and a chain mail vest. A black Three Musketeers' hat with an enormous red plume was tipped forward over his eyes. Subtle. All he lacked was a sign saying THE PIMP IS IN.

"Excuse me," I said, "I'm looking for Violet."

The pimp looked down at me from on top of his shoes and said, "Why?"

"I was told he could give me information about a girl."

"Someone's talking shit to you, man. I don't know nothing about no girl."

"You Violet?"

He shrugged and looked down Third Avenue.

"I'm looking for information about a girl named Donna Burlington," I said.

The Lincoln started up, backed away from the curb, U-turned, and drove away.

"You federal?" Violet said. "I ain't seen you around."

"I'm not anything," I said. "Just a guy looking to buy some information."

"Well, I hope you got a license for that piece on your right hip then."

Violet paid attention to detail. "Okay." I took a card from my breast pocket and gave it to him. "I'm a private cop. From Boston. But I'm still buying information."

"Baaahston." Violet laughed. "Shit. What Donna do, steal some beans?"

"No, she stole some teenybopper clothes from a ladies' dress shop and I think you're wearing some of them."

Violet laughed again. "Hey, man, you want me to dress like one of you tight-assed honkies?" He slapped one hand down on the hood of the Cadillac and whooped with laughter. "Look at that little mother-loving Buster Brown suit. Shit." Tears were forming in his eyes.

"Look, Violet," I said. "I didn't come down here to write a sonnet about your Easter bonnet. How about I buy you a beer and we talk a little?"

"Yeah, why not, man? You said something about buying information?"

We went in the Casa Grande and sat at the bar. There was a Mets game on television down the bar. The bartender, a middle-aged man in a clean white shirt who looked like Gilbert Roland, came down and wiped the bar off in front of us.

"What'll it be, gentlemen?" he asked, looking carefully at a spot between my head and Violet's.

"Two drafts," I said.

Violet said, "Be cool, Hec, he's okay. We just talking a little business."

The bartender looked at me then. "Okay, Violet," he said and drew the beers.

Violet took his hat off. His head was stark bald and smooth. "Hec figured you for fuzz too. I hope you don't think you working in disguise, man."

I shook my head. "You either," I said. Violet whooped again.

"What you want to know, man?"

I took out my picture of Donna Burlington and showed it to Violet. "Know her eight years younger?"

"You mentioned buying. How much you buying for?"

"Fifty bucks."

"That's not much bread, man."

"You don't have to work very hard for it," I said. "It'll cover your next tankful in that brontosaurus out front."

Violet nodded, drank half his beer, and said, "Yeah, I remember Donna. Remembered her when you said her name."

"Tell me about her."

"A shit kicker," Violet said. "Come from somewhere out in the woods. Real young when she worked for me. Worked for me maybe six months."

"How'd you meet her?"

"Her boyfriend was pimping her on my turf, man. I chased him off and she stayed with me."

"She have any choice?"

Violet grinned. "Not in this neighborhood, man."

"How come you remember her so well?"

"She was white, man. Most of my chicks are black."

"What happened to her?"

Violet shrugged. "Moved uptown, fancy stuff, appointment only." He finished the beer. The bartender brought us two more without being asked.

"She work on her own?"

"Naw, she work for another broad, a madame, baby. Very classy. Probably screwed only Baaahston dudes, dig?" And again the whooping laugh.

"Can you give me the name?"

"I can get it, but that's extra."

"Another fifty?"

"That's cool." Violet got up and went to a pay phone by the door. He was back in five minutes. "Patricia Utley," he said. "Fifty-seven East Thirty-seventh Street."

"Thanks, Violet." I took a $100 bill out of my wallet and handed it to him. "If you're ever in Boston . . ."

Violet laughed again. "Yeah, baby, if I ever want some beans . . ."

I finished the beer and got up. Violet turned and leaned his elbows on the bar. "Hey, Spenser," he said. "Utley works for very heavy people, dig?"

"That's okay," I said. "I don't mind heavy work."

"Well, you built for it, I give you that. But you walk around Utley careful, baby, this ain't Boston."

"Violet," I said, "I'm not sure this is even earth."

13

Midtown East Side in Manhattan is the New York they show in the movies. Elegant, charming, clean, "I bought you violets for your furs." Patricia Utley occupied a four-story town house on East Thirty-seventh, west of Lexington. The building was stone, painted a Colonial gray with a wrought-iron filigree on the glass door and the windows faced in white. Two small dormers protruded from the slate mansard roof, and a tiny terrace to the right of the front door bloomed with flowers against the green of several miniature trees. Red geraniums and white patient Lucys in black iron pots lined the three granite steps that led up to the front door.

A well-built man with gray hair and a white mess jacket answered my ring. I gave him my card. "For Patricia Utley," I said.

"Come in, please," he said and stepped aside. I entered a center hall with a polished flagstone floor and a mahogany staircase with white risers opposite the door. The black man opened a door on the right-hand wall, and I went into a small sitting room that looked out over Thirty-seventh Street and the miniature garden. The walls were white-paneled, and there was a Tiffany lamp in green, red, and gold hanging in the center of the room. The rugs were Oriental, and the furniture was Edwardian.

The butler said, "Wait here, please," and left. He closed the door behind him.

There was a mahogany highboy on the wall opposite the windows with four cut-glass decanters and a collection of small crystal glasses. I took the stoppers out of the decanters and sniffed. Sherry, cognac, port, Calvados. I poured myself a glass of the Calvados. On the wall opposite the door was a black marble fireplace, and on either side floor-to-ceiling bookcases. I looked at the titles: *The Complete Works of Charles Dickens, A History of the English-Speaking Peoples* by Winston Churchill, *Longfellow: Complete Poetical and Prose Works,* H. G. Wells's *The Outline of History,* Chaucer's *The Canterbury Tales,* with illustrations by Rockwell Kent. The door opened behind me, and a woman entered. The butler closed it softly behind her.

"Mr. Spenser," she said, "I'm Patricia Utley," and put out her hand. I shook it. She looked as if she might have read all the books and understood them. She was fortyish, small and blond with good bones and big black-rimmed round glasses. Her hair was pulled back tight against her head with a bun in the back. She was wearing an off-white sleeveless linen dress with blue and green piping at the hem and along the neckline. Her legs were bare and tanned.

"Please sit down," she said. "I see you have a drink. Good. How may I help you?" I sat on the sofa. She sat opposite me on an ottoman. Her knees together, ankles crossed, hands folded in her lap.

"I'm looking for information about a girl named Donna Burlington who you probably knew about eight years ago." I showed her the picture.

"And why would you think I know anything about her, Mr. Spenser?"

"One of your colleagues suggested that she had left his employ and joined your firm."

"I'm sorry, I don't understand." Her blue eyes were direct and steady as she looked at me. Her face without lines.

"Well, ma'am, I don't mean to be coarse, but an East Village pimp named Violet told me she moved uptown and went to work for you in the late fall of nineteen sixty-six."

"I'm afraid I don't know anyone named Violet," she said.

"Tall, thin guy, aggressive dresser, but small-time. No reason for you to know him. The Pinkerton Agency has never heard of me either."

"Oh, I'm sure you're well known in your field, Mr. Spenser." She smiled, and a dimple appeared in each cheek. "But I really don't see how I can help you. This Violet person has misled you, I suppose for money. New York is a very grasping city."

The room was cool and silent, central air conditioning. I sipped the Calvados, and it reminded me that I hadn't eaten since about seven thirty. It was now almost four thirty. "Ms. Utley," I said, "I don't wish to rock your boat and I don't want anything bad to happen to Donna Burlington, I just need to know about her."

"Ms. Utley," she said. "That's charming, but it's Mrs., thank you."

"Okay, Mrs. Utley, but what I said stands. I need to know about Donna Burlington. Confidential. No harm to anyone, and I can't tell you why. But I need to know." I finished the brandy. She stood, took my glass, filled it, and set it down on the marble-topped coffee table in front of me. Her movements were precise and graceful and stylish. So was she.

"I have no quarrel with that, Mr. Spenser, but I can't help you. I don't know the young lady, nor can I imagine how anyone could think that I might."

"Mrs. Utley, I know we've only met, but would you join me for dinner?"

"Is that part of your technique, Mr. Spenser? Candlelight and wine and perhaps I'll remember something about the young lady?"

"Well, there's that," I said. "But I hate to eat alone. The only people I know in the city are you and Violet, and Violet already had a date."

"Well, I don't know about being second choice to—what was it you said—an East Village pimp?"

"I'll tell you about my most exciting cases," I said. "Why, I remember one I call the howling dog caper . . ."

The dimple reappeared.

"And I'll do a one-hand push-up for you, and sing a dozen popular songs, pronouncing the lyrics so clearly that you can hear every word."

"And if I still refuse?"

"Then I go down to Foley Square and see if I can find someone in the DA's office that knows you and might put in a word for me."

"I do not like to be threatened, Mr. Spenser."

"Desperation," I said. "Loneliness and desire make a man crazy. Here, look at the kind of treat ahead of you." I put my glass on the end table, got down on the rug, and did a one-hand push-up. I looked up at her from the push-up position, my left hand behind my back. "Want to see another one?" I said.

She was laughing. Silently at first with her face serious but her stomach jiggling and giving her away, and then aloud, with her head back and the dimples big enough to hold a ripe olive.

"I'll go," she said. "Let me change, and we'll go. Now, for God sakes, get off the floor, you damn fool."

I got up. "The old one-hand push-up," I said. "Gets them almost every time."

She didn't take long. I had time to sip one more brandy before she reappeared in a backless white dress that tied around the neck and had a royal blue sash around the middle. Her shoes matched the sash, and so did her earrings.

I said, "Hubba, hubba."

"Hub-ba, hub-ba? What on earth does that mean?"

"You look very nice," I said. "Where would you like to go?"

"There's a lovely restaurant uptown a little ways we could try, if you'd like."

"I'm in your hands," I said. "This is your city."

"You are not, I would guess, ever in anyone's hands, Spenser, but I think you'll like this place."

"Cab?" I said.

"No, Steven will drive us."

When we went out the front door, there was the same well-built black man, sitting at the wheel of a Mercedes sedan. He'd swapped his mess jacket for a blue blazer.

We drove uptown.

The restaurant was at Sixty-fifth Street on the East Side and was called The Wings of the Dove.

"Do you suppose they serve the food in a golden bowl?" I said.

"I don't believe so. Why do you ask?"

"Henry James," I said. "It's a book joke."

"I guess I haven't read it."

It was only five thirty when we went in. Too early for most people to go to dinner, but most people had probably eaten lunch. I hadn't. It was a small restaurant, with a lavish dessert table in the foyer and two rooms separated by an archway. The ceiling was frosted glass that opened out, like a greenhouse, and the walls were used brick, some from the original building, some quite artfully integrated with the original. The tablecloths were pink, and there were flowers and green plants everywhere, many of them in hanging pots.

The maître d' in a tuxedo said, "Good evening, Mrs. Utley. We have your table."

She smiled and followed him. I followed her. One wall of the restaurant was mirrored, and it gave the illusion of a good deal more space than there was. I checked myself as we filed in. The suit was holding up, I'd had a haircut just last week. If only a talent scout from *Playgirl* would spot me.

"Would you care for cocktails?"

Patricia Utley said, "Campari on the rocks with a twist, please, John."

I said, "Do you have any draft beer?"

The maître d' said, "No."

I said, "Do you have any Amstel in bottles?"

He said, "No."

I said to Patricia Utley, "Is Nedick's still open?"

She said to the maître d', "Bring him a bottle of Heineken, John."

The maître d' said, "Certainly, Mrs. Utley," and stalked toward the kitchen.

She looked at me and shook her head slowly. "Are you ever serious, Spenser?"

"Yes, I am," I said. "I am serious, for instance, about discussing Donna Burlington with you."

"And I am serious when I say to you, why should you think I'd know her?"

"Because you are in charge of a high-priced prostitution operation and are bankrolled with what my source refers to as heavy money. Now I know it, and you know it, and why not stop the pretense? The truth, Mrs. Utley, will set us free."

"All right," she said, "say you are correct. Why should I discuss it with you?"

A waiter brought our drinks and I waited while he put them down. Mine rather disdainfully, I thought.

"Because I can cause you aggravation—cops, newspapers, maybe the feds—maybe I could cause you trouble, I don't know. Depends on how heavy the bankrollers really are. If you talk with me, then it's confidential, there's no aggravation at all. And I might do another one-arm push-up for you."

"What if my bankrollers decided to cause you aggravation?"

"I have a very high aggravation tolerance."

She sipped her Campari. "It's funny, or maybe it's not funny at all, but you're the second person who's come asking about Donna."

"Who else?"

"He never said, but he was quite odd. He was, oh, what, in costume, I guess you'd say. Dressed all in white, white suit and shirt, white tie, white shoes and a big white straw hat like a South American planter."

"Tall and slim? Chewed gum?"

"Yes."

I said, "Aha."

"Aha?"

"Yeah, like Aha I see a connection, or Aha I have discovered a clue. It's detective talk."

"You know who he is then."

"Yes, I do. What did he want?"

She sipped some more Campari. I drank some Heineken. "Among my enterprises," she said, "is a film business. This gentleman had apparently seen Donna in one of our films and wanted the master print."

"Aha, aha!" I said. "Corporate diversification." The waiter came for our order. When he was gone, I said, "Start from the beginning. When did you meet Donna, what did she do for you, what kind of film was she in, tell me all."

"Very well, if you promise not to keep saying Aha."

"Agreed."

"Donna came to me through a client. He'd picked her up down in the East Village when he was drunk." She grimaced. "She was working for Violet then; her boyfriend had pimped for her before but had run from Violet. I don't know what happened to the boyfriend. The client thought she was too nice a girl to be hustling out of the back of a car with a two-dollar pimp like Violet. He put her in touch with me."

The waiter came with our soup. I had gazpacho; Patricia Utley had vichyssoise.

"I run a very first-rate operation, Spenser."

"I can tell that," I said.

"Of course, I would deny this to anyone if it ever came up."

"It won't. I don't care about your operation. I only care about Donna Burlington."

"But you disapprove."

"I don't approve or disapprove. To tell you the truth, Mrs. Utley, I don't give a damn. I think about one thing at a time. Right now I'm thinking about Donna Burlington."

"It's a volunteer business," she said. "It exists because men have needs." She said it as if the needs had a foul odor.

"Now who's disapproving?"

"You don't know," she said. "You've never seen what I've seen."

"About Donna Burlington," I said.

"She was eighteen when I took her. She didn't know anything. She didn't know how to dress, how to do her hair, how to wear makeup. She hadn't read anything, been anyplace, talked to anyone. I had her two years and taught her everything. How to walk, how to sit, how to talk with people. I gave her books to read, showed her how to make up, how to dress."

The waiter brought the fish. Sole in a saffron sauce for her. Scallops St. Jacques for me.

"You and Rex Harrison," I said.

"Yes," she said. "It was rather like that. I liked Donna, she was a very unsophisticated little thing. It was like having a, oh not a daughter, but a niece perhaps. Then one day she left. To get married."

"Who'd she marry?"

"She wouldn't tell me—a client, I gathered, but she wouldn't say whom, and I never saw her again."

"When was this?"

Patricia Utley thought for a moment. "It was the same year as the Cambodian raids and the great protest, nineteen seventy. She left me in winter nineteen seventy. I remember it was winter because I watched her walk away in a lovely fur-collared tweed coat she had."

The waiter cleared the fish and put down the salad, spinach leaves with raw mushrooms in a lemon and oil dressing. I took a bite. So-so. "I assume the films were what I used to call dirty movies when I was a kid."

She smiled. "It is getting awfully hard to decide, isn't it? They were erotic films. But of good quality, sold by subscription."

"Black socks, garter belts, two girls and a guy? That kind of stuff?"

"No, as I said, tasteful, high quality, good color and sound. No sadism, no homosexuality, no group sex."

"And Donna was in some?"

"She was in one, shortly before she left me. The pay was good, and while it was a lot of work, it was a bit of a change for her. Her film was called *Suburban Fancy.* She was quite believable in it."

"What did you tell the man who came asking?"

"I told him that he was under some kind of false impression. That I knew nothing about the films or the young lady involved. He became somewhat abusive, and I had to call for Steven to show him out."

"I heard this guy was pretty tough," I said.

"Steven was armed," she said.

"Oh," I said. "How come you didn't have Steven show me out?"

"You did not become abusive."

The entrée came. Duck in a fig and brandy sauce for me, striped bass in cucumber and crabmeat sauce for her. The duck was wonderful.

I said, "You sell these films by subscription." She nodded. "How's chances on a look at the subscription list?"

"None," she said.

"No chance?"

"No chance at all. Obviously you can see my situation. Such material must remain confidential to protect our clients."

"People do sell mailing lists," I said.

"I do not," she said. "I have no need for money, Mr. Spenser."

"No, I guess you don't. Okay, how about I name a couple of people and you tell me if they're on your list? That doesn't compromise any but those I suspect anyway."

There were carrots in brown sauce with fresh dill and zucchini in butter with the entrée, and Patricia Utley ate some of each before she answered. "Perhaps we can go back to my home for brandy after dinner and I'll have someone check."

For dessert we had *clafoutis,* which still tastes like blueberry pancakes to me, and coffee. The coffee was weak. The bill was $119 including tip.

14

At Patricia Utley's home I returned to the Calvados. Patricia Utley had some sherry.

"Would you care to see the film, Spenser?" she said.

"No, thank you."

"Why not? I never met a man that didn't care for eroticism."

"Oh, I'm all for eroticism." I was thinking of Linda Rabb in her Church Park apartment in her clean white jeans. "It's movies I don't like."

"As you wish." She sipped some sherry. "You were going to mention some names to me."

"Yeah, Bucky Maynard—I don't know the real first name, maybe that's it—and Lester Floyd." I was gambling she'd never followed sports and had never heard of Maynard. I didn't want to tie Donna Burlington to the Red Sox, but I needed to know. If she'd ever heard of Bucky Maynard, she gave no sign. Lester didn't look like a self-starter. If he was in on this, it was a good bet he represented Maynard.

"I'll see," she said. She picked up a phone on the end table near the couch and dialed a three-digit number. "Would you please check the subscription list, specifically on *Suburban Fancy,* and see if we have either a Bucky Maynard or a Lester Floyd, and the address and date? Thank you. Yes, call me right back, I'm in the library."

"How many copies of that film are there?" I asked.

"I won't tell you," she said. "That's confidential."

"Okay, it doesn't matter anyway. The real question is can I get all the copies?"

"No, I offered to show you the film and you didn't want to."

"That's not the point."

The phone rang and Patricia Utley answered, listened a moment, wrote on a note pad, and hung up.

"There is a Lester Floyd on our subscription list. There is no Bucky Maynard."

"What's the address on Floyd?"

"Harbor Towers, Atlantic Avenue, Boston, Mass. Do you need the street number?"

"No, thank you, that's fine." I finished my brandy and she poured me another.

"The point I was making before is that I don't want the films to look at. I want them to destroy. Donna Burlington has a nice life now. Married, kid, shiny oak floors in her living room, all-electric kitchen. Her husband loves her. That kind of stuff. These films could destroy her."

"That is hardly my problem, Spenser. The odds are very good that no one who saw these films would know Donna or connect her with them. And this is not eighteen seventy-five. Queen Victoria is dead. Aren't you being a little dramatic that someone who acted once in an erotic movie would be destroyed?"

"Not in her circles. In her circles it would be murder."

"Well, even if you are right, as I said, it is not my problem. I am in business, not social work. Destroying those films is not profitable."

"Even if purchased at what us collectors like to call fair market value?"

"Not the master. That would be like killing the goose. You can have all the prints you want, at fair market value, but not the master."

I got up and walked across the room and looked out the windows at Thirty-seventh Street. The streetlights had come on, and while it wasn't full dark yet, there was a softening bronze tinge to everything. The traffic was light, and the people who strolled by looked like extras in a Fred Astaire movie. Well dressed and good-looking. Brilliant red flowers the size of a trumpet bell bloomed in the little garden.

"Mrs. Utley," I said, "I think that Donna's being blackmailed and that the blackmailer will eventually ruin her life and her husband's and he's using your films."

Silence behind me. I turned around and put my hands in my hip pocket. "If I can get those films, I can take away his leverage." She sat quietly with her knees together and her ankles crossed as she had before and took a delicate sip of sherry. "You remember Donna, don't you? Like a niece almost. You taught her everything. Pygmalion. Remember her? She started out in life caught in a mudhole. And she's climbed out. She has gotten out of the bog and onto solid ground, and now she's getting dragged back in. You don't need money. You told me that."

"I'm a businesswoman," she said. "I do not follow bad business practices."

"Is that how you stay out of the bog?" I said.

"I beg your pardon?"

"You climbed out of the mudhole a bit too, is that how? You keep telling yourself you're a businesswoman and that's the code you live by. So that you don't have to deal with the fact that you are also a pimp. Like Violet."

There was no change in her expression. "You lousy no-dick son of a bitch," she said.

I laughed. "Now, baby, now we are getting it together. You got a lot of style and great manners, but you and I are from the same neighborhood, darling, and now that we both know it maybe we can do business. I want those goddamned films, and I'll do what I have to to get them."

Her face was whiter now than it had been. I could see the makeup more clearly.

"You want her back in the mudhole?" I said. "She got out, and you helped her. Now she's got style and manners, and there's a man that wants to dirty her up and rub her nose in what she was. It'll destroy her. You want to destroy her? For business? When I said you were like Violet, you got mad. Think how mad it would make Violet." She reached over and picked up the phone and pressed the intercom button.

"Steven," she said, "I need you."

By the time the phone was back in the cradle, Steven was in the room. He had a nice springy step when he walked. Vigorous. He also had a .38 caliber Ruger Black Hawk.

Patricia Utley said, "I believe he has a gun, Steven."

Steven said, "Yeah, right hip, I spotted it when he came in. Shall I take it away from him?" Steven was holding the Ruger at his side, the barrel pointing at the floor. As he spoke, he slapped it absent-mindedly against his thigh.

"No," Patricia Utley said, "just show him to the street, please."

Steven gestured with his head toward the door. "Move it," he said.

I looked at Patricia Utley. Her color had returned. She was poised, still controlled, handsome. I couldn't think of anything to say. So I moved it.

Outside, it was a warm summer night. Dark now, the bronze glow gone. And on the East Side, midtown, quiet. I walked over to Fifth Avenue and caught a cab uptown to my motel. The West Side was a little noiser but nowhere near as suave. When I got into my room, I turned up the air conditioner, turned on the television, and took a shower. When I came out, there was a Yankee game on and I lay on the bed and watched it.

Was it Lester? Was it Maynard with Lester as the straw? It had to be something like that. The coincidence would have been too big. The rumor that Rabb is shading games, the wife's past, Marty knew something about it. He lied about the marriage circumstances, and Lester Floyd showing up asking about the wife and Lester Floyd's name being on the mailing list. It had to be. Lester or Maynard had spotted Linda Rabb in the film and put the screws on her husband. I couldn't prove it, but I didn't have to. I could report back to Erskine that it looked probable Rabb was in somebody's pocket and he could go to the DA and they could take it from there. I could get a print of the film and show Erskine and we could brace Rabb and talk about the integrity of the game and what he ought to do for the good of baseball and the kids of America. Then I could throw up.

I wasn't going to do any of those things, and I knew it when I started thinking about it. The Yankee game went into extra innings and was won by John Briggs in the tenth inning, when he singled Don Money in from third. Milwaukee was doing better in New York than I was.

15

I spent a good deal of time thinking about how to get the master print of *Suburban Fancy* from Patricia Utley and consequently spent not very much time sleeping till about 4:00 A.M. I didn't think of anything before I fell asleep, and when I woke up, it was almost 10 and I hadn't thought of anything while I slept. I was shaving at 10:20 when there was a knock at the door. I opened it with a towel around my middle, and there was a porter with a neat square package.

"Mr. Spenser?"

"Yeah."

"Gentleman asked me to give this to you."

I took it, went to the bureau, found two quarters, and gave them to the porter. He said thank you and went away. I closed the door and sat on the bed and opened the package. It was a canister of film. In the package was a note typed on white parchment paper.

Spenser,
This is the master print of *Suburban Fancy.* I have destroyed the remaining two copies in my possession. My records show a copy sold to the gentleman we discussed last night. There are ten other copies outstanding, but I can find no pattern in their distribution. You will have to deal with the gentleman mentioned above. I wish you success in that.

Doing this violates good business practice and has cost me a good deal more than the money involved. Violet would not have done it.

Yours,
Patricia C. Utley

She had signed it with a black felt-tipped pen in handwriting so neat it looked like type. I'd wasted a sleepless night.

I got out the Manhattan Yellow Pages from the bedside table and looked under "Photographic Equipment" till I found a store in my area that rented projectors. I was going to have to look at the film. If it turned out to be a film on traffic safety, or VD prevention, I would look like an awful goober. Patricia Utley had no reason particularly to lie to me but I was premising too much on the film's authenticity to proceed without looking.

I had mediocre eggs Benedict in the hotel coffee shop and went out and got my projector. Walking back up Fifty-seventh Street with it, I felt furtive, as if the watch and ward society had a tail on me. Going up in the elevator, I tried to look like an executive going to a sales conference. Back in my room I set up the projector on the luggage rack, pulled the drapes, shut off the lights, and sat on one of the beds to watch the movie. Wasteful practice giving me a room with two beds. Motels did that to me often. Alone in a two-bed room. A great song title, maybe I'd get me a funny suit and a guitar and record it. The projector whirred. The movie showed up on the bare wall.

Patricia Utley was right, it was a high-class operation. The color was good, even on the beige wall. I hadn't bothered with sound. The titles were professional, and the set was well lit and realistic-looking. The plot, as I got it without the sound, was about a housewife, frustrated by her church, children, and kitchen existence, who relieves her sense of limitation in the time-honored manner of skin flicks immemorial. The housewife was, in fact, Linda Rabb.

Watching in the darkened motel room, I felt nasty. A middle-aged man alone in a motel watching a dirty movie. When I got through here, I could go down to Forty-second Street and feed quarters into the peep show Movieolas. After the first sexual contact had established for sure what I was looking at, I shut off the projector and rewound the film. I went into the bathroom and stripped the film off the reel into the tub. I got the package of complimentary matches from the bedside table and lit the film. When it had burned up, I turned on the shower and washed the remnants down the drain. It was close to noon when I checked out of the hotel. Before I caught the shuttle back to Boston, I wanted to visit the Metropolitan Museum. On the way uptown in a cab, I stopped at a flower shop and had a dozen roses delivered to Patricia Utley. I checked my overnight bag at the museum, spent the afternoon walking about and throwing my head back and squinting at paintings, had lunch in the fountain room, took a cab to La Guardia, and caught the six o'clock shuttle to Boston. At seven forty-five I was home.

My apartment was as empty as it had been when I left, but stuffier. I opened all the windows, got a bottle of Amstel out of the refrigerator, and sat by the front window to drink it. After a while I got hungry and went to the kitchen. There was nothing to eat. I drank another beer and looked again, and found half a loaf of whole wheat bread behind the beer in the back of the refrigerator and an unopened jar of peanut butter in the cupboard. I made two peanut butter sandwiches and put them on a plate, opened another bottle of beer and went and sat by the window and looked out and ate the sandwiches and drank the beer. *Bas cuisine.*

At nine thirty I got into bed and read another chapter in Morison's *History* and went to sleep. I dreamed something strange about the colonists playing baseball with the British and I was playing third for the colonists and struck out with the bases loaded. In the morning I woke up depressed.

I hadn't worked out during my travels, and my body craved exercise. I jogged along the river and worked out in the BU gym. When I was through and showered and dressed, I didn't feel depressed anymore. So what's a strikeout? Ty Cobb must have struck out once in a while.

It was about ten when I went into the Yorktown Tavern. Already there were drinkers, sitting separate from each other smoking cigarettes, drinking a shot and a beer, watching *The Price Is Right* on TV or looking into the beer glass. In his booth in the back, Lennie Seltzer had set up for the day. He was reading the *Globe.* The *Herald American* and the New York *Daily News* were folded neatly on the table in front of him. A glass of beer stood by his right hand. He was wearing a light tan glen plaid three-piece suit today, and he smelled of bay rum.

He said, "How's business, kid?" as I slid in opposite him.

"The poor are always with us," I said. He started to gesture at the bartender, and I shook my head. "Not at ten in the morning, Len."

"Why not, tastes just as good then as any other time. Better, in fact, I think."

"That's what I'm afraid of. I got enough trouble staying sober now."

"It's pacing, kid, all pacing, ya know. I mean, I just sip a little beer and let it rest and sip a little more and let it rest and I do it all day and it don't bother me. I go home to my old lady, and I'm sober as a freaking nun, ya know." He took an illustrative sip of beer and set the glass down precisely in the ring it had left on the tabletop. "Find out if Marty Rabb's going into el tanko yet?"

I shook my head. "I need some information on some betting habits, though."

"Uh-huh?"

"Guy named Lester Floyd. Ever hear of him?"

Seltzer shook his head. "How about Bucky Maynard?"

"The announcer?"

"Yeah. Floyd is his batman."

"His what?"

"Batman, like in the British army, each officer had a batman, a personal servant."

"You spend too much time reading, Spenser. You know more stuff that don't make you money than anybody I know."

" 'Tis better to know than not to know," I said.

"Aw bullshit, what is it you want to know about Maynard and what's'isname?"

"Lester Floyd. I want to know if they bet on baseball and, if they do, what games they bet on. I want the dates. And I need an idea of how much they're betting. Either one or both."

Seltzer nodded. "Okay, I'll let you know."

16

Lennie Seltzer called me two days later at my office. "Neither Maynard nor Floyd does any betting at all I can find out about," he said.

"Sonovabitch," I said.

"Screw up a theory?"

"Yeah. How sure are you?"

"Pretty sure. Can't be positive, but I been in business here a long time."

"Goddamn," I said.

"I hear that Maynard used to bet a lot, and he got into the hole with a guy and couldn't pay up and the guy sold the paper to a shylock. Pretty good deal, the guy said. Shylock gave him seventy cents on the dollar."

I said, "Aha."

Seltzer said, "Huh?"

I said, "Never mind, just thinking out loud. What's the shylock's name?"

"Wally Hogg. Real name's Walter Hogarth. Works for Frank Doerr."

"Short, fat person, smokes cigars?"

"Yeah, know him?"

"I've seen him around," I said. "Does he always work for Doerr, or does he free-lance?"

"I don't know of him free-lancing. I also don't know many guys like me ever made a profit talking about Frank Doerr."

"Yeah, I know, Lennie. Okay, thanks."

He hung up. I held the phone for a minute and looked up at the ceiling. Seventy cents on the dollar. That was a good rate. Doerr must have had some confidence in Maynard's ability to pay. I looked at my watch: 11:45. I was supposed to meet Brenda Loring in the Public Garden for a picnic lunch. Her treat. I put on my jacket, locked the office, and headed out.

She was already there when I arrived, sitting on the grass beside the swan boat pond with a big wicker basket beside her.

"A hamper?" I said. "A genuine wicker picnic hamper like in Abercrombie and Fitch?"

"I think you're supposed to admire me first," she said, "then the food basket. I've always been suspicious of your value system."

"You look good enough to eat," I said.

"I think I won't pursue that line," she said. She was wearing a pale blue linen suit and an enormous white straw hat. All the young executive types looked at her as they strolled by with their lunches hidden in attaché cases. "Tell me about your travels."

"I had a terrific blackberry pie in Illinois and a wonderful roast duck in New York."

"Oh, I'm glad for you. Did you also encounter any clues?" She opened the hamper as she talked and took out a red and white checked tablecloth and spread it between us. The day was warm and still, and the cloth lay quiet on the ground.

"Yeah. I found out a lot of things and all of them are bad. I think. It's kind of complicated at the moment."

She took dark blue glossy-finish paper plates out of the hamper and set them out on the cloth. "Tell me about it. Maybe it'll help you sort out the complicated parts."

I was looking into the hamper. "Is that wine in there?" I said. She took my nose and turned my head away.

"Be patient," she said. "I went to a lot of trouble to arrange this and bring it out one item at a time and impress the hell out of you, and I'll not have it spoiled."

"Instinct," I said. "Remember I'm a trained sleuth."

"Tell me about your trip." She put out two sets of what looked like real silver.

"Okay, Rabb's got reason to be dumping a game or two."

"Oh, that's too bad."

"Yeah. Mrs. Rabb isn't who she's supposed to be. She's a kid from lower-middle America who smoked a little dope early and ran off with a local hotshot when she was eighteen. She went to New York, was a whore for a while, and went into acting. Her acting was done with her clothes off in films distributed by mail. She started out turning tricks in one-night cheap hotels. Then she graduated to a high-class call girl operation run, or at least fronted, by a very swish woman out of a fancy town house on the East Side. That's when I think she met her husband."

Brenda placed two big wine goblets in front of us and handed me a bottle of rosé and a corkscrew. "You mean, he was a—what should I call him—a customer?"

"Yeah, I think so. How can I talk and open the wine at the same time? You know my powers of concentration."

"I've heard," she said, "that you can't walk and whistle at the same time. Just open the wine and then talk while I pour."

I opened the wine and handed it to her. "Now," I said, "where was I?"

"Oh, giant intellect," she said, and poured some wine into my glass. "You were saying that Marty Rabb had met his wife when she was—as we sociologists would put it—screwing him professionally."

"Words," I said, "what a magic web you weave with them. Yeah, that's what I think."

"How do you know?" She poured herself a half glass of wine.

"Well, he's covering up her past. He lied about how he met her and where they were married. I don't know what he knows, but he knows something."

Brenda brought out an unsliced loaf of bread and took off the transparent wrapping.

"Sourdough?" I said.

She nodded and put the loaf on one of the paper plates. "Is there more?" she said.

"Yeah. A print of the film she made was sold to Lester Floyd." She looked puzzled. "Lester Floyd," I said, "is Bucky Maynard's gofer, and Bucky Maynard is, in case you forgot, the play by play man for the Sox."

"What's a gofer?"

"A lackey. Someone to go-for coffee and go-for cigarettes and go-for whatever he's told."

"And you think Maynard told him to go-for the film?"

"Yeah, maybe, anyway, say Bucky got a look at the film and recognized Mrs. Rabb. Is that smoked turkey?"

Brenda nodded and put a cranshaw melon out beside it, and four nectarines.

"Oh, I hope she doesn't know," she said.

"Yeah, but I think she does know. And I think Marty knows."

"Some kind of blackmail?"

"Yeah. First I thought it was maybe Maynard or Lester of the costumes getting Rabb to shave a game here and there and cleaning up from the bookies. But they don't seem to bet any these days, and I found out that Maynard owes money to a shylock."

"Is that like a loan shark?"

"Just like a loan shark," I said.

A large wedge of Monterey Jack cheese came out of the hamper, and a small crystal vase with a single red rose in it, which Brenda placed in the middle of the tablecloth.

"That hamper is like the clown car at the circus. I'm waiting for the sommelier to jump out with his gold key and ask if Monsieur is pleased with the wine."

"Eat," she said.

While I was breaking a chunk off the sourdough bread, Brenda said, "So what does the loan shark mean?"

I said, "Phnumph."

She said, "Don't talk with your mouth full. I'll wait till you've eaten a little and gotten control of yourself."

I drank some wine and said, "My compliments to the chef."

She said, "The chef is Bert Heidemann at Bert's Deli on Newbury Street. I'll tell him you were pleased."

"The shylock means that maybe Maynard can't pay up and they've put the squeeze on him and he gave them Rabb."

"What do you mean, gave them Rabb?"

"Well, say Maynard owes a lot of bread to the shylock and he can't pay, and he can't pay the vig, and—"

"The what?"

"The vig, vigorish, interest. A good shylock can keep you paying interest the rest of your life and never dent the principal . . . like a revolving charge. . . . Anyway, say Maynard can't make the payments. Shylocks like Wally Hogg are quite scary. They threaten broken bones, or propane torches on the bottoms of feet, or maybe cut off a finger each time you miss a payment."

Brenda shivered and made a face.

"Yeah, I know, okay, say that's the case and along comes this piece of luck. Mrs. Rabb in the skin flick. He tells the shylock he can control the games that Marty Rabb pitches, and Rabb, being probably the best pitcher now active, if he's under control can make the shylock and his employers a good many tax-free muffins."

"But would he go for it?" Brenda asked. "I mean it would be embarrassing, but the sexual revolution has been won. No one, surely, would stone her to death."

"Maybe so if she were married to someone in a different line of work, but baseball is more conservative than the entire city of Buffalo. And Rabb is part of a whole ethic: Man protects the family, no matter what."

"Even if he has to throw games? What about the jock ethic? You know winning isn't everything, it's the only thing. Wouldn't that be a problem?"

"That's not the real jock ethic, that's the jock ethic that people who don't know a hell of a lot about jocks believe. The real jock ethic's a lot more complicated."

"My, we're a little touchy about the jock ethic, aren't we?"

"I didn't mean you," I said.

"Maybe you haven't outgrown the jock ethic yourself."

"Maybe it's not something to outgrow," I said. "Anyway, some other time I'll give my widely acclaimed lecture on the real jock ethic. The thing is that unless I misjudged Rabb a lot, he's in an awful bind. Because his ethic is violated whichever way he turns. He feels commitment to play the game as best he can and to protect his wife and family as best he can. Both those commitments are probably absolute, and the point when they conflict must be sharp."

Brenda sipped some wine and looked at me without saying anything.

"A quarter for your thoughts if you accept Diners Club?"

She smiled. "You sound sort of caught up in all this. Maybe you're talking some about yourself too. I think maybe you are."

I leered at her. "Want me to tell you about the movie Mrs. Rabb was in and what they did?"

"You think I need pointers?" Brenda said.

"When we stop learning, we stop growing," I said.

"And you got us off that subject nicely, didn't you?"

I had once again qualified for membership in the clean plate club by then, and we had begun a second bottle of wine. "You have to get back to work?" I said.

"No, I took the afternoon off. I had the feeling lunch would stretch out."

"That's good," I said, and filled my wineglass again.

17

It was a classic summer morning when I dropped Brenda Loring off at her Charles River Park apartment. The river was a vigorous and optimistic blue, and the MDC cop at Leverett Circle was whistling "Buttons and Bows" as he directed traffic. Across the river Cambridge looked clean and bright in sharp relief against the sky. I went around Leverett Circle and headed back westbound on Storrow Drive. The last hurrah of the rush-hour traffic was still to be heard, and it took me twenty minutes to get to Church Park. I parked at a hydrant and took the elevator to the sixth floor. I'd called before I left that morning, so Linda Rabb was expecting me. Marty wasn't home; he was with the club in Oakland.

"Coffee, Mr. Spenser?" she said when I came in.

"Yeah, I'd love some," I said. It was already perked and on the coffee table with a plate of assorted muffins: corn, cranberry, and blueberry; all among my favorites. She was wearing pale blue jeans and a blue and pink striped man-tailored shirt, open at the neck with a pink scarf knotted at the throat. On her feet were cork-soled blue suede slip-on shoes. The engagement ring on her right hand had a heart-shaped diamond in it big enough to make her arm weary. The wedding ring on her left was a wide gold band, unadorned. A small boy who looked like his father hung around the coffee table, eyeing the muffins but hesitant about snatching one from so close to me. I picked up the plate and offered him one, and he retreated quickly back behind his mother's leg.

"Marty's shy, Mr. Spenser," she said. And to the boy: "Do you want cranberry or blueberry, Marty?" The boy turned his head toward her leg and mumbled something I couldn't hear. He looked about three. Linda Rabb picked up a blueberry muffin and gave it to him. "Why don't you get your crayons," she said, "and bring them in here and draw here on the floor while I talk with Mr. Spenser?" The kid mumbled something again that I couldn't hear. Linda Rabb took a deep breath and said, "Okay, Marty, come on, I'll go with you to get them." And to me: "Excuse me, Mr. Spenser."

They went out, the kid hanging onto Linda Rabb's pants leg as they went. No wonder so many housewives ended up drinking Boone's Farm in the morning. They were back in maybe two minutes with a lined yellow legal-sized pad of paper and a box of crayons. The kid got down on the floor by his mother's chair and began to draw stick-figured people in various colors, with orange predominant.

"Now, what can I do for you, Mr. Spenser?" she asked.

I hadn't counted on the kid. "Well, it's kind of complicated, Mrs. Rabb, maybe I ought to come back when the boy isn't . . ." I left it hanging. I didn't know how much the kid would understand, and I didn't want him to think I didn't want him around.

"Oh, that's all right, Mr. Spenser, Marty's fine. He doesn't mind what we talk about."

"Well, I don't know, this is kind of ticklish."

"For heaven's sake, Mr. Spenser, say what's on your mind. Believe me, it is all right."

I drank some coffee. "Okay, I'll tell you two things; then you decide whether we should go on. First, I'm not a writer, I'm a private detective. Second, I've seen a film called *Suburban Fancy.*"

She put her hand down on the boy's head; otherwise she didn't move. But her face got white and crowded.

"Who hired you?" she said.

"Erskine, but that doesn't matter. I won't hurt you."

"Why?" she said.

"Why did Erskine hire me? He wanted to find out if your husband was involved in fixing baseball games."

"O my God Jesus," she said, and the kid looked up at her. She smiled. "Oh, isn't that a nice family you're drawing. There's the momma and the daddy and the baby."

"Would it be better if I came back?" I said.

"There's nothing to come back for," Linda Rabb said. "I don't know anything about it. There's nothing to talk about."

"Mrs. Rabb, you know there is," I said. "You're panicky now and you don't know what to say, so you just say no, and hope if you keep saying it, it'll be true. But there's a lot to talk about."

"No."

"Yeah, there is. I can't help you if I don't know."

"Erskine didn't hire you to help us."

"I'm not sure if he did or not. I can always give him his money back."

"There's nothing to help. We don't need any help."

"Yeah, you do."

The kid tugged at his mother's pants leg again and held up his drawing. "That's lovely, Marty," she said. "Is that a doggie?" The kid turned and held the picture so I could see it.

I said, "I like that very much. Do you want to tell me about it?"

The kid shook his head. "No," I said, "I don't blame you. I don't like to talk about my work all that much either."

"Marty," Linda Rabb said, "draw a house for the doggie." The boy bent back to the task. I noticed that he stuck his tongue out as he worked.

"Even if we did need help, what could you do?" Linda Rabb said.

"Depends on what exactly is going on. But this is my kind of work. I'm pretty sure to be better at it than you are."

My coffee cup was empty, and Linda Rabb got up and refilled it. I took a corn muffin, my third. I hoped she didn't notice.

"I've got to talk with Marty," she said.

I bit off one side of my corn muffin. Probably should have broken it first. Susan Silverman was always telling me about taking small bites and such. Linda Rabb didn't notice. She was looking at her watch. "Little Marty goes to nursery school for a couple of hours in the afternoon." She looked at the telephone and then at the kid and then at her watch again. Then she looked at me. "Why don't you come back a little after one?"

"Okay."

I got up and went to the door. Linda Rabb came with me. The kid came right behind her, close to her leg but no longer hanging on. As I left, I pointed my finger at him, from the hip, and brought my thumb down like the hammer of a pistol. He looked at me silently and made no response. On the other hand, he didn't run and hide. Always had a way with kids. The Dr. Spock of the gumshoes.

Outside on Mass Ave, I looked at my watch: 11:35. An hour and a half to kill. I went around the corner to the Y on Huntington Ave where I am a member and got in a full workout on the Universal, including an extra set of bench presses and two extra sets of wrist rolls. By the time I got showered and dressed my pulse rate was back down under 100 and my breathing was almost under control. At 1:15 I was back at Linda Rabb's door. She answered the first ring.

"Marty's at school, Mr. Spenser. We can talk openly," she said.

18

The coffee and muffins were gone. Linda Rabb said, "Has it been raining somewhere? Your hair's wet."

"Shower," I said. "I went over to the Y and worked out."

"Oh, how nice."

"Sound mind in a healthy body and all that."

"Could you show me some identification, Mr. Spenser?"

I got out the photostat of my license in its little plastic case and handed it to her. Also my driver's license. She looked at them both and gave them back.

"I guess you really are a detective."

"Thanks," I said, "I need reassurance sometimes."

"Just what do you know, Mr. Spenser?"

"I've been to Redford, Illinois, I've talked with Sheriff Donaldson and with your mother and father. I know you got busted there in 'sixty-six for possession of marijuana. I know you ran away with a guy named Tony Reece and that you haven't been back. I know you went to New York, that you lived in a rooming house on Thirteenth Street in the East Village, that you were hustling for a living first for old Tony, then for a pimp named Violet. I know you moved uptown, went to work for Patricia Utley, made one pornographic movie, fell in love with one of your customers, and left to get married in the winter of nineteen seventy, wearing a lovely fur-collared tweed coat. I've been to New York, I've talked with Violet and with Patricia Utley. I preferred Mrs. Utley."

"Yes," Linda Rabb said without any expression, "I did too. Did you see me in the movie?"

"Yeah."

She was looking past me out the window. "Did you enjoy it?"

"I think you're very pretty."

She kept staring out the window. There wasn't anything to see except the dome of the Christian Science Mother Church. I was quiet.

"What do you want?" she said finally.

"I don't know yet. I told you what I know; now I'll tell you what I think. I think the client you married was Marty. I think someone got hold of *Suburban Fancy* that knows you and is blackmailing you and Marty, and that Marty is modifying some of the games he pitches so that whoever is blackmailing you can bet right and make a bundle."

Again silence and the stare. I thought about moving in front of the window to intercept it.

"If I hadn't made the film," she said. "It was just a break, in a way, from turning tricks with strangers. I mean there was every kind of sex in it, but it was just acting. It was always just acting, but in the movie it was supposed to be acting and the guy was acting and there were people you knew around. You didn't have to go alone to a strange hotel room and make conversation with someone you didn't know and wonder if he might be freaky, you know? I mean, some of them are freaky. Christ, you don't know." She shifted her stare from the window to me. I wanted to look out the window.

"One film," she said. "One goddamned film for good money under first-class conditions and no S and M or group sex, and right after that I met Marty."

"In New York?"

"Yes, they were in town to play the Yankees, and one of the other players set it up. Mrs. Utley sent three of us over to the hotel. It was Marty's first time with a whore." The word came out harsh and her stare was heavy on me. "He was always very straight."

More silence.

"He was a little drunk and laughing and making suggestive remarks, but as soon as we were alone, he got embarrassed. I had to lead him through it. And afterward we had some food sent up and ate a late supper and watched an old movie on TV. I still remember it. It was a Jimmy Stewart western called *Broken Arrow.* He kissed me good-bye when I left, and he was embarrassed to death to pay me."

"And you saw him again?"

"Yes, I called him at his hotel the next day. It was raining and the game with the Yankees was canceled. So we went to the Museum of Natural History."

"Yes."

"How about the other two players that night? Didn't they recognize you?"

"No, I had on a blond wig and different makeup. They didn't pay much attention to me anyway. Nobody looks at a whore. When I met Marty the next day, he didn't even recognize me at first."

"When did you get married?"

"When we said, except that we changed it. Marty and I worked out the story about me being from Arlington Heights and meeting in Chicago and all. I'd been to Chicago a couple of times and knew my way around okay if anyone wanted to ask about it. And Marty and I went out there before we were married and went to Comiskey Park, or whatever it's called now, and around Chicago so my story would sound okay."

"Where'd you get Arlington Heights?"

"Picked it out on a map."

We looked at each other. I could hear the faint hum of the refrigerator in the kitchen. And somewhere down the corridor a door opened and closed.

"That goddamned movie," she said. "When the letter came, I wanted to confess, but Marty wouldn't let me."

"What letter?"

"The first blackmail letter."

"Do you know who sent it?"

"No."

"I assume you don't have it."

"No."

"What did it say?"

"It said—I can remember it almost exactly—it was to Marty and it said, 'I have a copy of a movie called *Suburban Fancy.* If you don't lose your next ball game, I'll release it to the media.' "

"That's all?"

"That's all. No name or return address or anything."

"And did he?"

Linda Rabb looked blank. "Did he what?"

"Did Marty lose his next game?"

"Yes, he hung a curve in the seventh inning with the bases loaded against the Tigers, on purpose. I woke up in the middle of the night, that night, and he wasn't in bed, he was out in the living room, looking out the window and crying."

Her face was very white, and her eyes were puffy.

"And you wanted to confess it again."

"Yes. But he said no. And I said, 'It will kill you to throw games.' And he said a man looked out for his wife and his kid, and I said, 'But it will kill you.' And he wouldn't talk about it again. He said it was done and maybe there wouldn't be another letter, but we both knew there would."

"And there was."

She nodded.

"And they kept coming?"

She nodded.

"And Marty kept doing what they said to do?"

She nodded again.

"How often?" I said.

"The letters? Not often. Marty gets about thirty-five starts a year. There were maybe five or six letters last year, three so far this year."

"Smart," I said. "Didn't get greedy. Do you have any idea who it is?"

"No."

"It's a hell of a hustle," I said. "Blackmail is dangerous if the victim knows you or at the point when the money is exchanged. This is perfect. There is no money exchanged. You render a service, and he gets the money elsewhere. He never has to reveal himself. There are probably one hundred thousand people who've seen that film, and you can't know who they are. He mails his instructions, bets his money, and who's to know?"

"Yes."

"And furthermore, the act of payment is itself a blackmailable offense so that the more you comply with his requests, the more he's got to blackmail you for."

"I know that too," she said. "If there was a hint of gambling influence, Marty would be out of baseball forever."

"If you look at it by itself, it's almost beautiful."

"I've never looked at it by itself."

"Yeah, I guess not." I said, "Is it killing Marty?"

"A little, I think. He says you get used to anything—maybe he's right."

"How are you?"

"It's not me that has to cheat at my job."

"It's you that has to feel guilty about it," I said. "He can say he's doing it for you. What do you say?"

Tears formed in her eyes and began to run down her face. "I say it's what he gets for marrying a whore."

"See what I mean?" I said. "Wouldn't you rather be him?"

She didn't answer me. She sat still with her hands clenched in her lap, and the tears ran down her face without sound.

I got up and walked around the living room with my hands in my hip pockets. I'd found out what I was supposed to find out, and I'd earned the pay I'd hired on at.

"Did you call your husband?" I said.

She shook her head. "He's pitching today," she said, and her voice was steady but without inflection. "I don't like to bother him on the days he's pitching. I don't want to break his concentration. He should be thinking about the Oakland hitters."

"Mrs. Rabb, it's not a goddamned religion," I said. "He's not out there in Oakland building a temple to the Lord or a stairway to paradise. He's throwing a ball and the other guys are trying to hit it. Kids do it every day in schoolyards all over the land."

"It's Marty's religion," she said. "It's what he does."

"How about you?"

"We're part of it too, me and the boy—the game and the family. It's all he cares about. That's why it's killing him because he has to screw us or screw the game. Which is like screwing himself."

I should be gone. I should be in Harold Erskine's office, laying it all out for him and getting a bonus and maybe a plaque: OFFICIAL MAJOR LEAGUE PRIVATE EYE. Gumshoe of the stars. But I knew I wasn't going to be gone. I knew that I was here, and I probably knew it back in Redford, Illinois, when I went to her house and met her mom and dad.

"I'm going to get you out of this," I said.

She didn't look at me.

"I know who's blackmailing you."

This time she looked.

19

I told her what I knew and what I thought.

"Maybe you can scare him off," she said. "Maybe when he realizes you know who he is, he'll stop."

"If he's wearing Frank Doerr's harness, I'd say no."

"Why?"

"Because he's got to be more scared of Frank Doerr than I can make him of me."

"Are you sure he's working for Frank What's'isname?"

"I'm not sure of anything. I'm guessing. Right after I started looking around the ball club, Doerr came to my office with one of his gunbearers and told me I might become an endangered species if I kept at it. That's suggestive, but it ain't definitive."

"Can you find out?"

"Maybe."

"Marty makes a lot of money. We could pay you. How much do you charge?"

"My normal retainer is two corn muffins and a black coffee. I bill the rest upon completion."

"I'm serious. We can pay a lot."

"Like Jack Webb would say, you already have, ma'am."

"Thank you."

"You're welcome."

"But I don't want you to start until we get Marty's approval."

"Un-unh. Your retainer doesn't buy that. I'm still also working for Erskine, and I'm still looking into the situation. I'm now looking with an eye to getting you unhooked, but you can't call me off."

"But you won't say anything about us?" Her eyes were wide and her face was pale and tight again and she was scared.

"No," I said.

"Not unless Marty says okay."

"Not until I've checked with you and Marty."

"That's not quite the same thing," she said.

"I know."

"But, Spenser, it's our life. It's us you're frigging around with."

"I know that too. I'll be as careful as I can be."

"Then, damn it, you have got to promise."

"No. I won't promise because I may not be able to deliver. Or maybe it will turn out different. Maybe I'll have to blow the whistle on you for reasons I can't see yet. But if I do, I'll tell you first."

"But you won't promise."

"I can't promise."

"Why not, goddamn you?"

"I already told you."

She shook her head once, as if there were a horsefly on it. "That's bullshit," she said. "I want a better reason than that for you to ruin us."

"I can't give you a better reason. I care about promises, and I don't want to make one I can't be sure I'll keep. It's important to me."

"Bullshit, bullshit, bullshit." She was leaning forward, and her nostrils seemed to flare wider as she did.

"My game has rules too, Mrs. Rabb."

"You sound like Marty," she said.

I didn't say anything.

She was looking at the Christian Science dome again. "Children," she said to it. "Goddamned adolescent children."

My stomach felt a little funny, and I was uncomfortable as hell.

"Mrs. Rabb," I said, "I will try to help. And I am good at this. I'll try."

She kept looking at the dome. "You and Marty and all the goddamned game-playing children. You're all good at all the games." She turned around and looked at me. "Screw," she said, and jerked her head at the door.

I couldn't think of much to say to that, so I screwed. She slammed the door behind me, and I went down in the elevator feeling like a horse's ass and not sure why.

It was almost three o'clock. There was a public phone outside the drugstore next to the apartment building entrance. I went in and called Martin Quirk.

"Spenser," he said. "Thank God you called. I've got this murder took place in a locked room. It's got us all stumped and the chief said; 'Quirk,' he said, 'only one man can solve this.' "

"Can I buy you lunch or a drink or something?"

"Lunch? A drink? Christ, you must be in deep trouble."

I did not feel jolly. "Yes or no," I said. "If I wanted humor, I'd have called Dial-A-Joke."

"Yeah, okay. I'll meet you at the Red Coach on Stanhope Street."

I hung up. There was a parking ticket neatly tucked under the wiper blade on the driver's side. The string looped around the base. A conscientious meter maid. A lot of them just jam it under the wiper without looping the string, and sometimes on the passenger side where you can't even see it. It was nice to see samples of professional pride. I put the ticket in a public trash receptacle attached to a lamppost.

I drove down Boylston Street past the Prudential Center and the new public library wing and through Copley Square. The fountain in the square was in full spray, and college kids and construction workers mingled on the wall around it, eating lunch, drinking beer, taking the sun. A lot of them were shirtless. Beyond the fountain was the Copley Plaza with two enormous gilded lions flanking the entrance. And at the Clarendon Street end of the square, Trinity Church gleamed, recently sandblasted, its brown stones fresh-looking, its spires reflecting brightly in the windows of the Hancock Building. A quart of beer, I thought, and a cutlet sub. Shirt off, catch some rays, maybe strike up a conversation with a coed. Would you believe, my dear, I could be your father? Oh, you would.

I turned right on Clarendon and left onto Stanhope, where I parked in a loading zone. Stanhope Street is barely more than an alley and tucked into it between an electrical supply store and a garage is the Red Coach Grill, looking very old world with red tile roof and leaded windows. It was right back of police headquarters, and a lot of cops hung out there. Also a lot of insurance types and ad men. Despite that, it wasn't a bad place. Quiet lighting, oaken beams, and such. Quirk was at the bar. He looked like I always figured a cop ought to. Bigger than I am and thick. Short, thick black hair, thick hands and fingers, thick neck, thick features, a pockmarked face, and dressed like he'd just come from a summit meeting. Today he had on a light gray three-piece suit with a pale red plaid pattern, a white shirt, and a silk-finish wide red tie. His shoes were patent leather loafers with a gold trim. I slipped onto a barstool beside him.

"You gotta be on the take," I said. "Fuzz don't get paid enough to dress like that."

"They do if they don't do anything else. I haven't been on vacation in fifteen years. What are you spending your dough on?"

"Lunch for cops," I said. "Want to sit in a booth?"

Quirk picked up his drink, and we sat down across from the bar in one of the high-backed walnut booths that run parallel to the bar front to back and separate it from the dining room.

I ordered a bourbon on the rocks from the waitress. "Shot of bitters and a twist," I said, "and another for my date." The waitress was young with a short skirt and very short blond hair. Quirk and I watched her lean over the bar to pick up the drinks.

"You are a dirty lecherous old man," I said. "I may speak to the vice squad about you."

"What were you doing, looking for clues?"

"Just checking for concealed weapons, Lieutenant."

She brought the drinks. Quirk had Scotch and soda.

We drank. I took a lot of mine in the first swallow. Quirk said, "I thought you were a beer drinker."

"Yeah, but I got a bad taste I want to get rid of and the bourbon is quicker."

"You must be used to a bad taste in your line of business."

I finished the drink and nodded at the waitress. She looked at Quirk. He shook his head. "I'll nurse this," he said.

"I thought you guys weren't supposed to drink on duty," I said.

"That's right," he said. "What do you want?"

"I just thought maybe we could rap a little about law enforcement theory and prison reform, and swap detective techniques, stuff like that."

"Spenser, I got eighteen unsolved homicides in my left-hand desk drawer at this moment. You want to knock off the bullshit and get to it."

"Frank Doerr," I said. "I want to know about him."

"Why?"

"I think he owns some paper on a guy who is squeezing a client."

"And the guy is squeezing the client because of the paper?"

"Yes."

"Doerr's probably free-lance. Got his own organization, operates around the fringe of the mob's territory. Gambling, mostly, used to be a gambler. Vegas, Reno, Cuba in the old days. Does loan sharking too. Successful, but I hear he's a little crazy, things don't go right, he gets bananas and starts shooting everybody. And he's too greedy. He's going to bite off too big a piece of somebody else's pie and the company will have him dusted. He's looking flashy now, but he's not going to last."

"Where do I find him?"

"If you're screwing around in this operation, he'll find you."

"But say I want to find him before he does, where?"

"I don't know, exactly. Runs a funeral parlor, somewhere in Charlestown. I get back to the station I'll check for you."

"Has he got a handle I can shake him with?"

"You? Scare him off? You try scaring Doerr and they'll be tying a tag on your big toe down at Boston City."

"Well, what's he like best? Women? Booze? Performing seals? There must be a way to him."

"Money," Quirk said. "He likes money. Far as I know he doesn't like anything else."

"How do you know he doesn't like me?" I said.

"I surmise it," Quirk said. "You met him?"

"Once."

"Who was with him?"

"Wally Hogg."

Quirk shook his head. "Get out of this, Spenser. You're in with people that will waste you like a Popsicle on a warm day." The waitress brought us another round. She was wearing fishnet stockings. Could it be Ms. Right? I drank some bourbon.

"I wish I could get out of this, Marty. I can't."

"You're in trouble yourself?" Quirk asked.

"No, but I gotta do this, and it's not making anyone too happy."

"Wally Hogg," Quirk said, "will kill anyone Doerr tells him to. He doesn't like it or not like it. Slow or fast, one or a hundred, whatever. Doerr points him and he goes bang. He's a piece with feet."

"Well, if he goes bang at me," I said, "he'll be Wally Sausage."

"You're not as good as you think you are, Spenser. But neither is Captain Marvel. I've seen people worse than you, and maybe you got a chance. But sober. Don't go up against any of Doerr's group half-gassed. Go bright and early in the morning after eight hours' sleep and a good breakfast." He stirred the ice in his new drink. I noticed he hadn't finished the old one.

"Slow," I said. "Always knew you were a slow drinker." I reached over and picked up his old drink and finished it. "I can drink you right out of your orthopedic shoes, Quirk."

"Christ, this thing really is bugging you, isn't it?" Quirk said. He stood up. "I'm going back to work before you start to slobber."

"Quirk," I said.

He stopped and looked at me.

"Thanks for not asking for names."

"I knew you wouldn't tell me," Quirk said. "And watch your ass on this, Spenser. There must be someone who'd miss you."

I gave him a thumbs-up gesture, like in the old RAF movies, and he walked off. I drank Quirk's new drink and gestured to the waitress. There'll always be an England.

By five thirty in the afternoon I was sitting at the desk in my office, drinking bourbon from the bottle neck. Brenda Loring had a date, Susan Silverman didn't answer her phone. The afternoon sun slanted in at my window and made the room hot. I had the sash up, but there wasn't much breeze and the sweat was collecting where my back pressed against the chair.

Maybe I should get out of this thing. Maybe it bothered me too much. Why? I'd been told to screw before. Why did this time bother me? "Goddamned adolescent children." I'd heard worse than that before. "Goddamned game-playing children." I'd heard worse than that too. I drank some bourbon. My nose felt sort of numb and the surface of my face felt insulated. Dumb broad. Promises. Shit, I can't promise what I don't know. World ain't that simple, for crissake. I said I'd try. What the hell she want, for crissake? By God, I would get her out of it. I held the bottle up toward the window and looked at how much was left. Half. Good. Even if I finished it, there was another one in the file cabinet. Warm feeling having another one in the file cabinet. I winked at the file cabinet and grinned with one side of my mouth like Clark Gable used to. He never did it at file cabinets, though, far as I could remember. I drank some more and rinsed it around in my mouth. Maybe my teeth will get drunk. I giggled. Goddamned sure Clark Gable never giggled. Drink up, teeth. Hot damn. She was right, though, it was a kind of game. I mean, you played ball or something and whatever you did there had to be some kind of rules for it, for crissake. Otherwise you ended up getting bombed and winking at file cabinets. And your teeth got drunk. I giggled again. I was going to have Frank Doerr's ass. But sober, Quirk was right, sober, and in shape. "I'm coming, Doerr, you sonovabitch." Tongue wasn't drunk yet. I could still talk. Have a drink, tongue, baby. I drank. "Only where love and need are one," I said out loud. My voice sounded even stranger. Detached and over in the other corner of the room. "And the work is play for goddamned mortal stakes/Is the deed ever really done." My throat felt hot, and I inhaled a lot of air to cool it. "Mortal goddamned stakes," I said. "You got that, Linda Rabb/Donna Burlington, baby?" I had unclipped my holster, and it lay with my .38 detective special in it on the desk beside the bourbon bottle. I drank a little more bourbon, put down the bottle, picked up the gun still in its holster, and pointed it at one of the Vermeer prints, the one of the Dutch girl with a milk pitcher. "How do you like them goddamned games, Frank?" Then I made a plonking sound with my tongue.

It was quiet then for a while. I sipped a little. And listened to the street sounds a little and then I heard someone snoring and it was me.

20

The next day it took me five miles of jogging and an hour and a half in the weight room to get the swelling out of my tongue and my vital signs functioning. I had breakfast in a diner, nothing could be finer, took two aspirin, and set out after Frank Doerr. A funeral parlor in Charlestown, Quirk had said. I brought all my sleuthing wiles to bear on the problem of how to locate it and looked in the Yellow Pages. Elementary, my dear Holmes. There it was, under "Funeral Directors": Francis X. Doerr, 228 Main Street, Charlestown. There's no escape, Doerr.

With the top down I drove my eight-year-old Chevy across the bridge into City Square. Charlestown is a section of Boston. Bunker Hill is there, and *Old Ironsides,* but the dominant quality of Charlestown is the convergence of elevated transportation. The Mystic River Bridge, Route 93, and the Fitzgerald Expressway all interchange in Charlestown. Through the maze run the tracks of the elevated MBTA. Steel and concrete stanchions have flourished in the City Square area as nowhere else. If the British wanted to attack Bunker Hill now, they wouldn't be able to find it.

From City Square I drove out Main Street under the elevated tracks. Doerr was maybe a half mile out from City Square toward Everett. Parking in that area of Charlestown was no problem. Most of the stores along that stretch of Main Street are boarded up. And urban renewal had not yet brought economic renewal. My car looked just right in the neighborhood.

Doerr's Funeral Parlor was a two-story brick house with a slate roof. It was wedged in between an unoccupied grocery store with plywood nailed over the windows and a discount shoe store called Ronny's Rejects. Across the street a vacant lot, not yet renewed, supported a flourishing crop of chicory and Queen Anne's lace. Nature never betrayed the heart that loved her.

I brushed my hand over the gun on my hip for security and rang the bell at the front door. Inside, it made a very gentle chime. Full of solicitude. The door was opened almost at once by a plump man with a perfectly bald head. Striped pants, white shirt, dark coat, black tie. The undertaker's undertaker.

"May I help you," he said. Soft. Solicitous. May I take your wallet, may I have all your money? Leave everything to us.

"Yes," I said. "I'd like to speak with Mr. Doerr." Mr. Doerr? He had me talking like him. I felt the scared feeling in my stomach.

"Concerning what, sir?"

I gave Baldy my card, the one with just my name on it, and said, "Tell Doerr I'd like to continue the discussion we began the other night." Dropping the "Mr." made me feel more aggressive.

"Certainly, sir, won't you sit down for a moment?"

I sat in a straight-back chair with a velvet seat, and the bald man left the room. I thought he might genuflect before he left but he didn't, just left with a dignified and reverent nod. It didn't help my stomach. Getting the hell out would have helped my stomach but would have done little for my self-image. Doerr probably wasn't that tough anyway. And Big Wally looked out of shape. Course you don't have to be in really great shape to squeeze off, say, two rounds from a nine-millimeter Walther.

The building was absolutely silent and had a churchy smell. The entry hall where I sat was papered in a dim beige with palm fronds on it. Very understated and elderly. The rug on the floor was Oriental, with dull maroon the dominant color, and the ceiling fixture was wreathed in molded plaster fruit.

The bald man came back. "This way, please, sir," he said, and stood aside to let me precede him through the door. Well, Spenser, I said, it's your funeral. Sometimes I'm uncontrollably droll.

Doerr's office was on the second floor front and looked out at the elevated tracks. Just right if you wanted to make eye contact with commuters. Apparently Doerr didn't because he sat behind a mahogany desk with his back to the window. His desk was cluttered with manila file folders. There were two phones, and a big vase of snapdragons flourished on a small stand beside the window.

"What do you want?" Doerr said.

I sat in one of the two straight chairs in front of the desk. Doerr didn't waste a lot of bread on decor.

"Why don't you get right to the point, Frank?" I said. "Don't hide behind evasive pleasantries."

"What do you want?"

"I want to answer some of the questions you asked me the other day."

"Why?"

"Openness and candor," I said. "The very hallmark of my profession."

Doerr was sitting straight, hands resting on the arms of his swivel chair. He looked at me without expression. Without comment. A train clattered by outside the window, headed for Sullivan Square. Doerr ignored it.

"Okay," I said. "You asked me what I was doing out at the ball park besides playing pepper."

Doerr continued to look at me.

"I was hired to see if someone was going into the tank out there."

Doerr said, "And?"

"And someone is."

"Who?"

"I think we both know."

"Why do you think that?"

"Several things, including the fact you came calling with your gunslinger right after I was out there."

"So?"

"So you heard from someone. I know who's dumping the games, I know who's blackmailing him into it, and I know what shylock the blackmailer owes. And that brings us right back here to you. Okay if I call you Shy for short? We get on so well and all."

"Names, Spenser. I'm not interested in a lot of bullshit about who you know and what anonymous whosis is doing what. Gimme a name and maybe I'm interested."

"Marty Rabb, Bucky Maynard, and you, Blue Eyes."

"Those are serious allegations. You got proof?"

"Serious allegations." I whistled. "That's very good for a guy whose lips move when he reads the funnies."

"Look, you piece of turd, don't get smart with me. I can have you blown away before you can scratch your ass. You understand? Now gimme what you got or you're going to get hurt."

"That's better," I said, "that's the old glib Frankie. Yeah, I got some proof, and I can get some more. What I haven't got for proof yet is the tie between you and Maynard, but I can get it. I'll bet Maynard might begin to ooze under pressure."

"Saying you're right, saying that's the way it is, and you can get some proof out of Maynard. Why don't I just waste Maynard or, maybe better, waste you?"

"You won't waste Maynard, because I'll bet you don't know what he's got on Rabb and I'll bet even more that he's got it stashed somewhere so if something happens to him, you'll never know. You won't waste me because I'm so goddamned lovable. And because there's a homicide cop named Quirk that knows I'm here. Besides, I'm not sure you got the manpower."

"You're doing a lot of guessing."

As far as you could tell from Doerr's face, I might have been in there arranging a low-budget funeral. And maybe I was.

"I'm licensed to," I said. "The state of Massachusetts says I'm permitted to make guesses and investigate them."

"So what do you want?"

"I want it to stop. I want Maynard to give me the item he's using for blackmail, and I want everyone to leave the Rabbs alone."

"Or what?"

"I don't suppose you'd accept 'or else.' "

"I'm getting sick of you, Spenser. I'm sick of the way you look, and the way you dress, and the way you get your hair cut, and the way you keep shoving your face into my work. I'm sick of you being alive and making wise remarks. You understand what I'm saying to you, turd?"

"What's wrong with the way I dress?"

"Shut up." Doerr's face had gotten a little red under the health club tan. He swung his chair sideways and stared out the window. And he had begun to fiddle with a pencil. Tapping it against his thigh until it had slid through his fingers and then reversing it and tapping it again. Tap-tap-tap. Reverse. Tap-tap-tap. Reverse. Lead end. Erasure end. Tap-tap-tap. Another train went by, almost empty, heading this time from Everett Station toward City Square. I slid my gun out of the hip holster and held it between my legs under my thighs with my hands clasped over it so it looked like I was leaning forward in concealed anxiety. I had no trouble at all simulating the anxiety.

Doerr swung his chair back around, still holding the pencil. He pointed it at me.

"Okay," he said. "I'm going to let you walk out of here. But before you go, I'm going to give you an idea of what happens when I get sick of someone."

There must have been a button under the desk that he could hit with his knee, or maybe the room was bugged. Either way a door to the left of the desk opened and Wally Hogg came in. He had on another flowered shirt, hanging outside the double knit pants, and the same wraparound sunglasses. In his right hand was one of those rubber truncheons that French cops use for riot control. He reminded me of one of the nasty trolls that used to lurk under bridges.

"Wally," Doerr said, looking at me while he said it, "show him what hurts."

Wally came around the desk. "You want it sitting down or standing up," he said. "It don't make no difference to me." He stood directly in front of me, looking down as I leaned over in even greater anxiety. I brought the gun up from between my thighs, thumbed the hammer back while I was doing that, and put the muzzle against the underside of his jaw, behind the jawbone, where it's soft. And I pressed up a little.

"Wally," I said, "have you ever thought of renting out as a goblin for Halloween parties?"

Wally's body was between Doerr and me, and Doerr couldn't see the gun. "What the hell are you waiting for, Wally? I want to hear him yelling."

I stood up and Wally inched back. The pressure of the gun muzzle made him rise slightly on the balls of his feet.

"Overconfidence," I said. "Overconfidence again, Frankie. That's twice you said ugly things to me and then couldn't back them up. Now I am thinking about whether I should shoot Wally in the tongue or not. Put the baton in my left hand, porklet," I said to Wally. He did. Our faces were about an inch apart, and his was as blank as it had been when he'd walked into the room. Without looking, I tossed it into the corner behind me.

"Of course, you could try me, Frank. You could rummage around in your desk maybe and come up with a weapon and have a go at me. Pretty good odds, Frankie. I have to shoot the Hog first before I can get you. Why not? It's quicker than scaring me to death." I kept the pressure of the gun barrel up under Wally's chin and looked past his shoulder at Doerr. Doerr had his hands, palms down, on the desk in front of him. His face was quite red and his lips were trembling. But he didn't move. He stared at me and the lines from his nostrils to the corners of his mouth were deep and there was a very small tic in his left eyelid. With my left hand I patted Wally down and found the P .38 in its shoulder holster under his belt. All the time I watched Doerr. His mouth was open maybe an inch, and a small bubble of saliva had formed in the right-hand corner. I could see the tip of his tongue and it seemed to tremble, like the tic in his eye and in counterpoint to the movement of his lips. It was kind of interesting. But I was getting sick of standing that close to Wally.

"Turn around, Wall," I said. "Rest your hands on the desk and back away with your feet apart till all your weight is on your arms. You probably know the routine." I stepped away from him around the desk closer to Doerr, and Wally did as he was told.

"Okay, Frank," I said. "So much for what hurts. Are you going to climb down from Marty Rabb's back, or am I going to have to take you off?"

Doerr's mouth had opened wider and his tongue was quivering against his lower lip much more violently than it had been. The small bubble had popped and a small trickle of saliva had replaced it. His head had dropped, and as he began to look at me, he had to roll his eyes up toward his eyebrows. His mouth was moving too, but he wasn't making any noise.

"How about it, Frank? I like standing around watching you drool, but I got things to do."

Doerr opened his middle drawer and came out with a gun. I

slammed my gun down on the back of his wrist, and it cracked against the edge of the desk. The gun rattled across the desk top and fell on the floor. Wally Hogg raised his head and I turned the gun at him. Doerr doubled up over his hand and made a repetitive grunting noise. Rocking back and forth in the swivel chair, grunting and drooling and making a sound that was very much like crying.

"Am I to interpret this as a rejection, Frank?"

He kept rocking and moaning and crying. "Aw balls," I said. I picked up Doerr's little automatic and stuck it in my pocket and said to Wally, "If you try to stop me, I'll kill you," and walked out the door. No one was downstairs. No one let me out. No one pursued me as I drove off.

21

There's a bird I read about that lives around rhinos and feeds on the insects that the rhinos stir up when they walk. I'd always figured that my work was like that. If the rhinos were moving, things would happen. This time, though, the rhino had started to cry and I wasn't too sure how to deal with that. I had a feeling, though, how Doerr would deal with that once he stopped crying. I didn't like the feeling. Maybe the technique only worked with real birds and real rhinos. Maybe I was doing more harm than good. Maybe I should get back on the cops and do what the watch commander said. I could get rid of a lot of maybes that way. I drove out Main Street, past the candy factory and around the circle at Sullivan Square, and back in toward Boston on Rutherford Ave. The sweet smell from the factory masked the smoke that billowed out of the skyscraper chimneys at the Edison plant across the Mystic River. Past the community college I turned right over the Prison Point Bridge, which had been torn down and rebuilt and called the

Somebody T. Gilmore Bridge. The traffic reporters called it the Gilmore Bridge, but I remembered when it led to the old prison in Charlestown, where the walls were red brick like the rest of the city, and on execution nights people used to gather in the streets to watch the lights dim when they turned on the current in the chair. Now state prison was in Walpole and electrocutions were accidental. Ah sweet bird of youth.

It was before lunchtime still and traffic was light. In five minutes I was at my office and sliding into a handy tow zone to park. I bought a copy of the *Globe* at a cigar store and went up to my office to read it. The Sox had an off day today and opened at home against Cleveland tomorrow. Marty Rabb had beaten Oakland 2 to 0 yesterday on the coast, and the team had flown into Logan this morning early.

I called Harold Erskine and got Bucky Maynard's home address. It was what I thought it would be.

"Why do you want to know?" Erskine asked.

"Because it's there," I said.

"I don't want you screwing around with Maynard. That's the surest way to have this whole thing blow wide open."

"Don't worry, I am a model of circumspection."

"Yeah," Erskine said, "sure. You find out anything yet?"

"Nothing I can report on yet, I need to put some things together."

"Well, for crissake, what have you found out? Is Marty or isn't he?"

"It's not that simple, Mr. Erskine. You'll have to give me a little more time."

"How much more? You're costing me a hundred a day. What do your expenses look like?"

"High," I said. "I been to Illinois and New York City and spent a hundred and nineteen bucks buying dinner for a witness."

"Jesus Galloping Christ, Spenser. I got a goddamned budget to work with, and I don't want you appearing in it. How the Christ am I going to bury that kind of dough? Goddamn it, I want you to check with me before you go spending my money like that."

"I don't work that way, Mr. Erskine, but I think I won't run up much more expense money." I needed to stay on this thing. I couldn't afford to get fired and shut off from the Sox. Also I needed the money. My charger needed feed and my armor needed polish. "I'm closing in on the truth."

"Yeah, well, close in on it quick," Erskine said, and hung up.

The old phrasemaker, Closing In on the Truth. I should have been a poet. If I went back on the cops, I wouldn't need to worry about charger feed and armor polish.

Harbor Towers is new, a complex of high-rise apartments that looks out over Boston Bay. It represents a substantial monument to the renaissance of the waterfront, and the smell of new concrete still lingers in the lobbies. The central artery cuts them off from the rest of the city, penning them against the ocean, and they form a small peninsula of recent affluence where once the wharves rotted.

I parked in the permanent shade under the artery, on Atlantic Ave, near Maynard's apartment. It was hot enough for the asphalt to soften and the air conditioning in the lobby felt nice. I gave my name to the houseman, who called it up, then nodded at me. "Top floor, sir, number eight." The elevator was lined with mirrors and I was trying to see how I looked in profile when we got to the top floor and the doors opened. I looked quickly ahead, but no one was there. It's always embarrassing to get caught admiring yourself. Number 8 was opposite the elevator and Lester Floyd opened it on my first ring.

He had on white denim shorts, white sandals, a white headband, and sunglasses with big white plastic frames and black lenses. His upper body was as smooth and shiny as a snake's, tight-muscled and flexible. Instead of a belt, there was what looked like a black silk scarf passed through the belt loops and knotted over his left hip. He was chewing bubble gum. He held the door open and nodded his head toward the living room. I went in. He shut the door behind me. The living room looked to be thirty feet long, with the far wall a bank of glass that opened onto a balcony. Beyond the balcony, the Atlantic, blue and steady and more than my eye could fully register. Lester slid open one of the glass doors, went out, slid it shut behind him, settled down on a chaise made from filigreed white iron, rubbed some lotion on his chest, and chewed his gum at the sun. Mr. Warm.

I sat in a big red leather chair. The room was full of pictures, mostly eight-by-ten framed glossy prints of Maynard and various celebrities. Ballplayers, politicians, a couple of movie types. I didn't see any private eyes. Discriminatory bastard. Or maybe just discriminating. The sound of a portable radio drifted in faintly from Lester's sun deck. The top forty. Music with the enchantment and soul of a penny gum machine. Ah when you and I were young, Sarah.

Bucky Maynard came into the living room from a door in the far right-hand wall. He was wearing bright yellow pajamas under a maroon silk bathrobe with a big velvet belt. He needed a shave and his eyes were puffy. He hadn't been awake long.

"Y'all keep some early hours, Spenser. Ah didn't get to bed till four A.M."

"Early to bed," I said, "early to rise. I wanted to ask you what Lester was doing down in New York talking with Patricia Utley."

The collar of Maynard's robe was turned up on one side. He smoothed it down carefully. "Ah can't say ah know what you mean, Spenser. Ah can ask him."

"As us kids say out in the bleachers, don't jive me, Bucko. Lester was down there on your business. I've talked with Utley. I've talked with Frank Doerr and Wally the bone breaker. I've seen a film called *Suburban Fancy* and I've talked with Linda Rabb. Actually I guess I asked the wrong question. I know what Lester was doing down there. What I want to know is what we do now that I know."

"Lester." Maynard showed no change in expression. Lester left the radio playing and came into the living room and blew a pink bubble that nearly obscured his face.

"Criminentlies, Lester," I said. "That's a really heavy bubble. I think you're my bubble-blowing idol. Zowie." Lester chewed the bubble back into his mouth without even a trace sticking to his lips. "Hours," I said. "It must take hours of practice."

Lester looked at Maynard. "Spenser and ah are going to talk, and ah want you to be around and to listen, Lester." Lester leaned against the edge of the sliding door and crossed his arms and looked at me. Maynard sat in one of the leather chairs and said, "Now what exactly is the point of your question, Spenser?"

"I figure that we've got a mutual problem and maybe we could conspire to solve it. Conspire, Lester. That means get together."

"Get to the point, Spenser. Lester gonna get mad at you."

"You owe Frank Doerr money and you can't pay, so you're blackmailing Marty Rabb into going into the tank for you and you're feeding the information to Doerr so he won't hurt you."

"Frank Doerr gotta deal with me before he hurts anybody," Lester said.

"Yeah, that's a big problem for him," I said. "Flex at him next time he and the Hog come calling. See if he faints."

"I'm getting goddamned sick of you, you wise bastard." Lester unfolded his arms and moved a step toward me.

"Lester," Maynard said, "we're talking." Lester refolded, stepped back, and leaned on the door again. Like reversing a film sequence.

"Ah don't know why you think all that stuff, Spenser. But say y'all was right. What business would that be of yours? You being a writer and all?"

"You know and I know that I'm not a writer."

"Ah do? Ah don't know any such thing. You told me you was a writer." The cornpone accent had gotten thicker. I didn't know if it was the real one coming through under duress or a fake one getting faker. Actually I couldn't see that it mattered much.

"Yeah, and you hollered to Doerr and he looked me up and we both know I'm a private cop."

"How about that?" Maynard raised both eyebrows. "A private detective. That still leaves the question, though, Spenser. What is your interest?"

"I would like you to stop blackmailing the Rabbs."

"And if ah was blackmailing them, and ah stopped, what would ah get out of that?"

"Well, I'd be grateful."

From his post by the sliding door, Lester said, "Shit," drawing it out into a two-syllable word.

"Anything besides that?" Maynard said.

"I'll help you with Frank Doerr."

Lester said, "Shit," again. This time in three syllables.

"Well, Spenser, that's awful kind of you, but there's some things wrong with it all. One, ah don't much give a rat's ass for your gratitude, you know? And number two, ah don't figure, even if ah was having trouble with Frank Doerr, that you'd be the one ah'd ask to help me. And of course, number three, ah'm not blackmailing anybody. Am I, Lester?"

Lester shook his head no.

"So, ah guess you wasted some time coming up here. Interesting to know about you being a detective, though. Isn't that interesting, Lester?"

Lester nodded his head yes. From the radio on the sun deck the disk jockey was yelling about a "rock classic."

I said, "Y'all seem to be takin' the short view." Christ, now he had me doing it.

"Why do you say so?"

"Because you have only a short-term solution. How long will Marty Rabb pitch? Five more years. You think that when he's through with baseball, Doerr will be through with you? Doerr will feed on you till you die."

"I can handle Doerr," Lester said. He didn't get too much variety into the conversation.

"Lester," I said, "you can't handle Doerr. Handling Doerr is different from beating up some tourist in a bar or breaking bricks with your bare hand. Wally Hogg is a professional tough guy. You are an amateur. He would blow you away like a midsummer dandelion."

Lester said, "Shit." You find a line that works for you, I suppose you ought to stick with it.

Maynard said, "If these people are so tough, Spenser, what makes you think you can help?"

"Because I'm a professional too, Bucko, and that means I know what I can do and also what I can't do. It means I don't walk around thinking I can go up against the likes of Frank Doerr, head-on, without getting my body creased. It means I know how to even things up a bit. It means I know what I'm doing and you two clowns don't."

"You don't look so frigging tough to me," Lester said.

"That's the difference between you and me, Lester. Aside from our taste in music. I don't worry about how things look. You do. I don't have to prove whether I'm tough. You do. You'll say something like that to Wally the Hog and he'll shoot you three times or so in your nose, while you're posing and blowing bubbles."

Lester had gone into the stance, legs bent, left fist forward, right drawn back, clenched palms up, a little like the old pictures of the great John L. "Why don't you try me, you mother?"

I stood up. "Lester, let me show you something," I said. And brought my gun out and aimed it at his forehead. "This is a thirty-eight caliber Colt detective special. If I pull the trigger, your mastery of the martial arts will be of very little use to you."

Maynard said, "Now, Spenser . . ."

Lester looked at the gun.

"Now put that thing down, Spenser," Maynard said. "Lester. Y'all just relax over there."

Lester said, "If you didn't have that gun."

"But that's the point, Les, baby, I do have the gun. Wally Hogg has a gun. You don't have a gun. Professionals are the people with the guns who get them out first."

"Now relax, y'all, just relax," Maynard said.

"You won't always have that gun, Spenser."

"See, boy, see what a baby you are," I said. "You're wrong again. I will always have the gun. You'd forget the gun, you wouldn't have it where you could get at it, but I will always have it."

"Lester," Maynard said again. This time loud. "Y'all just settle down. You hear me. Now you settle down. Ah don't want no more of this."

Lester eased out of his attack stance and leaned back against the doorjamb, but he kept his eyes on me and one of the eyelids seemed to flicker as he stared. I put the gun away.

I said to Maynard, "You keep him away from me or I will hurt him badly."

"Now, Spenser," Maynard said. "Lester excites kind of prompt, but he's not a fool. Right, Lester?"

Lester didn't speak. I noticed that there was a glisten of sweat on Maynard's upper lip. "Suppose ah was interested in joining forces with you," Maynard said. "What would be your plan? How would you keep Doerr from coming around and killing me?"

"I'd tell him that right now we call off the scheme and end the blackmail and he's out some bread, but no one's incriminated. If he causes trouble, it'll mean the cops, and then someone will be incriminated. And it'll be him, because we've stashed evidence where the cops will find it if anything happens to you."

"What about the money I owe him, Ah mean hypothetically?"

"You've paid that off long ago if Doerr got any bread down at all on Rabb's pitching."

"But maybe Doerr will want more, and ah don't have it."

"It'll be my job to convince him not to want more."

"That's it. That's the part ah want to know," Maynard said, and his face looked very moist. "How you going to convince him of anything?"

"I don't know. Appeal to his business sense. Dropping the scheme is a lot less trouble than sticking to it. He can pick up dough a lot of other ways. You and Rabb aren't the only goobers in the patch."

Maynard took a deep breath. The top forty played on outside on the deck. Lester glared at me from the doorjamb. Whitecaps continued to pattern the bay. Maynard shook his head. "Not good enough, Spenser. What you say may be so, but right now ah'm not getting hurt. And what you say makes getting hurt more likely."

"I can handle Doerr, Bucky." Lester sounded almost plaintive from the doorjamb.

"Maybe yes, maybe no, Lester. You couldn't have handled Spenser here, if it had been for real. Ah'm saying right now, no. Ah'm not going to take the chance. Things have worked out so far."

"But it's different now, Buck," I said. "I'm in it now. And I'm going to poke around and aggravate the hornets. It's not safe anymore to go along with the program."

"Maybe that's true too." Maynard said. "But ah got a choice between you and Frank Doerr, and right now ah'm betting on Frank Doerr. But ah'll tell you this. If you come up with something better than you have, ah'm willing to listen."

He had me. Maybe if I were he, I'd go that way too.

"Lester," Maynard said, "show Mr. Spenser out."

I shook my head. "I'll show myself out. I want Lester to stay there. Mad, like he is, he might slam the door on my foot."

Maynard nodded. There was a little drip of sweat at the tip of his beaky little canary nose. It was the last thing I saw as I backed out.

22

The Aquarium is near Harbor Towers, and I walked to it. Inside, it was nearly empty at midday, dark and cool and unconnected with the city outside. I went up the spiral walkway around it and watched the fish glide in silent pattern around and around the tank, swimming at different strata, sharks and groupers and turtles and fish I didn't know in the clear water. They were oblivious of me and seemed oblivious of each other as they swam in a kind of implacable order around and around the tank. The spiral walk was open and the rest of the aquarium was spacious. Below the flat pool, bottom lit and cool green, silhouetted other, smaller fish, black and quick in the bright water.

A small group of children, perhaps a second-grade class on a field trip, came in, shepherded by a plump little nun with hornrimmed glasses. After a fast inspection of the fish, the children ignored them and began to enjoy the building and the space as if the real occasion for the visit was not the fish but the feel of the aquarium. The kids ran up and down the spiral and looked over the balcony and yelled at each other from above and below. The nun made no serious attempt to shush them, and the open space and the darkness seemed to absorb the noise. It was still nearly quiet.

I stood and stared in through the six-inch-thick glass windows of the tank and watched the sharks, small, well fed, and without threat, as they glided in their endless circle. I had screwed up the situation. I knew that. I had made Frank Doerr mad and Doerr was a cuckoo. Maynard was right not to buy what I was selling. Doerr wouldn't let Maynard off the hook and he wouldn't bargain with me. Maybe he never would have, but his honor was at stake now and he'd die before he let me talk him into, or scare him into, doing anything.

A small boy pushed in front of me to stare through the glass. His belt was too long, I noticed, and the surplus had been tucked through his belt loops halfway around his body. Another kid joined him and I found myself being moved away from the fish tank. Kids already know how to block out, I thought. I walked off the spiral and looked at the penguins on the first balcony. They were the false note in the place. There was no glass wall, no separation between us except six feet of space. The smell of fish and, I supposed, penguin was rank and uninsulated. I didn't like it. The silent fish in the lucid water were fantasy. The smelly penguins were real.

I went on back down the spiral and out into the bright hot day that met me with a clang as I came out of the aquarium. I could put Doerr and Maynard away by going to the cops. But that would humiliate Linda Rabb and probably get Marty Rabb barred from baseball. I could disarm Doerr and Maynard by getting Linda to make a public confession. But that would have the same results. The top was down on my car and the seats were hot and uncomfortable when I got in. I couldn't shake Maynard loose from Doerr. Doerr was the key and I had handled him wrong. If I got near him again, he'd try to kill me. It made negotiations difficult.

Back to the Rabbs. The lobby attendant called up, and Marty Rabb was waiting for me at the apartment door. His face was white, and the hinge muscles of his jaw were bunched.

"You sonovabitch," he said. His voice was hoarse.

"Maybe," I said, "but that won't help."

"What do you want now, plant a bug in our bedroom maybe?"

"I don't want to talk about it out in the corridor."

"I don't give a shit what you don't want. I don't want you in my goddamned house, stinking up the place."

"Look, kid, I feel lousy and I understand how you feel, and I don't blame you, but I need to talk and I can't do it out here in the hall with you yelling at me."

"You're lucky I'm yelling, you bastard. You're lucky I don't knock you on your ass."

Linda Rabb came to the door beside her husband. "Let him in, Marty," she said. "We're in trouble. Yelling won't change that. Neither will hitting him."

"The sonovabitch caused it. We were doing all right till he came sticking his goddamned nose into things."

"I caused it as much as he did, Marty. I'm the whore, not Spenser."

Rabb turned at her. "I don't want to hear you say that again," he said. "Not again. I won't have any talk like that in my house. I don't want my son hearing that kind of talk."

Linda Rabb's voice sounded as if she were tired. "Your son's not home, Marty; he's at nursery. You know that. Come in, Spenser." She pulled Rabb away from the door, holding his right arm in both her hands. I went in.

I sat on the edge of the sofa. Rabb didn't sit. He stood looking at me with his hands clenched. "Be goddamned careful what you say, Spenser. I want to belt you so bad I can feel it in my guts, and if you make one smart remark, I'm going to level you."

"Marty, you are the third person this morning who has offered to disassemble my body. You are also third in order of probable success. I can't throw a baseball like you can, but the odds are very good that I could put you in the hospital before you ever got a hand on me." I was getting sick of people yelling at me.

"You think so."

I was proud of myself. I didn't say, "I know so."

Linda Rabb let go of his arm and came around in front of him and put both her arms around his waist. "Stop it, Marty. Both of you, grow up. This isn't a playground where you little boys can prove to each other how tough you are. This is our home and our future and little Marty and our life. You can't handle every problem as if it were an arm-wrestling contest." Her voice was getting thicker and she pressed her face against Rabb's chest. I knew she was crying, and I bet it wasn't the first time today.

"But, Jesus Christ, Linda, a man's gotta—"

She screamed at him, the voice muffled against his chest. "Shut up. Just shut up about a man's gotta."

I wished I smoked. It would have given me something to do with my hands. Rabb put his arms around his wife and rubbed the top of her head with his chin.

"I don't know," he said. "I don't know what in hell to do."

"Me either," I said. "But if you'd sit down, maybe we could figure something out."

Linda Rabb said, "Sit down, Marty," and pushed him away from her with both hands against his chest. He sat. She sat beside him, her head turned away, and wiped her eyes with a Kleenex.

"I don't know," Rabb said again. He was sitting on the edge of the couch, his elbows on his thighs, his hands clasped together between his knees, staring at his thumbnails. Then he looked up at me.

"How much does Erskine know?" he said.

"Nothing. He had heard just the hint that something might not be square. He hired me to prove it was square. He wants to believe it's square and you're square."

"Yeah," Rabb said, "I'm square okay. You got any good ideas?"

"Your wife's told you what I said yesterday?" He nodded. "I've talked with Doerr and I've talked with Maynard. Doerr won't let go of Maynard and Maynard won't let go of you. He's too scared."

"Maynard really is in debt to a loan shark?"

"Yes."

"I can't see anything else to do but keep on the way we have been," Rabb said.

"If you can stand it," I said.

"You can stand what you can't change," Rabb said. "You got a better idea?"

"You could blow the whistle."

Linda Rabb had finished with her Kleenex and was looking at us again.

"Yes," she said.

"No," Rabb said.

"Marty," she said.

"No."

"Marty," she said again, "we can't stand it. I can't stand it. I can't stand the guilt and watching how you feel every time you lose a game so they can make money."

"I don't always have to lose," he said. "Sometimes I give up a run or two for the inning pools."

"Don't quibble, Marty. You're in a funk for a week after every letter. You have lived too long believing in do-or-die for dear old Siwash. It's killing you and it's killing me."

"I'm not having your name blabbed all over the country. You want your kid to hear that kind of talk about his mother. Maybe we should show him the movie."

"It will pass, Marty. He's only three."

"And it'll make nice talk in the bullpen, you know. You want me to listen to those bastards laughing in the dugout when I go out to pitch? Or maybe that doesn't matter either because if it gets out that I been dumping games I won't be pitching anyway. You want that?"

"No, but I don't want this either, Marty."

"Yeah, well maybe you should have thought of that when you were spreading your legs in New York."

I felt a jangle of shock in my solar plexus. Linda Rabb never flinched. She looked at her husband steadily. The silence hung between them. It was Rabb who broke it. "Jesus, honey, I'm sorry," he said and put his arms around her. She didn't pull away, but her body was as stiff and remote as a wire coat hanger and her eyes were focused on something far beyond the room as he held her.

"Jesus," he said again, "Jesus Christ, what is going to happen to us? What are we going to do?"

23

"What would you do if you didn't play ball?" I said.

"Coach."

"And if you didn't coach?"

"Scout, maybe."

"And if you couldn't scout and couldn't coach? If you were out of baseball altogether?"

Rabb was looking at his thumbnails again. "I don't know," he said.

"What did you major in in college?"

"Phys ed."

"Well, what would you like to do?"

"Play ball and then coach."

"I mean, if you couldn't play ball." Rabb stared harder at his thumbnails. Linda Rabb looked at the coffee table. Neither one spoke.

"Mrs. Rabb?"

She shook her head.

"How sure are you that if this all comes out you'll be suspended?" I said to Rabb.

"Sure," he said. "I threw some games. If the commissioner's office finds out, I'm finished for life."

"What if I confessed," Linda Rabb said. "If I told everyone about my past and no one said anything about the gambling part. I could say Marty didn't even know about me."

"They could still blackmail me with the fact I dumped the games," Rabb said.

"Not necessarily," I said. "If I could find a way to get Doerr out of it, we might be able to bargain with Maynard. If Maynard told about you, he'd have to tell about himself. He'd be out of work too. With Maynard you'd have a standoff."

"Doesn't matter," Rabb said. He looked up from his thumbnails. "I won't let her." Linda Rabb was looking at me too.

"Could you get Doerr out of it, Spenser?"

"I don't know, Mrs. Rabb. If I can't, we're stuck. I guess I'll have to."

"She's not saying anything about it. What the hell kind of a man do you think I am?"

"How can you?" Linda Rabb said, and I realized we weren't paying attention to Marty.

"I don't know," I said.

"If you can, I'll do it," she said.

"No," Rabb said.

"Marty, if he can arrange it, I'll do it. It's for me too. I can't stand watching you pulled apart like this. You love two things, us and baseball, and you have to hurt one to help the other. I can't stand knowing that it's my fault, and I can't stand the tension and the fear and the uncertainty. If Spenser can do something about the other man, I will confess and we'll be free."

Rabb looked at me. "I'm warning you, Spenser."

"Grow up, Marty," I said. "The world's not all that clean. You do what you can, not what you oughta. You're involved in stuff that gets people dead. If you can get out of it with some snickers in the bullpen and some embarrassment for your wife, you call that good. You don't call it perfect. You call it better than it was."

Rabb was shaking his head. Linda Rabb was still looking at me. She nodded. I noticed that her body was still stiff and angular, but there was color in her face. Rabb said, "I . . ." and shook his head again.

I said, "We don't need to argue now. Let me see what I can do about Doerr. Maybe I can't do anything about him. Maybe he'll do something about me. But I'll take a look."

"Don't do anything without checking here," Rabb said.

I nodded. Linda Rabb got up and opened the door for me. I got up and walked out. No one said be careful, or win this one for the Gipper, or it counts not if you win or lose but how you play the game. In fact, no one said anything, and all I heard as I left was the door closing behind me.

Outside on Mass Ave I looked at my watch: 1:30. I went home.

In my kitchen I opened a can of beer. I was having trouble getting Amstel these days and was drinking domestic stuff. Didn't make a hell of a lot of difference, though. The worst beer I ever had was wonderful. The apartment was very quiet. The hum of the air conditioner made it seem quieter. Doerr was the key. If I could take him out of this, I could reason with Maynard. All I had to do was figure out what to do about Doerr. I finished the beer. I didn't know what to do about Doerr. I applied one of Spenser's Rules: When in doubt, cook something and eat it. I took off my shirt, opened another can of beer, and studied the refrigerator.

Spareribs. Yeah. I doused them with Liquid Smoke and put them in the oven. Low. I had eaten once in a restaurant in Minneapolis, Charlie's something-or-other, and had barbecued spareribs with Charlie's own sauce. Since then I'd been trying to duplicate it. I didn't have it right yet, but I'd been getting close. This time I tried starting with chili sauce instead of ketchup. What did Doerr like? I'd been through that: money. What was he afraid of? Pain? Maybe. He hadn't liked me whacking his hand. I put a little less brown sugar in with the chili sauce this time. But maybe he hadn't liked me standing up to him. He was a weird guy and his reaction might be more complicated than just crying because his hand hurt. Two cloves of garlic this time. But first another beer, helps neutralize the garlic fumes. Either way I had got to him today. So what? I squeezed a couple of lemons and added the juice to my sauce. The smell of the spareribs was beginning to fill the kitchen. Even with the air conditioner on, the oven made the kitchen warm and sweat trickled down my bare chest.

Getting to Doerr and getting him to do what I wanted were

different things. I had a feeling that right now if I saw him, I'd have to kill him. I never met a guy before who actually foamed at the mouth. If I killed, I'd have to kill the Hog. Maybe a little red wine. I hadn't tried that before. I put in about half a cupful. Or would I? If Doerr were dead, the Hog might wither away like an uprooted weed. Best if I never found out. One dash of Tabasco? Why not? I opened another beer. If I were dead, I'd shrivel up like an uprooted weed. I put the sauce on to cook and began to consider what else to have. Maybe I could call Wally and Frank over and cook at them until they agreed to terms. Way to a man's heart and all that.

There was zucchini squash in the vegetable drawer, and I sliced it up and shook it in flour and set it aside while I made a beer batter. It always hurt me to pour beer into a bowl of flour, but the results were good. That's me. Mr. Results. Lemme see, what was I going to do about Frankie Doerr? The barbecue sauce began to bubble, and I turned the gas down to simmer. I put two dashes of Tabasco into the beer batter and stirred it and put it aside so the yeast in the beer would work on the flour.

I looked in the freezer. Last Sunday Susan Silverman and I had made bread all afternoon at her house while we watched the ball game and drank Rhine wine. She had mixed and I had kneaded and at the end of the day we had twelve loaves, baked and wrapped in foil. I'd brought home six that night and put them in the freezer. There were four left. I took one out and put it in the oven, still in the foil. Maybe old Suze would have an idea about what to do with Frankie Doerr, or how to get my barbecue sauce to taste like Charlie's, or whether I was drinking too much lately. I looked at my watch: 3:30 She'd be home from school. I called her and let it ring ten times and she didn't answer, so I hung up. Brenda Loring? No. I wanted to talk about things I had trouble talking about. Brenda was for fun and wisecracks and she did a terrific picnic, but she wasn't much better than I was at talking about hard things.

The spareribs were done and the bread was hot. I dipped my sliced zucchini in the beer batter and fried it in a little olive oil. I'd eaten alone before. Why didn't I like it better this time?

24

I ate and drank and thought about my problem for the rest of the afternoon and went to bed early and woke up early. When I woke up, I knew what I was going to do. I didn't know how yet, but I knew what.

It was drizzly rainy along the Charles. I ran along the esplanade with my mind on other things, and it took a lot longer to do my three miles. It always does if you don't concentrate. I was on the curb by Arlington Street, looking to dash across Storrow Drive and head home, when a black Ford with a little antenna on the roof pulled alongside and Frank Belson stuck his head out the window on the passenger side and said, "Get in."

I got in the back seat and we pulled away. "Drive around for a while, Billy," Belson said to the other cop, and we headed west toward Allston.

Belson was leaning forward, trying to light a cigar butt with the lighter from the dashboard. When he got it going, he shifted around, put his left arm on the back of the front seat, and looked at me.

"I got a snitch tells me that Frank Doerr's going to blow you up."

"Frank personally?"

"That's what the snitch says. Says you roughed Frank up yesterday and he took it personally." Belson was thin, with tight skin and a dark beard shaved close. "Marty thought you oughta know."

We stayed left where the river curved and drove out Soldiers Field Road, past the 'BZ radio tower.

"I thought Wally Hogg did that kind of work for Doerr."

"He does," Belson said. "But this one he's gonna do himself."

"If he can," I said.

"That ain't to say he might not have Wally around to hold you still," Belson said.

Billy U-turned over the safety island and headed back in toward town. He was young and stylish with a thick blond mustache and a haircut that hid his ears. Belson's sideburns were trimmed at the temple.

"Reliable snitch?"

Belson nodded. "Always solid in the past."

"How much you pay him for this stuff?"

"C-note," Belson said.

"I'm flattered," I said.

Belson shrugged. "Company money," he said.

We were passing Harvard Stadium. "You or Quirk got any thoughts about what I should do next?"

Belson shook his head.

"How about hiding?" Billy said. "Doerr will probably die in the next ten, twenty years."

"You think he's that tough?"

Billy shrugged. Belson said, "It's not tough so much. It's crazy. Doerr's crazy. Things don't work out, he wants to kill everybody. I hear he cut one guy up with a machete. I mean, cut him up. Disgoddamn-membered him. Crazy."

"You don't think a dozen roses and a note of apology would do it, huh?"

Billy snorted. Belson didn't bother. We passed the Kenmore exit.

I said to Billy, "You know where I live?"

He nodded.

Belson said, "You got a piece on you?"

"Not when I'm running," I said.

"Then don't run," Belson said. "If I was Doerr, I coulda aced you right there at the curb when we picked you up."

I remembered my lecture to Lester about professionals. I had no comment. We swung off at Arlington and then right on Marlborough. Billy pulled up in front of my apartment.

"You're going up a one-way street," I said to Billy.

"Jeez, I hope there's no cops around," Billy said.

I got out. "Thanks," I said to Belson.

He got out too. "I'll walk up to your place with you."

"With me? Frank, you old softy."

"Quirk told me to get you inside safe. After that you're on your own. We don't run a baby-sitting service. Not even for you, baby."

When I unlocked my apartment door, I noticed that Belson unbuttoned his coat. We went in. I looked around. The place was empty. Belson buttoned his coat.

"Watch your ass," he said and left.

From my front window I looked down while Belson got in the car and Billy U-turned and drove off. Now I knew what and was getting an idea of how. I took my gun from the bureau drawer and checked the load and brought it with me to the bathroom. I put it on the toilet seat while I took a shower and put it on the bed while I dressed. Then I stuck the holster in my hip pocket and clipped it to my belt. I was wearing broken-in jeans and white sneakers with a racing stripe and my black polo shirt with a beaver on the left breast. I wasn't up in the alligator bracket yet. I put on a seersucker jacket, my aviator sunglasses, and checked myself in the hall mirror. Battle dress.

I unlocked the front hall closet and got out a 12-gauge Iver Johnson pump gun and a box of double-aught shells. Then I went out. In the hall I put the shotgun down and closed a toothpick between the jamb and the hinge side of the door, a couple of inches up from the ground. I snapped it off so only the edge was visible at the crack of the door. It would be good to know if someone had gone in.

I picked up the shotgun and went out to my car. On the way down I passed another tenant. "Hunting season so early?" he said.

"Yeah."

Outside I locked the shotgun and the box of shells in the trunk of my car, got in, put the top down, and headed for the North Shore. I knew what and how, now I had to find where.

I drove Route 93 out of Boston through Somerville and Medford. Along the Mystic River across from Wellington Circle, reeds and head-high marsh grass still grew in an atmosphere made garish with neon and thick exhaust fumes. Past Medford Square, I turned off 93 and took the Lynn Fells Parkway east, looking at the woods and not seeing what I was looking for. Medford gave way to Melrose. I turned off the Fellsway and drove up around Spot Pond, past the MDC Zoo in Stoneham, and back into Melrose. Still nothing that looked right to me. I drove through Melrose, past red clay tennis courts by the lake, past the high school and the Christian Science Church. Just before I got to Route 1, I turned off into Breakhart Reservation. Past the MDC skating rink the road narrows to a single lane and becomes one way. I'd been there on a picnic once with Susan Silverman, and I knew that the road looped through the woods and returned here, one way all the way. There were saddle trails, and lakes, and picnic areas scattered through thick woods.

Thirty yards into the reservation I found the place. I pulled off the narrow hot top road, the bushes scraping my car fenders and crunching under the tires, and got out. A small hill sloped up from the road, and scooped out of the side of it was a hollow the size of a basketball court and the shape of a free-form pool. About in the middle was a flat-planed granite slab, higher than a man's head at one end that tapered into the ground in a shape vaguely like a shark fin.

The sides of the gully were yellow clay, streaked with erosion troughs, scattered with small white pines. The sides sloped steeply up to the somewhat gentler slope of the hill, which was thick with white pine and clustered birch saplings and bunches of sumac. I walked into the hollow and stood by the slab of granite. The high end was a foot above my head. There was a high hum of locust in the hot, still woods and the sound of birds. A squirrel shot down the trunk of a birch tree and up the trunk of a maple without pausing. I took my coat off and draped it over the rock. Then I scrambled up the slope of the gully and looked down. I walked around the rim of the hollow, looking at the woods and at the sun and down into the hollow. It would do. I looked at my watch: 2:00.

I went back down, put my coat on again, got in my car, and drove on around the loop and out of the reservation. There was a small shopping center next to the exit road and I parked my car in among a batch of others in front of a Purity Supreme Supermarket.

There was a pay phone in the supermarket, and I used it to call Frank Doerr.

He wasn't in, but the solicitious soft-voiced guy that answered said he'd take a message.

"Okay," I said, "my name is Spenser. S-p-e-n-s-e-r, like the English poet. You know who I am?"

"Yeah, I know." No more solicitude.

"Tell Frank if he wants to talk to me, he should drive up to the Breakhart Reservation in Saugus. Come in by the skating rink entrance, drive thirty yards down the road. Park and walk into the little gully that's there. He'll know it. There's a big rock like a shark fin in the middle of the gully. You got that?"

"Yeah, but why should he want to see you? Frank wants to see someone he calls them into the office. He don't go riding around in the freaking woods."

"He'll ride around in them this time because if he doesn't, I am going to sing songs to the police that Frank will hate the sound of."

"If Frank does want to do this, and I ain't saying he will, when should he be there?"

"Six o'clock tonight."

"For crissake, what if he ain't around at that time? Maybe he's busy. Who the Christ you think you're talking to?"

"Six o'clock tonight," I said, "or I'll be down on Berkeley Street crooning to the fuzz." I hung up.

25

I bought a pound of Hebrew National bologna, a loaf of pumpernickel, a jar of brown mustard, and a half gallon of milk and walked back to my car. I opened the trunk and got an old duffel bag from it. I put the shotgun, the shells, and my groceries in the duffel bag, closed the trunk, shouldered the duffel bag, and walked back toward Breakhart.

It took about fifteen minutes for me to walk back to my gully in the hillside. I climbed up the hill past it, halfway to the top of the hill, and found a thick stand of white pine screened by some dogberry bushes that let me look down into the hollow and the road below it. I took my groceries, my shotgun, and my ammunition out of the duffel bag, took off my coat, and put it in the duffel bag. I spread the bag on the ground, sat down on it, and loaded the shotgun. It took six shells. I put six extras in my hip pocket and cocked the shotgun and leaned it against the tree. Then I got out my groceries and made lunch. I spread the mustard on the bread with my pocketknife and used the folded paper bag as a plate. I drank the milk from the carton. Not bad. Nothing like dining al fresco. I looked at my watch: 2:45. I ate another sandwich. Three o'clock. The locusts keened at me. Some sparrows fluttered above me in the pines. On the road below cars with children and mothers and dogs and inflatable beach toys drove slowly by every few minutes but less often as the afternoon wore on.

I finished the milk with my fourth sandwich and wrapped the rest of the bread and bologna back up in the paper sack and shoved it in the duffel bag. At four fifteen a silver gray Lincoln Continental pulled off the road by the gully and parked for a long time. Then the door opened and Wally Hogg climbed out. He was alone. He stood and looked carefully all over the hollow and up the hill at where I sat behind my bushes and everywhere else. Finally he looked up and down the road, reached back into the car, and came out with a shoulder weapon. He held it inconspicuously down along his leg and stepped away from the car and in behind the trees along the road. The Lincoln started up and drove away.

In the shelter of the trees Wally was less careful with the weapon, and I got a good look at it. An M-16 rifle. Standard U.S. infantry weapon. 7.62 millimeter. Twenty rounds. Fancy carry handle like the old BARs and a pistol grip back of the trigger housing like the old Thompsons. M-16? Christ, I was just getting used to the M-1.

Wally and his M-16 climbed the gully wall about opposite me. He was wearing stacked-heel shoes. He slipped once on the steep sides and slid almost all the way back down. Hah! I made it first try. When the Lincoln had arrived, I'd picked up the shotgun and held it across my lap. I noticed that my hands were a little sweaty as I held it. I looked at my knuckles. They were white. Wally didn't climb as high as I had. Too fat. Ought to jog mornings, Wally, get in shape. A few yards above the gully edge he found some thick bushes and settled in behind them. From the hollow he would be invisible. Once he got settled, he didn't move and looked like a big toad squatting in his ambush.

I looked at my watch again. Quarter of five. Some people went by on horseback, the shod hooves of the horses clattering on the paved road. It was a sound you didn't hear often, yet it brought back the times when I was small and the milkman had a horse, and so did the trash people. And manure in the street, and the sparrows. All three of the horses on the road below were a shiny, sweat-darkened chestnut color. The riders were kids. Two girls in white blouses and riding boots, a boy in jeans and no shirt.

The draft horses that used to pull the trash wagons were much different. Big splayed feet and massive, almost sumptuous haunches. Necks that curved in a stolid, muscular arch. When I was very small, I remembered, horses pulling a scoop were used to dig a cellar hole on the lot next to my house.

The riders disappeared and the clopping dwindled. Wally Hogg still sat there, silent and shapeless, watching the road. I heard a match scrape and smelled cigarette smoke. Careless Wally, what if I were just arriving and smelled the smoke? It carries out here in the woods. But Wally probably wasn't all that at home in the woods. Places Wally hung out you could probably smoke a length of garden hose and no one would smell it. The woods were dry, and I hoped he was careful with the cigarette. I didn't want this thing getting screwed up by a natural disaster.

I checked my watch again: 5:15. My chest felt tight, as if the diaphragm were rusty, and I had that old tingling toothache feeling in behind my navel. There was a lump in my throat. Above me the sky was still bright blue in the early summer evening, dappling through the green leaves. Five thirty, getting on toward supper. The road was empty now below me. The mommas and the kids and the dogs were going home to get supper going and eat with Daddy. Maybe a cookout. Too hot to eat in tonight. Maybe a couple of beers and some gin and tonic with a mint leaf in the glass. And after supper maybe the long quiet arc of the water from the hoses of men in shirt sleeves watering their lawns. My stomach rolled. Smooth. How come Gary Cooper's stomach never rolled? Oh, to be torn 'tween love and duty, what if I lose . . . Five forty. My fingertips tingled and the nerves along the insides of my arms tingled. The pectoral muscles, particularly near the outside of my chest, up by the shoulder, felt tight, and I flexed them, trying to loosen up. I took two pieces of gum out of my shirt pocket and peeled off the wrappers and folded the gum into my mouth. I rolled the wrappers up tight and put them in my shirt pocket and chewed on the gum. Quarter of six. I remembered in Korea, before we went in at Inchon, they'd fed us steak and eggs, not bologna and bread, but it hadn't mattered. My stomach rolled before Inchon too. And at Inchon I hadn't been alone. Ten of six.

I looked down at Wally Hogg. He hadn't moved. His throat

wasn't almost closed, and he wasn't taking deep breaths and not getting enough oxygen. He thought he was going to sit up there and shoot me in the back when Frank Doerr gave the nod, which would be right after Frank Doerr found out exactly what I had on him and if I'd given anything to the cops. Or maybe Doerr wanted to fan me himself and Wally was just backup. Anyway, we'd find out pretty soon, wouldn't we? Seven of six. Christ, doesn't time flit by when you're having a big time and all?

I stood up. The shotgun was cocked and ready. I carried it muzzle down along my leg in my right hand and began to move down the hill in a half circle away from where Wally Hogg was. I was about 100 yards away. If I was careful, he wouldn't hear me. I was careful. It took me ten minutes to get down the slope to the road, maybe 50 yards down the road beyond the gully.

Still daylight and bright, but under the trees along the road a bit dimmer than midday. I stayed out of sight behind some trees just off the road and listened. At five past six I heard a car stop and a door open and close. With the shotgun still swinging along by my side, I walked up the road toward the dell. High-ho a dairy-o. The car was a maroon Coupe de Ville, pulled off on the shoulder of the road. No one was in it. I went past it and turned into the hollow. The sun was shining behind me and the hollow was bright and hot. Doerr was standing by the shark-fin rock. Maroon slacks, white shoes, white belt, black shirt, white tie, white safari jacket, black-rimmed sunglasses, white golf cap. A really neat dresser. Probably a real slick dancer too. His hands were empty as I walked in toward him. I didn't look up toward Wally. But I knew where he was, maybe thirty yards up and to my left. I kept the rock on his side of me as I walked into the gully. I kept the shotgun barrel toward the ground. Relaxed, casual. Just had it with me and thought I'd bring it along. Ten feet from Doerr, with the shark-fin rock not yet between me and Wally Hogg, I stopped. If I got behind the rock, Wally would move.

"What the hell is the shotgun for, Spenser?" Doerr said.

"Protection," I said. "You know how it is out in the woods. You might run into a rampaging squirrel or something."

I could feel Wally Hogg's presence up there to my left, thirty yards away. I could feel it along the rib cage and in my armpits and behind the knees. He wasn't moving around. I could hear him if he did; he wasn't that agile and he wasn't dressed for it. You can't sneak around in high-heeled shoes unless you take them off. I listened very hard and didn't hear him.

"I hear you have been bad-mouthing me, Frankie."

"What do you mean?"

"I mean you been saying you were going to blow me up."

Still no sound from Wally. I was about five feet from the shelter of the rock.

"Who told you that?"

I wished I hadn't thought about Wally taking his shoes off.

"Never mind who told me that. Say it ain't so, Frankie."

"Look, shit-for-brains. I didn't come out here into the freaking woods to talk shit with a shit-for-brains like you. You got something to say to me or not?"

"You haven't got the balls, Frankie."

Doerr's face was red. "To blow you up? A shit-for-brains pimple like you? I'll blow you up anytime I goddamned feel like it."

"You had the chance yesterday in your office, Frankie, and I took your piece away from you and made you cry."

Doerr's voice was getting hoarse. The level of it dropped. "You got me out here to talk shit at me or you got something to say?"

I was listening with all I had for Wally. So hard I could barely hear what Doerr was saying.

"I got you out here to tell you that you're a gutless, slobbering freak that couldn't handle an aggressive camp fire girl without hiring someone to help you." I was splitting my concentration, looking at Doerr as hard as I was listening for Wally, and the strain made the sweat run down my face. I almost grunted with the effort.

Doerr's voice was so hoarse and constricted he could barely talk. "Don't you dare talk to me that way," he said. And the oddly quaint phrase squeezed out like dust through a clogged filter.

"You gonna cry again, Frankie? What is it? Did your momma toilet-train you funny? Is that why you're such a goddamned freak-o?"

Doerr's face was scarlet and the carotid arteries stood out in his neck. His mouth moved, but nothing came out. Then he went for his gun. I knew he would sometime.

I brought the pump up level and shot him. The gun flew from his hand and clattered against the shark-fin rock and Doerr went over backwards. I didn't see him land; I dove for the rock and heard Wally's first burst of fire spatter the ground behind me. I landed on my right shoulder, rolled over and up on my feet. Wally's second burst hit the rock and sang off in several directions. I brought the shotgun down over the slope end of the rock where it was about shoulder-high and fanned five rounds into the woods in Wally Hogg's area as fast as I could pump.

I was back down behind the rock, feeding my extra rounds into the magazine, when I heard him fall. I looked and he came rolling through the brush down the side of the gully and came to a stop at the bottom, face up, the front of him already wet with blood. Leaves and twigs and dirt had stuck to the wetness as he rolled. I looked at Doerr. At ten feet the shotgun charge had taken most of his middle. I looked away. A thick and sour fluid rose in my throat and I choked it down. They were both dead. That's the thing about a shotgun. At close range you don't have to go around checking pulses after.

I sat down and leaned back against the rock. I hadn't planned to, and I didn't want someone to find me there. But I sat down anyway because I had to. My legs had gotten weak. I was taking deep breaths, yet I didn't seem to be getting enough oxygen. My body was soaking wet and in the early evening I was feeling cold. I shivered. The sour fluid came back and this time I couldn't keep it down. I threw up with my head between my knees and the two stiffs paying no attention.

Beautiful.

26

It was quarter to seven. I had the shotgun back in the duffel bag and the duffel bag back in the trunk of my car and my car on the overpass where the Fellsway meets Route 1. I drove north on 1 toward Smithfield. On the way I stopped and bought a quart of Wild Turkey bourbon. Turning off Route 1 toward Smithfield Center, I twisted the top off, took a mouthful, rinsed my mouth, spit out the window, and drank about four ounces from the bottle. My stomach jumped when the booze hit it, but then it steadied and held. I was coming back. I drove past the old common, with its white church and meetinghouse, and turned left down Main Street. I'd been up here a year or so back on a case and since then had learned my way around the town pretty well. At least I knew the way to Susan Silverman's house. She lived 100 yards up from the common in a small weathered shingle Cape with blue window boxes filled with red petunias. Her car was in the driveway. She was home. It hadn't occurred to me until now that she might not be.

I walked up the brick path to her front door. On either side of the path were strawberry plants, white blossoms, green fruit, and some occasional flashes of ripe red. A sprinkler arced slowly back and forth. The front door was open and I could hear music which sounded very much like Stan Kenton. "Artistry in Rhythm." Goddamn.

I rang her bell and leaned against the doorjamb, holding my bottle of Wild Turkey by the neck and letting it hang against my thigh. I was very tired. She came to the door. Every time I saw her I felt the same click in my solar plexus I'd felt the first time I saw her. This time was no different. She had on faded Levi's cutoffs and a dark blue ribbed halter top. She was wearing octagonal hornrimmed glasses and carried a book in her right hand, her forefinger keeping the place.

I said, "What are you reading?"

She said, "Erikson's biography of Gandhi."

I said, "I've always liked Leif's work."

She looked at the bourbon bottle, four ounces gone, and opened the door. I went in.

"You don't look good," she said.

"You guidance types don't miss a trick, do you?"

"Would it help if I kissed you?"

"Yeah, but not yet. I been throwing up. I need a shower. Then maybe we could sit down and talk and I'll drink the Wild Turkey."

"You know where," she said. I put the bourbon down on the coffee table in the living room and headed down the little hall to the bathroom. In the linen closet beside the bathroom was a shaving kit of mine with a toothbrush and other necessaries. I got it out and went into the bathroom. I brushed and showered and rinsed my mouth under the shower and soaped and scrubbed and shampooed and lathered and rinsed and washed for about a half an hour. Out, out, damned spot.

When I got through, I toweled off and put on some tennis shorts I'd left there and went looking for Susan. The stereo was off, and she was on the back porch with my Wild Turkey, a bucket of ice, a glass, a sliced lemon, and a bottle of bitters.

I sat in a blue wicker armchair and took a long pull from the neck of the bottle.

"Were you bitten by a snake?" Susan said.

I shook my head. Beyond the screen porch the land sloped down in rough terraces to a stream. On the terraces were shade plants. Coleus, patient Lucy, ajuga, and a lot of vincas. Beyond the stream were trees that thickened into woods.

"Would you like something to eat?"

I shook my head again. "No," I said. "Thank you."

"Drinking bourbon instead of beer, and declining a snack. It's bad, isn't it?"

I nodded. "I think so," I said.

"Would you like to talk about it?"

"Yeah," I said, "but I don't quite know what to say."

I put some ice in the glass, added bitters and a squeeze of lemon, and filled the glass with bourbon. "You better drink a little," I said. "I'll be easier to take if you're a little drunk too."

She nodded her head. "Yes, I was thinking that," she said. "I'll get another glass." She did, and I made her a drink. In front of the house some kids were playing street hockey and their voices drifted back faintly. Birds still sang here and there in the woods, but it was beginning to get dark and the songs were fewer.

"How long ago did you get divorced?" I asked.

"Five years."

"Was it bad?"

"Yes."

"Is it bad now?"

"No. I don't think about it too much now. I don't feel bad about myself anymore. And I don't miss him at all anymore. You have some part in all of that."

"Mr. Fixit," I said. My drink was gone and I made another.

"How does someone who ingests as much as you do get those muscle ridges in his stomach?" Susan said.

"God chose to make me beautiful instead of good," I said.

"How many sit-ups do you do a week?"

"Around a zillion," I said. I stretched my legs out in front of me and slid lower in the chair. It had gotten dark outside and some fireflies showed in the evening. The kids out front had gone in, and all I could hear was the sound of the stream and very faintly the sound of traffic on 128.

"There is a knife blade in the grass," I said. "And a tiger lies just outside the fire."

"My God, Spenser, that's bathetic. Either tell me about what hurts or don't. But for crissake, don't sit here and quote bad verse at me."

"Oh damn," I said. "I was just going to swing into *Hamlet.*"

"You do and I'll call the cops."

"Okay," I said. "You're right. But bathetic? That's hard, Suze."

She made herself another drink. We drank. There was no light on the porch, just that which spilled out from the kitchen.

"I killed two guys earlier this evening," I said.

"Have you ever done that before?"

"Yeah," I said. "But I set these guys up."

"You mean you murdered them?"

"No, not exactly. Or . . . I don't know. Maybe."

She was quiet. Her face a pale blur in the semidarkness. She was sitting on the edge of a chaise opposite me. Her knees crossed, her chin on her fist, her elbow on her knee. I drank more bourbon.

"Spenser," she said, "I have known you for only a year or so. But I have known you very intensely. You are a good man. You are perhaps the best man I've ever known. If you killed two men, you did it because it had to be done. I know you. I believe that."

I put my drink on the floor and got up from the chair and stood over her. She raised her face toward me and I put one hand on each side of it and bent over and looked at her close. She had a very strong face, dark and intelligent, full of kinetic suggestion, with faint laugh lines at the corners of her mouth. She was still wearing her glasses, and her big dark eyes looked bigger through the lenses.

"Jesus Christ," I said.

She put her hands over mine and we stayed that way for a long time.

Finally she said, "Sit."

I sat and she leaned back on the chaise and pulled me down beside her and put my head against her breast. "Would you like to make love?" she said.

I was breathing in big low inhales. "No," I said. "Not now, let's just lie here and be still."

Her right arm was around me and she reached up and patted my cheek with her left hand. The stream murmured and after a while I fell asleep.

27

It was a hot, windy Tuesday when I finished breakfast with Susan and drove back into Boston. I stopped on the way to look at the papers. The *Herald American* had it, page one, below the fold: GANGLAND FIGURE GUNNED DOWN. Doerr and Wally Hogg had been found after midnight by two kids who'd slipped in there to neck. State and MDC police had no comment as yet.

Under the expressway, street grit was blowing about in the postcommuter lull as I pulled up and parked in front of Harbor Towers. I went through the routine with the houseman again and went up in the elevator. Bucky Maynard let me in. He was informal in a Boston Red Sox T-shirt stretched over his belly.

"What do you want, Spenser?" Informal didn't mean friendly. Lester leaned against the wall by the patio doors with his arms folded across his bare chest. He was wearing dark blue sweat pants and light blue track shoes with dark blue stripes. He blew a huge pink bubble and glared at me around it.

"It's hard to look tough blowing bubbles, Lester," I said. "You ever think about a pacifier?"

"Ah asked what you want, Spenser." Maynard still had his hand on the door.

I handed him the paper. "Below the fold," I said, "right side."

He looked at it, read the lead paragraph, and handed it to Lester. "So?"

"So, maybe your troubles are over."

"Maybe they are," Maynard said.

"So are Marty Rabb's troubles over too?"

"Troubles?"

"Yeah, maybe you'll stop sucking on him now that Frank Doerr's not going to suck on you anymore."

"Spenser, y'all aren't making any sense. Ah'm not doing anything to Marty Rabb. Ah don't know, for a fact, what you are talking of."

"You're going to recoup your losses," I said. "You mean, stupid sonovabitch."

"No reason to stand there shaking your head, Spenser. Ah'm the one should be offended."

"Doerr bled Rabb through you, and you never got any blood. Now he's dead, you want yours."

"Ah think you ought to leave now, Spenser. You're becoming abusive."

Lester popped his bubble gum and tittered. There were newspapers on the coffee table, the *Globe* and the *Herald American.* They'd known before I got here, and Maynard had already figured out that he had the money machine now.

"Don't you want to know why I think you're stupid?" I said.

"No, ah don't."

"Because you were off the hook, clean. And you won't take the break."

"Move out," Lester said. "And just keep in mind, Spenser, if anybody was blackmailing Rabb, they could get him for throwing games just as much as for marrying a whore."

"Never mind, Lester," Maynard said sharply. "We don't know anything about it and Spenser is on his way out."

"I'd be glad to make him go faster, Buck."

"He's on his way, Lester. Aren't you, Spenser?"

"Yeah, I am, but as they say in all the movies, Bucky, I'll be back."

"Ah wouldn't if ah were you. Ah can't restrain Lester too much more."

"Well, do what you can," I said. "I don't want to kill him." Maynard opened the door. He'd never taken his hand off the knob.

"Hey, Spenser," Lester said, "I got something you haven't seen before." He put his hands behind his back and brought them back out front. In his right hand was a nickel-plated automatic pistol. It looked like a Beretta. "How's that look to you, Mr. Pro?"

I said, "Lester, if you point that thing at me again, I'll take it away from you and shoot you with it." Then I stomped out. The door closed behind me and I headed for the street.

Outside, the wind was hotter and stronger. I drove home in such a funk that I didn't even check the skirts on the girls, something I did normally as a matter of course, even on still days. Across the street from my apartment was a city car, and in it were Belson and the cop named Billy.

I walked over to the car. "You guys want something or are you hiding from the watch commander?"

"Lieutenant wants you," Billy said.

"Maybe I don't want him."

Belson was slumped down in the passenger seat with his hand over his eyes. He said, "Aw knock off the bullshit, Spenser. Get in the car. Quirk wants you and we both know you're going to come."

He was right, of course. The way I felt if someone said up I'd say down. I got in the back seat. In the two minutes it took us to drive to police headquarters no one said anything.

Quirk's office had moved since last time. He was third-floor front now, facing out onto Berkeley Street. With a view of the secretaries from the insurance companies when they broke for lunch. On his door it said COMMANDER, HOMICIDE.

Belson knocked and opened the door. "Here he is, Marty."

Quirk sat at a desk that had nothing on it but a phone and a clear plastic cube containing pictures of his family. He was immaculate and impervious, as he had been every other time I ever saw him. I wondered if his bedroom slippers had a spit shine. Probably didn't own bedroom slippers. Probably didn't sleep. He said, "Thanks, Frank. I'll see him alone."

Belson nodded and closed the door behind me. There was a straight chair in front of the desk. I sat in it. Quirk looked at me without saying anything. I looked back. There was a traffic cop outside at the Stuart Street intersection and I could hear his whistle as he moved cars around the construction.

Quirk said, "I think you burned those two studs up in Saugus."

I said "Uh-huh."

"I think you set them up and burned them."

"Uh-huh."

"I went up and took a look early this morning. One of the MDC people asked me to. Informal. Doerr never fired his piece. Wally Hogg did, the magazine's nearly empty, there's a lot of brass up above the death scene in the woods, and there's ricochet marks on one side of the big rock. There's also six spent twelve-gauge shells on the ground on the other side of the rock. The shrubs are torn up around where the M-sixteen brass was. Like somebody fired off about five rounds of shotgun into the area."

"Uh-huh."

"You knew that Doerr was gunning for you. You let him know you'd be there and you figured they'd try to back-shoot you and you figured you could beat them. And you were right."

"That's really swell, Quirk, you got some swell imagination."

"It's more than imagination, Spenser. You're around buying me a drink, asking about Frank Doerr. Next day I get a tip that Doerr is going to blow you up, and this morning I was looking at Doerr and his gunsel dead up the woods. You got an alibi for yesterday afternoon and evening?"

"Do I need one?"

Quirk picked up the clear plastic cube on his desk and looked at the pictures of his family. In the outer office a phone rang. A typewriter clacked uncertainly. Quirk put the cube down again on the desk and looked at me.

"No," he said. "I don't think you do."

"You mean you didn't share your theories with the Saugus cops?"

"It's not my territory."

"Then why the hell am I sitting here nodding my head while you talk?"

"Because this is my territory." The hesitant typist in the outer office was still hunting and pecking. "Look, Spenser, I am not in sorrow's clutch because Frank Doerr and his animal went down. And I'm not even all that unhappy that you put them down. There's a lot of guys couldn't do it, and a lot of guys wouldn't try. I don't know why you did it, but I guess probably it wasn't for dough and maybe it wasn't even for protection. If I had to guess, I'd guess it might have been to take the squeeze off of someone else. The squeezee, you might say."

"You might," I said. "I wouldn't."

"Yeah. Anyway. I'm saying to you you didn't burn them in my city. And I'm kind of glad they're burnt. But . . ." Quirk paused and looked at me. His stare was as heavy and solid as his fist. "Don't do it ever in my city."

I said nothing.

"And," he said, "don't start thinking you're some kind of god-damned vigilante. If you get away with this, don't get tempted to do it again. Here or anywhere. You understand what I'm saying to you?"

"Yeah. I do."

"We've known each other awhile, Spenser, and maybe we got a certain amount of respect. But we're not friends. And I'm not a guy you know. I'm a cop."

"Nothing else?"

"Yeah," Quirk said, "something else. I'm a husband and a father and a cop. But the last one's the only thing that makes any difference to you."

"No, not quite. The husband and father makes a difference too. Nobody should be just a job."

"Okay, we agree. But believe what I tell you. I won't bite this bullet again."

"Got it," I said.

"Good."

I stood up, started for the door and stopped, and turned around and said, "Marty?"

"Yeah?"

"Shake," I said.

He put his hand out across his desk, and we did.

28

No one drove me home. It's a short walk from Berkeley Street to my place, and I liked the walk. It gave me time to think, and I needed time. A lot had happened in a short while, and not all of it was going my way. I hadn't thought it would, but there's always hope.

It was afternoon when I got home. I made two lettuce and tomato sandwiches on homemade wheat bread, poured a glass of milk, sat at the counter, and ate and drank the milk and thought about where I was at and where the Rabbs were at and where Bucky Maynard was at. I knew where Doerr and his gunner were at. I had a piece of rhubarb pie for dessert. Put the dishes in the dishwasher, wiped the counter off with a sponge, washed my hands and face, and headed for Church Park.

It was in walking distance and I walked. The wind was still strong, but there was less grit in the air along Marlborough Street, and what little there was rattled harmlessly on my sunglasses. Linda Rabb let me in.

"I heard on the radio that what's'isname Doerr and another man were killed," she said. She wore a loose sleeveless dress, striped black and white like mattress ticking, and white sandals. Her hair was in two braids, each tied with a small white ribbon, and her face was without makeup.

"Yeah, me too," I said. "Your husband home?"

"No, he's gone to the park."

"Your boy?"

"He's in nursery school."

"We need to talk," I said.

She nodded. "Would you like coffee or anything?"

"Yeah, coffee would be good."

"Instant okay?"

"Sure, black."

I sat in the living room while she made coffee. From the kitchen came the faintly hysterical sounds of daytime television. The set clicked off and Linda Rabb returned, carrying a round black tray with two cups of coffee on it. I took one.

"I've talked with Bucky Maynard," I said, and sipped the coffee. "He won't let go."

"Even though Doerr is dead?" Linda Rabb was sitting on an ottoman, her coffee on the floor beside her.

I nodded. "Now he wants his piece."

We were quiet. Linda Rabb sipped at her coffee, holding the cup in both hands, letting the steam warm her face. I drank some more of mine. It was too hot still, but I drank it anyway. The sound of my swallow seemed loud to me.

"We both know, don't we?" Linda Rabb said.

"I think so," I said.

"If I make a public statement about the way I used to be, we'll be free of Maynard, won't we?"

"I think so," I said. "He can still allege that Marty threw some games, but that implicates him too and he goes down the tube with you. I don't think he will. He gets nothing out of it. No money, nothing. And his career is shot as bad as Marty's."

She kept her face buried in the coffee cup.

"I can't think of another way," I said.

She lifted her face and looked at me and said, "Could you kill him?"

I said, "No."

She nodded, without expression. "What would be the best way to confess?"

"I will find you a reporter and you tell the story any way you wish, but leave out the blackmail. That way there's no press conferences, photographers, whatever. After he publishes the story, you refer all inquiries to me. You got any money in the house?"

"Of course."

"Okay, give me a dollar," I said.

She went to the kitchen and returned with a dollar bill. I took out one of my business cards and acknowledged receipt on the back of it and gave it to her.

"Now you are my client," I said. "I represent you."

She nodded again.

"How about Marty?" I said. "Don't you want to clear it with him or discuss it? Or something?"

"No," she said. "You get me the reporter. I'll give him my statement. Then I'll tell Marty. I never bother him before a game. It's one of our rules."

"Okay," I said. "Where's the phone?"

It was in the kitchen. A red wall phone with a long cord. I dialed a number at the *Globe* and talked to a police reporter named Jack Washington that I had gotten to know when I worked for the Suffolk County DA.

"You know the broad who writes that *Feminine Eye* column? The one that had the Nieman Fellowship to Harvard last year?"

"Yeah, she'd love to hear you call her a broad."

"She won't. Can you get her to come to an address I'll give you? If she'll come, she'll get a major news story exclusively. My word, but I can't tell you more than that."

"I can ask her," Washington said. There was silence and the distant sound of genderless voices. Then a woman's voice said, "Hello, this is Carol Curtis."

I repeated what I'd said to Washington.

"Why me, Mr. Spenser?"

"Because I read your column and you are a class person when you write. This is a story that needs more than who, what, when, and where. It involves a woman and a lot of pain, and more to come, and I don't want some heavy-handed slug with a press pass in his hatband screwing it up."

"I'll come. What's the address?"

I gave it to her and she hung up. So did I.

When I hung up, Linda Rabb asked, "Would you like more coffee? The water's hot."

"Yes, please."

She put a spoonful of instant coffee in my cup, added hot water, and stirred.

"Would you care for a piece of cake or some cookies or anything?"

I shook my head. "No, thanks," I said. "This is fine."

We went back to the living room and sat down as before. Me on the couch, Linda Rabb on the ottoman. We drank our coffee. It was quiet. There was nothing to say. At two fifteen the door buzzer buzzed. Linda Rabb got up and opened the door.

The woman at the door said, "Hello, I'm Carol Curtis."

"Come in, please. I'm Linda Rabb. Would you like coffee?"

"Yes, thank you."

Carol Curtis was small with brown hair cut short and a lively, innocent-looking face. There was a scatter of freckles across her nose and cheekbones, and her light blue eyes were shadowed with long thick lashes. She had on a pink dress with tan figures on it that looked expensive.

Linda Rabb said, "This is Mr. Spenser," and went to the kitchen. I shook hands with Carol Curtis. She had a gold wedding band on her left hand.

"You are the one who called," she said.

"Yeah."

"Jack told me a little about you. It sounded good." She sat on the couch beside me.

"He makes things up," I said.

Linda Rabb came back with coffee and a plate of cookies, which she placed on the coffee table in front of the couch. Then she sat back down on the ottoman and began to speak, looking directly at Carol Curtis as she did.

"My husband is Marty Rabb," she said. "The Red Sox pitcher. But my real name is not Linda, it's Donna, Donna Burlington. Before I married Marty, I was a prostitute in New York and a performer in pornographic films when I met him."

Carol Curtis was saying, "Wait a minute, wait a minute," and rummaging in her purse for pad and pencil. Linda Rabb paused. Carol Curtis got the pad open and wrote rapidly in some kind of shorthand. "When did you meet your husband, Mrs. Rabb?"

"In New York, in what might be called the course of my profession," and off she went. She told it all, in a quiet, uninflected voice the way you might read a story to a child when you'd read it too often. Carol Curtis was a professional. She did not bat one of her thick-lashed eyes after the opening sentence. She asked very little. She understood her subject and she let Linda Rabb talk.

When it was over, she said, "And why are you telling me this?"

Linda Rabb said, "I've lived with it too long. I don't want a secret that will come along and haunt me, later, maybe when my son is older, maybe . . ." She let it hang. Listening, I had the feeling that she had given a real reason. Not the only reason, but a real one.

"Does your husband know."

"He knows everything."

"Where is he now?"

"At the park."

"Does he know about this . . . ah . . . confession?"

"Yes, he does," Linda said without hesitation.

"And he approves?"

"Absolutely," Linda said.

"Mrs. Rabb," Carol Curtis said. And Linda Rabb shook her head.

"That's all," she said. "I'm sorry. Mr. Spenser represents me and anything else to be said about this he will say." Then she sat still with her hands folded in her lap and looked at me and Carol Curtis sitting on the couch.

I said, "No comment," and Carol Curtis smiled.

"I bet you'll say that often in the future when we talk, won't you?"

"No comment," I said.

"Why is a private detective representing Mrs. Rabb in this? Why not a lawyer or a PR man or perhaps a husband?"

"No comment," I said. And Carol Curtis said it silently along with me, nodding her head as she did so. She closed the notebook and stood up.

"Nice talking with you, Spenser," she said, and put out her hand.

We shook. "Don't get up," she said. Then she turned to Linda Rabb.

"Mrs. Rabb," she said and put out her hand. Linda Rabb took it, and held it for a moment. "You are a saint, Mrs. Rabb. Not a sinner. That's the way I'll write this story."

Linda Rabb said, "Thank you."

"You are also," Carol Curtis said, "a hell of a woman."

29

When Carol Curtis left, I said to Linda Rabb, "Shall I stay with you?"

"I would rather be by myself," she said.

"Okay, but I want to call Harold Erskine and tell him what's coming. I took some of his money and I don't want him blindsided by this. I probably better resign his employ too."

She nodded.

"I'll call him from my office," I said. "Would you like me around when you tell Marty?"

"No," she said. "Thank you."

"I think this will work, kiddo," I said. "If you hear from Maynard, I want to know, right off. Okay?"

"Yes, certainly."

"You know what Carol Curtis said to you?"

She nodded.

"Me too," I said. "Me too."

She smiled at me slightly and didn't move. I let myself out of the apartment and left her sitting on her ottoman. Looking, as far as I could tell, at nothing at all.

I caught a cab to my office and called Harold Erskine. I told him what Linda Rabb had said in the papers and that it was likely to be on the street in the morning. I told him I'd found not a trace of evidence to suggest that Marty Rabb gambled or threw games or chewed snuff. He was not happy about Linda Rabb, and he was not happy that I didn't know more about it. Or wouldn't tell.

"Goddamnit, Spenser. You are not giving it to me straight. There's more there than you're saying. I hire a man I expect cooperation. You are holding out on me."

I told him I wasn't holding out, and if he thought so, he could refuse to pay my bill. He said he'd think about that too. And we hung up. On my desk were bills and some letters I should get to. I put them in the middle drawer of my desk and closed the drawer. I'd get to them later. Down the street a construction company was tearing down the buildings along the south side of Stuart Street to make room for a medical school. Since early spring they had been moving in on my building. I could hear the big iron wrecking ball thump into the old brick of the garment lofts and palm-reading parlors that used to be there. By next month I'd have to get a new office. What I should do right now is call a real estate broker and get humping on relocation. When you have to move in a hurry, you get screwed. That's just what I should do. Be smart, move before I had to. I looked at my watch: 4:45. I got up and went out of my office and headed for home. Once I got this cleared up with the Rabbs, I'd look into a new office.

As I walked across the Common, the Hare Krishnas were chanting and hopping around in their ankle-length saffron robes, Hush Puppies and sneakers with white sweat socks poking out beneath the hems. Did you have to look funny to be saved? If Christ were around today, He'd probably be wearing a chambray shirt and flared slacks. There were kids splashing in the wading pool and dogs on leashes and squirrels on the loose and pigeons. In the Public Garden the swan boats were still making their circuit of the duck pond under the little footbridge.

At home I got out a can of beer, read the morning *Globe,* warmed up some leftover beef stew for supper, ate it with Syrian bread while I watched the news, and settled down in my living room with my copy of Morison. I'd bought it in three-volume softcover and was halfway through the third volume. I stared at it for half an hour and made no progress at all. I looked at my watch: 7:20. Too early to go to bed. Brenda Loring? No. Susan Silverman? No. Over to the Harbor Health Club and lift a few and talk with Henry Cimoli? No. Nothing. I didn't want to talk with anyone. And I didn't want to read. I looked at the TV listings in the paper. There was nothing I could stand to look at. And I didn't feel like woodcarving and I didn't feel like sitting in my apartment. If I had a dog, I could take him for a walk. I could pretend.

I went out and strolled along Arlington to Commonwealth and up the mall on Commonwealth toward Kenmore Square. When I got there, I turned down Brookline Ave and went into a bar called Copperfield's and drank beer there till it closed. Then I walked back home and went to bed.

I didn't sleep much, but after a while it was morning and the *Globe* was delivered. There it was, page one, lower left, with a Carol Curtis by-line. SOX WIFE REVEALS OTHER LIFE. I read it, drinking coffee and eating corn bread with strawberry jam, and it was all it should have been. The facts were the way Linda Rabb had given them. The writing was sympathetic and intelligent. Inside on the sports page was a picture of Marty, and one of Linda, obviously taken in the stands on a happier occasion. Balls.

The phone rang. It was Marty Rabb.

"Spenser, the doorman says Maynard and another guy are here to see me. Linda said to call you."

"She there too?"

"Yes."

"I'll be over. Don't let them in until I come."

"Well, shit, I'm not scared . . ."

"Be scared. Lester's got a gun."

I hung up and ran for my car. In less than ten minutes I was in the lobby at Church Park and Bucky and Lester were glaring at me. The houseman called up and we three went together in the same elevator. No one said anything. But the silence in the elevator had the density of clay.

Marty Rabb opened the door and the three of us went in. Me first and Lester last. Linda Rabb came out of the bedroom with her little boy holding on to her hand. Rabb faced us in the middle of the living room. Legs slightly apart, hands on hips. He had on a short-sleeved white shirt, and his lean, wiry arms were tanned halfway up the forearms and pale thereafter. Must pitch with a sweat shirt on, I thought.

"Okay," he said. "Get it done, and then get the hell out of here. All three of you."

Bucky Maynard said, "Ah want to know just what in hell you think you gonna accomplish with that nonsense in the newspapers. You think that's gonna close the account between you and me? 'Cause if you think so, you better think on it some more, boy."

"I thought on it all I'm going to think on it, Maynard," Rabb said. "You and me got nothing else to say to each other."

"You think ah can't squeeze you some more, boy? Ah got records of every game you dumped, boy. Every inning you fudged a run for the office pools, and ah can talk just as good as your little girl to the newspapers, don't you think ah can't."

Lester was leaning bonelessly against the wall by the door with his arms across his chest and his jaws working. He was doing Che Guevara today, starched fatigue pants, engineer boots, a fatigue shirt with the sleeves cut off, and black beret. The shirt hung outside the pants. I wondered if he had the nickel-plated Beretta stuck in his belt.

"You can," I said. "But you won't."

Linda and the boy stood beside Marty, Linda's left hand touching his arm, her right holding the boy's.

"Ah won't?"

"Nope. Because you can't do it without sinking yourself too. You won't make any money by turning him in and you can't do it without getting caught yourself. Marty will be out of the league, okay. But so will you, fats."

Maynard's face got bright red. "You think so?" he said.

"Yeah. You say one word to anybody and you'll be calling drag races in Dalrymple, Georgia. And you know it."

Everybody looked at everybody. No one said anything. Lester cracked his gum. Then Rabb said, "So it looks like I got you and you got me. That's a tie, you fat bastard. And that's the way it'll end. But I tell you one time: I'll pitch and you broadcast, but you come near me or my wife or my kid and I will kill you."

Lester said, "You can't kill shit."

Rabb kept looking at Maynard. "And keep that goddamn freak away from me," he said, "or I'll kill him too."

Lester moved away from the wall, the slouch gone. He shrugged into his tae kwon do stance like a man putting on armor.

The little boy said, "Momma," not very loud, but with tears in it.

Marty said, "Get him out of here, Linda." And the woman and the boy backed away toward the bedroom. Maynard's face was red and sweaty.

"Hey, kid," Lester said, "your momma's a whore."

Rabb swung a looping left hand that Lester shucked off his forearm. He planted his left foot and swung his right around in a complete circle so that the back of his heel caught Rabb in the right side, at the kidneys. The kick had turned Lester all the way around. But he spun back forward like an unwinding spring. He was good. The kick staggered Rabb but didn't put him down. The next one would, and if it didn't, Lester would really hurt him. Maybe he already had. A kick like that will rupture a kidney.

Linda Rabb said, "Spenser." And grabbed hold of her husband, both arms around him. "Stop it, Marty," she said, "stop it." The boy pressed against her leg and his father's. Marty Rabb dragged his wife and son with him as he started back toward Lester. Lester was back in his stance, blowing a big bubble and chewing it back in again. He was about three feet to my left. I took one step and sucker-punched him in the neck, behind the ear. He fell down, his legs folding under him at the knees so that he sank to the floor like a penitent in prayer.

"Marty," I said, "get your wife and kid out of here. You don't want the kid seeing this. Look at him."

The kid was in a huddle of terror against his mother's leg. Marty reached down and picked him up, and with his other arm tight around Linda Rabb, he hustled them into the bedroom.

"I will say to you what Rabb did, you great sack of guts," I said. "You and your clotheshorse stay away from Rabb as long as you live or I will put you both in the hospital."

Lester came off the floor at me, but he was wobbly. He tried the kick again, but it was too slow. I leaned away from it. I moved in behind the kick and drove a left at his stomach. He blocked it and hit me in the solar plexus. I tensed for it, but it still made me numb. A good punch turning the fist over as it came, but there wasn't as much steam as there should have been behind it, and I was inside now, up against him. I had weight on him, maybe fifteen pounds, and I was stronger. As long as I stayed up against him, I could neutralize his quickness and I could outmuscle him. I rammed him against the wall. My chin was locked over his shoulder, and I hit him in the stomach with both fists. I hurt him. He grunted. He hammered on my back with both fists, but I had a lot of muscle layer to protect back there. Twenty years of working on the lats and the lateral obliques. I got hold of his shirtfront with both hands and pulled him away from the wall and slammed him back up against it. His hand whiplashed back and banged on the wall. It was plasterboard and it broke through. I slammed him again and he sagged. I brought my left fist up over his arms and hit him on the side of the face, at the temple, with the side of my clenched fist. Don't want to break the knuckles. A kind of pressure was building in me, and I saw everything indistinctly. I slammed him on the wall and then stepped back and hit him left, left, right, in the face. I could barely see his face now, white and disembodied in front of me. I hit it again. He started to sag, I got hold of his collar with my left hand and pulled him up and hit him with my right. He sagged heavier, and I jammed him against the wall with my left and hammered him with my right. His face was no longer white. It was bloody, and it bobbled limply when I hit him. I could feel my whole self surging up into my fist as I held him and hit him. The rhythm of the punches thundered in my head, and I couldn't hear anything else. I was vaguely aware of someone pulling at me and I brushed him away with my right hand. Then I could hear voices. I kept punching. Then I could hear Linda Rabb's voice. The pounding in my head modified a little.

"Stop it, Spenser. Stop it, Spenser. You're killing him. Stop it."

Someone had hold of my arm, and it was Marty Rabb, and Lester's face was a bloody mess, unconscious in front of me. Maynard was sitting openmouthed on the floor, blood trickling from his nose. It must have been him I brushed away.

"Stop it, stop it, stop it." Linda Rabb had hold of my left arm and was trying to pry my hand loose from Lester's shirtfront. I opened the fingers and stepped away, and Lester slid to the floor. Maynard slid over to him without getting up and with a handkerchief began to wipe the blood from Lester's face. I could see Lester's chest rising and falling as he breathed. I noticed I was breathing heavy too. Marty and Linda Rabb both stood in front of me, the kid holding Linda's hand. Tears were running down his cheeks and his eyes were wide with fright, but he was quiet.

"Jesus, Spenser," Rabb said. "What happened? You were crazy."

I was sweating now, as if a fever had broken. I shook my head. "A lot of strain," I said. "We've all had a lot of strain. I'm sorry the kid saw it."

Maynard had gone to the bathroom and come back with wet towels and was cleaning Lester up and putting a cold compress on his forehead. "Pay attention to what happened, Bucky boy," I said. "Don't irritate me."

Lester moved a little. His lips were swollen and one eye was closed. Maynard kept washing his face with the damp towel.

"It's okay, Lester," he said. "It's okay."

Lester sat up and pushed the towel away. "Help me up," he mumbled.

Maynard got up and got Lester on his feet.

"Let's get out of here," Lester said.

Maynard started to take him toward the door, his arm around Lester's back.

"Bucky," I said, "we agree about the tie? And how we got no further business?"

Maynard nodded. There was no color left in his face, just the slight smear of brown, drying blood on his lip.

"I want to go home, Bucky," Lester mumbled, and Bucky said, "Yeah, yeah, Lester, we'll go home." And out they went.

Linda Rabb sat on the floor with her son and held him against her and put her face in his hair. They rocked back and forth slightly on the floor, and Marty Rabb and I stood awkwardly above them and said nothing at all. Finally I said, "Okay, Marty. I think we've done all there is to do."

He put his hand out. "Thank you, Spenser, I guess. We were in a mess we couldn't have gotten out of without you. I can't say quite where we're at now, but thank you for what you did. Including Lester. I think probably he's too good at tae kwon dong or whatever it is for me."

"He might have been too good for me if I hadn't sucker-punched him first."

We shook hands. Linda Rabb didn't look up. I went out the front door. She didn't say good-bye.

I never saw her again.

30

"And you kept hitting him," Susan Silverman said.

We were sitting in a back booth in The Last Hurrah, looking at the menu and having the first drink of the evening. Mine was a stein of Harp; hers, a vodka gimlet.

"It all seemed to bubble up inside me and explode. It wasn't Lester; it was Doerr and Wally Hogg and me and the case and the way things worked out so everyone got hurt some. It all just exploded out of me, and I damn near killed the poor creep."

"From what you say he probably earned the beating."

"Yeah, he did. That's not what bothers me. I'm what bothers me. I'm not supposed to do that."

"I know, I've seen the big red *S* on your chest."

"That ain't all you seen, sweet patooti."

"I know, but it's all I remember."

"Oh," I said.

She smiled at me, that sunrise of a smile that colored her whole face and seemed to enliven her whole body. "Well, maybe I can remember something else if I think on it."

"Perhaps a refresher course later on tonight," I said.

"Perhaps."

The waiter came and took our order, went away, and returned shortly with another beer for me.

"The irony is," I said, "that Linda Rabb is married to one of the all-time greats of jockdom, and she's being helped by me, with the red *S* on my chest and the gun in my pocket, and she's the one that saves them. She's the one, while us two stud ducks are standing around flexing, that does what had to be done. And it hurt and I couldn't save them and her husband couldn't save them. She saved herself and her husband."

"Maynard has stopped the blackmail?"

"Sure, he had to. He had nothing to gain and everything to lose." I drank some beer. The waiter brought us each a plate of oysters and a bottle of Chablis.

"The papers have been kind to Mrs. Rabb."

"Yeah, pretty good. There's been a lot of mail, some of it really ugly, but the club publicity people are handling it and she hasn't had to read much of it."

"How about Marty?"

"He went into the stands for some guy out in Minnesota and got a three-day suspension for it. Since then he's kept his mouth shut, but you can tell it hurts."

"And you?"

I shrugged. The waiter took away the empty oyster plates and put down two small crocks of crab and lobster stew.

"And you?" she said again.

"I killed two guys, and almost killed another one."

"Killing those two was what made it possible for Linda Rabb to do what she did."

"I know."

"You've killed people before."

"Yeah."

"They would have killed you."

"Yeah."

"Then it had to be, didn't it?"

"I set them up," I said. "I got them up there to kill them."

"Yes, and you walked in on them from the front, two of them to one of you, like a John Wayne movie. How many men do you think would have done that?"

I shook my head.

"Do you think they would have done it? They weren't doing it. They were trying to ambush you. And if they'd succeeded, would they be agonizing about it now?"

I shook my head again.

"You'd have had to kill them," Susan said. "Sometime. Now it's done. What does it matter how?"

"That's the part that does matter. How. It's the only part that matters."

"Honor?" Susan said.

"Yeah," I said. The waiter came and took the crocks and returned with scrod for Susan and steak for me. We ate a little.

"I am not making fun," Susan said, "but aren't you older and wiser than that?"

I shook my head. "Nope. Neither is Rabb. I know what's killing him. It's killing me too. The code didn't work."

"The code," Susan said.

"Yeah, jock ethic, honor, code, whatever. It didn't cover this situation."

"Can't it be adjusted?"

"Then it's not a code anymore. See, being a person is kind of random and arbitrary business. You may have noticed that. And you need to believe in something to keep it from being too random and arbitrary to handle. Some people take religion, or success, or patriotism, or family, but for a lot of guys those things don't work. A guy like me. I don't have religion or family, that sort of thing. So you accept some system of order, and you stick to it. For Rabb it's playing ball. You give it all you got and you play hurt and you don't complain and so on and if you're good you win and the better you are the more you win so the more you win the more you prove you're good. But for Rabb it's also taking care of the wife and kid, and the two systems came into conflict. He couldn't be true to both. And now he's compromised and he'll never have the same sense of self he had before."

"And you, Spenser?"

"Me too, I guess. I don't know if there is even a name for the system I've chosen, but it has to do with honor. And honor is behavior for its own reason. You know?"

"Who has it," Susan said, "he that died a Wednesday?"

"Yeah, sure, I know that too. But all I have is how I act. It's the only system I fit into. Whatever the hell I am is based in part on not doing things I don't think I should do. Or don't want to do. That's why I couldn't last with the cops. That's the difference between me and Martin Quirk."

"Perhaps Quirk has simply chosen a different system," Susan said.

"Yeah. I think he has. You're catching on."

"And," Susan said, "two moral imperatives in your system are never to allow innocents to be victimized and never to kill people except involuntarily. Perhaps the words aren't quite the right ones, but that's the idea, isn't it?"

I nodded.

"And," she said, "this time you couldn't obey both those imperatives. You had to violate one."

I nodded again.

"I understand," she said.

We ate for a bit in silence.

"I can't make it better," she said.

"No," I said. "You can't."

We ate the rest of the entrée in silence.

The waiter brought coffee. "You will live a little diminished, won't you?" she said.

"Well, I got a small sniff of my own mortality. I guess everyone does once in a while. I don't know if that's diminishment or not. Maybe it's got to do with being human."

She looked at me over her coffee cup. "I think maybe it has to do with that," she said.

I didn't feel good, but I felt better. The waiter brought the check.

Outside on Tremont Street, Susan put her arm through mine. It was a warm night and there were stars out. We walked down toward the Common.

"Spenser," she said, "you are a classic case for the feminist movement. A captive of the male mystique, and all that. And I want to say, for God's sake, you fool, outgrow all that Hemingwayesque nonsense. And yet . . ." She leaned her head against my shoulder as she spoke. "And yet I'm not sure you're wrong. I'm not sure but what you are exactly what you ought to be. What I am sure of is I'd care for you less if killing those people didn't bother you."

At Park Street we crossed to the Common and walked down the long walk toward the Public Garden. The swan boats were docked for the night. We crossed Arlington onto Marlborough Street and turned in at my apartment. We went up in silence. Her arm still through mine. I opened the door and she went in ahead of me. Inside the door, with the lights still out, I put my arms around her and said, "Suze, I think I can work you into my system."

"Enough with the love talk," she said. "Off with the clothes."